SECRETS OF DESIRE

"Julia, stop this!" He brought her close to him and kissed her.

At first she was paralyzed with surprise and shock, then she began to struggle against his embrace. But as his lips moved on hers, familiar yet strange, frightening yet persuading, she felt that sense of helpless bewitchment engulf her. Without wishing it or intending it, she found she was lost in that same sweet rapture that his first, well-remembered kiss had brought her.

This time he was the one to draw away. He released her, but he did not move far. A great weight of emotion lay heavily between them, separating them, yet drawing them somehow together. Julia, released from the spell of his lips and his arms, had a queer feeling of confusion that weakened her knees again. She placed a hand once more on the chair back for support and tried to steady her breathing.

"I must have your promise of silence, Julia." His voice was low, urgent, steel-edged.

She stood looking at him silently. Her head gave a small shake, as much in bafflement as refusal. He put his hands on her shoulders and looked steadily into her eyes.

Other Leisure Books by Faye Summers:

STORMSPELL

Winterhall

Faye Summers

Chapter One

In the early-morning hours of June 20, 1837, Alexandrina Victoria was awakened from her slumber and informed that she was now the Queen of England. The undistinguished life and reign of her uncle, William IV, had ended, unlamented by most of his subjects, though most *would* agree that he was less objectionable a king than his brother had been. Now the kingdom was presented with the rather romantic notion of a queen. And a youthful queen at that.

Unlamented or not, the decencies for His Late Majesty would be observed, and this fact would be of importance—and perhaps some inconvenience —even as far away as the city of York.

"Mama, the king is dead. We are to have a queen."

5

Frances turned emerald eyes to the parlor door as her daughter came into the room.

"Yes, dear. Mrs. Woodland and I were just discussing this news, as well as another event much closer to home."

"Oh!" Julia looked up from the paper and closed the door behind her. "I am sorry, Mrs. Woodland. How rude of me not to see that we have a guest."

Mrs. Woodland smiled her gracious forgiveness and said, "I was just saying to Mrs. Forrest that Mr. Grant, I mean Sir William, told me this morning that he had hoped to bid farewell to all of us with a large party at the Beatrice, but he thinks he must reconsider in view of the death of the king."

Julia looked in confusion from Mrs. Woodland to her mother.

Frances said, "You had best tell her, Mrs. Woodland. You have heard the news from the gentleman himself."

"Well, my dear Miss Forrest," the lady began eagerly, "it is the most amazing thing. Our own Mr. Grant is now to be Sir William Grant. A baronet!"

"What? Indeed, ma'am, you have surprised me. I have never heard that Mr. Grant had such expectations."

"He had no idea of it himself. He told me so."

"It would seem, then," Frances contributed, "that he cannot have been very intimate with these lofty relations of his."

"Well, of course, Mrs. Forrest, Mr. Grant is such an unpretentious man. He would not like to *presume*."

Frances lifted skeptical eyebrows but said nothing.

"He knew, of course, of his cousin's death some

weeks ago, but he thought there must be other, closer male heirs. It seems they have all died out, however, and he is now to inherit the title and quite a grand estate."

"I am very happy for him, certainly," said Julia, "but I fear it will require some time to think of Mr. Grant as a baronet." She turned with a thoughtful face to look at her mother, but Frances was engaged in snipping a thread from her needlepoint and would not look up.

"I do agree with him that a large party would be most inappropriate at this sad time." Mrs. Woodland accepted another tea cake from the plate Julia offered. "Indeed, I am not certain it would be quite suitable in any case, in view of his profession."

"But he is not, strictly speaking, our clergyman, Mr. Grant, any longer," Frances pointed out. "He is already Sir William and may think such a gesture befitting, perhaps requisite, of his new position."

Mrs. Woodland sniffed and looked doubtful and said she thought Sir William's friends and neighbors could bid him farewell quite nicely at a small gathering in the vicarage. "Or perhaps in my own home, for it is much larger. I could not accommodate so many as the Beatrice, naturally." Mrs. Woodland stared vacantly before her to consider which members of the parish might be reasonably excluded from this chaste and proper gathering.

"I confess I should very much like to see the improvements that have been done to the Beatrice," Julia said. "Miss Pierce has seen it recently and declared it to be quite as elegant as a London hotel."

"Then I am sure we may believe it, my dear," Frances remarked, "for Miss Pierce is certainly a young lady with a taste for the elegant." With a dazzling smile, she turned her green eyes on Mrs. Woodland. "Do you not agree, Mrs. Woodland?"

Mrs. Woodland came back from her calculations. "I do, indeed, Mrs. Forrest. And such a lively, pretty girl, I always think. I would certainly include Miss Pierce in any gathering for Mr. Grant. Oh! I wonder if he means to take MacKenzie with him?" An eager light came into Mrs. Woodland's eyes. "If not, I shall certainly offer to take him into my employment, for he is an excellent and most versatile servant."

Frances suppressed an exasperated sigh. "Well, and so we are to have a queen. Do you think, Mrs. Woodland, that the kingdom will receive her happily?"

"I'm sure I hope so, Mrs. Forrest, though the monarchy has given us little to admire these past years. She is quite shockingly young, of course."

"In fact," Julia said, "she is just my own age. Exactly so, for we have the very same birthday."

"Born on the same day as the new queen! Just think of that. Still," Mrs. Woodland went on, "as she is so young, I daresay there will be a regent."

"Unless," Frances said as she spread her needlepoint in her lap, "she is as mature and sensible at eighteen as Julia is." She eyed the material critically—a beautiful work in blue and silver, destined for some as yet undetermined use.

"Very true, indeed, Mrs. Forrest. Robert and I were saying just the other evening how mature and sensible Miss Forrest is."

"Mr. Woodland keeps well, I hope?" Frances asked with as much warmth as she could muster.

"Yes, thank you. Robert has always enjoyed

excellent health." Mrs. Woodland turned to Julia with a reassuring smile. "There has never been the slightest hint of the sad affliction that took his father from me."

"He seems to have recovered nicely from his little mishap," Frances said, glancing innocently at her daughter. "He was walking quite normally again on Sunday."

"But, Mrs. Woodland," Julia asked hurriedly, "where is this estate Mr. Grant is to have? Is it far from York?"

"A day's journey to the south, I believe he said. The place is called 'Winderfields.' "

"Winderfields?" Frances looked up suddenly. "Mrs. Woodland, are you certain?"

"Well, reasonably certain, my dear. Though I confess I was so surprised at hearing the news, I may not have attended to the name as well as I should. Do you know the place?"

Frances's eyes were back on her needlework. "Oh, now that I consider, I believe the place I am thinking of was called Windwood or perhaps Windy Hill. But tell me, Mrs. Woodland, what is the name of the family he will now succeed?"

"Why I cannot say. Though I believe I heard the name when he was mourning them some weeks ago. It was a carriage accident, I remember. The father and the only son most tragically lost."

Frances tucked up a stray red curl, untouched by gray. "Oh, yes, now I recall. Very sad, indeed."

Mrs. Woodland suddenly remembered that there were other members of Mr. Grant's flock who had yet to be told the wonderful news. She finished her tea, said her good-byes and hurried away to fulfill this happy mission.

"Heavens!" said Frances when she and Julia were alone, "I hope, Julia, that being courted by Robert Woodland is not as tedious as being visited by his mother."

"Mama," Julia smiled, "you know that where Mr. Woodland might speak five words, *she* may well say twenty thousand. And I'm not entirely certain I am being courted at all."

"Nonsense!"

"His mother would prefer that he marry Miss Pierce."

"Certainly. Miss Pierce is a cousin and is to have a few thousand pounds to add to their fortunes."

"And I believe Mrs. Woodland finds Miss Pierce more . . . companionable."

"A woman like Mrs. Woodland will always prefer flattery and gossip to sensible conversation, but . . ." Frances stopped as the parlor door opened once again and Mimmie came in breathlessly.

"Mercy!" Mimmie exclaimed as she dropped her parcels on the table. "I just heard the most surprising news at the milliner's." She sat down heavily and accepted the cup of tea Julia poured for her.

"If you mean the news of Mr. Grant," Frances said as she folded her needlework, "I assure you we have already heard it. Mrs. Woodland has been here nearly an hour speaking to me of nothing else. She professed great surprise that he had not called on me himself." And Frances did look puzzled about it.

"*She* only heard it at the bank. According to Mrs. Harris, whom I met at the milliner's, Mrs. Woodland was there with her son when Mr. Grant called to keep an appointment."

"Ah," said Frances.

"Oh, Julia," Mimmie said as she stirred herself and rustled among her packages, "Miss Pierce stopped me as I was passing and asked if I would bring home the book you had lent her."

"With all you had to carry?" Julia frowned. "I must say that Miss Pierce, for all her celebrated liveliness, is wanting manners. I suppose she thought to spare herself my questions as to how she enjoyed the book. I doubt she even opened it, despite all her eager interest when Mr. Woodland and I were discussing it that evening. Don't you agree, Mama, that this was most impolite of Miss Pierce?"

But Frances was gazing thoughtfully out the window and did not answer. When asked again, she turned, made a vague reply, then rose and drifted out of the room, leaving her needlepoint on the chair.

Julia and Mimmie watched her go. When the door closed, their eyes met and Julia asked the question that was in both their minds. "Mimmie, do you think Mr. . . . . I mean Sir William will ask her to marry him now?"

"I cannot say, my dear."

"I believe he surely will. Even *I* have known that he has been in love with her since the day he arrived in the parish. Seven years. Nearly eight. Now that he can afford to take a wife. . . ."

"A good many men have admired your mother, Julia."

"*All* men admire her!" Julia got up restlessly and went to the mirror that hung above a table near the parlor door. She studied her reflection discontentedly. "Do I . . . I *must* look like my father, for I am nothing like her."

Mimmie shook her graying head sympathetically and repositioned the silver comb she always wore. She said nothing but silently agreed. Where Frances was small and delicately curvaceous, Julia was tall and rather angular. Instead of the vivid red hair and bewitching green eyes of her mother, Julia had pale, almost silvery blond hair and eyes that were icy-blue. It made no difference that Julia had features more classically beautiful than Frances, for no one was likely to notice. Julia was too solemn where Frances was vivacious; introverted where Frances was gregarious; unpretentious where Frances was accomplished; cautious and retiring where Frances was determined, witty, temperamental. It had been painful, Mimmie knew, for Julia to grow up in the shadow of such a mother, but of course, Frances could not help it. She was as she was—the beautiful, the beguiling, the enchanting Frances. Nothing could change that.

Julia turned from the mirror. The often asked childhood question was in her eyes.

"Your father was a very handsome man, dear Julia. Very tall. Most striking in his uniform. And a brave and worthy man as well."

The same description Julia had heard from Mimmie so many times before. The same words, even. From this meager information she had tried to form a picture of the father who, without ever having known him, she missed terribly.

"My mother must have loved him very much, to have remained unmarried after all these years. And it is still so—so difficult for her even to speak of him."

Mimmie did not answer; she was moving back to her packages.

"If only there were a painting, some likeness of him," Julia persisted.

"Yes. That is a very great pity. Julia, I believe I have seen the very lace for your new gown. I asked Mrs. Tuttle to put it aside until you can go to look at it, for she had very little of it left."

Julia sighed. The subject was to be dismissed as usual.

"Thank you, Mimmie. You have had a busy morning." Julia went to pick up her book to return it to its place on the shelf. Unlike her mother, Julia was a tidy and methodical person.

Sir William called that afternoon. He was admitted by Polly, the maid of all work, and expressed dismay that Mrs. Forrest was not at home, having gone out to look at a new shipment of baskets just arrived at Mrs. Tuttle's store. The other ladies were in the parlor, however, and received him with congratulations and a glass of the special sherry Frances kept for festive observances.

At forty-seven years of age, the new baronet was a man neither fat nor thin, tall nor short, dark nor fair. He was in every way extremely ordinary except for his eyes. These were black and at times seemed to glow with a special light. When she first met him, Julia had supposed it was the intensity of his religious calling that gave him this quality, but his sermons had never reflected any such fervor. Perhaps it was an unsuspected passion of a more earthly kind. Julia wondered whether this idea had ever occurred to her mother.

Sir William had just finished relating the tale of

wonderment that had raised him to his new station when Frances returned and the whole account was heard again.

When a happy toast had been raised and drunk, Mimmie asked for a description of Winderfields.

"Indeed, Miss Chappel," Sir William replied, "I remember very little of it. I was hardly more than a child when I saw it last. My late cousin was just a boy then, several years younger than myself, and his grandfather was still alive. A proper old rake that old gentleman was. Quite a character. The son who succeeded him, my late cousin's father, was nothing like him—all business and determination."

"I daresay the estate would fare better under such a steward," Frances remarked. "I hope for your sake, Sir William, that the son was like his father rather than his grandfather. Children sometimes *do* spurn the habits of their parents and revert to those of the previous generation."

Sir William shifted uncomfortably and searched for a charitable comment that would do justice to all three generations of his cousins.

Julia spared him the trouble. "But tell us, Sir William, what do you think of our new queen? I hope you are not one of those who believes a regent, perhaps her mother, should be appointed."

"I am not, Miss Forrest. I have little opinion of the duchess or of anyone else closely related to our new monarch. A foolish and avaricious lot they are. I believe the queen will be better served and better advised by members of the present government. And so shall we all."

Frances gave a charming shake of her head and asked, "Do you think, Sir William, that radical elements will use the ascension of a woman to stir up old troubles? One does hear just lately that such extremist movements may be at work again."

Sir William looked disappointed at the turn the conversation seemed to be taking, but he smiled kindly at Mrs. Forrest. "I do not think it likely, ma'am. I rather think the kingdom is in a state of hopefulness. Having rarely in our history been subjected to two such inept kings in a row, we may certainly, in an average pattern, expect better this time."

"As I was shopping today," Frances said, her voice pensive and absorbed, "someone mentioned the rumors we all heard just before the last King George was to come to the throne, of a movement to prevent it. Do you recall such rumors, Sir William?"

"I do, though not very clearly." He laughed humorlessly. "And why there should be any vexation at having George IV as king, I cannot think. We had, after all, endured the man a good many years as Prince Regent."

Frances said, "The rumors I refer to held that a band of discontented individuals had formed and were at work creating agitation, dissension, and unrest among the populace. The goal, it was reported, was the complete overthrow of the monarchy."

"How dreadful!" Julia was already a fierce supporter of the new Queen Victoria. "What pitiful, misguided creatures those persons must have been to conceive of such a thing."

Frances looked at her daughter in mild surprise that her usual calm demeanor and quiet voice were replaced by something approaching heated words.

Sir William shrugged. "Well, perhaps. Though some might call their motives lofty, placing power in the hands of the people."

"Meaning themselves!" said Frances sharply.

"But, after all, it came to nothing." Sir William smiled mildly. "King George ascended the throne, the rumors eventually died away, and the monarchy is still very much extant."

"But was nothing done to stop such a thing?" Julia wanted to know. "Were these individuals not caught and punished?"

Sir William frowned and said, "I do not precisely recall hearing of any settlement in the matter."

Frances said, "This occurred around the time I lost my husband, so my memory may not be perfect, but it seems to me that there was a serious search made for the leader of the movement. An odd name—Bellwether, was it not? But he eluded capture. Was there not some theft and even a death involved?"

Julia heard Mimmie draw in her breath.

"I forget the exact circumstances," Sir William replied. "I daresay these persons simply left the country, taking with them the proceeds of their thievery. It was a very long time ago. These are far more settled times." Sir William took up the newspaper from the table beside him. "Our new queen is not precisely handsome, I would say, but she has a pleasant face."

"Or perhaps," Frances said, "the artist who made this sketch, like the rest of the kingdom, is anxious to show Her New Majesty every possible charity at this time."

Sir William smiled and mentioned the party he planned to host at the Beatrice.

"But it must be delayed. I think it best if I go at once to Winderfields," he said, "to see the condition of the estate and determine what, if anything, needs immediate attention. When I return to York in five or six weeks, we may then have a pleasant party without fear of offense to the memory of the king or my poor cousin, either."

This was greeted by murmurs of approval.

"It is a very sad thing about your cousin," said Frances thoughtfully. "Were all the family lost in the accident?"

"My cousin's wife died some years ago. There remains an unmarried female cousin who will now be my responsibility."

"I see. It must be a great comfort to Miss—"

"Miss Sennett."

". . . to know that she is not to be entirely alone."

"I hope to make Winderfields a happy home for everyone who dwells there."

Frances looked up to meet his gaze briefly, then her glance flickered away.

Julia remembered that moment later that night in her bedroom. How very different life would be if Mama should marry Sir William. New sights, new friends, a life in the country—very probably a life of ease and pleasure. Julia wondered if she would regret leaving any of the places and people of York. After a few minutes' consideration, she decided that she would not. Except for Mr. Woodland, of course.

"I do hope, Miss Forrest, that we shall get a new neighbor who is not so very fond of cats."

"Your flowers will be the better for their absence, certainly."

The two women stood at the window of the parlor in old Mrs. Ponder's house next door to Julia's. (Mrs. Ponder was a widow and loved to be visited.) They were watching with interest the commotion in the street as Mr. Haskel's family, owing to a windfall from Mrs. Haskel's uncle's will, vacated the house across the street to move to a more fashionable neighborhood.

"I don't suppose we are likely to get a truly agreeable family." Mrs. Ponder sighed. "Those who can afford it will settle elsewhere."

"It is true that we have not had such a pleasant neighbor there since Dr. Baines died. I confess I should like to see some children on this street again."

"Ah," said Mrs. Ponder offering tea and cakes as they sat down, "perhaps our new queen will soon marry and give us royal children to occupy our interest."

"Perhaps so. Did I mention, Mrs. Ponder, that Her Majesty and I were born on the very same day?"

Mrs. Ponder expressed suitable amazement and delight at this news, then fell to speculating which youngling of European royalty might be the most desirable consort for the queen. Julia listened thoughtfully.

"Then you do not share Mrs. Woodland's view that Queen Victoria is too young to be left without a regent?"

"Nonsense!" Mrs. Ponder snorted. "Mature years certainly did not make our last king a wise and worthy man. Even less his brother before him."

Julia, still troubled by what she had heard the previous day, now asked Mrs. Ponder if she recalled any rumors of an anti-monarchist movement some nineteen or twenty years before.

Mrs. Ponder did remember, even to the name of Bellwether. "There were all sorts of stories about him. Some held that he was the agent of a foreign power. Others thought he must certainly be an Englishman—the castoff son of a noble family. Or a gentleman fallen on hard times and seeking revenge on a system that had disappointed him."

"But—but did no one ever see him? How could he attract a following if he were never known or seen?"

"I suppose, of course, that it was his underlings who did the real work! And, except for the thievery, much of their activity was confined to publishing outrageous notices that would appear mysteriously on walls and trees, urging the people to unite, to be ready for the day Bellwether would lead them in the overthrow of the crown and establish a new and rightful order with unbounded prosperity. Prosperity for themselves, very likely!"

"So my mother said. And, with a woman coming to the throne, she wonders if there might be a similar plot being hatched at this moment."

"My dear, there are always men to do the hatching, whatever their motives may be. Hotheads and thieves, most of them. And there are those who undertake such a plot in a grasp at power they do not have. Very often that is the real reason people do things they hope will be thought noble deeds.

Although there *are* always *some* who become associated with such a scheme out of altruistic motives. They are the most dangerous of all."

"Sir William gave the opinion that these are more settled times and that such a movement now would have a hard time finding a foothold."

"Dear Sir William, like a good many men, will always expect the best without any substantial reason for doing so. I, for one, am very glad we have a sound and skeptical woman on the throne. Now we may hear some sense from London, which will be a very welcome change."

Mr. Woodland called that afternoon on a small matter of business with Frances. Mr. Woodland and his father before him had, at the Woodland family bank, prudently and successfully managed and invested Frances's meager resources over the years, enabling her, with care, to maintain her modest household in the manner of a gentlewoman. Frances was grateful, even wished she could look happily on the prospect of having such a prosperous young gentleman marry her daughter, but it was no use. Julia, Frances knew in her heart, deserved better, was entitled to better, and it cost Frances many hours of agonizing and regrets that life might cheat her daughter of a more stimulating life companion than Mr. Woodland.

In fact, Mr. Woodland was an inoffensive and sensible young man of greater than average height, agreeable manners, and a pleasant face with thoughtful gray eyes. When the papers were signed, he lingered to sit by Julia and to announce his latest good fortune. Sir William had asked him to go along to Winderfields to help assess the condition of the estate's affairs.

"Do you believe, Mr. Woodland," Frances asked, "that Sir William expects to spend *some* time in York even after he takes up residence at Winderfields?"

"I should not be at all surprised, ma'am. It cannot be an easy thing to leave long-known friends and places behind, even for a grand estate."

It was, perhaps, imagination, but Julia thought she heard an accusing note in the words.

"Sir William expected to be away some five or six weeks," Julia said. "Do you think you must also be absent so long?"

"I cannot say. Sir William has not seen the place in many years, and it has, after all, been without a master for some weeks, just at the time of year when a farming estate needs most attention. And there is his cousin, Miss Sennett, to be considered. It is not yet clear what her situation or desires may be."

Frances said, "It sounds as though Sir William means to rely heavily upon you, Mr. Woodland. This should be very good for the bank." And here she kindly took herself away so that Mr. Woodland's courting, if courting it was, could continue undistracted by her presence. Frances knew that her presence *could* be distracting, and that was hardly fair to Julia. And anyway, when conversing with Mr. Woodland after a heavy tea, one was always in danger of committing the ultimate rudeness of nodding off.

After half an hour of vaguely disturbing conversation with Mr. Woodland, Julia told him good-bye and went to her bedroom, taking a parcel with her. Inside was a froth of white lace, purchased that morning from Mrs. Tuttle and destined to adorn her new dress. This was a gown of palest blue silk, certainly the most elegant she had ever owned. The cloth had been given to her by Mimmie on her eighteenth birthday. It was not new cloth, of course. Julia knew it had come from the chest in Mimmie's bedroom—another scrap of a former life when Mimmie and Frances had been girls together. A life of which, to this day, Julia knew very little.

But what a remarkable friendship theirs was Julia thought, not for the first time. How remarkable Mimmie's devotion to Frances was for her to leave her family, her expectations behind and to go with her newly widowed and expectant cousin into a strange city and an uncertain future. And then to remain, year after year when the mourning was long over. Julia smoothed the sleeves of her gown and was grateful that this kindly and devoted woman *had* remained. It had been Mimmie, after all, who had been the careful nurse through childhood illnesses. It had been Mimmie who had listened most patiently to the frustrations and the delights that every little girl must encounter. Julia loved her mother and knew that love was returned, but it was an affection that was understood rather than spoken or demonstrated. Mimmie, on the other hand, was openly doting, absorbed by, concerned in everything, however trivial, that occupied Julia's time or thoughts. Doting but never indulgent, always enforcing discipline and decorum, always dispensing wisdom and clear thinking. So

22

great was her devotion that Mimmie had lost, for practical purposes, her own name. As a baby learning to speak, Julia had, from constant association, tried to call her "Mama." This could not be permitted, of course, and Frances had at last settled for a corruption of the word. Miss Clara Chappel was "Mimmie" to Julia ever after, and now even Frances called her that.

Julia sat down in a chair by the window and wondered whether she should be concerned about a new rival for Mr. Woodland's attentions. This Miss Sennett, of whom he had spoken in terms of curiosity and sympathy, was, no doubt, a young lady of some wealth, and she and Mr. Woodland would, it seemed, be much together during his stay at Winderfields.

And if Julia did not marry Mr. Woodland, what would become of her? She had no fortune to tempt a suitor, and she was not likely to find another so agreeable a young man around *here* very soon. And as much as she loved her mother and Mimmie, Julia did not want, could not bear to think of, this life stretching on for years into the future. She wanted, above all, a home and family—a real family—of her own.

In truth, Julia liked Mr. Woodland very much. Their temperaments and interests were so much alike. He was kind, intelligent, industrious, wealthy; he would certainly be an excellent husband. Julia closed her eyes and tried to picture married life in the Woodland home. She did not consider long. The problem, of course, was his mother.

No doubt Mrs. Woodland would still preside, in

name and in fact, in that household. Julia sighed as she pictured evenings with the three of them at home with Mr. Woodland and herself so solemn and Mrs. Woodland so noisy. She wondered if they wouldn't bore each other beyond endurance.

On the other hand, if Mama should marry Sir William, a great many things might be different.

Chapter Two

Sir William was gone a good deal longer than five or six weeks. Mr. Woodland came back to York in mid-July to attend to pressing business at the bank, but he would not be in town a week before a summons would send him hurrying back to the country and Sir William's affairs.

While he *was* in town, Mr. Woodland paid a brief call at the Forrest home where, under persistent questioning, he parted with a few details of the wonders of Winderfields. Julia listened with only half an ear as she observed how carefully her mother listened and then questioned Mr. Woodland on certain points of information about the estate. This display of curiosity persuaded Julia that her mother would certainly accept Sir William's proposal when it came, but she could not get Mimmie to agree.

Life in Julia's corner of York went on much the

same with or without Mr. Woodland's presence, and it surprised her a great deal that this should be so. She visited at the orphanage, attended work parties to assist the poor, called on her neighbors and ran errands for her mother. In her almost daily chats with Mrs. Ponder, she listened to her fears and doubts that the house across the street would ever be taken.

"And then you will see, my dear Miss Forrest, how the neighborhood's decline will accelerate!" Mrs. Ponder had assured her.

Mr. Woodland returned from Winderfields for good at the beginning of September, with Sir William to follow in two weeks' time. The affair at the Beatrice was most definitely to be held, and, since there was to be no dancing, Mrs. Woodland gave her grudging approval of the plan.

Mr. Woodland, when he called at the Forrest home one early evening, brought other news, too.

"I had word of a quite disturbing occurrence today," he said with a shake of his head. "A client was in the bank who had spent all of yesterday in Leeds. He told me that he had seen a most disgusting notice affixed to the wall of a bank—a bank!—in the very center of the town."

"A notice?" Frances asked with a twinkle. "What sort of notice? Or was it of such a nature that—"

"Oh, no!" Robert said quickly, then, realizing that he was being teased, actually managed a little smile. "It was of a political nature, Mrs. Forrest, espousing a cause that the gentleman could only describe as treasonous, if not entirely anarchist."

"Oh!" Julia drew in her breath sharply. "Bell-wether!"

Robert turned to look at her and nod. "So said

Mr. . . . my client. I mentioned this to the new vicar, who, as you know, has just come from Leeds. He said that he had seen such notices, too, just before he moved here from that city."

"Mr. Woodland," Julia said anxiously, "what can this mean?"

"Why, I suppose it could mean that Bellwether is alive after all, or has returned from his hiding, and is at work again. Mrs. Forrest, do *you* think such a thing is possible?"

"I cannot say, of course, Mr. Woodland." Frances shook her head, looking more puzzled than anxious. "Though I find the idea . . . quite surprising. Did you say that you had heard from Sir William?"

Robert had received a letter that very morning from Winderfields, and was able to give the ladies a piece of news even more stimulating than that of the notices at Leeds. Sir William, when he returned to York, would be accompanied by his cousin, Miss Sennett.

Julia told herself that she was pleased; she was anxious to have a look at this possible rival, and, besides, as she said confidently to Mimmie, "It is very likely that he is bringing her along to meet us all. He may even mean to take Mama with him when he returns to Winderfields!"

Mimmie was very doubtful about this suggestion and said so. And elsewhere in the neighborhood, the impending arrival of Miss Sennett was unwelcome news.

"Coming from such a fine place as Winderfields, she is sure to be most elegantly dressed," Miss Pierce complained as she sat with Julia in Mrs. Woodland's drawing room at work in altering and repairing a collection of castoff clothing destined for the orphans. "And no doubt she will bring several maids and hairdressers to turn her out. It hardly seems fair. Miss Sennett must have any number of opportunities to be the favorite belle of the evening, while this is the only party of any consequence I have attended in ever so long."

"Perhaps she is still wearing mourning," Julia pointed out. "She has lost most of her family quite recently, you know."

Miss Pierce found this to be of some comfort and went on to speak more cheerfully of the new vicar who had arrived to fill Mr. Grant's place. "Truly a most pleasing and *contemplative* young gentleman. It is a great pity about his accident, though one hardly notices his disfigurement after a time."

Julia, knowing it was wicked, but unable to help herself, said, "My mother thinks the scar on Mr. Simmons's cheek is quite romantic. Almost like a dueling scar."

Miss Pierce, horrified at the prospect of *another* rival from the Forrest family, spoke firmly. "Surely Mrs. Forrest can't think Mr. Simmons to have been dueling! You must assure her, my dear Miss Forrest, that it was a fall from a horse! Some years ago now." She lowered her voice to a confidential tone. "Mrs. Woodland has told me that his leg was broken in two places, and one can see that it gives him pain, still. No, no. There is no question of dueling."

Julia smiled mildly into Miss Pierce's anxious face and said that she thought the most appealing thing about Mr. Simmons was his preaching.

"There certainly is more passion and intensity in his sermons than Sir William ever gave us as the

Reverend Mr. Grant. And Mr. Simmons never mumbles. Every word is pronounced distinctly and can be heard even at the back of the church. I think there should be a course of study at all the universities which turn out our preachers, perhaps taught by a professional actor, to instruct the young men in proper speaking. Then, perhaps, a clergyman like Mr. Simmons would not be such a rarity."

Miss Pierce, relieved that Miss Forrest had no designs on Mr. Simmons, and hopeful that she had turned aside any threat from the beauteous Mrs. Forrest, turned the conversation back to the question of Miss Sennett.

Julia listened halfheartedly, though she was more and more anxious to see Miss Sennett for herself. She had not cared to question Mr. Woodland about her beyond an expression of civil concern for her well-being. Mr. Woodland, reticent as ever, volunteered no information. His manner toward Julia *seemed* unchanged; he was quietly attentive. Still, it would be good to judge for oneself.

Miss Sennett notwithstanding, Julia was even more concerned about her mother's prospects for marriage than her own. And Frances, if not thinking of marriage to Sir William, was certainly preoccupied about something.

As it happened, no one need have feared Miss Sennett. Had it occurred to anyone to have asked the specific question, it might easily have been learned that Miss Sennett was the elder sister of the late baronet, and not his daughter. She was four or five years older than Frances and, unlike the dazzling Mrs. Forrest, looked every day of it. All the same, Julia wondered why Miss Sennett had never married. Though plain, she must have a sizeable fortune to bring to the man who married her.

Frances had her own thoughts about Miss Sennett. To her practiced eye, it was quite obvious that the lady was in love with her cousin. Frances wondered very much how long this had been so.

The party at the Beatrice began very well. There was the rush of excitement to greet the new baronet and to be introduced to his cousin. There was an undercurrent of excitement as many wondered whether an engagement would be announced that very evening.

There were gowns to be admired and whispered about. Frances, resplendent in anything she wore, appeared in a gown of deep green that was several years old but outrageously becoming to her. Her glowing red curls were dressed away from her face except for a few cleverly placed wisps on the forehead which accented her beautiful eyes. Julia wore her new blue gown and, having learned by experience that it was futile to expect her own heavy blond hair to hold curls through an entire evening, had drawn it into a coil at her neck, forsaking her usual fancy braid.

After a sumptuous dinner—Sir William loved good food—which was accompanied by the playing of some stately chamber music, the party, to Julia's way of thinking, threatened to sink into dullness. Except for Miss Sennett, these were, after all, the same people she saw at church each week, at the decorous teas and dinners she attended with Frances and Mimmie. Around her, the groups of chattering people were having the same conversations she heard at each of the usual functions. Even more disappointing, the proper moment for an announcement of an engagement—while they were all seated at dinner—had come and gone. This much anticipated evening, which she had, perhaps foolishly, expected to be special, magical, was ordinary after all.

How unfair it seems, Julia told herself silently, *though I suppose I was courting disappointment. My expectations were too grand.*

And another thing—except for the grand entry and this particular reception room, she still had seen nothing of the hotel. That, at least, could be remedied. She looked around for someone to go with her on an exploration.

Mimmie was her first choice of companion, but Mimmie was kindly engaged in conversation with poor Miss Sennett, whom everyone else except Frances had seemed to forget after the first introductions. Frances herself was standing apart with Sir William, and the two of them seemed to be discussing something serious. It would not do to disturb that conversation. And Mr. Woodland, who had been harnessed by Miss Pierce, seemed to be enjoying very much whatever lively things she was saying to him, for he smiled at every whispered remark. It was further proof of Julia's inflated expectations; everyone else seemed to be having a fine time.

Mrs. Woodland was disengaged, to be sure, but Julia was not that desperate for company. The musicians reappeared, and another round of chamber music seemed to be imminent. Though it was not, perhaps, entirely seemly, she would simply go unescorted.

There were steps leading up to the landing by which one entered the room. Too public, she decided; she would rather not be noticed leaving. But near her elbow was another, smaller door that must lead somewhere. Perhaps she could get out that way.

The door was unlocked. With a glance over her shoulder and an unfamiliar sense of daring, she slipped through and closed it softly behind her.

In the moonlight from a high window, Julia could see that she was in a sort of closet, full of shelves stacked high with linen and serving trays. Her heart sank momentarily until she spied the other door. She opened it carefully.

Again there was only moonlight to show her another reception room, darkened and empty, identical, so far as she could see, to the one Sir William had engaged. She crossed the room, climbed the stairs and let herself out.

She found herself in a wide carpeted hallway, standing opposite a tastefully executed sign directing guests to the main dining room. Here was luck, for this was one room Julia was especially anxious to see. It was, Miss Pierce had told her, fashion itself, with large palm trees growing actually in pots, so that the diners found themselves having their meals beneath the trees. Just imagine!

Julia's plan was simply to step to the door and look around, as though she were looking for someone, just to catch a glimpse of the famous room. In the doorway she collided with a gentleman.

She had seen this man when she had first entered the hotel and had mentally named him "the brown man," for he was dressed all in that color, and his hair, crisply curling, was also brown. She had seen him only at a distance and only from the back, but had made note for some reason that, for a large man, he moved with astonishing grace. His stride as he had gone up the main staircase was purposeful yet light, almost cautious. It had occurred to Julia as she had unaccountably stood and watched him that he would move silently through a ballroom or boulevard or barn. She had caught herself then and wondered why she had noticed.

Now she saw that he was indeed very tall, and his eyes were green. Not the emerald shade of her mother's, but apple green, pools of luminous color in his brown face. And to those eyes there leapt an appreciative glimmer, a sensual, almost indecent look which made Julia wish she had not been persuaded by the seamstress, Mrs. Carter, to have such a low neckline on this particular gown. But very quickly, the look was gone, replaced by aloof gentility as he helped her to right herself.

"I do beg your pardon, sir."

"It was entirely my fault, madam," came a silky, drawling, almost caressing voice. "I apologize for my clumsiness."

Polite words, smoothly said. Meaningless, of course. But after a moment his expression of well-bred civility faded to something that looked like puzzlement. He was looking at her carefully, and Julia felt herself begin to blush, although instinct told her it was not *that* kind of look.

It seemed to Julia that they stood together a long time before he stepped back, bowed with that grace of movement she had noticed before, and turned away. Julia stood where he had left her, and saw him turn back for another glance before he disappeared around a corner in the hallway.

She supposed he was a guest of the hotel for he was alone, coming from the dining room and did not seem to be bound for any of the party rooms. She turned and took a few steps into the dining room. Very likely he was a visitor from another city, perhaps here on business. As she surveyed the wonders of the potted palms that hung over the few patrons lingering over their dinners, she amused herself by speculating as to what sort of business might bring a dark and handsome gentleman to the Beatrice. She decided to think of him as someone with money to invest in the vigorous industries of the neighboring area. Perhaps at Leeds.

Sir William's reception in one of the several large public rooms which the Beatrice now boasted was not the only room in use. The grand ballroom was engaged this evening as well. Julia had seen many elegantly dressed ladies and gentlemen walking in that direction when she had first entered the hotel. She wanted very much to have a look at this room, too, and knew that tonight might be her only chance. If she just went and stood inside the door for a few moments, no one would know that she was not one of the party. It would be a breach of etiquette and entirely out of character for Julia to enter the ballroom, but something drew her on.

She stood just inside the doorway at the top of the wide and graceful stairs that descended to the ballroom floor where couples twirled to the strains of a waltz. In the loft to her left, a group of perspiring musicians labored heavily. The room was beautifully lighted and hung with gold-and-white festooning. Across the room a bride and groom stood with a group of laughing friends and family near a window open to admit the evening breeze. It was an appealing, very novel sight to Julia, who lived so quietly, and she could not help thinking that parties such as this might take place rather often at a place like Winderfields.

A man standing next to the bride turned to look at her, and Julia decided she must stay no longer. She went out again into the hallway.

She looked around, wondering whether to explore further or to return to Sir William's party. At the end of the hallway was a French door which opened onto a terrace. A breath of air would be welcome, and Julia stepped outside.

She found herself on a small terrace. Several yards away was another, longer terrace which probably led to the ballroom. She could not hear music now, and thought that someone must be making a speech, for there were periods of silence followed by bursts of laughter and applause from inside. It was mid-September, but the evening was mild and smelled of summer. She took a deep breath of the air scented with late roses that bloomed in the garden below.

"This will be the last summer night."

She turned, startled, at the sound of the strange, yet familiar, voice, and oddly was not surprised to see that it was the brown man. She wondered fleetingly if he had followed her onto the terrace or if he had been there in the shadows all along.

Her mind, always sensible, and all her years of careful upbringing, told her to go at once. Just to curtsy, apologize for having disturbed the gentleman's solitude, and go back to the party where she belonged.

She did none of these things.

"Why do you say so?" she asked.

"I feel a change is coming." He moved from the shadows to join her at the balcony railing. "But it cannot matter. You do not seem to be a creature of the summer."

"What do you mean, sir?"

"I mean that you seem to be a princess of a northern, frosty land." The music from the ballroom began again, and he held out his hand to her.

"Will the princess consent to dance with one of her subjects?"

Julia thought silently, *Oh, dear, this* is *a gentleman whom Mimmie would describe as a rascal.* Therefore, it was most peculiar that, almost without realizing what she was doing, she placed her hand in his. He gathered her into his arms and began to dance with her, his green eyes gazing steadily into hers as they waltzed. Curiously, Julia did not feel uneasy or foolish; instead, she felt a strange suspension of reality, as though she were in a dream or a fantasy which would disappear at the first word or sigh.

She had no idea how long they danced; time seemed to have little meaning. But she felt great desolation when the music ended and he released her, though he still held her hand. He raised it slowly to his lips, and his eyes held a message that made Julia catch her breath. Feeling both weak and exhilarated, she sat down on a stone bench and studied the face that looked down at her.

Those eyes seemed almost familiar, and she wondered for a passing moment if she might have seen them in her dreams. This was a crazy notion, which brought her out of the trance into which she somehow had fallen. She reclaimed her hand and stood up quickly.

"I must go back now."

He nodded and extended his arm.

"Oh, no." She drew back. "I cannot return to my party on the arm of an unknown gentleman."

Julia saw the flash of humor in his eyes, but it was quickly gone. He was again the well-bred gentleman, perhaps now a little bored with this unsophisticated local girl.

"I have no wish to intrude, I do assure you. I mean only to see you to your doorway, nothing more." He extended his arm again. "In which room is your party assembled?"

"In the East Room." She would not take his arm, but allowed him to follow her through the terrace door and to walk silently by her side to the door of the East Room, from which the strains of the chamber music could be heard very plainly. Here Julia faltered.

"I did not actually come out this way," she said, her eyes averted, for she did not *want* to see what expression this information would provoke. "I wish to return without being noticed."

His hand made a motion that said, "Lead on." She turned with resignation and led the way to the door of the next reception room, which was, of course, known as the West Room.

"Ah"—he grinned—"like Columbus before you, you sail west to arrive in the east."

"I can find my way from here. Thank you very much."

Silently he opened the door and followed her

into and across the path of moonlight on the floor until they reached the closet door. As they stood there together, Julia recognized with a start that she did not want to leave him. But, of course, she must; so she extended her hand.

"Thank you again, sir, and good-bye. I hope . . ." She searched for the proper formality to suit a situation like this one.

He took her hand in both of his. "You hope I understand that you do not make a habit of cavorting on a moonlit terrace with unnamed gentlemen. Good. It is not a wise practice in most instances."

He still held her hand as they gazed into each other's face. Julia felt intuitively that he was debating, deciding, perhaps, whether to say something more. Slowly, almost hesitantly, he drew her close and kissed her startled mouth.

Julia had never been kissed by a man. Once she had thought that Mr. Woodland was going to kiss her, but the moment had passed somehow. And Julia knew in her belly that a kiss from Mr. Woodland would be nothing like this. It made her breathless, dizzy, weak with an ill-defined longing.

And her companion, who may have told himself he intended only a flirtatious, teasing embrace to give this very beautiful, very guileless young woman a secret thrill to remember, or perhaps to describe to an awe-struck friend, found himself unwilling to have it end. Her red lips were soft and berry sweet, and her slim, delicate, regal body was strangely arousing.

But Julia, with great difficulty, came to her senses. Just as he began to pull her more closely into his arms, she drew away. Her wide, astonished eyes, vivid blue even in the moonlight, were aghast at what she had done. She turned quickly, evading his reaching hands, and slipped into the closet. As she closed the door she heard him whisper, "Goodbye, Frost Princess."

The music was still in progress when she entered the room, and she took a seat at the back without being seen. She was still trying to catch her breath when the music ended. The audience applauded and began to stand and stir. The concert was over.

Frances, looking around the room, saw her daughter, and, heeding the silent summons, Julia went to where her mother stood, talking again with Miss Sennett.

"Miss Sennett and I have had quite interesting conversations this evening. She has just told me that this is her first visit to York."

"Is it indeed? I suppose, though, Miss Sennett, that you go often to London."

"We did go fairly often in former times." And here Miss Sennett seemed to run out of conversation and fell awkwardly silent.

Frances said, "Miss Sennett has most kindly given me a description of the house and estate which is her home. It sounds quite charming. Do you think, Miss Sennett, that Sir William will undertake any great changes or improvements there? Gentlemen always seem to like to improve whatever comes into their hands, be the object ever so perfect in the first place."

Miss Sennett almost smiled and seemed to warm a little more. "I cannot say, Mrs. Forrest. My brother, and our father before him, had always some project in mind or in hand that seemed to keep at least some portion of the property in a state of uselessness at all times."

Frances gave her a dazzling smile and said, "No doubt Sir William will be grateful to have you advise him of what changes have already been tried, and with what results. In this way he can avoid repeating costly mistakes."

"Perhaps," said Miss Sennett a little doubtfully.

"I think it most unlikely," Julia said with a smile, "that Sir William will do anything too peculiar just because he now has the means. Those of us in his parish have always considered him a cautious and sensible man."

"I do agree that he seems much more . . . deliberate than I recall him as a younger man. The influence of his profession, I daresay, although I suppose that all of us at this age may have the same said of us." She turned the question to Frances, who was horrified that Miss Sennett would think her old enough to be concerned with such a thought. On the other hand, Frances's grown-up daughter stood before them. She let it pass.

"And certainly he could not have been kinder these last weeks," Miss Sennett continued. "I am so very grateful that he has offered me a home at Winderfields."

Frances, her emerald eyes narrowed, began to ask about the history of the estate and the family, but Julia did not listen to Miss Sennett's modestly proud replies, for Julia realized with uncharacteristic insight that Miss Sennett might be a problem after all.

When Sir William had come to claim his cousin to say farewell to Mrs. Ponder, Julia turned to her mother. "Mama! Do you think it possible that Miss Sennett is in love with Sir William?"

"Oh, yes, dear. I should say most certainly," was her vague and preoccupied reply.

Sometimes Mama could be quite maddening! She *must* be conscious that all the guests, with the possible exceptions of Miss Sennett and Sir William himself, were wondering, not whether, but when, Sir William's engagement to the exquisite Mrs. Forrest would be announced. Though Miss Sennett could not be considered, even by the kindest soul, as a rival to Mama, Sir William must feel some regard or fondness for her if he meant to keep her at Winderfields, as he surely had enough resources to provide for her at a separate establishment. What sort of difference would a marriage make in this arrangement? Julia wondered.

As she searched for words to say to her mother, she stopped suddenly. Something was not quite right here. Julia now saw her mother's eyes widen in mild surprise, then her winglike brows knit in puzzlement. Was she debating the question of Miss Sennett, after all? In another moment, Julia realized her mother's reactions had nothing to do with Miss Sennett; Frances was staring over her daughter's shoulder. Julia turned to see what had caught her mother's attention, and her heart sank with dismay and an undeniable pang of jealousy.

Standing on the landing of the staircase down into the room was the brown man, *her* brown man. He was staring in their direction, but not at Julia. His eyes were on Frances and his gaze was intent, curious, captivated.

Julia could not help the angry disappointment

that welled up in her heart. True, Frances always had this affect on men; every man who looked at her was a victim of her beauty. But with this particular man Julia felt betrayed.

It seemed a long and breathless eternity before he turned abruptly and climbed the stairs to leave the room.

When he left the East Room, the man in brown walked thoughtfully along the hallway, thinking that he almost wished he had not followed his impulse to see where the beautiful Frost Princess had come from, or who her people were. He wished he had not obeyed that small urgent voice that had said, *Just see. Just be sure. You won't rest if you don't make certain.* Now it was too late. He must find a place to wait and watch until this decorous party was ended. Having made a most astonishing discovery, he must think, ask questions, and then decide what must be done.

Chapter Three

The garden was still and heavy with the musk of the summer night. Julia stood at the window and breathed deeply of the fragrance of the bouquet he had given her. (She must get them into water soon.) Behind her, he swept the silvery hair from her neck, and his lips brushed her silky skin. Julia could not prevent the tiny shiver that coursed through her quickened flesh. His fingers moved lightly on her skin from her shoulders along her arms, paused, returned to lift and to cup her breasts in hands that, through the thin nightgown, felt firm and large and practiced. Julia sighed and leaned against him, savoring this new and irresistible sensation.

His hands, impatient now, untied the ribbon at the bodice of her gown and slipped inside. Flesh upon flesh. A stroking, circling, persuading enfold-ment, while his lips moved in a warm path of eagerness along her throat. Julia could not speak or even breathe as the passion he had kindled rose irrepressibly from she knew not where.

His hands moved again to take the flowers from her, and flung them onto the bed. He turned her to face him and kissed her, long and deeply, no longer persuasive, but urgent, compelling, confident. His hands held her tightly as he moved against her and Julia could only cling to him in a daze of bewilderment and longing. Then he was raising her nightgown over her legs until he held her bare flesh in a clasp that was fire and confusion and sweetness.

He lifted the gown over her head and studied her nakedness. Julia, released from the madness of his arms, felt suddenly abandoned and knew with a piercing sting of torment that he was comparing her beauty with her mother's. That knowledge made her cry out in pain, and the sound of her own voice made her sit straight up in bed.

It was just a dream. All a dream. Her bedroom was still in darkness, and Julia knew she could not have been asleep very long. Shaken and a little horrified, she got up to wash her face and to try to read the hands of the clock that ticked quietly on the corner of the mantel.

She thought the clock read half past two. They had returned from the Beatrice at half past eleven, and Julia, along with Mimmie, had gone straight to bed, leaving Frances alone in the parlor to settle the excitement of the evening with work on her needlepoint. Julia and Mimmie had exchanged glances at this, but the name of Sir William was not mentioned between them.

Julia shivered and realized that the night had turned chilly and damp; a layer of fog had gathered in the trees outside her window. He was right, after all; it was the last summer night.

She got back beneath the covers and lay staring into the darkness, trying not to remember her dream's still vivid sensations of lust and surrender that had seemed so real. Where had such feelings, such knowledge come from? Certainly not from experience, or books, or from the rather barren explanations of life she had had from Mama and Mimmie. She wondered for a brief moment if the brown man had imagined or dreamed such a scene, and if she had somehow read his thoughts. Impossible of course, but. . . . Oh, all this was madness! It was not logical and certainly not decent that a man whom she had seen only once, whose name she did not even know, could arouse such intense and traitorous feelings inside her.

It is because he is the first man to kiss me. That is all! she reassured herself as she settled on her pillows and prepared to go back to sleep. This dream, like other disturbing dreams, she decided, must be put aside and perhaps examined in the safety of daylight, then must certainly be forgotten, for something told her that a memory of this dream, like the memory of the man, could be very dangerous.

Frances came into the breakfast room, carrying something unfamiliar. She placed it on the table and sat down.

"Oh, Mama, so this is what you have made." Julia's voice was hushed. "It is quite—quite beautiful."

It was beautiful. The blue-and-silver needlepoint

had been incorporated into the construction of a flat oval basket. The material, folded so that the design was the same inside and out, lined the basket and stood just beneath the handle, gathered into folds that closed by drawing tight a heavy silver ribbon. Frances opened the folds so that Julia and Mimmie could see inside. It was fitted out as a sewing basket, complete with thread, needles, pins in their own matching cushion, and a pair of dainty silver scissors.

"But this is much too elegant to be used as a sewing basket," Julia said as she ran admiring hands over the beautiful fabric.

"I thought you meant it for some article of clothing," Mimmie added. "The trim of a cloak, perhaps, if you had made it larger."

Frances said, "I see no reason that everyday things should not be as lovely as we can make them. Indeed, they should be the most beautiful of our possessions if we use them so constantly." With a sudden movement she placed the basket before her daughter. "And I hope, Julia, that you will use it very constantly."

Julia stared unbelieving from the basket to her mother.

"Yes," Frances said with her radiant smile, "it is for you."

"But—but why?" Julia looked at Mimmie, as though she had the answer, but Mimmie was just as surprised.

"Why? Because you need a new basket to replace the shabby thing you have used since you first learned to embroider. And because"—Frances leaned over to give the folds of the basket's closure a smoothing stroke—"these colors remind me of you."

Julia found herself suddenly close to tears of delighted gratitude. She put her hand out to her mother. "Is it really true? Oh, I do thank you, Mama!"

"You see," Frances went on with sudden brisk-ness, "that when the basket is grown old, you can simply remove the fabric here where it is fastened and attach the whole thing to a new basket, so long as it is about the same size and shape." She looked up smiling. "In fact, I will do it for you when the time comes or sooner if I find a nicer basket of the right size. This one is not so well made as it might be and probably will not last more than a year or two."

"What a clever idea," Mimmie said warmly. "And so practical."

"You needn't be so astonished." Frances laughed. "You know that I can be practical when it is necessary."

"Yes. I know," Mimmie said softly.

Julia could not take her eyes from the beautiful and quite astonishing gift. "It is so lovely, Mama. I will treasure it always."

"My dear Julia, I know that your instinct will be to wrap it up carefully and put it away, only to be taken out and admired at special times. That is not why I gave it to you. I insist that you go this minute and transfer your materials from the old basket. Take this one with you this morning when you go to Mrs. Woodland's."

"Oh!"

"If you *must* put something away, let it be the old

47

basket. Then you may take *it* out from time to time to remind yourself of the dreariness of using it rather than the new one."

With a sudden smile, half-delight, half-rueful recognition of this description of her prudent nature, Julia rose, gave her mother a kiss and embrace, then hurried with the basket to her bedroom.

Frances stared at the door for several moments after it had closed behind her daughter, then refilled her teacup and sat thoughtfully silent. Mimmie, too, was silent, waiting for Frances to tell her what she had done about Sir William. He was to leave York this morning. Probably he was already on the road to Winderfields.

Frances turned to her abruptly. "Clara," she said, forsaking the familiar 'Mimmie,' "at the reception last evening, did you notice a young man, not of our party, who came for a few moments into the room? He stood on the landing and observed the group for a time. He was dressed all in brown."

Mimmie put aside her surprise to answer, "No, I did not observe him. Why?"

"He seemed . . ." Frances paused to consider, then abruptly changed her mind. "Oh, it is nothing. I merely wondered if you had noticed him." She sat turning her teacup round and round on its saucer. "Clara," she said suddenly, gravely, "you do remember where I have put the brooch? And—and what to do if—"

"Frances"—Mimmie put a hand on her cousin's arm—"of course I remember. Why do you ask me now?"

"Oh," and now came the dazzling smile and a little shrug, "it must be the change in the weather.

48

It makes one . . . pensive."

With that, Frances rose and drifted from the room, leaving Mimmie with the great question of Sir William still unanswered.

Frances examined her watch as she entered the tiny park on the hotel grounds which would afford her a short cut to the front entrance of the Beatrice. Not yet one o'clock. She would be on time. She put up a gloved hand to hold her hat safely on her head against the little wind that blew here where there was no protection of buildings. There was, to be sure, a hint of the coming autumn in the air, and she looked up idly to see if the leaves of the enormous maple tree that was the pride of this particular patch of parkland had started to turn.

Another gust of wind sent the still-green leaves dancing, perhaps an especially strong one, for, out of the corner of her eye, even the gnarled and massive trunk of the maple seemed to be swaying. Oh, no. It was just someone moving out from its shelter and onto the path behind her. A waiter, by his short white coat, on his way to work at the hotel.

It was already too late when she felt the vague flash of recognition of the stride and bearing of this waiter. The knife, a long, thin, silver dagger, gleamed for an instant before her eyes as it was plunged unerringly into her heart.

She hardly felt it, the thrust was so quickly done. She even walked a few steps more before falling to her knees, then pitching sideways onto the gravel path. And in the recognition of that figure, so certain now, as he moved away quickly, calmly, Frances cursed herself for a fool.

Julia's new sewing basket was duly noticed and admired that day at Mrs. Woodland's, though Sir William's reception was the primary topic of conversation.

As she listened to Miss Pierce's lamentations that there had been no dancing the previous evening, Julia's mind was very much elsewhere. Her mother had said nothing—*nothing*—about Sir William that morning. Indeed, Julia, in the excitement of her gift and the lingering confusion over her dream, had quite forgotten Sir William herself.

But now she must face the fact that it did not look promising; Sir William's departure was imminent, if not already accomplished. She must assume that either he had not spoken to her mother—difficult to believe!—or her mother had not accepted him.

So it looked as though there would be no move to Winderfields, no life in the country, no new sights and experiences. Julia looked absently around the Woodland drawing room where the group of ladies was at work. It was a prosperous, not to say an ostentatious room, a little fussier than Julia cared for. Would she be permitted to change it in any particular if she came to live here? Not likely.

But that could hardly matter. She and Mr. Woodland were most compatible and comfortable with each other. That was the important thing. They would be quietly happy together. And there would be guests, of course, and some entertainments, surely. And in time, even children. Children always made a home more lively.

"Well, Miss Forrest," Miss Pierce was now saying, "Sir William and Miss Sennett are surely gone from York by now. I wonder if *any* of us shall see them again."

"Mr. Woodland expects that Sir William will find it necessary to spend a day or two here from time to time."

"And I suppose," Miss Pierce continued fretfully, "Mr. Woodland will find it convenient to spend a like amount of time at the estate, since he appears to have become so necessary to Sir William. I daresay he will find quite a gay life there, a lively set of people. From Miss Sennett's accounts, Winderfields was accustomed to host several large house parties each year. Do you think it possible that Sir William might invite some of his old friends to such a gathering? Think how delightful, Miss Forrest."

"I rather think it likely that Mrs. Woodland would be asked to accompany her son at some time or other."

"Oh, yes, of course!" Miss Pierce rose and went to the table to place her finished garment with the others.

Poor Miss Pierce. Her interest in Robert Woodland clearly was not entirely overcome by the tragic charm of the new vicar. Julia wondered if Mr. Woodland might conceivably be moved to do so mad a thing as to marry the flirtatious and imprudent Miss Pierce. It would be a most uncharacteristic step for that cautious gentleman; still, so long as no engagement to Julia was announced, who could blame Miss Pierce for her hopes?

Julia did not have long to consider the question, for Robert himself now appeared, accompanied by Major Forbisher, the justice of the peace.

"Have we missed Mr. Simmons?" Julia heard Robert ask his mother.

"No, indeed," Mrs. Woodland replied. "I have been expecting him this half hour."

"I have brought Major Forbisher to see him most particularly—"

"It is a most alarming thing, madam," Major Forbisher interrupted, his gray moustache bristling. "I will show you this nasty thing, and the other ladies, too, and ask that if any of you see such a thing about the town, you will send word to me at once."

He drew from his pocket a rectangle of rough grayish paper on which Julia could see were printed the crude words, "Death to Victoria." Julia left her chair and hurried to examine the notice and hear more of it.

"Major Forbisher, where did such a thing come from?"

"It was found on the very grounds of the Beatrice, Miss Forrest." Major Forbisher's moustache quivered indignantly. "A young lad discovered it just before noon today and brought it to me directly."

Julia fingered the rough paper, then raised her eyes to meet Mr. Woodland's. He shook his head slightly, then turned with an expression of relief to the drawing-room door, where Mr. Simmons was arriving.

"Oh, Mr. Simmons, just come and look at this, will you?"

The new vicar, who was greeting Miss Pierce, regretfully left her side and did as he was asked.

Mr. Simmons, though rather too intense for

Julia's tastes, was a young, rather appealing, but unfortunately impoverished, gentleman, to whom, in Julia's opinion, Miss Pierce's modest fortune would be most welcome.

"Can you tell us, Mr. Simmons," Mr. Woodland was asking, "if this disgusting notice is like those you have seen in Leeds?"

Mr. Simmons peered at the paper for several moments, then allowed that it did seem to be much the same.

"That is just what I feared!" Mr. Woodland spoke urgently. "It is not a condition or a problem confined to Leeds. It may be—it must be—that Bellwether is at work again."

"Perhaps." Major Forbisher, who was old enough to remember the business of Bellwether quite distinctly, was skeptical. "But if you read the smaller lettering, you will see that, unlike Bellwether, those who published this atrocity offer no proposals for an alternative to the monarchy. Nor do they accuse the queen of any misdeeds that might be thought to justify her death."

"How could there be such misdeeds?" Julia cried. "She has been queen much too short a time to have committed any."

"When one considers the wording carefully, it appears more and more fanatical," Major Forbisher said with a thoughtful frown. "These cannot be rational men."

"But if not Bellwether, who?" was Robert's question.

They could only shrug and look at each other with raised eyebrows, though the word "anarchists" was muttered among them. When the conversation died away, Mr. Simmons took the opportunity to return to Miss Pierce, and the others turned to other, less troublesome news.

Mr. Woodland and Mr. Simmons had breakfasted early with Sir William at the Beatrice and seen him and Miss Sennett on their way to Winderfields by eight o'clock. Both had seemed happy and eager to be away, though Sir William declared that he meant to keep in very close touch with his old friends in York. When Mr. Woodland had imparted this information sufficiently, tea was served, and Mr. Simmons made a handsome little speech in well-chosen, distinctly spoken words thanking the ladies for their work on behalf of the orphans. When the party broke up half an hour later, Mr. Woodland had said nothing more than a "Good afternoon, Miss Forrest," to Julia.

Julia walked homeward, feeling uncertain of where to turn her thoughts. To the troubling notice found on the grounds of the Beatrice? to the question of her mother and Sir William? to the matter of Miss Pierce and Mr. Woodland? Certainly her thoughts must not stray back to that disturbing and mystifying dream.

As she turned the corner, she was grateful for the novelty of the sight of a carriage standing in front of the vacant house across from Mrs. Ponder's. She was almost certain that it was the agent's carriage; perhaps there would be a new neighbor after all.

Suddenly a second carriage swung around the corner into view. It drew abreast of her, and she heard her name shouted. It was a familiar voice, and now she saw Mimmie hailing her from within the carriage.

Mimmie in a carriage! It could mean only one thing. The three of them were to go to Winderfields! It had happened at last!

Mimmie threw open the carriage door without waiting for assistance from the driver. Julia saw her face, streaked and tear-stained, red-eyed and pinched, and Julia's heart froze. Mimmie did not look as though they were leaving for Winderfields. Something was wrong.

"Get in!" Mimmie cried. "Quickly!"

"What has happened?" Julia hurried to obey. "Where is my mother?"

"Drive on!" Mimmie commanded the driver. "As quickly as you can!"

The door slammed, the driver disappeared, and in an instant they were underway.

"Mimmie, where are we going? What has happened? Tell me!"

Mimmie burst into tears.

"Please, Mimmie." Julia forced down her own emotions to reason with her. "Please don't cry. You must tell me what has happened."

Mimmie nodded but continued to sob and hiccup. Fighting rising panic, Julia waited the several minutes before Mimmie could begin.

"It is—it is Frances. Julia, your mother is dead."

It took a few moments for the words to sink in. "Impossible! It cannot be!" It was not blind denial; Julia truly did not believe it. Mama, of course, would never die. She would live on, year after year, never growing old, ever beautiful, charming, exasperating, wonderful.

"It is true, my dearest Julia. She was discovered this afternoon on the grounds of the Beatrice. It was thought at first that she had been taken suddenly ill, for she had been walking toward the hotel. When she was taken up from the path by passersby, it was seen that she had been . . . had been struck with a dagger to the heart."

Julia gave an incoherent cry and sank back into the cushions. The words could not be understood, even less believed, but they struck like a blow all the same. In fact, this was another bizzare and most unwelcome dream from which she could wake herself. One *could* wake oneself if one made the effort, and it would be best to do so now, before it got any worse.

But she did not wake. Long minutes went by with no sudden return to blessed consciousness. There was only the sound of Mimmie's sobs and the rattles and creaking of the carriage and the soft clop of the horses along the road.

And surely this was wrong. Snatching at this diversion, Julia sat up and looked out of the window. It was the absence of city sounds that had brought her to herself; they were passing quiet pastures and ripe fields where the harvest was well under way.

"Mimmie, where are we going?"

"Away," Mimmie murmured between sobs. "Away from York."

"We must stop! We must go home! I want—I must see my mother." Tears of fear and confusion were in Julia's eyes.

"No! We cannot go back."

"Mimmie, this is madness. Even if what you say is—is true, we must go back. I must be with her and so must you. There are arrangements to be made. We cannot leave her with strangers."

"We must! I have promised her, time and again, that if . . . when . . . that I would take you to safety. It was her command to me, Julia. I must not fail her."

"What do you mean?" Julia nearly screamed in her panic. "I don't understand! Mimmie, what do you mean by 'taking me to safety'? Where are we going?"

"I am taking you to your father."

For a long time, Julia could say nothing. She sat stunned but in a state of intense awareness. She could feel every bump of the rutted road, every swaying, lurching motion of the carriage. She could hear clearly the clatter of hooves and the rattle of wheels, even smell the earth and vegetation of the farms they passed. So this was real and not a dream.

"To my father?" she breathed at last.

Mimmie nodded silently.

Julia could focus on none of the questions that darted through her mind. She sat back again and stared out the window, hoping by watching the fields and workers to seize some strands of rational thought.

At length the carriage drew to a stop; it was time to change the horses. Julia and Mimmie stepped down from the carriage and stood beneath a tree, not speaking for all the time that fresh horses were hitched.

When they were under way again, Julia asked, "Whose carriage is this?"

"I hired it from Mr. Higgins's stables."

Julia wondered silently why she did not demand

to be taken back. Why she had not simply remained behind at the post stop? Why she was tolerating this impossible tale of her mother being dead and her father alive when only this morning the opposite was true? But the answer was simple: It was because it was Mimmie who said so.

They continued some time in silence, except for Mimmie's sighing and occasional weeping. Julia was too numbed, too confused to cry, and any questions she tried to ask brought on another fit of incoherent sobs from her companion. The September day drew to a close. Night came, but in the moonlight that lent a sheen of eerie beauty to the countryside, the carriage continued on its journey. It was not until past midnight by Julia's watch, when the moon was near setting, that they stopped at a small village inn and the two women stumbled stiffly from the carriage.

"We can rest a few hours," Mimmie said, "but we must be off again at daybreak."

The inn was not a large establishment and the two travelers had to share a bed. Julia lay awake, staring silent and bewildered into the darkness. Mimmie, she knew, was not sleeping either, but still they did not speak of what had happened.

They left the inn at dawn, both Julia and Mimmie declining breakfast as they had declined a meal the night before. Mimmie had been watchful as they paid for their lodging, looking constantly about her as if fearing the appearance of any of the other lodgers. When the carriage drew away from the door, she thrust her head from the window several times, looking backward.

When it seemed she was satisfied no other carriage or horseman followed, she settled back against the cushions with a sigh. Then, without question or prompting from Julia, and in a voice that bespoke weariness as much as sorrow, Mimmie began to speak. "We are going to a village to the southwest of London. That is where your father lives, or rather, near there. His property is called Fainway."

"This is where my father lives when he is not at sea?"

"Mr. Townes is never at sea. He is not and has never been a naval officer."

"Why was I told so?"

"Julia, dear, it was simply a part of the history which Frances created to protect herself. To protect all of us."

"Protect us? From what? From whom?" Fear lodged in the pit of Julia's stomach. "From my father?"

Mimmie shook her head. "She did not fear him, except that he would find her—that anyone might find her. Her fear was of others, of one man in particular."

As Mimmie fumbled for her handkerchief, Julia tried to absorb this strange new perception of her mother.

Mimmie took a deep breath, seemed mentally to square her shoulders, and in a moment, continued. "Some of what Frances told you of her own history was quite true. She *was* the daughter of a clergyman, and orphaned at the age of fifteen. That was when she came to live with a family of cousins at Winterhall, an estate near Fainway, where we became friends.

"She was a great beauty, even then, and the son of the household—his name was Richard—Richard Payne—was in love with her from a very early time. Frances loved him, too, but his mother, and to a lesser extent, his father, were opposed to the match. They had decided, you see, that he would marry a certain young lady with a very large fortune. Frances and Richard were forced to meet secretly, and I helped them. I would walk with her to a special place on the grounds of Winterhall, called the Druid's Circle, where Richard would join us. There I would leave them for an hour or two while I walked in the woods nearby. Their love grew, and they were determined to marry. When his parents were told, they were very angry, and Richard was sent away to Canada. Undaunted, the two young lovers promised to be faithful to each other and to marry when he returned, whether or not his parents relented and gave their consent.

"While in Canada, his letters to Frances were intercepted by his mother, and when he had been gone just over a year, his parents told Frances, indeed, told everyone, that he had died there. There was a great show of mourning by the family and the neighborhood, for everyone believed the story.

"A few months later, a neighbor, Mr. Townes, who had long admired Frances, asked for her hand. After many weeks of badgering, threatening and even mistreatment, her cousins forced her to accept him."

"Mimmie, did—did Mr. Townes know this?"

"I do not know, Julia. Frances always hoped not. In due time, when the wedding was safely accomplished, Richard was permitted to return, with a great show of rejoicing by his parents at the miracle which had restored their son to them.

"Richard's anger, when he returned and learned the truth, was a terrible thing. It extended to his parents, who were well-connected and landed people, and was turned against all members of the upper classes, whom he had come to see as greedy, grasping idlers, unworthy of their status and privilege, only interested in gaining more wealth by whatever means. In this state of mind, Richard left his family and fell in with a group of radical young men of like thinking, who undertook to change the establishment by whatever means were required. They turned, I am afraid, to theft and even to violence as they engaged to overthrow the government, even the crown."

"Oh, my God! Bellwether! And this . . . Richard . . . took part in the deeds of theft and violence? Mimmie, was he Bellwether?"

"No. But Richard was completely under the sway of the man and the movement. He soon became Bellwether's protege and gained his confidence. A mysterious man, Bellwether. His real name was unknown, even, I believe, to Richard, though I have always believed that he told Frances *something* about Bellwether.

"It was more than a year, indeed, nearly two years before Richard became disenchanted with the movement and its leader, recognizing at last that Bellwether was nothing more than a charlatan and an imposter, who sought power for himself rather than reform of the government or relief for the common man. Richard left the movement and was actively hunted, not only by the authorities for his part in the criminal activities the group had engaged in, but by Bellwether as well, who feared that Richard would betray him, disclose whatever he knew of Bellwether that might somehow lead the authorities to find him."

"What did he do? Richard, I mean."

"He came to Fainway, to Frances. He chose a time when Mr. Townes was away and Frances was alone. He begged for her help in escaping the country, and she did not refuse him. But she went even further. She decided to go with him." Mimmie sighed and stared into her lap, unwilling now to meet Julia's eyes. "There had to be money, of course, and Frances took from Mr. Townes's home everything of value that could be carried."

It was a long time before Julia could say, "And she took me with her?"

Mimmie shook her graying and untidy head.

"Frances did not know she carried you. It was only after she had departed Fainway that she discovered she was to have a child. It was, of course, too late to return.

"They had intended to go to France, taking me with them. Frances and I traveled separately from Richard. He insisted on it for our safety. We managed to elude the authorities and had all arrived at Portsmouth. But Bellwether was too clever. He found Richard, after all."

Mimmie paused, sighed and continued in a soft and vacant voice, as though the words were too painful to tell in a normal tone. "Richard had gone to the docks to arrange our passage. As he was returning to the inn, he was set upon by Bellwether or by one of his agents and struck down with a dagger, just as—"

"Oh . . . oh, Mimmie!"

"When he did not return after two hours, I went in search of him. It was always easier for me than for Frances to go about unnoticed. I followed the exact route he had told us he would take. I found him dead just behind the inn's stables. I found in his pocket the tickets he had bought. I took them and returned at once to the inn, leaving . . ." Mimmie had to stop and recover herself. "Leaving Richard there in the dust, as I knew I must do."

Seeing the tears now flowing unheeded from Mimmie's eyes, Julia held her gently until the storm had passed. "What did you do next?" Julia asked as Mimmie dried her eyes.

"Frances and I left that very evening for France. We engaged a serving man to attend us and disguised ourselves as a lady and her French-speaking maid. It was in France, in Orleans, that you were born."

"In France?" Julia was shaken and astonished.

"When you were two years old we returned to England. We settled first in Hornsea, but stayed only long enough to establish a history there as a widow of a naval officer, her young daughter and an impoverished cousin living with them. We accounted for our final move to York by saying that Hornsea, a seaside town, brought memories of the poor widow's husband which were too painful to permit us to remain there. York, of course was a fairly large and impersonal city, far enough, we reasoned, from any persons in the south of England who might recognize us."

"And in York we all remained," Julia breathed. Memories of her childhood came unbidden now— the quiet, reclusive life which had seemed always incongruous for a woman like her mother. It made sense now in the light of these revelations. But. . . .

"Mimmie, why did you go with her? Why did you stay?"

"Because Frances was my friend. And Richard was my brother."

"Oh, my God!"

"And I, like Frances, had taken from my own home whatever of value I could remove. I could not return there, even had I wanted to live with my parents who had caused such misery to my most beloved brother."

Julia sat thoughtful for a long time. "But, Mimmie," she said finally, "this Mr. Townes, the man you say is my father, why should he believe it? As I understand it, he had no information as to my being expected."

"That is true. He does not know, even to this day, of your existence."

"And . . . and truly, Mimmie, is there not a very good chance that he is not my father at all? That you are, in fact, not my cousin, but my aunt?"

Mimmie shook her head. "Mr. Townes is your father."

It was said decidedly, and Julia, though not persuaded, said no more for the moment.

As the journey continued through the long day, more pieces of the incredible tale were supplied: the decisions about their new names and histories; the journeys from France to Hornsea to York; the search for lodgings; the careful selection of old Mr.

Woodland and his bank to hold and invest their meager resources; the struggle to live; and the fears for their safety which subsided only after years had passed without discovery or incident.

Frances had used her beauty and her charm to obtain help and good treatment for them. How could the most hardened landlord demand more than she could afford to pay for a suitable house? How could tradesmen deny her credit while old Mr. Woodland labored to make her solvent? Their little nest egg grew, though never so large as to make them entirely at ease about money. Caution, so foreign to Frances's nature and to Mimmie's upbringing, had always been necessary where money was concerned.

And, of course, Frances could not marry—not Sir William or any of the other prosperous gentlemen who had wished for her hand.

They traveled again until the near midnight hour brought the setting of the moon. They ate a scanty meal in the room the innkeeper assigned to them, and as they settled down for a few hours of sleep, the inconvenience of having left York with nothing in the way of clothing or belongings became more apparent. Julia washed herself in the tepid water the maidservant had brought, and wished for a comb. Mimmie had fallen into bed after placing a chair before the locked door, and was already asleep. Julia was wearier than she had ever been in her life, but the cold, bitter apprehension and the burning ache of sorrow were stronger still.

And suddenly the grief overwhelmed her. The tears that had not come, strangely, during all those many hours now welled up in huge, heartbroken sobs. She clutched her precious new sewing basket, the only tangible link remaining to the beautiful, fascinating, mysterious Frances, and until the sleep of sheer exhaustion overtook her, Julia cried for her mother.

Again they set out at dawn. On this day of travel, Julia and Mimmie, victims of accumulated fatigue and emotion, slept intermittently. But it was a day of questions and reflection, too, for Julia had now come to accept the unthinkable fact that her mother had died a violent and mysterious death at the hand of the villian, Bellwether. He had found her somehow, and had believed, as Mimmie did, that Frances knew something that could do him harm, even after all these years. Was this a signal that the evil movement was reborn and the new queen in danger? The notices Julia had seen in Major Forbisher's hands told her that it must be so.

At one point, when both she and Mimmie were awake and disposed to talk, Julia asked for an accounting of Frances's last day.

"I saw nothing of her after breakfast," Mimmie said. "It seems quite disturbing now, but . . ." Her voice died away, then she said, "She reminded me that very morning of my promise to deliver you to your father should it be necessary."

Julia felt a little prick of apprehension at the mention of their destination, but she forced it aside. "What else did she say?"

"Nothing else that seemed out of the ordinary, then or now. We spoke of Sir William's gathering, of course. She asked me . . . I remember now . . . she asked if I had noticed a young, dark man who stood a few moments on the stairs that evening."

A sensation of cold dread ran down Julia's spine. "And did you notice him?"

Mimmie shook her head. "No. I did not see him."

"Mimmie, how did she come to be at the Beatrice? Sir William had departed early that morning. Who else was she thinking of visiting there?"

Mimmie could only puzzle over it, but Julia recalled vividly and with a heavy heart the look that had passed between her mother and the brown man. Recognition? Puzzlement? Surprise? She could not say precisely which of these responses— perhaps all—had been present when those two had looked at each other, but the memory of that instant was like a knife—not of jealousy now, but of fear. The brown man was too young to be Bellwether himself, of course, but. . . .

In the late afternoon they had a final change of horses, and the driver received detailed directions to their destination. An hour later, when dusk had fallen, the carriage stopped before a high gate. The coachman, as weary as his passengers, stepped to the carriage door. "The gate appears to be open, madam."

"Very well," Mimmie replied. "Just wait nearby. We shall be going on in a moment."

The driver disappeared and Mimmie turned to Julia. "I cannot take you further. I cannot linger here at all."

"What? But you must not leave me! How will I—"

"Take this," Mimmie interrupted, opening her

little handbag and drawing out a piece of jewelry. "Go to Mr. Townes. Give him this. He will know that it has come from Frances. If you must, you may tell him that I have brought you, but implore that he say nothing of it to anyone."

"I cannot do this, Mimmie!" Julia was very near to panic. "Please let me come with you!"

Mimmie shook her head firmly, though Julia could see tears in her eyes. "It would be madness, Julia. It would endanger me to a degree that cannot be imagined. Indeed, it would endanger both of us." She put out a hand to touch Julia's cheek. "Hurry, my dearest child. You must go now."

"But where are you going? When will I see you?"

"I will write to you when—if I can. And I will pray for you always, as you must do for me."

Fighting back tears, Julia embraced this woman who was the last remnant of anything that embodied life as she had known it until three days—it seemed an eternity—ago. She then drew away and stepped down from the carriage. She stood watching as the door closed and the driver, who had been waiting, walking off the hours of stiffness a few feet up the road, climbed into his seat and took up the reins. She stood watching a long time after the carriage had driven out of sight.

At last she turned toward the gate. She saw a sloping gravel drive that led into the distance toward a dim glow of lighted windows. Then, because she knew not what else to do, she began to walk toward the house that sat at the top of the drive.

Chapter Four

Charles stood in the hallway, his hand still on the knob of the dining-room door which he had just closed behind him. He waited, willing his heartbeat and his breathing to slow. Half of his attention was drawn to the voices of his dinner guests, muffled but still distinguishable: the shrill, affronted bleating of Mrs. Merryweather, punctuated by the nasal, apprehensive giggle of her daughter; and the deep, arrogant tones of Mrs. Todd. Charles told himself that he should have waited, remained in the dining room until dinner was over, but even as he formed the thought, he knew how impossible it would have been to delay. Now to his ears came Mary's soothing, well-bred voice—reconciling words, a gentle laugh at the end, followed by other, masculine-timbred voices, speaking quickly. More laughter. Mary had turned the dispute aside; she could always be depended upon, though, of course, she would be disappointed that Charles had not been present to admire her tact and skill.

He touched the sharp object in his pocket and gave his full attention to the question of whether he should go and fetch his aunt. He doubted she would be asleep. Charles knew that it was only Mrs. Todd's presence which had kept Aunt Julia from presiding in her customary way at dinner this evening. But, confound it, the woman was a neighbor and had to be asked to dine once in a while!

No. He would not fetch his aunt, he decided, squaring his shoulders and moving on along the hall.

He came into the library very quietly, for the heavy oak doors moved silently and the latch with nary a click or groan. He saw a woman dressed in blue standing by the fire. He supposed it was a young woman—Cobb had said so—but the room was dimly lighted, and though she stood erect, there was a trace of great weariness in the line of her back. She made a slight movement, and the light of the lamp on the table illuminated her more fully.

She was not precisely tall, about six or seven inches above five feet, he guessed; perhaps her slimness made her seem a little taller. A bright spark from the fire now showed that she had a mass of heavy straight hair of palest blonde, dressed in a braid beginning at the crown and doubled back on itself.

He let the door make a muted thud as he closed it; she turned sharply.

"Good evening," he said.

"Good evening, sir."

She had a soft and pleasing voice, though there was a trace of a Northern accent.

"I am told you . . ." He stopped as he stood in the lamplight and saw her face clearly. The blue of her eyes and the planes of her face made him catch his breath. Her wide eyes widened even more as she studied his features in turn. They stood silent for several moments.

"Are you Mr. Townes?" she asked finally.

"Yes." His own voice seemed oddly strained to him, as though he heard it as a stranger's voice and from a great distance.

"I—" The tiny shake of her head betrayed her perplexity. "I am told that I am your daughter, sir. My name is Julia Forrest."

"Julia," he breathed, and then fell silent once again. He remained so for what seemed to Julia a very long time, then he asked, "Where is your mother?"

"She is dead, sir." Tears welled in her eyes. "Or so I am told, for I have not seen her."

"When? When did she die?"

"Some days ago, sir. Three days, I think."

"And where?"

"In the city of York, which was our home."

"York. But I . . ." He took a long breath. "Please, Miss . . . Miss Julia, let us be seated."

Though stiff from three days in a carriage, Julia complied. Mr. Townes strode to a cabinet and poured two glasses of Madeira. He brought one of them to Julia before sitting in a chair to face her.

"You must tell me everything. And especially"— he drew from his pocket the gold-and-ruby brooch —"how you came to bring this to me."

Julia took a sip of the unfamiliar beverage and placed the glass on a table beside her chair. She sighed with weariness and sorrow; Mr. Townes turned to look at her more closely.

"Have you had any supper?"

"No, sir."

He rang a bell, ordered a tray to be brought and when the servant had departed, resumed his seat. Julia took another sip of wine and, finding it helpful, began the tale.

It was more than an hour later when she stopped speaking, having told at the last of the flight from York at the insistence of Mimmie, the woman Mr. Townes decided must be Clara Payne, daughter of a farmer proprietor of Winterhall. The narrative had been interrupted only with the arrival of the supper tray, and Julia had continued her revelations even as she ate the tasty dishes brought to her, surprised that she had such an appetite. As she had spoken, as she had eaten and drunk, Mr. Townes had watched her intently, studying the pale hair, so like his own before it had turned more truly silver. And the eyes. Though softened by feminine features and long lashes and arching brows of a soft brown that was almost gray, the color of those eyes was the same as those which stared at him each morning from his shaving mirror. She had not been able to account for the brooch. She had seen it for the first time when Mimmie had handed it to her this evening, but he thought he understood its part in this affair.

Julia stopped speaking, took the last sip from the glass of wine and settled back into the deep cushions of her chair. There was a heavy silence in the room broken only by the stately tick tock of the clock that hung on the far wall. Julia listened to it drowsily, noticing for the first time that it had not chimed in all the time she had been in the room. Perhaps in a study, such as this surely was, one did not wish for the interruptions that came at each quarter hour.

"I see that you are very tired," he said. "I'll have you shown to a bedroom." Again he rang the bell, and when Cobb appeared, he sent for the housekeeper.

Mrs. Holmes, if she felt surprise or any other emotion when told that the young lady would stay the night, did not betray it.

"Miss . . . Miss Forrest has had supper, Mrs. Holmes," Mr. Townes said. "See that she has whatever else she may require or wish."

"Yes, sir."

Julia rose from her chair and took up the sewing basket which sat beside it on the floor. She turned to say a word of relief and gratitude to Mr. Townes, but he was already moving away from her.

"Thank you, sir," she called after him.

He only nodded abruptly and was gone.

"Have you no boxes or belongings, ma'am?"

Julia shook her head silently.

"Ah, well. We can find what you need. This way, ma'am."

Julia followed Mrs. Holmes into the hallway and up the staircase, too weary to notice much detail of the house where she would spend at least this one night. She was shown into a bedroom that was not overlarge, but to Julia it looked like a paradise of comfort. A housemaid who had been collected along the way hurried to light a fire.

"Do you wish to have a bath, ma'am?"

"Oh, yes, Mrs. Holmes, if you please."

"Just sit here by the fire, then, and I will return in a few minutes' time." Mrs. Holmes took the blue-and-silver basket from Julia, placed it on a table and took a moment to examine its contents. Then she left the room.

Julia did as she was told, and she found that she had, in fact, been fast asleep in the chair when Mrs. Holmes returned, accompanied by a small band of servants bringing tub, water and a bundle of clothing and implements.

Julia was undressed, put into the tub, her hair and body scrubbed by two diligent maids, then dressed in a soft white nightdress that was disentangled from the bundle of garments that lay on a chair. Her hair was then toweled vigorously and combed dry before the fire. That done, she was tucked into bed like a child, and never was a child more willing or more grateful to lay its head on the softest of feather pillows. Julia was instantly asleep.

It was raining. Julia could hear the pelting of large drops even before she opened her eyes. Lying on her side in a bed that had no bed curtains, she was facing a large window hung with a white-patterned drapery. She lay still, remembering slowly where she was and the events of the past days that had brought her here. Tears came as she thought of her mother, but she forced them aside, turned onto her back and sat up against the pillow.

"Who are you?" she cried with a gasp at the elderly, white-haired lady who sat knitting in the rocking chair drawn up beside the bed.

"I am Mrs. Carlyle. I am Mr. Townes's aunt. I live here."

"How do you do?" Julia could think of nothing else to say.

"I wanted to see you before any of the others. They know only that another guest has arrived, but Charles came to my bedroom last night to give me a full account of your arrival."

"Others. Are there more family, then?"

"Oh, I daresay Mary Belleville chooses to think herself family, though, of course, she is not. We have a family by the name of Dalton here as houseguests. They will leave tomorrow."

"I see." Julia fell silent, knowing instinctively that Mrs. Carlyle was not a lady for idle chatter, and, anyway, she had no idea what to say.

Mrs. Carlyle spent long silent moments staring hard into Julia's face before she spoke again. "You have the family features, I must admit. What is the exact date of your birth?"

Now here was a question that Julia had kept expecting from Mr. Townes all during their interview the previous evening, but he had never asked it.

"I was born on the twenty-fourth of May in the year 1819, ma'am. On the same day as our queen."

"Were you, indeed?" Mrs. Carlyle seemed to fall into a state of careful calculation. Finally she said, "Well, it is possible."

Julia met steadily the eyes that studied her. Presently, Mrs. Carlyle stood up.

"I shall tell Mary the whole of your story, as Charles has given me leave to do. Very likely she will be along to see you quite soon thereafter, for she loves to make herself useful. In the meantime, you will want your breakfast. I'll have them bring it."

"Thank you, ma'am."

Mrs. Carlyle departed without acknowledging the thanks, leaving Julia with the precious scrap of information that her father, if father he was, was called Charles.

When she was alone, Julia washed her face and hands and explored the room. Looking into the wardrobe, she discovered that her dress was not hanging there, nor was it anywhere in the room. She shivered and wished for a dressing gown and slippers, but she discovered to her delight that the comb from last night had been left. She took it back to bed with her and set about bringing order to her tangled tresses.

Before she had finished, a maid came into the room to draw the drapes and make up the fire. Hard on her heels came a second maid bearing a tray from which came the wondrous smell of breakfast.

"Can you tell me," Julia asked as the tray was placed on her knees, "what has become of my clothing?"

"Everything is being laundered, madam. Mrs. Holmes is looking for something for you to wear until your own things are ready."

"I see. Thank you." It appeared that Julia was confined to bed or at least to this room for the time being.

She had finished her breakfast and was standing barefoot by the window when the next visitor arrived.

"Miss . . . Miss Forrest?" Mary asked as she closed the bedroom door.

"Yes."

"I am Miss Belleville. Mary Belleville. I have just spoken with Mrs. Carlyle and . . . Oh, dear, have you no slippers?"

"No. Nor anything of my own except what is being laundered. Even my shoes have disappeared."

"I imagine they are being cleaned as well."

Julia murmured something about the efficiency of the household staff.

"Mrs. Holmes is said to be most particular." Mary smiled and Julia felt encouraged by the mild and friendly expression of her visitor's face.

Mary Belleville was not precisely a pretty woman, and at thirty-six was past her first bloom, to be sure, but she was tall and straight, with a regal carriage. She had quiet hazel eyes and light brown hair that was blessed with a touch of natural wave. She was not over intelligent or overeducated, just a pleasant, well-spoken, ladylike woman, mistress of a modest fortune from her late father which enabled her to live and do as she pleased. And it pleased her to visit, as often as invited, her very agreeable connection, Mr. Townes.

"Do get back into bed, my dear," Mary said. "This floor must be cold, and, indeed, you do not look as though you are completely rested."

Julia was glad to obey; after that large breakfast, she did feel rather drowsy again.

"There must be questions you are wishing to ask of someone," Mary said softly. "Should you care to ask them of me?"

"I would, indeed." Julia nodded. "But I hardly know where to begin."

"Perhaps," Mary said, "I should begin by telling you who I am."

"Mrs. Carlyle said that you are thought of as family."

"Not quite." Mary laughed a little self-consciously. "Mrs. Carlyle, least of all, I am sure, thinks of me in that way, though she is always kind to me. My brother, he is actually my stepbrother, *is* a relative, however. His father was a cousin to Mr. Townes."

"Then your brother is not a Mr. Belleville?"

"Mr. Christian. Lawrence Christian. He is a few years younger than I. But you will meet him yourself. Even now he is traveling home from the north and is expected here at any time."

Julia was thinking that, though she had always wished for a brother, she would be happy enough with a cousin, distant though this one might be. That is, if she were permitted. . . .

"And that," Mary was saying, "is all of the family, I am afraid, besides Mrs. Carlyle and Mr. Townes. Mrs. Carlyle is the sister of Mr. Townes's father. She was married to a naval officer who died some years ago, and she returned here at that time. She is rather fierce to behold from time to time, but I believe her to be kind of heart." Another bright and friendly smile lit Mary's face. "You must never let her know that she is suspected of such a thing."

"And do you and Mr. Christian live here at . . ." She had to search her mind for a moment. "At Fainway?"

"Oh, no. We are Londoners, both of us. Our homes are within a brief walk of each other, but in fact, we see each other most often on our visits here."

"Then the only occupants of this house are Mr. Townes and Mrs. Carlyle?"

"That is so. Though Mr. Townes often entertains guests for a week or a month at a time." Mary smiled again at Julia. "He is especially fond of asking families who have children."

Julia flushed and said, "I wonder if you would ask Mr. Townes when I might see him. I mean, of course, when my clothes are fit to appear in."

"Oh, my dear, I fear it will be some days before you will see Mr. Townes."

"What? But I must see him! I cannot bear not knowing what is to become of me. Am I to stay? Must I go elsewhere? Why may I not see him?"

"Mr. Townes left Fainway very early this morning. He was not certain when he might return." Mary hesitated, then said, "He has gone to York, you see."

Julia fell back against the pillows. "To York. Of course."

Mary turned to the window and watched the rain. "He will have had a wet ride today. I pray he may not catch a cold."

Chapter Five

Julia remained all day in her bedroom; in fact, she slept a good deal. The rain continued in a monotonous drizzle and the day in an unremitting grayness, sapping what little energy she had after the ordeal of the past several days. In sleep, there was forgetfulness, although dreams of an uncomfortable ordinariness intruded.

At about five o'clock she was roused by the sound of a carriage on the gravel drive below. She rose and went to the window in time to see a gentleman, caped and hatted, emerge and step promptly into a puddle. She heard a faint bark of self-conscious laughter before he hurried up the steps and out of sight.

Julia was moving restlessly around the room, from window to dressing table (she combed her hair again) to fireside chair, when the maid, who had appeared throughout the day to tend the fire, bring fresh water, meals and tea, now arrived bringing an armload of books.

"Miss Belleville asked that I bring these, madam. She begs your pardon for not coming herself. She was on her way to your room when her brother arrived."

"Thank you. What is your name, please?"

"I am Rosie, madam. And I am to tell you that Miss Belleville will come to see you before dinner."

"Thank you, Rosie. It is very kind of Miss Belleville."

Rosie, ever diligent, built up the fire, inspected the water pitcher, asked if there was anything madam might wish for, then Julia was left alone again.

Julia sorted through the books. Most she had read, but there was one that she had not, nor even heard of. *Oliver Twist.* She took the book to the large chair near the fire, curled her bare feet into her nightgown and began to read.

But it was impossible, futile even to try to concentrate. Her mother was dead! How unreal it still seemed. Perhaps if she were at home now and not here in a house that seemed almost a wonderland, it would be easier to believe it. If she could see with her own eyes that Mama was not in her usual chair in the parlor, looking up with that smile that always warmed Julia clear to her toes, then it might seem real. Then she might somehow grasp the idea that Mama had been . . . murdered. Murdered, it would seem, by shadowy, unknown, evil people because . . . because of something she knew— some secret from a long ago time. What could it be? And here her musings could take her no further.

Julia knew rather than felt that she was grieving

for her mother. When she thought of never again seeing that beautiful, maddening, dearest of humans, she felt a great emptiness in her soul. And to lose her in a manner so unthinkable. . . .

Perhaps it was best not to think of it just yet, she thought as she took up the book and began again at page one.

But her thoughts refused to allow her to concentrate on the words.

What of Mimmie? Where was she this wet, unwelcoming day? Hiding? Devising a second new identity? Seeking for another dwelling place? Perhaps she had returned to France.

And Mr. Townes had gone to York. Would he find satisfaction there that Frances Forrest was in truth Frances Townes? And if he did not?

Then she would very likely be turned out as an imposter. Mr. Townes appeared to be a man of means, even a man of great wealth, if Mimmie's description was accurate. He was wise to be cautious. She would have thought him a fool if he had done otherwise. Of course he had gone to York. She sighed and began a paragraph again, and again her eyes stared blankly at the page.

If he returned unsatisfied or even uncertain, she would go without delay. Perhaps she should go anyway, for she was not at all sure that she belonged here with these kind, but distant strangers.

Brave thoughts, but where, after all, could she go?

She could return to York and seek a position as a governess. She was educated, and Sir William would assist her, she was sure. And Mrs. Woodland.

Mrs. Woodland. Yes, indeed. And what of her son? What would Robert think of all this? And would it be dangerous to return? Mimmie believed that here she would be safe.

Round and round, over and over, the same questions, the same want of answers. Julia closed the book, rose to stand again at the window and watched the shadows of evening gather on the lawns below.

She was still there when a light tap on the door brought the return of Miss Belleville.

"Oh, my dear, there you are again on the cold floor with bare feet! Now here. I have brought you a couple of things that I hope will insure I see no more of this."

Mary draped the rose-colored garment she carried over one shoulder and held out a pair of slippers. "Put these on at once. They are not things of beauty, I know, but I do believe they will fit you."

After a long moment of hesitation, Julia took the slippers. "Thank you, Miss Belleville. And thank you for sending the books. You have been extremely kind to me. I shall be grateful for that always, no matter what happens."

"Oh, my dear Miss . . . Miss Forrest, you must trust that all will be well. I have not heard the whole of the events which have brought you here, but I know in my heart that you are a well-bred and kindly young woman, not . . ." Miss Belleville's delicacy prevented her from saying more.

"I am thankful for your encouragement, Miss Belleville," Julia said, fighting back a sudden urge for sarcasm.

"Would you like to come downstairs to dinner? Mrs. Carlyle has said that she will join us this evening."

Julia, uncomfortable at the thought of a room full of strangers and the piercing eyes of Mrs. Carlyle, asked to be excused.

"Of course. I quite understand," Mary said. "You are to do just as you like. Tomorrow the Daltons will be gone, and perhaps my brother as well. It will be easier for you when there is not such a houseful. In the meantime, I hope you will try not to be gloomy and that you will ask for whatever you may need."

"Thank you, Miss Belleville." It occurred to Julia that she had done little since coming to this house but thank people.

It was all very well, she thought to herself when she was once more alone, for Miss Belleville and anyone else she should encounter in the dining room to tell her that all would be well, and to try not to be "gloomy." *They* had not been cut adrift, as though by a sword stroke, from everything that was precious or even familiar. It was ungracious, she knew, but she could not help thinking that Miss Belleville's excessive kindness might become a little irritating if one were showered with it for days on end. With a guilty sigh, she put on the rose-colored dressing gown.

It fit her well enough, though loosely, and she *was* grateful to have it. She took her book to the chair by the fire where the light was better and began once more at page one.

Her dinner tray was brought by Mrs. Holmes, and Julia, on hearing her knock, was surprised to see the number of pages she had read.

"I thought it best that I explain the customs of the household to you, Miss Forrest," said Mrs. Holmes, "as you will be with us for several more days," the trace of a smile, "at the very least."

"I should like to know of them, Mrs. Holmes," Julia replied in a noncomittal voice.

"When we have no guests in residence, and Miss Belleville and Mr. Christian are not considered guests for such purposes, breakfast is not served downstairs at all. All parties have breakfast served in their own bedrooms. You may simply ring"— she pointed to the bell cord—"whenever you wish to have breakfast brought to you."

"Yes, I see."

"We do not serve a midday dinner. It is Mr. Townes's opinion, and Mrs. Carlyle's as well, that a large meal in the middle of the day makes one unfit for further usefulness without a long nap. A luncheon, therefore, is served at one o'clock, a very light tea at five, and dinner, a large meal for which it is customary to dress, is served at eight-thirty."

"I see," Julia said again.

"This is the custom on every day except Sunday, when a large dinner is served at two o'clock. Usually there are guests on Sunday—neighbors, perhaps the Reverend Mr. Witherspoon."

Julia nodded, then said, "Mrs. Holmes, you will think me quite mad, but what is the day of the week today?"

"It is Friday, Miss Forrest."

"Friday."

"There is no footman remaining awake all night. If you require a servant after the house is closed— this will be at midnight unless we are entertaining —you may go to Mrs. Carlyle's maid, who has a small bedroom in her mistress's suite."

The idea of taking such a liberty with Mrs. Carlyle's maid left Julia speechless. She nodded silently.

"Otherwise, the kitchen maid is always at hand in the kitchen by five o'clock, and the cook an hour later."

"That is very clear, Mrs. Holmes. Thank you."

Mrs. Holmes nodded and removed the covers from the dishes that had been set on the table near the fire, and Julia sat down.

"Mrs. Holmes," she said with sudden daring, "do you mind telling me how long you have been housekeeper here at Fainway?"

"Very nearly thirty years, Miss Forrest."

Julia met the housekeeper's kindly eyes, but nothing more was said as Julia opened her napkin and placed it in her lap. Mrs. Holmes made yet another tour of the room to insure that no error or omission had occurred, then, with a "Good night, Miss Forrest," she was gone.

Julia ate her dinner, which was excellent, reflecting that she had had quite a parade of visitors in and out of the room this day—maids, the housekeeper and the kind Miss Belleville. But the one person she really wanted to see again had not come.

What does *Mrs. Carlyle make of me*? she wondered. She had no idea.

Julia finished her dinner, the maid came to remove the tray, and she was left alone, she presumed, for the night. Suddenly she wondered whether she was locked in this room. After all, they had no reason to trust her. She might be a thief. Was Mrs. Holmes's mention of the absent footman meant to put her off guard?

She went to the door and tried the knob. It turned smoothly, and the door opened without protest. Cautiously, she put her head out to look.

The door opened, not into a hallway, but to an open gallery through which she dimly remembered passing on the previous night. It was wide and silent, lit by lamps placed on tables at intervals along its length and by the reflected glow of the lamps in the entry hall below. The wooden floor gleamed with polish in the lamplight, and there was a patterned carpet to hush the footsteps of passers-by. From below she could hear, very faintly, the laughter and chatter of the dinner guests.

She closed the door and went to her bed in preparation for her second night under Mr. Townes's roof.

But she could not fall asleep. The extreme fatigue of the previous evening was not at hand, and the fears and confusion that haunted her were in full display as she lay restlessly, listening to the rain falling against her window. She thought of Mr. Townes on his journey. What would he find in York, and what would happen when he returned? What, for that matter, would tomorrow bring for her? Above all, was Mimmie safe? The fire was dead and long cold before Julia's whirling brain released her to a fitful dozing.

When she woke, her first thought was that it was still raining. The room was damp and chilly, and she was grateful to slip into the rose dressing gown after she had washed her face. Then, remembering Mrs. Holmes's instructions, she rang for the maid.

Rosie appeared almost instantly, bringing Julia's dress and undergarments, now laundered and fresh, and her shoes as well.

When she had breakfasted and dressed and had watched from the window as the family of guests— she had forgotten their name—drove away in their carriage, she went to the dressing table and combed her hair. There was a tap on the door.

Julia called, "Come in," fairly certain who her visitor would be.

She was right. Mary came in smiling.

"Good morning, Miss Forrest. I hope that you slept well."

"Good morning, Miss Belleville. I hope the same for you."

"What perfectly beautiful hair you have. And that braided arrangement is so becoming. You must teach me how to do it."

"Yes, certainly, if you wish."

"Now, if you are feeling up to it, I should like to have you meet my brother. He should be stirring soon and will surely join me in the small salon this morning. He declares that he means to stay a few days despite the absence of Mr. Townes, and indeed, he thinks that Mr. Townes will return quite soon."

"York is a full three days' journey from here," Julia pointed out. "Still, I hope it will be completed as quickly as possible."

"And you mustn't brood here alone, my dear Miss Forrest." Mary tucked a tortoiseshell comb more firmly into her own coiffure. "You may talk to us or not, as you please, but I do think that a change will be to your benefit."

"Indeed, Miss Belleville, I should very much like a change." Julia smiled. "Perhaps while we wait for Mr. Christian you will show me about the house."

A sudden qualm. "Unless you think Mrs. Carlyle will object."

"Object? Mercy no! Of course not."

So Julia had a tour of the house. She had never seen anything to compare with it.

"This is the guest wing," Mary said as she led Julia beyond the neighboring door and into the gallery. Peering over the railing, Julia could see the large entry hall below. "Here on this floor are the guest bedrooms," Mary went on as she made a grand sweep of her arm to include the rooms that continued all along this wing, even beyond where the gallery ended and became an ordinary hall. "The Waltons were given rooms down there. Bedrooms on the left, and on the right where, of course, there are no windows except on the very end, are storage rooms and that sort of thing."

"I see. How many bedrooms are there in this wing?"

"There are ten, I believe." Mary did not lead her down the hallway portion, but turned right where the gallery continued at a right angle, still overlooking the entry hall. "This doorway leads into the family's portion of the house."

To Julia, the double doors just beyond the point where the grand staircase reached the gallery appeared very firmly closed. "We shall see that portion of the upstairs later," Mary said as she turned to descend the stairs.

"This of course is the main entry, where I expect you were admitted the night before last."

Julia paused to study it. A very wide hallway seemed to cut right through the house. At each end was a large imposing double door. The one she could see closely, presumably the front door, was of carved wood, and she expected somehow that its opposite in the distant, shadowy other end was its twin.

Mary threw open the doors of the first room to the left of the front door. "This is the small reception room. I expect this is the room you were shown to when you arrived."

Julia shook her head. "It does not look familiar."

Mary looked puzzled for a moment, then dismissed the problem and said, "Come in and I will show you something remarkably clever."

Julia obeyed.

"Do you see this paneled wall? It is removable!"

Julia felt certain some response was expected. "Indeed?" she said, hoping the word expressed sufficient amazement.

"Yes. Removable. When a very large ball is to be held, the wall is removed in panels and this space," another sweep of her arm, "can be added to the ballroom. The furniture must be removed, of course."

"Of course. Mr. Townes must employ a hardy lot of men."

"Just come along next door into the ballroom and you will see a little better how it is arranged."

Sure enough, when they entered the ballroom through a very large and beautiful set of doors, Julia could see the same paneling on the removable wall that separated this room from its neighbor.

Julia went to examine the panels more closely. "I do think this a very sensible use of space," she said thoughtfully. "It was a clever man who thought of this idea."

"The house was built by Mr. Townes's grandfather after the old mansion was destroyed in a fire. Most would say this house is ugly in its exterior, I admit that I am one of them, but within the walls, nothing could be more comfortable and elegant. But look," yet another sweep of her arm, "you see that there is another paneled wall on the other side of the room. When that wall is removed, the drawing room may also be used to accommodate an extremely large crowd, though I have never known all three rooms to be used. For a ball, it is customary to remove the panels between the drawing room and the ballroom and store them in the reception room."

"I see. Well, they must be placed somewhere, of course."

Mary led the way back into the hallway, then along it, where the ceiling went beyond the gallery. At the far end of the hall, near the back door which proved to be identical to the front, she opened the door into the drawing room.

Here the curtains were drawn open on the large windows on two of the walls. Through the windows Julia could see a terrace, and below it a precisely planted flower garden where a few hardy roses had survived the pelting rain.

"The Mr. Townes who built this house had quite a large hand in its design," Mary was saying. "Our own Mr. Townes has told me that the old gentleman was still alive when Mr. Townes was a boy. He thought him a wonderfully interesting and clever gentleman."

Julia felt a pang of longing for a family who had memories of such ancestors. Of real people who had lived lives of adventure or of ordinariness, of worth or of worthlessness, of happiness or tragedy —all the things that contribute to one's own self. With a sudden start, she put these thoughts aside. There was still too much danger of disappointment to permit them, and, besides, she felt that such wishes might be somehow disloyal to her mother.

The tour of the house continued. Mary led her charge through cloakrooms for ladies and gentlemen, the library, which Julia recognized as the room she had been in previously, the dining room —or rooms, for here again the panel wall system had been used to allow conversion of the large dining room to one even larger by removing the wall that separated it from the more intimate family dining room. They were now in the family's wing of the house on the main floor. Besides the family dining room, there were a large and a small sitting room which were separate, distinct rooms, with no panels employed here. There was another staircase by which the family could reach the bedroom floor without returning to the main hallway, and, at the end of the wing, another exterior door, just like the other two, which Mary called the family entrance.

The hallway in this wing was two stories high, with another gallery above by which the bedrooms were reached.

Julia and Mary climbed the family stairs to the bedroom floor. Here Mary pointed out the two bedrooms at the end as Mr. Townes's and Mrs. Carlyle's, a couple of empty rooms, then hers and her brother's. Julia duly took note that Miss Belleville and Mr. Christian, therefore, were considered more family than guests in this household. And she wondered, but did not ask, which bedroom had been her mother's.

The tour being over, they went below to the smaller of the sitting rooms. Mr. Christian was there.

He rose from his chair as the ladies came into the room, and it seemed to Julia that it took an eternity for him to stand up, for Mr. Christian was very tall. He was very handsome, too, she observed, as she heard, seemingly from a great distance, Miss Belleville's voice making a graceful introduction. His hair was blond, but not quite the true family blond. It was almost golden and softly waving, and his eyes were quite surprisingly brown. He smiled, showing white even teeth, and his face seemed to light from within.

Julia extended her hand. He took it and held it in both of his as he studied her face intently.

"How do you do, Mr. Christian?"

"How do you do, Miss . . . I know that I must call you Miss Forrest for now, but I trust I will soon have the very great pleasure of calling you cousin."

Julia flushed with pleasure and, for the first time since coming into this house, felt truly warm and welcome.

Chapter Six

The office was not pretentious, for which Charles was oddly grateful. It was a comfortable room, tasteful and quietly well appointed, though devoid of any personal touches, as was, perhaps, suitable for a banker's office. He had been studying the room in order to give the young man opposite him the time to recover from his surprise and consternation.

"Do you mean to say, Mr. Townes," Robert asked in wonderment, "that you are the *husband* of Mrs. Forrest? Actually her husband?"

"I believe that is the case."

"And *Miss* Forrest is therefore your daughter?"

"Yes, sir."

Silence.

"Upon my soul," Robert said at last, "it is the most astonishing thing I have yet heard in all these last astonishing and most distressing days."

"If you will be so kind, Mr. Woodland, as to look at this"—Charles began to unwrap the paper parcel he had carried into the office—"I believe much of the mystery of Mrs. . . . Mrs. Forrest can be made clear."

He turned the portrait toward Mr. Woodland, who gave an audible gasp.

"Merciful heaven! It is the same woman! I . . . You must forgive me, sir, but I scarcely can believe it."

"Mr. Woodland, I do understand."

More silence.

After a time, Robert, ever the man of business, cleared his throat and said, "It is certainly timely that you should have come just now, Mr. Townes. Mrs. . . . I must continue to call her Mrs. Forrest . . . did not leave a will, you see. We had spoken of it from time to time, but she did not take steps to take care of the matter. She said always that she was in the best of health and that there was no one to leave any of her possessions to other than her daughter, who would inherit in any case. Now this . . ." Mr. Woodland shook his head and looked grave.

"I am interested, of course, in whether any other items of the family jewelry may have remained in her possession, but that is not the matter uppermost in importance just now. I wish first, if I may, to have others who knew the lady—neighbors and acquaintances—to view this portrait. I must be quite certain before I proceed further. The matter of Mrs. Forrest's possessions can be settled in due course."

"Quite so." Robert took out a handkerchief and dabbed at his brow. "My mother will be glad to

oblige you in the matter of the portrait, I am sure."
Then a sudden thought came to Robert. "But it
would be best, in my view, to go at once to the
Beatrice. Sir William—Sir William Grant—plans
to leave again tomorrow, so we must see him today.
He is one who must be shown the portrait, and in
any case he must be told of—of this development."

"I have heard the name of Sir William Grant
from Miss Forrest, though from her account, I did
not expect to find him in York."

"Well, you see, sir"—Robert's eyes shifted awkwardly from those of his visitor—"I sent a messenger after him when I heard of what had happened to
Mrs. Forrest. He was . . . It seemed fitting that he
should know without delay."

"I see," Charles said thoughtfully. "I shall certainly go to see him at once if you think it best."

"Perhaps I had best . . . that is, I will be happy to
come with you, sir, if you wish it."

Mr. Townes accepted, and the two gentlemen set
off in Mr. Townes's carriage, which Robert was
interested to see was far grander than even the new
carriage Sir William had ordered for himself.

They found Sir William at the Beatrice, where he
had just returned from a morning walk. As explanations proceeded and the situation became clear,
Sir William's distress was more acute than his
astonishment. Robert understood and sympa-
thized. To have the woman Sir William had long
loved so nearly in his grasp and then to lose her in
such an abrupt and painful way was ordeal enough,
but here was Mr. Charles Townes, a wealthy and
sensible gentleman, who claimed, apparently in all
legitimacy, to be the lady's husband!

It was a shocking, even a sordid history of the lady which Mr. Townes related to poor Sir William, all the more so for being told in a flat, sober voice from which the emotion for this tale had long ago been drained away. And when Sir William was shown the portrait, he turned away abruptly and walked over to the window to stare down into the park below. Robert felt it prudent to send Sir William's servant, the versatile MacKenzie, for brandy.

When this restorative had been drunk and Sir William was looking more himself, Mr. Townes returned to the matter of Bellwether and the long ago movement to overthrow the crown.

"Miss Forrest has been persuaded to believe that her mother was murdered by Bellwether, who had somehow discovered her after all these years and still feared she might endanger him. In fact, Sir William, I have been told by Miss Forrest that her mother actually mentioned Bellwether to you and asked your opinion whether others like him might be at work again."

Sir William, who had been shaking his head in disbelief, now put down his brandy glass and ran his hand across his eyes. "I do recall," he said softly. "It was just before I first went to Winderfields. But I say now as I said then that such a thing seems most unlikely. The events of which Mrs. Forrest spoke to me were very long ago. Times are different now. And why should this Bellwether return to England to take up a cause that failed once and has even less chance of succeeding now?"

"Perhaps," Charles said quietly, "he never left England at all, but has been hiding among us all these years."

"How could such a thing be possible?" Sir William demanded. "He would surely have been found out."

"Not if his appearance and identity were unknown to the authorities," Charles replied, "which I understand to be the case."

Robert sighed heavily. "I agree, Sir William, that it seems almost too fantastic an idea to be believed, beyond even the bizarre events we have heard of today. But I *do* believe it. I will tell you now of something that occurred the very day of Mrs. Forrest's death, after you had left for Winderfields."

Charles and Sir William listened intently as Robert told of the notice brought to Major Forbisher, and Mr. Simmon's confirmation that it was the same as those which had appeared previously in Leeds. Charles nodded silently from time to time, but Sir William only looked more and more stupified.

"Well," Sir William at last said grudgingly, "I believe this Bellwether was an uncommonly clever man."

But he had no chance to say whether he was now persuaded, because at that moment, the arrival of Miss Sennett was announced.

She came into the sitting room with apologies and a tiny frown of consternation. A letter had come just that minute from Winderfields. Mrs. Ferguson, the housekeeper, wrote, with many regrets for disturbing Miss Sennett, that the new harp had *not* arrived on the previous Friday as promised, and Mrs. Ferguson thought Sir William should be informed, as he had made such a point of the harp and might wish to look into the matter before he left the city.

Sir William, grateful to have an ordinary problem to deal with, excused himself to send round an inquiry to the unfortunate harp dealer.

Robert made a proper introduction of Mr. Townes and explained the circumstances which had brought him to York and to Sir William. Miss Sennett, true to the rule that a lady is never surprised or shocked, merely said, "Ah, the poor lady. How beautiful she was. It is a very great shame."

Mr. Townes showed her the portrait and asked if Miss Sennett had known Mrs. Forrest well.

"Very slightly, I fear. I had met her only the evening before her death, here at the reception in this hotel."

After a thoughtful pause, Charles asked, "Miss Sennett, do you happen to recall any of your conversations with Mrs. Forrest on that evening that would suggest anything unusual? Any fears or suspicions that she might be in danger?"

"Why no. We spoke only of ordinary things. Of the people who were there . . . Oh, we did actually speak of disfigurements." She turned to Mr. Woodland. "Because of poor Mr. Simmons, you know. She thought it a great shame that he must have that scar so prominently on his face, when each of us could name persons with similar or even worse imperfections which might be hidden by ordinary clothing. Let me see. We discussed the music we heard. She inquired about Winderfields. I found her very pleasant company."

"Did you see her speak to anyone not of your

party? A waiter, a guest here in the hotel?"

"No. No one."

"Miss Forrest mentioned a man who came into the room during the reception. A young man dressed in brown. Did you see him?"

"Oh, yes! He did not actually come into the room, but merely stood on the stairs. But now that you mention it, I did see him look with a great deal of interest at Mrs. Forrest, and she at him. It is not, of course, unusual that a gentleman would look with interest at Mrs. Forrest"—Miss Sennett tittered self-consciously—"but it did make me wonder if they knew each other. Ah! But her daughter would know. She was there at the time and was looking at the gentleman quite as hard as her mother."

Mr. Townes turned to Robert and asked if he had seen this gentleman, but he had not. "We might ask some of the other ladies. My mother and Miss Pierce, perhaps."

Charles fell silent and Robert sought to fill the conversational blank by asking Miss Sennett if she was anxious to be at home again.

"Yes," she replied, though a little uncertainly, "but I fear it may seem rather too quiet after York. I do not, of course, refer to the excitement surrounding poor Mrs. Forrest. That is sad, indeed. But I find on the whole that city life agrees with me." She smiled at Robert.

"It is fortunate, then, that Winderfields is not so very great a distance from the city, although it is quite a full day's journey and must be wearisome, especially now that you have had a partial trip there and back again within so few days."

"It is not so at all, Mr. Woodland. We had made little progress toward Winderfields when the messenger you sent caught up to us. The carriage, wretched thing, took us only to a village some four or five miles outside the limits of York before it gave notice of an extremely dangerous condition. We were quite on the point of losing a wheel entirely. Had MacKenzie not been alert and given us warning, there might have been a nasty accident, just as . . . as my poor brother suffered."

"My God!" Robert gasped. "This is not the same carriage, surely, as that in which your brother met his end!"

"Not the same, no. The other carriage was destroyed beyond repair. This is an older carriage which belonged to our father. Sir William has ordered a new one, but in the meantime, I hope at least that this one will take us safely home."

The eyes of Mr. Woodland and Mr. Townes met as Miss Sennett fanned herself with some vigor. When Sir William rejoined them, Mr. Townes invited him to go along to the house Mrs. Forrest had occupied.

Sir William hesitated at the awkwardness of the situation and he came close to excusing himself by pleading the expectation of the harp merchant's arrival. But perhaps it was more circumspect to agree. So Miss Sennett was instructed to detain the harp merchant until Sir William's return, and the gentlemen departed.

In the carriage, which Sir William admired in silence, Robert hurried to ask the question which had been burning for the last few minutes. "Sir William, we understand from Miss Sennett that you came near to having an accident in your carriage when you left York on that morning."

"Yes. Quite a nuisance, though I suppose it worked out for the best. The messenger you sent found us without difficulty, and it was a very short return to the city. I felt, under the circumstances" —he cast an uneasy glance at Mr. Townes—"that it was only proper to return."

Charles replied with only a nod.

"And it was an accident in a carriage that took the life of your cousin, I believe?" Robert now asked.

"So it was."

"And was a wheel lost in that circumstance?"

"I couldn't say. Why do you ask?"

Robert replied with yet another question. "Sir William, was your carriage housed in the hotel's stables while you stayed here?"

"Yes, of course, it was. Where else should it be kept? Woodland, why are you asking me these questions?" Sir William's brow was knitted in a sharp frown. "Are you suggesting . . ." He looked from one to the other of his companions with eyes that spoke of astonishment and outrage. "Are you suggesting that someone wished to do *me* harm?"

"Not exactly that, Sir William," Robert replied cautiously, "but I think in this case we must not mince words. There are many in my acquaintance, and in yours, Sir William, who thought it likely that when you left York you would take Mrs. Forrest with you."

"My God!" Sir William turned to Charles in acute distress. "I assure you, sir, that I had no idea . . . I admit that I admired Mrs. Forrest and did hope that . . ." His voice trailed off.

Charles paid scant attention to Sir William's discomfort. "I believe I agree with what you are suggesting, Mr. Woodland. Bellwether first attempted what would appear to be an accident. When Frances did not depart with Sir William, more drastic means were employed."

"That is exactly what I am suggesting."

"And another carriage accident," Charles continued thoughtfully, "so soon in the same family would have shifted attention from the lady who died to the death of the gentleman." He gave a long sigh. "This Bellwether is a devil. And a clever one."

"I cannot agree with you!" Sir William protested. "Why the worst that might have happened had we actually lost the wheel would have been a few bruises. There are no steep embankments on that stretch of road for us to pitch into."

"Not near the city, it is true," said Robert. "But what of further on, as you had drawn nearer to Winderfields? It is quite a treacherous bit of road there."

"I fear we must believe it, Sir William," Charles said not unkindly. "I am very much in fear that Bellwether is at work again."

Sir William snorted and said that it seemed more the work of a madman to him. And in view of this new idea about the carriage and the fact that an unidentified waiter had been seen hurrying from the spot where Mrs. Forrest had fallen, the entire hotel staff should be questioned again.

After Sir William's emphatic declaration, they continued in silence until the carriage stopped. In a moment they stood before Frances's house.

"Here I am, Mr. Woodland, sir!" Polly came running from Mrs. Ponder's house, where she had been keeping watch for them. "I brought the key, sir, just as you said." She shifted her feet. "I didn't care to go inside alone, sir."

"Very well, Polly. But open the door now, please."

"Yes, sir."

No key was necessary, for the door was not locked. It was apparent as soon as they stepped inside that the house had been thoroughly ransacked. The hall tree had been overturned in the haste of the visitor to tear off the cloak that had once hung upon it. That garment, one of Mimmie's, lay in a heap where it seemed to have been kicked aside.

Every room was the same as they went through the house, silent except for Polly, who could not stifle the gasps and cries of shock and perhaps fear that she might somehow be blamed. Books had been taken from the shelves and flung aside to land wherever they might fall. Cushions had been torn from the sofa and chairs, some slashed, some merely crumpled. Every drawer had been opened and removed.

Sir William let out a long breath and said, "Gentleman, there *has* been a madman at work here."

Robert shook his head.

"I would say rather that it was a man entirely sane. How long has the house been empty?" Charles asked.

"Since the very day of Mrs. Forrest's death," Robert replied. "Polly was the only servant who

104

resided here, and she refused absolutely to stay here alone. I had the house locked up, and Polly came into service with my mother."

"So we may say that this happened at any time in the last six days. Or, more likely, nights. There should be an inquiry made as to any strangers who might have been seen in the neighborhood, though, if it is Bellwether who has done this, I doubt there will be any result."

When Polly showed them to the bedroom that had been Mrs. Forrest's, the three men could only gasp with the maid. Here the devastation was complete. Not only drawers, cushions, books had been violated, but every garment in the wardrobe had been removed, pockets turned out, hems and seams ripped, every shoe, slipper, handbag and hat ravaged beyond hope of repair.

Charles picked his way through the wreckage, stopping once or twice to touch or examine an item of clothing or jewelry, a flower torn from a hat, a bit of lace, a silken ribbon. At length he turned to Polly.

"Will you see what clothing of Miss Forrest's can be salvaged? Pack them, along with whatever of her personal belongings that can be found."

"Yes, sir."

When Polly was gone, Charles turned to his companions. "There is no point in looking through this house. If the intruder was looking for something, he must surely have found it, if, indeed, it was ever here at all."

An awkward silence followed as the men moved among the debris in the bedroom. Each had thoughts of his own as he viewed the ruination, but no words or even will to express them. Soon, by common, silent consent, they turned to leave the disturbing place behind.

As they stepped into the hallway there came a clatter and commotion from the floor below them. At the sound, they saw Polly's head appear from the doorway of Julia's room a few doors away.

"Robert! Polly? Are you here?" The voice boomed from the entry hall, then was followed by mutterings of surprise and distress.

"It is my mother," Robert said to his companions, then he leaned over the banister to call, "yes, Mama. We are just coming down."

They settled themselves in the dining parlor, which had suffered somewhat less damage than the other rooms. Mrs. Woodland, after introductions and explanations, was shocked into total silence for several moments, and she had to be asked by Mr. Townes a second time if she recalled seeing a dark young man enter the reception room on the night of Sir William's party.

"Dressed all in brown, you say?" she asked when she had at last recovered herself.

"Yes, madam. So said Miss Forrest and Miss Sennett."

Difficult as it was for Mrs. Woodland to be outdone in such a matter, she could not, in all honesty—and she was essentially an honest woman—recall having seen the gentleman. Perhaps Miss Pierce had noticed him.

The portrait was brought from the carriage. Mrs. Woodland confirmed the opinions of her son and Sir William that the painting was that of Mrs. Forrest, without doubt.

106

Polly now appeared to announce that such of Miss Forrest's belongings as were suitable had been packed in a trunk that she had found in the attic storeroom.

"The attic, sir, has been ransacked as well."

The party broke up. Mrs. Woodland and Polly went home, though Polly took a more direct route than her new mistress. Mrs. Woodland was obliged to stop en route to confide to Miss Pierce all that she had seen and learned, and to voice her shock and amazement at this latest turn of events in the matter of Mrs. Forrest. "And I must say, my dear, that I believe and trust we have seen the last of *that* household."

Miss Pierce expressed suitable distress and consoled her visitor with tea and a slice of especially tasty plum cake.

Sir William was now returned to the Beatrice to deal with the unhappy harp merchant. He made a half-hearted offer to remain in York and at the service of Mr. Townes and Mr. Woodland in this matter, and could only hide his relief very poorly when the offer was declined with thanks.

Mr. Townes and Mr. Woodland were occupied together for all the rest of the day. Mr. Townes was obviously satisfied now as to the identity of Mrs. Forrest, and Robert could not be sure whether that knowledge brought the man sorrow. He could see that it most certainly brought relief.

Charles took rooms at the Beatrice. There were arrangements to be seen to and there were questions—many questions to be answered. He hardly knew how to begin.

"Should you care to ride about the property, Miss Forrest?"

"Do you mean on a horse, Mr. Christian?"

"Why, yes, of course on a horse." Lawrence's eyes crinkled with his smile.

"You will think it odd, I daresay, but I have never actually ridden a horse. The idea rather frightens me."

"Never ridden? Then you must certainly begin at once. There is the gentlest of ponies in Mr. Townes's stable. The rain has stopped and it is a splendid day which must not be wasted, for they grow ever fewer at this time of year. Please say you will be so good as to bear me company. It will be an honor as well as a very great pleasure to see that you survive your first experience on a horse. You will forgive me if I say that, although you have suffered a most tragic loss, you need to get out of the house."

"Well . . ." It was impossible to resist that smile, those engaging brown eyes. "Yes. I will come. Oh, but I have no riding clothes."

This was not allowed to be a problem. The omnipotent Mrs. Holmes was summoned and asked by Mr. Christian if riding clothes might be found in the stores of the household that would permit Miss Forrest to take some exercise. Half an hour later a maid appeared in Julia's bedroom with an acceptable, if rather musty, riding dress.

Julia was mounted on the pony with little difficulty, and they set out, accompanied at a proper distance by a stable groom. They began with a stately tour of the grounds near the house. The various outbuildings were identified in answer to

Julia's questions, and the fields which could be seen from a little hilltop were admired and an explanation provided by the groom as to which crops each had produced this year. Julia's pony was as gentle as promised, and she grew more comfortable and even a little enthusiastic for riding as her fear disappeared.

They rode next into a stand of woods. At their approach, a small flock of birds, disturbed from the place where they rested in their autumn migration, rose with a flutter and a commotion and flew noisily away.

"On the other side of these woods is the boundary of Fainway's grounds with that of its only neighbor," Lawrence told her.

Julia's heart gave a leap. "What is the name of the other estate?"

"It is called 'Winterhall.' Quite a large place. It surrounds Fainway on two sides. The other boundaries, of Fainway, I mean, are the river and the limits of the village."

"May we ride to the boundary and see the other estate?"

"Well . . ." Lawrence was doubtful. "It is nearly a mile. We may certainly go if you do not think it too great a distance for your first outing."

But Julia was too eager to see the estate where her mother had lived before her enforced marriage to wait for another time. She asked that they ride on.

Julia was very thoughtful as they made their way through the trees, did not notice the beginning of the autumn colors, did not ask questions about the age or extent of the grove. She was about to see another fragment of her mother's past. This excited her, drew her on eagerly, even as she felt the tears of emptiness that threatened each time she saw again in her mind the beautiful face, the emerald eyes of her mother.

The timber finally began to thin, there was more light ahead in the distance, and at last they emerged from the woods into the sunlight. They found themselves on a small rise that overlooked a broad, flat plain that stretched away toward a river in the distance. Julia was disappointed that the house could not be seen from there.

"No," Lawrence replied to her question. "The house sits on a hillside above the river, but it is hidden by those woods."

Julia looked where he pointed. It was indeed a quite large woods, almost a forest, all the way to the line of small hills that bordered the plain.

"But here is something far more interesting than a house," Lawrence said. "Look there below us."

Julia did as she was told and felt a shiver of excitement as she saw the circle of large stones standing upright at the edge of the trees. She turned inquiring eyes to her companion.

"It is a Druid's Circle," he said. "Not a very large one, of course, but it is in a fine state of preservation. You can see that only one of the stones has fallen in all these many centuries."

Julia was awe-struck. This was, it must be, the place Mimmie had mentioned. This was where the doomed lovers had met. She had to struggle to control her voice. "I have heard of such things, of course," she said. "I never thought to see one for myself."

"It is possible to see even the Druids," Lawrence

said. "Not at this time of year, but Mr. Parke permits the fools who affect to practice these ancient and barbaric rites to come here to do so. He insists that it is less troublesome to allow it and insure that the proceedings are supervised than to try to prevent their sneaking onto his land without his knowledge."

"I suppose that is the most sensible attitude." Julia studied the circle more carefully. "I should like to have a closer look at it sometime, if it is possible. And with the owner's permission, of course."

"I would take you now, with pleasure, Miss Forrest, but I believe I see someone coming." Lawrence took his field glass and gazed at the speck in the distance which Julia could now see was moving ever closer. "Yes, it is a rider, and he seems to be coming to the circle. Odd. I doubt that the steward, much less any of the workers, would have business so far away from the fields."

They watched intently as the rider, who was moving at a fine pace, covered the distance very quickly. He did seem to be making for the circle or for the edge of the forest that grew near it.

"Ah!" said Lawrence, looking again through his glass. "I believe it is Philip Sommerville."

"Sommerville. It is not the owner, then? Mr. Parke?"

"His nephew. I wonder what brings Sommerville to Winterhall. I thought he was . . ." Lawrence stopped speaking and peered intently through his glass.

The rider arrived at the circle of stones and he rode around its perimeter in a casual way.

"Would you care to have a look?" Lawrence passed her the glass.

Julia put the glass to her eye and could not hold back the gasp that escaped.

"It is quite startling, isn't it," Lawrence said with a smile, "how clearly one can see even small detail through a really good glass?"

"Yes. Quite amazing." Mr. Christian could not know that her gasp was not for the strength of the glass or the clarity of the scene before her. She thought, she was almost certain, that she had recognized the rider, and her heart beat so quickly she could barely speak. If her eyes were not playing some strange trick, it was the brown man!

But before she could be sure, his face was obscured as he raised a glass of his own. It was as though he had felt their eyes upon him, for he gazed unerringly to the rise where they sat. Lawrence lifted a hand in greeting and the groom doffed his cap. But the greetings were not returned. Julia felt uneasily that the glass was trained upon her, and she felt herself blush at the thought of his eyes studying her.

At long last the man lowered his glass, raised a hand in a belated acknowledgment of their presence, then turned his horse and rode away.

Chapter Seven

"Rosie!"

"Yes, madam?"

"See that Miss Forrest has a hot bath at once. And another this evening before dinner. Quite as hot, mind you, as she can bear."

"Yes, madam." Rosie hurried away to do as she was bidden, and Mrs. Carlyle approached the unhappy girl on the bed.

"See that you remain in the bath at least a full half-hour," she told Julia. "And mind that the water is kept hot!"

"Yes, Mrs. Carlyle."

"Very foolish to ride so long one's first time upon a horse! It is a wonder you can walk at all."

Julia's only reply was a long unhappy sigh.

"I shall have something to say to Lawrence about this."

"Indeed, ma'am, Mr. Christian is not to blame. I

was the one who wished to continue."

"That is nonsense. Lawrence was responsible for you, and he certainly knows better. Though I daresay he meant no harm, like all young people he is inclined to be thoughtless. All the same, it will be best for *you,* my dear, if you learn that you must be responsible for yourself. This is true of the trivialities of life as well as for the most weighty issues."

"Yes, Mrs. Carlyle."

The old woman appeared to hesitate, debating whether to deliver further wisdom on this point. At length she decided against it, nodded to Julia and withdrew.

When she was alone, Julia lay quite still. If she lay quite still, if not a muscle moved, it almost didn't hurt. She moaned inwardly when she thought of rising, moving, walking, sitting down, even in a tub of hot water. But rise she must for Rosie soon returned with two colleagues, and the business of the bath was undertaken.

And when she was dried and wrapped cozily in the rose dressing gown and eating a light luncheon from a tray, she had to admit that she did feel better. It had been a wakeful, restless night, tormented not only by stiff, aching limbs, but by questions for which there seemed to be no answers.

What was Mr. Sommerville—and she was certain that it *was* Mr. Sommerville—a neighbor of Fainway, doing in York at the Beatrice hotel? And just on the night before the impossible, the unthinkable had happened to her mother! *Had* they recognized each other? He could not have been more than eight or ten years old when Frances Townes had fled her home. Unless he had seen a portrait in the house where he now lived or visited.

Or more likely in *this* house. Julia was certain that her mother had changed very little from her girlhood. Certainly she had not aged enough as to be unrecognizable.

Even so, what did it mean? Here her thoughts became frayed. To speculate on the meaning of it was confusing, disturbing, frightening.

Where was Mimmie? How she missed her. Would she ever see that dear face again? At the thought that she might not, tears of immense loneliness could not be held back. Exhausted and frustrated with these quandaries and misgivings, she looked for something to divert her weary brain. At length she fell asleep, reading *Oliver Twist*.

After her nap and another hot bath, Julia was able to appear at dinner without too great a risk of moaning or of sudden grimacing from startled pain when a certain movement did not please her offended extremities.

Mrs. Carlyle was still inclined to be severe with Lawrence. "It was quite remiss of you, indeed. Half an hour is the very most a young lady should be permitted to ride on the first occasion. I should, myself, advise only twenty minutes. It was extremely thoughtless, Lawrence, quite, quite as bad as that awful Mrs. Todd might do!"

And this, Julia supposed, must be the ultimate reprimand.

"I apologize most grovelingly, madam," Lawrence said, "to yourself as well as to Miss Forrest. I can only plead that the day was so fine and the company so delightful that I quite lost track of time."

Julia's conscience required her to say again that she had asked to be taken to the boundary of the woods but Mrs. Carlyle was not softened.

Lawrence said, "I pledge, madam, if Miss Forrest will permit me, to accustom her to the job of riding in a proper way. Tomorrow, Miss Forrest, we will ride for twenty minutes, as Mrs. Carlyle advises so wisely, and the next day for five and twenty, and so on, until you are both accomplished and comfortable."

Julia, meeting his smiling eyes, thought in this moment that she had never met any man with such, well, finesse. But then she dropped her eyes and turned away.

"Thank you, Mr. Christian, but . . ." Julia paused, wondering how it would be taken if she were to mention that she might well be gone from this household long before she had mastered the equestrian art. "But I fear it may take a good deal more time than you can spare for instruction."

"Yes, Lawrence," Mary said. "Do not promise what you cannot perform. Did you not tell me that you must return to London by Thursday?"

"That is merely business, Mary." Lawrence's eyes twinkled with that irresistible humor. "You have heard Mrs. Carlyle scold me, rightly so, for this transgression. My good character can only be restored by making proper amends. A gentleman can do no less." He smiled again into Julia's eyes, and she felt herself strangely beginning to blush.

"Besides"—Lawrence turned to Mrs. Carlyle—"I have been here some three days, and I think it would be quite uncivil to depart now without greeting my host. I shall wait for Mr. Townes's return."

The next day brought no riding lessons, after all. The rain returned in heavy sheets, accompanied by wind which thrashed the lawns and lanes and filled the air with wet brown leaves. Mr. Christian did not flee, however, at this opportunity to escape to his business in London. He remained to teach Julia the game of whist and to talk to her by the hour of an afternoon. Emboldened by his easy manner, Julia dared to ask him who the much-censured Mrs. Todd was.

"Mrs. Todd is an elderly lady who lives on the other side of the village. I know no harm of her beyond a tiresome self-importance and fanciness of taste."

"But Mrs. Carlyle seems to think very ill of her. Is there an old injury there?"

"How astute you are, Miss Forrest. I believe, though, that the injury was done by the late Mr. Todd to the late Admiral Carlyle. Did him out of a certain property, as I recall." His voice took on a tone of mock menace as he shuffled the cards. "We are a family of long memories, Miss Forrest, and unforgiving natures."

Lawrence was an amusing companion, with far greater wit and quickness than his sister, yet he appeared to possess all of her benevolence, especially where Julia was concerned. He read to her, sketched amusing pictures for her, and he talked to her of life in York, asked questions about the neighborhood where she had lived, the entertainments, the daily occupations of that existence.

"It is kind of you to listen to my reminiscences, Mr. Christian," Julia told him one rainy afternoon. "I know they must seem very trivial and dull."

"I expect it is a relief for you to speak of those days and to recall them with something like a normal attitude," Lawrence replied. "You may

117

have been thinking it somehow indelicate to mention that life in the presence of Mrs. Carlyle or even of Mary."

That was exactly how Julia had been feeling, and she told him so, thinking that she had never met a man so perceptive.

Lawrence went on, "There is certainly nothing dull or trivial about what has happened to you in these recent days. Are you now fearful that this . . . this Bellwether may find you here and wish to do you harm?"

"I have thought about it a good deal." Julia turned to the drawing-room window and stared through the drops alighting and cascading on the pane. "I believe that as time passes I will be in less and less danger. If it was Bellwether who killed my mother, he will see that I have no information which can be a threat to him." She struck her fist suddenly on the windowsill. "I wish I did! He must—somehow he must—pay for this."

Lawrence got up from his chair and came to the window where she stood. He handed her the sketch he had been making.

"Oh! It is a drawing of me!"

"So it is! I wish you to keep it to remember me."

She looked up from the picture. "Should it not then be a drawing of yourself?"

"It should. But I do not wish you to think me vain."

Julia smiled, the first smile of genuine pleasure that had touched her face since leaving York. "Mr. Christian," she said softly, "there are only one or two gifts I have received in my lifetime that have pleased me as much. I hope . . ." She gave a tiny shake of her head as she looked into his eyes. "It will be a very great sorrow if I find that you are not my cousin."

When that rainy week had passed, a letter arrived for Mrs. Carlyle. It announced that Mr. Townes's business in York was nearly concluded and he expected to set out for Fainway within a day or two.

"I should say," Mrs. Carlyle announced at dinner, "that we shall see him on Friday next. Or, failing that, the day following."

That was all. No mention of what he had found in York, no word as to what Julia could expect on his return. The omission did not appear to disturb Mary and Lawrence; they expressed their delight at the news and turned to Julia expectantly. Julia forced her voice to remain calm as she said that she hoped the weather might clear for Mr. Townes's journey homeward.

Charles was an entire day later than Mrs. Carlyle had predicted. He arrived after dark on Sunday evening, to the great relief of a household which was beginning to think, if not to speak, of sending a servant to scour the highway for his master.

Charles joined a gathering of the household in the drawing room, to which Mrs. Holmes had been summoned. He began without preamble. "I am satisfied that this young lady's mother was none other than Frances Townes, my wife. I believe further that Julia is my own child and not that of Richard Payne, with whom Mrs. Townes departed this house some nineteen years ago. I have sent a man to France to verify the date of Julia's birth, but only as a formality and to see that the birth is registered in the proper name."

Julia heard the words but felt only numbness.

Where was the relief, the joy, the gratitude she should be feeling, indeed had expected to feel if these happy words should ever be uttered? Even as she wondered, she realized that it was because none of these emotions were present in Mr. Townes's voice or in his face.

Charles continued. "The strong family resemblance which she displays cannot have escaped your notice any more than mine." He strode now to the chair where Julia sat. He placed his hand on the high chair back but did not touch the girl who sat there. "This is my daughter, Julia Townes. Mrs. Holmes, you will please see that the staff is informed."

"Yes, sir."

Mrs. Holmes received a nod of dismissal. She smiled kindly at Julia and left the room.

A silence fell—expectant, uncertain. In a few moments Charles cleared his throat. "We all know," he said, "that this young lady has endured a great loss in recent days at the death of her mother. I am sure we all hope that she can at length put aside the sorrow she carries and find happiness here within a new family."

Kind words, but said, to Julia's ear, so impersonally, so unlike the happy murmurs of agreement from Lawrence and Mary, even different from the smile, quite warm, really, on Mrs. Carlyle's face.

All eyes were on Charles, whose face seemed to reflect some inner struggle, but he said nothing more.

Julia had only a moment to be pained by his coldness. Now Mary Belleville was on her feet, rushing to Julia, embracing her.

"Oh, my dear Miss . . . Miss Townes, as I now

120

may rightly call you. How very happy I am!" There were indeed tears in Mary's mild eyes. "I knew, I just knew, that all would be well."

"Thank you, Miss Belleville." Julia had stood to receive Mary's embraces.

Lawrence, who was standing nearby, took Julia's hand. "You see, cousin, we shall have all the time we need for riding lessons."

Mrs. Carlyle now rose from her chair and came to Julia, actually put an arm around her and kissed her cheek. "You are to call me 'Aunt Julia.'"

"Yes, ma'am," Julia managed to whisper through her astonished gratitude. "Yes, Aunt Julia."

"Lawrence," the old woman said, "ring for a servant. Have him bring champagne. We must mark this occasion in a fitting way."

Charles drank half a glass of champagne with the others, then said that his journey had left him extremely weary and he retired.

The next day a funeral service was held at the graveyard of the village church. Charles had brought Frances home with him to Fainway. After removing the coffin and the earth that surrounded it from the little churchyard in York, and placing it all in a wagon and covering it with heavy canvas, the earthly remains of the late Mrs. Townes made the slow journey behind his carriage. She had been reburied the very evening of his arrival, without anyone in attendance except the Reverend Mr. Witherspoon, who had received notice by letter of Charles's wishes and intentions.

Now at the private gravesite service, only the family was included; however, some of the village people, who had heard the truth of whose grave was to be solemnized, had gathered on the fringes of the churchyard to stare and wonder.

There *was* one person at the funeral who was not part of the Fainway family. Mr. Parke was present at Mr. Townes's invitation. Though the name was not the same, Julia told herself as she received the introduction that Mr. Parke must be a relative of Mimmie's parents, the Paynes. He must also be a relation, however distant, of her mother's. And, therefore, of hers. That was somehow not a comforting thought.

Mr. Parke was a gaunt man, a little older, Julia guessed, than Mr. Townes. He was nearly bald, though the fringe of brown hair had not grayed. He wore spectacles that gave him an owlish appearance, but his expression was more of irritability than of wisdom.

Mr. Witherspoon read a brief and not very appropriate service. Julia placed a bouquet of flowers on the grave and turned away, and with this act came the sudden pain, the inescapable realization that her mother was gone forever. As they walked from the churchyard past the eyes of the curious, Lawrence took her arm.

Riding in the carriage from the church back to Fainway, Julia studied Mr. Townes through lowered lashes. She had said good-bye to her mother this morning. Had he done the same to his wife? she wondered.

Had he loved her? What had become of that love when he had been abandoned? Whatever his other emotions, it had to be a great relief for him to *know* what had become of Frances, to put that unhappy question to rest. That might explain the reason for this ceremony, which could have been avoided, surely, by merely leaving her buried in the little churchyard at York. Julia could not begin to guess at the motives of her father—how strange to call him that—but for all her uncertainty, she was grateful to have her mother's grave nearby.

Mr. Parke returned to Fainway for tea. Sitting in the drawing room, Julia could feel his eyes on her from time to time, and she wondered what he must make of her, of this whole affair. With a start, she realized that her father was asking him about his nephew, Philip.

"Philip was here the week before last for just one day," Mr. Parke said. "In fact, he was quite disappointed to find that you were not at home. He had some information or message to give you, I believe. I daresay he will be back before many days pass. He never stays in one place for two days, it seems."

"Is Mr. Sommerville still living in London?" Mary asked.

"Oh, yes, indeed!" Mr. Parke clearly was not pleased about it. "An idle life. Not suitable at all in my view to prepare him to manage property, though I will say he learns quickly when he spares time to come and employ himself at home."

Mary gave a soothing little laugh. "I daresay he finds the city amusing. It is to a young man, of course." She turned to smile at Lawrence.

"Yes," Lawrence said. "And I have noticed Mr. Sommerville in the city a good deal more often in the past months. Even so, I know for a fact that he has far more invitations than he accepts or even wishes for."

"I shouldn't wonder," said Mary, "for he is quite

a charming young gentleman. I am sure you will agree, Miss For—excuse me, Miss Townes, when you meet him."

Julia's teacup gave a sudden unwelcome rattle, and it took great dexterity on her part to prevent an insult to the drawing-room carpet. She put down her cup and managed to murmur something civil in reply to Miss Belleville.

Mr. Parke was not done on the subject of his nephew. "I only wish he were a more *steady* man. Until the last year or two, I believed he had no taste for or interest in all the parties and foolishness these young people think so much of today. It seemed he would settle down happily to his proper life at Winterhall. But now I hardly ever see him. He always comes for the month of August, but this year even that visit was shortened. He is either in London or flying about the country on some nonsense. I confess I am most disappointed in him."

"You surprise me, sir," Charles said. "In my own dealings with your nephew, I have found him most competent. He is extremely intelligent and clever, and his judgment is quite exceptional."

Mr. Parke looked over his spectacles in astonishment at his host. Mary quickly turned the conversation by asking if there had been a gathering of the Druids lately.

This was a less personal but no less contentious topic; Mr. Parke scowled and said there had not.

"It seems to me most unfortunate," Mary said, "that these dreadful individuals should impose themselves on the neighborhood, and especially upon you, Mr. Parke, simply because that wretched circle of stones is on your property. I should think that, with the assistance of your neighbors, or even from martial forces, should they be needed, you might prevent them coming onto your land at all."

"There I do not agree with you, Mary," Lawrence said emphatically. "I believe that Mr. Parke has chosen the wisest course by far. If he made such an issue of this affair, it would arouse interest and perhaps even sympathy for these misguided creatures who have taken up this bizarre affectation. By treating them as the harmless fools they are, he has insured that they are, for the most part, ignored. Their numbers are dwindling already, and in a few years this foolish fancy will have given way to some other senseless notion. I should be more concerned about the gypsies."

"Quite right, Lawrence," Aunt Julia put in, "for it is known that they are nothing but a pack of thieves."

Here Mr. Parke testily took up his own cause. "I think we need not concern ourselves about the gypsies until we see if they intend to make a practice of coming back. Last summer was the first time they have appeared in my time at Winterhall. Perhaps it was a singular event and I shall not see them again."

"There used to be gypsies," Charles said thoughtfully. "Each winter Mr. Payne tried, with no success, I recall, to prevent them camping on his land."

"I was told many years ago that Winterhall came by its name because it was, even from very ancient times, a winter camping site for nomadic peoples," Aunt Julia informed them.

"I have heard the same stories," Mr. Parke growled. "A lot of nonsense, in my opinion."

"In any case," Charles finished his thought,

"since Mr. Payne's death, I do not recall that the gypsies have appeared at all until this past summer. Odd."

"I think gypsies sometimes go onto the continent," said Mary. "They may remain there throughout a generation before returning to this country. I do wish this particular band had seen fit to remain wherever they may have been. It was such a spectacle last summer, Miss Townes! With the Druids and their chanting, and the gypsies and their dancing, and the campfires and that vulgar singing, it was quite offensive. Lawrence and I viewed the scene with your father from the edge of the woods, and I found it quite shocking."

"*I* found it quite surprising that there was no trouble between the two groups encamped there together on the plain for four days," said Charles. "Anyway, that will likely not occur again. It was just at midsummer, you know, when the gypsies happened to come just as the Druids were conducting their most important ritual."

Mr. Parke spoke grudgingly. "Now, there Philip was most useful to me, for he was willing and able to mediate with them to keep matters peaceful. I never asked how he accomplished it. I only hope it did not cost him too dearly from his own pocket." But Mr. Parke's eyes held a malicious twinkle that belied his words.

At dinner that evening, Mary announced that she and Lawrence would depart for London the next day. Julia felt a surge of panic at the thought of their going, and Charles voiced his regret.

"Not a bit of it," Mary said firmly. "You and your daughter must have time now to get acquainted with each other. Lawrence and I are only in the way, however much we may wish to think otherwise. Isn't that so, Lawrence?"

Lawrence's frown said plainly that he did not agree, but he submitted to Mary's decision.

"I go reluctantly, for I am delighted beyond words to have come to know, albeit so briefly, my cousin, Julia."

Julia blushed with pleasure and dared to raise her eyes to see what reaction might be at work around the table. Lawrence's words *were* a trifle more emphatic than family warmth might require. As nearly as she could tell, her father, her aunt and Mary all displayed only thoughtful interest.

"We will, with your permission, sir, return at Christmastime as planned," Mary said to Charles.

"Yes, certainly."

"It will be a genuine celebration this year," Mary continued. "We have a most earnest cause for joy."

Julia wondered through that evening as she had her last whist lesson, whether Mary, and even Lawrence, really felt the joy they professed at finding themselves with a new relation. Her father's reaction, though painful to her, was, upon reflection, undoubtedly more logical. It was hardly reasonable to think that she, a stranger, the child of a marriage that had been ill-fated, even scandalous, could be immediately dear to him. He would do his duty by her, he would give her a home. It was the proper, the gentlemanly thing to do. But there was no reason to suppose that he, like herself, was lonely, hungering for a family connection of any sort.

She played her hand so stupidly that she feared

Lawrence would think her too empty-headed to retain the principles of the game.

Just as Aunt Julia declared that she was too weary to play on, a servant appeared to announce that Mr. Townes had a visitor waiting in the library.

Charles did not return, with or without his visitor, to the large sitting room that evening and after an hour, Mary said that she was going to bed and insisted that Lawrence do likewise.

"We must be on our way at some decent hour."

Lawrence protested that he was not tired and would continue the whist lessons without Mary, but Julia, uncomfortable at remaining alone with Lawrence just now, said that she would go to bed as well. They shook hands all around and went upstairs together, going around by the main staircase to leave Julia in the guest wing where she still slept. As she parted from brother and sister, Julia suddenly remembered something and turned back. "Oh, Miss Belleville! If you will just wait a moment, I will fetch the dressing gown you have lent me."

"Oh, please do not!" Mary said, coming along the gallery to take Julia's hand once more. "Keep it and wear it until I return at Christmastime. It will remind you of me, I hope. I assure you that I can well spare it, and I should like to think it will be put to good use until you have arranged your own wardrobe to your liking."

Julia was grateful and said so; there had been no dressing gown among the belongings that had come with her father from York. Good nights were said again and Julia went to her own bedroom.

Rosie was waiting to help her undress. The turned-down bed looked welcoming, but Julia was too unsettled to go to it at once. When her nightgown was donned, her hair brushed, and Rosie had left, Julia, wrapped snugly in the dressing gown, sat with a lamp and her book in a chair by the fire that warmed the room on this chilly night.

Staring into the fire, Julia knew that it would take more than a night's reflection to understand or even unravel the confusion of what had befallen her these recent weeks. She must wait, be patient, see what each day would bring now as she became familiar with this new life, this new family.

She opened *Oliver Twist* and began to read. Now she could turn the pages without anxiety. In her first days at Fainway, this tale of homeless, orphaned boys had been a painful, frightening reminder of her own situation. Now, though uncertain of a genuine welcome, she was at least safe from such a fate. A sense of peace fell unaccountably over the room, the only sounds the muted crackling of the fire and the flutter of pages turning. Once or twice Julia felt the book slip from her fingers as sleep encroached upon her in the quiet room.

"Julia."

As she heard the whispered calling of her name, she thought she must be dreaming and settled her head more deeply into the wing of her armchair; it promised to be a pleasant dream.

"Julia."

This was no dream. The soft, oddly familiar voice was there in the room—and very near.

She sat up with a start and would have screamed,

but a strong hand quickly covered her mouth to prevent it.

"Don't be afraid." Green eyes were intent on her face. "It was necessary that I see you tonight."

Julia nodded to show that she would not scream, and the hand was withdrawn. Philip pulled the opposite chair closer and sat down.

Julia's eyes were wide, startled and uncertain. He put out a hand to touch her own and instinctively she drew it back. As she did so, she noticed that her dressing gown had fallen open, revealing her nightgown and rather too much of her flesh. He watched intently as she drew it closed, and Julia could feel a flush creeping into her neck. Summoning calm, she folded her hands and looked at him, determined that he should speak first.

"My name is Philip Sommerville, but I expect you know that by this time."

"I had guessed it must be so."

"I was told your name before. In York. Now, of course, you have a new one."

"How did you get in here?"

"I was admitted very properly by the butler when I called to see your father. As to how I managed to get in *here,* I think I had best not say."

"What do you want?"

"I have come to tell you that you must not speak to anyone of having seen me in York."

"Why not, Mr. Sommerville?" She frowned at him.

A tiny smile touched his eyes. "I rather hoped you would do so because I ask it of you. I cannot tell you why I ask it, any more than I could tell your father why I asked for his assistance just now, but he will assure anyone who might inquire that I was with him on a fishing expedition on the very day in question."

Julia shook her head. "Even if Mr. Townes should do such a thing, you were seen by others at the hotel. You are registered as a guest, I should imagine."

"The gentleman who was a guest at the Beatrice was not Philip Sommerville."

Julia stood up uneasily, moved to stand behind her chair. "A false name is no protection. And why should Mr. Townes agree to profess to something that is not true?"

"Mr. Townes and I often do favors for one another."

Julia went suddenly white as a sickening thought came searing into her brain. "You did it for him." She said it softly because the idea was too terrible to be voiced in a normal tone. "You killed her for his revenge."

Her knees gave way; she held on to the back of the chair for support and was too dazed to resist when he came out of his chair and caught her to keep her from falling.

"Julia"—his green eyes glinted fiercely into hers—"you cannot believe this of me. Even less of your father."

"I don't know you!" she gasped. "Nor do I truly know him." She could not withstand his green gaze, and looked away from him, though he still held her upright. "You saw my mother that night, you recognized her, I am certain, and the next day she was dead. There is nothing—nothing to prove that it was Bellwether who found her! Nothing but Mimmie's fears that the long dreaded had finally happened!"

His hold on her loosened for the briefest of moments, then he gripped her arms more tightly, making her cry out softly as she looked again into his face.

"Julia, stop this!" He brought her close to him and kissed her.

At first she was paralyzed with surprise and shock, then she began to struggle against his embrace. But as his lips moved on hers, familiar yet strange, frightening yet persuading, she felt that sense of helpless bewitchment engulf her. Without wishing it or intending it, she found she was lost in that same sweet rapture that his first, well-remembered kiss had brought her.

This time he was the one to draw away. He released her, but he did not move far. A great weight of emotion lay heavily between them, separating them, yet drawing them somehow together. Julia, released from the spell of his lips and his arms, had a queer feeling of confusion that weakened her knees again. She placed a hand once more on the chair back for support and tried to steady her breathing.

"I must have your promise of silence, Julia." His voice was low, urgent, steel-edged.

She stood looking at him silently. Her head gave a small shake, as much in bafflement as refusal. He put his hands on her shoulders and looked steadily into her eyes.

"Very well. Since you are not inclined to give me your promise for my own sake, I will ask it for the sake of another. You were brought to this house by someone most dear to you."

"Mimmie! Where is she? What—"

"Let us say that she is under my protection. She will be safe so long as I continue that protection."

The pressure of his hands increased and the voice was not silky at all, but hard and cold and uncompromising.

Julia met his eyes defiantly. "I don't believe you."

"Yes, you do. But I will show you this all the same." He put a hand into the pocket of his coat, and when the hand was opened, Julia saw Mimmie's silver comb resting in his palm. As she gasped and took it from him, he said, "In exchange for your promise, I will see that she comes to no harm."

"You—you are a devil, Philip Sommerville." Julia's voice quavered with anger and the words were almost hissed.

"Perhaps. But sometimes it is necessary to bargain with the devil. Do we have a bargain?"

After a long time she nodded slowly.

As he looked at her, he sighed and shook his head, a little smile playing at the corner of his mouth. He touched a finger to her cheek, and the contact was like a lick of flame on her skin. His finger moved along her throat, across her collarbone, and stopped just where the swell of her breast began, then stroked her skin. "I wish that you . . ." His voice trailed off as he raised his eyes to look into hers. "As you are, I fear you may be very dangerous."

Julia never understood why she could not move, strike his hand away, turn from him. She stood rooted as he removed his hand, and without a word, he left the bedroom.

She rushed to the door to lock it, then had to lean against it to calm herself. She walked shakily to retrieve the lamp and move it to her bedside. She would leave it burning as long as the oil lasted.

Chapter Eight

"We must send for Miss Flagg," Aunt Julia said.

"Whatever for?" Charles lowered his newspaper. "The girl has said that she is educated."

"But how well?" She closed her book with a snap. "When her period of mourning her mother is over, she will be introduced to a society much different than she has known at York. Though Julia appears to be a clever and sensible girl, it is hardly fair to expect her to succeed or even to be comfortable among the people she will meet if she has not the proper background."

"My dear aunt, we cannot give her a background! She is eighteen years old. Her background is established."

"But we may determine what gaps there may be in her education and see that she is given the opportunity to prepare herself to enter society.

135

Miss Flagg is the very person to undertake this job."

"Providing that she is willing to do so, and I think it likely that she is not."

"She will do so if *I* ask it, which I shall do at once unless you give me a valid and serious objection."

Charles closed his paper in defeat. "Indeed, Aunt, I have no objection at all, providing Miss Flagg will come here. I do not think it wise to send the girl—"

"Julia."

"Julia to London at this time."

"I quite agree. It was my intention that Miss Flagg come here. I will write to her this morning."

Miss Narcissa Flagg was the daughter of a naval colleague of the late Admiral Carlyle. When she and her mother were left alone and with little money at the untimely death of Lt. Flagg, the girl, with the encouragement of her mother and the kindness of friends (principally Mrs. Carlyle), was educated far above ordinary achievements in order to enter the teaching profession. In an astonishingly short time she had become the much-prized governess to a couple of prominent families, commanding a very fine salary and giving full value for the price charged. She was now, again through the assistance of Mrs. Carlyle, established at her own day school in London, where she and her select staff supervised the education of about seventy young ladies of the highest social strata. An education by Miss Flagg had become a much-desired social credential, and there were far more applications for admission to her academy than she could possibly accommodate.

It was not at all convenient for Miss Flagg to

leave her school at this time, but, it was, after all, Mrs. Carlyle who asked it. Miss Flagg agreed to come to Fainway.

Miss Flagg was a lady of some thirty-three years, small and dainty, and, in fact, quite a beautiful woman. She was dressed and coiffed in the latest fashion and the most impeccable taste. Her chestnut hair was arranged in a pile of flirty curls, and she looked for all the world like a pampered and frivolous matron of London society. The curls notwithstanding, Miss Flagg was all business. Within an hour of being shown to the best guest room, she summoned Julia to the small reception room, which had been set aside for her use, and the examination of Julia's acquirements began.

Julia soon began to think that she hadn't many. She had progressed easily enough through the schooling she had received at Mrs. Grayson's academy in York. It had been a friendly, pleasant school, offering a course of study that was general in nature and deemed appropriate to prepare young ladies of moderate means for lives as the wives of lawyers, doctors, and bankers. There had been some supplemental education at home. Frances had taught her French and Mimmie had taught her to play the piano. But of architecture, of great art and artists, of exalted philosophers, Julia had only a scanty acquaintance.

It was a fortnight of great intensity. Julia would later describe it as feeling as though her head had been opened, its contents picked over, offending ideas or information ruthlessly excised and replaced with more enlightened notions, and the whole of her mind polished like a silver tray, with particular care given to the corners and crannies.

All the while Miss Flagg sat calmly still, except for her fingers, which, as though they belonged to some other being, were constantly busy. Miss Flagg never needed a reference, never required paper or pencil for even the most challenging mathematical problem. She questioned, she listened, she corrected. And she made lace—an intricate and exquisite pattern taught to her by her mother, whose design it was. Julia went to bed each night exhausted, and for the first time in a long time, her dreams were of Plato and Doric columns, and not of the tragedy that had happened at York, or the confusing and anguishing questions that rose from it, or, above all, what was happening to Mimmie.

At the end of her stay, Miss Flagg gave the opinion that Miss Townes had been decently, if not brilliantly, educated and would benefit from carefully chosen further study. She prepared a formidable list of books that were to be obtained and read, and suggested that, when her mourning was over, Miss Townes might come to London to be received at Miss Flagg's school and examined again.

"She is not at all a flighty girl, I am pleased to say, Mrs. Carlyle," Miss Flagg reported. "She is, indeed, rather too solemn and very much preoccupied, though some consideration must be given to her unfortunate situation just now. Her calm demeanor belies a ready wit . . ."

"Yes, I thought you would discover that," said Mrs. Carlyle, very pleased.

". . . and, I trust, more imagination than she displays at present. She is quite clever and has a most impressive grasp of mathematics. Her French is quite good, as well—very little trace of accent.

She writes a pretty paragraph, well reasoned and presented in an interesting way."

"Excellent."

"Though her penmanship requires more work."

"I see."

"In short, I like the young lady very much. I shall be happy to make room for her as a boarding student if she wishes to pursue further education, but I believe that she will do quite well with the course of study I have outlined. She has a quick and, more important, a retentive mind. I am quite pleased with her."

This was high approval indeed, and Mrs. Carlyle beamed her delight. Miss Flagg departed, and Julia took her first easy breath in two weeks. She went to her bedroom to look over several of the books from the list, which had been available in Charles's library.

Julia had moved from the guest wing into the family's portion of the house. Mrs. Holmes had helped her to select a bedroom; Julia had silently hoped to be given the bedroom that had been her mother's, but a discreet comment from the perceptive housekeeper had let her know that it was a room connected to Father's, which he now used as a private sitting room. And Julia, of course, had been scrupulous in not choosing those rooms which had been allocated to Mary and Lawrence. She settled at length on a large room overlooking the back garden, with two huge bay windows, just like those in her aunt's room a couple of doors away. Julia had seen Aunt Julia's room on one or two occasions when she had been invited to see which of Aunt Julia's many black dresses could be quickly altered to give Julia suitable mourning attire. Julia now called her "Aunt Julia" with slowly increasing ease and enjoyed quiet interludes of discussion with this interesting and very practical woman. Once, Aunt Julia had even mentioned Julia's mother, remarking on her surprise that Frances had named her daughter after her.

"We did not know each other well, you see. I had not yet returned to Fainway when Charles married her. I saw her on visits, of course, and once they came to stay with us in London."

"Did you like her?" Julia asked hesitantly.

"Yes, I did." The old woman touched Julia's hand for the briefest of moments, then turned to look thoughtfully out the bay window. "In many ways, Frances was like the heroine of a romantic story—so beautiful, so fiery, the victim of undeserved misfortune. But I liked her because she was never sorry for herself. In spite of everything that had happened to her, she was not a bitter woman. She accepted life on its own terms, and I believe she tried to be a good wife to Charles. Of course there were passions there which we could not guess at."

"Yes," Julia said softly, a little hesitantly. "Mimmie told me that there was never a love more intense than that between my mother and Richard Payne."

There was another thoughtful pause, then her aunt said, "I should not have liked to have her as an enemy."

"Why do you say so, Aunt Julia?"

"Richard Payne's parents found to their sorrow that she could extract a high measure of retribution for their treatment and deception of her."

"What? How did she do this?"

"By telling the simple truth about the financial condition of the estate of Winterhall. When the Paynes had applied for financing to Charles and one or two of the other gentlemen in the vicinity, she let it be known that they would most likely lose their money if it were placed into Mr. Payne's hands. As a result of her warning, careful investigation of the estate's condition was undertaken, and it was found to be on the verge of ruin. The loans were denied, the estate foundered and eventually had to be sold. The Paynes, in time, lost their place in society as well as their son and their daughter."

Julia released the breath she had been holding and said, "Perhaps it is not right to feel this way, but I am glad!"

"And so am I, my dear, for I always thought the Paynes odious people. How they came to have such fine children, I cannot fathom."

Julia sat thinking of what she had just learned. "Was the estate sold to Mr. Parke, then? I am surprised that it was not entailed in some way within the family."

"Yes, of course, it was and is entailed. I know of few estates which are not entailed on the nearest male relation. Actually, since Richard Payne had died, Mr. Parke is the gentleman who would have inherited anyway, in due time, the house and the portion of the land that was entailed. He chose to purchase the extensive property that had been acquired in Payne's lust for prestige and place among his neighbors. I believe he gave Payne a bit extra for the house and the entailed portion and took possession of the whole estate. The Paynes were reduced to living in rooms in Bath for the short time they both remained alive after this debacle."

"Mr. Parke is a near relative of the family?"

"No. Rather a distant one. And, of course, even a more distant relative of yours."

Julia turned this information over thoughtfully. "I know that Mr. Parke has a nephew," Julia said presently. "Are there no children of his own?"

"There *was* a son, but—"

"Yes?"

"He was a rather wild boy, I'm afraid. Much worse than Philip is said to be. I never knew him myself, but this is the opinion of acquaintances of mine who did know him. It was the usual story. Too much time on his hands, too much money, too appealing to the ladies, too little character. He fell in with a bad lot, never settled down properly to any one pursuit. There was a final breaking with his father over some event which was never disclosed. He left the country, went out to the West Indies, I believe, and was killed there in a most disgraceful way."

"I see. Mr. Parke's distress at Mr. Sommerville's manner of living makes more sense in the light of this knowledge," Julia said. "I suppose he fears that the nephew will go the way of the son."

"He is concerned, of course." Aunt Julia turned from the wardrobe, catching at the black dress which had fallen from its hook. "Philip is the son of a much younger sister, the last of the family now. He seemed always a steady and sensible young man until this last year or two. Now he seems to have taken up a very idle life, spending less and less time with his uncle. And he has, by some accounts, not all of which I consider valid, become quite a flirt. Of course, he is a very handsome young man. Perhaps that sort of thing must be, to some extent, expected."

Julia stood still for the seamstress and sighed.

"The principal families in this particular region seem to have uncommonly bad luck with their children."

"Julia," Charles said.

"Yes, sir." Julia still could not call him "Father."

"I have this morning received a letter from Sir William Grant. He and Miss Sennett and Mr. Woodland are traveling soon down to London. He asks that they be permitted to call here to pay their respects to you."

Julia was so taken aback by this news that she could not answer at once. The idea of seeing, actually seeing, someone from York, from a life that sometimes lately almost seemed to have happened to someone else, was overwhelming.

"Julia," Charles was saying with a little frown, "if you do not wish this visit, I will certainly write an excuse."

"Oh, no!" Julia was roused from her preoccupation. "I am sorry, sir, it is just that . . . Indeed, I should be very pleased to see them if it is not an inconvenience to you and my aunt."

"Sir William proposes to put up at the inn for a day or two while here, but I will invite them to stay at Fainway, of course. It is natural that Sir William should take an interest in your welfare."

His expression was unreadable; it crossed Julia's mind again to wonder how much he knew or guessed about Sir William and Mama.

"Sir William is an old friend and was for many years our clergyman. I think it very kind of him, of all of them, to pay this courtesy."

Before leaving to write the invitation, Charles handed Julia a couple of letters that had come for her by the same post from York.

The first letter was from Mr. Woodland. It was formal and understandably a little awkward, but it conveyed a sincere wish that Miss Townes was well, and the hope that he might be permitted to deliver in person the good wishes of her many friends in York.

Mr. Woodland! She had thought of him from time to time, of course, over these last turbulent weeks. How strange it would be to see him now, after so much had changed, so much had happened. She recalled with gentle fondness his kind, rather scholarly face, the gray eyes, and knew that she would be very glad to see him. And, of course, Sir William, too.

But what she wished most for in this visit was information. What was being done to bring Bellwether, or whatever fiend had killed her mother, to justice? There had been no word of any progress since her father had returned from York. Perhaps Mr. Woodland or Sir William would have fresh news.

The second letter was from Mrs. Ponder, who sent kind condolences and warm wishes and closed with the news that the house across the street had been taken at last by a gentleman.

"... *Although none of us have seen him in all these many weeks, and there is no satisfactory*

144

*information to be gained from his housekeeper
. . . My Hopkins has called on her twice and
come away with no information beyond the
fact that the gentleman is not yet determined
to settle here for good. But happily, I have seen
no sign of cats. . . ."*

Julia put aside the letter with her eyes full of tears
and her heart full of missing those bygone days on
that quiet street.

It was a long three weeks before the party from
the north arrived at Fainway. Sir William's new
carriage brought them all to the door on a blustery
November afternoon.

"Sir William. Mr. Woodland. Miss Sennett."
Julia met them at the front door herself and took
them to the drawing room. "Come and let me
introduce you to my aunt, Mrs. Carlyle. Aunt Julia,
these are my friends from York."

"Miss Sennet," Aunt Julia said, looking narrowly
at the new arrival, "you will forgive me if I say that
you look rather pale. I trust this kind journey has
not been too much for you."

"I confess, ma'am," Miss Sennett replied faintly,
"I am feeling still a little weak."

"My dear Miss Sennett, you needn't sit here and
make polite conversation with us. Come with me at
once and get settled in your room. You can have a
nice nap before dinner."

Undisguised relief appeared in Miss Sennet's
dark eyes, and she followed Aunt Julia to the door.
As they reached it, Lawrence entered.

Lawrence was presented to Miss Sennet, and

145

Julia was glad to see that he did not stint on his smile of courteous pleasure or on the charm of his words of welcome for this plain and unremarkable woman. Miss Sennett brightened noticeably, and it almost looked that she might prefer to stay in the drawing room after all, but Aunt Julia, when she judged that sufficient courtesies had been exchanged, led her firmly away.

Lawrence was now brought forward for presentation to the two gentlemen.

"How lucky it is that I am passing Fainway on this particular day," Lawrence said. "My cousin has spoken of you both, and I am pleased to have this opportunity of meeting you."

"Are you here for this day only, Mr. Christian?" Robert asked, his countenance brightening.

Lawrence looked at him with an expression of sudden surprise. "I am expected back in London by tomorrow evening."

"A pity," said Robert politely, but he did not really look as though he thought it unfortunate.

"Indeed," Lawrence replied with a thoughtful frown.

Julia could not help feeling some amusement as the two young men measured each other. She turned to glance at Sir William to see what he might make of it, but Sir William only looked uncomfortable.

"Well, perhaps," Lawrence was beginning, "I could send word and remain a day or two—"

He was interrupted by the arrival of Mr. Townes, who had just ridden home from Winterhall.

Charles greeted his guests warmly, made all the proper inquiries about their journey, expressed regret at Miss Sennett's fatigue, then, to Julia's gratitude, he exerted himself to chat cordially with Sir William in an effort to relieve the awkwardness that unfortunate gentleman must be feeling at being in this house.

At dinner it fell to Lawrence to entertain Miss Sennett, who had improved sufficiently to appear downstairs and he bore this duty manfully. On this evening, at her aunt's insistence, Julia sat for the first time at the head of her father's table and did the courtesies of official hostess of Fainway. Sir William, though still not entirely comfortable, found a topic of mutual interest to Aunt Julia—which London hotel was *really* the most prestigious (not, of course, to be confused with *fashionable*).

And so the evening passed pleasantly.

The next day Lawrence was gone—any intention he might have had of remaining circumvented by Charles giving him a letter that must go to London without delay. ". . . And as you must go tomorrow, it would be a great alleviation to have it entrusted to reliable hands," Charles had added.

After breakfast, Julia showed her guests about the house and wondered if she might have done Miss Sennett a disservice. Sir William was delighted with the system of wall panels and could not understand why his cousin did not agree that such an improvement would be just the thing at Winderfields. That afternoon, Julia and her father rode with Sir William and Robert (Miss Sennett was not feeling *that* much better) to show them the Druid's Circle. This outing seemed to contribute further to the easing of Sir William's strain, and when Charles offered to show him some alterations now underway in the carriage house, they went cheerfully out together. Julia and Robert were left alone. Unfortunately, he had no news of Bellwether to give her in answer to her questions, but Julia had another reason to be grateful to him.

"Thank you sincerely, Mr. Woodland, for bringing more of my belongings."

"I cannot pretend to have done this alone. Sir William returned again to York after your father left and assisted me in the making of a thorough inspection and inventory."

"Ah, Sir William. I hope he has not given himself more pain by this kind visit. I see the change in him—so drawn and anxious and weary. I always knew that he loved her."

Robert said, "I believe he has done the wise thing by coming here, putting it firmly to rest."

Julia met his eyes, wondering if Robert was also putting an affair of the heart to rest. His mild expression told her nothing, but he was the first to look away.

"I shall offer to take him to her grave," Julia said. "Perhaps that will help him to confront his sorrow, then lay it aside and enjoy himself in London."

Robert gave a little shake of his head. "He is concerned, too, about his cousin's health."

"Indeed?"

"One purpose of this visit to London is to permit Miss Sennet to consult a certain physician, and I expect that she will then go to Bath for some weeks."

Miss Sennett, it appeared, suffered from a condition too delicate for precise description, but which seemed to center upon the digestive system. She had been troubled by this malady in her early years, but not until just lately had the condition reappeared. It was most worrisome.

"I am very sorry," said Julia. "I hope she may find relief in the curative waters." She looked at him steadily. "And why have you come along, Mr. Woodland?"

If this was a moment of opportunity, Robert did not seize it. "I hope to make this my last effort in regard to Sir William's business. It is becoming more and more difficult to spare so much time from the bank to handle each question and crisis that arises. I shall put some last matters in order for him in London, then he must engage his own man of business. I shall help him to conduct interviews in the city, and I mean to insist that the man selected be willing to go permanently to Winderfields. I do not mean to speak unkindly, but I am afraid that Sir William enjoys more *being* a baronet than working at it."

"I confess that I have never quite understood the man. I always seemed to expect more energy and, oh, fire from Sir William than he ever demonstrated."

A comfortable little silence fell, then Julia asked about Mrs. Ponder.

"Ailing a bit, I am afraid. A new family has been found for your house, though she does not think very highly of them. I believe she would be wise to sell her own house and go to live with her daughter in Leeds."

"It is a hard thing to leave one's home," Julia said, not intending to give more meaning to her words than that associated with Mrs. Ponder.

"Very true. And Leeds is not so pretty a place as York. All the same, I believe that she is terribly lonely now. She depended upon your company a great deal."

, Julia now asked after all the friends and acquaintances she could recall; she received satisfactory reports on all, but rather more information regarding Miss Pierce than she particularly wanted.

Miss Sennett improved even more and came down to dinner that evening to sing the praises of a preparation that Aunt Julia had given her. Aunt Julia, who suffered from time to time from similar troubles, was a great joy to Miss Sennett, not only for providing genuine relief from this mysterious condition, but for her patience in listening to Miss Sennett's symptoms and fears.

After dinner, when Charles talked to Robert of banking and Miss Sennett talked to Aunt Julia about Bath, Sir William drew Julia to a distant corner of the room and asked her with a hushed voice and a frown of concern how she was.

"I am well enough, Sir William. I have had quite an adjustment, of course, but I daresay I shall survive it."

"I have heard from Mr. Townes today that Miss Chappell, that good lady, is not here. Has actually left you."

"That is so."

"You must miss her."

"Oh, yes!" For a moment tears filled Julia's eyes, and for a dizzying, crazy instant, she longed to throw herself onto Sir William's chest and weep for the loss of Mimmie with someone who would understand. To scream that Mimmie's fate lay in the hands of a devil who bargained that precious life for Julia's silence. But she composed herself to say, "Mr. Townes very likely told you that her real name was not Chappel, but Payne, and that she was the sister of the man with whom my mother left this house."

"He did, and I am most concerned. If I understand Mr. Townes correctly, Miss, er, Payne is actually hiding for her own protection, and she feared that if she remained with you, you might also be in danger."

"That is what Mimmie told me."

"How can this be? Even if it *is* this Bellwether, and not a madman who is to blame for your mother's death, why does she suppose that he is such a fiend that he would extract revenge upon an innocent young woman who had nothing to do with events of so long ago?"

"I rather think," Julia said thoughtfully, "her fear was that Bellwether might suspect that I know something. Something about him that my mother or Mimmie might have told me that could lead to his exposure."

Sir William seemed to be waiting to hear whether she *did* have such knowledge, but for reasons of her own, Julia chose to say nothing, and Sir William did not ask the question.

"It seems so bizarre," Sir William said after a moment. "I should have said confidently that the man was dead years ago."

"Someone ransacked our house. My father believes it was done in a search for, well, for that something."

151

"Ah, the house. What a dreadful business. I hope the things we have brought you will be of some use. There was little to be salvaged beyond what Mr. Townes brought with him before."

"I am grateful to have anything of that life, those days, Sir William. Thank you."

"I understand that you were spirited away from York with nothing."

"It is quite true. Mimmie found me on the street as I returned from Mrs. Woodland's home. We took nothing, did not even go to the house. I left with nothing but the clothes I was wearing."

Sir William made a sympathetic sound and said that it must have been a difficult trip.

"I pray I never have another like it," Julia said.

Charles now came to join them, and Sir William spoke at once of something that had been long on his mind.

"Sir," he said, "I hesitate to mention this, but if I intrude where I have no business, you must forgive me, for I mean well. I am gravely concerned about Miss Townes's safety. This Bellwether, if he is indeed the culprit in this filthy business, may well be searching for this young lady even now. I hope that steps have been taken to insure her safety."

"What measures would you recommend, Sir William?"

"Why, I hardly know. Is she attended when she goes into public? Are strangers who come here scrutinized? Is a watch being kept in the neighborhood for suspicious persons?"

"My daughter does not go out publicly just yet. She will be in mourning for a few weeks more. As for your other points, I assure you that we are extremely cautious in this way. I must say, however, that I do not think an attack on her very likely. She has done this man no injury, and if she had known anything to place him in danger, she has had ample time to report it. To stalk her at this time would merely endanger him to no good purpose."

Sir William sat in laborious consideration of this argument for several minutes, then he sighed and said, "Well, perhaps you are right. I am not sorry to have mentioned the subject, however. Both Mr. Woodland and I have given the question much thought. I shall tell him your views."

"I assure you, sir, I have just done so, for he posed me the same question. Miss Townes is most fortunate in her friends' concern for her welfare. I am pleased to see it. Should you care to hunt tomorrow?"

Julia was warmed by this display of concern from Robert and even Sir William but uncertain of her feelings about her father's stated lack of apprehension on her behalf. What he said made sense, even echoed her own assessment of the matter, but she could not help regretting that he was not capable of a bit more parental anxiety.

Would she always be a stranger to him? She did not want to consider the other possibility—that nagging, ugly suspicion that was so wretched, so unthinkable, but which would not quite go away— that he was responsible for her mother's death and knew that there could be no danger from Bellwether, who might well, as Sir William believed, be long dead anyhow.

Three days later Sir William's party was gone, conveying Miss Sennett to the London specialist, even though she now protested that she had little need of him and would just as soon go directly to Bath. Sir William insisted, however, and Aunt Julia added her voice on the side of prudence. Therefore, Miss Sennett went quietly to London, taking along several brown bottles containing Aunt Julia's wondrous remedy.

Julia took leave of Robert, wondering whether they would ever meet again and feeling rather sad at the thought that they might not. He would write, he promised, or perhaps his mother would, of news of York from time to time, and taking with him Julia's good wishes for the friends she had left behind, he entered the carriage behind Sir William. MacKenzie slapped the reins and called to the horses, and the group departed.

Chapter Nine

London! It was a place that Julia, not so very many weeks ago, had wondered if she ever might see. There had been some hope that, had she become Mrs. Woodland, her husband might, in due time, indulge her with a visit to this exotic capital. But here she was—not in the company of Robert or any other husband, but arriving in a carriage belonging to her father (another amazement), and accompanied by that same gentleman as well as her great aunt.

They arrived at a large and elegant hotel where a liveried doorman, more resplendent than any officer of the Queen's Regiment could possibly be, bowed them inside. They were shown to a spacious suite boasting accommodations for the three of them as well as for Charles's valet and the maid who would attend the ladies. Julia was a wide-eyed participant, though she had nearly come to expect to be overwhelmed on an almost daily basis in this new life of hers.

They dined that evening in one of the hotel's private dining rooms, which had no potted palms, but made up for this omission with its elegant furnishings, dazzling linens, expert service and, above all, the grandeur of the head waiter, whose mustache was the largest, sleekest, blackest Julia had ever dreamed of seeing. They went early to bed, and the next morning brought a lady more resplendent in her own way than even the head-waiter. Julia supposed that she must be a duchess, but she proved to be Mrs. Talmadge, dressmaker of merit, whose fashionable premises in the city employed more than twenty of the most skillful seamstresses to be found in the kingdom. She had brought a couple of her staff along, and Julia was soon measured, draped, turned this way and that before the mirror, then seated to look through a sheaf of sketches. With Aunt Julia's urging and persuading, she selected several designs and several fabrics, remembering at the end to ask if she might have a dressing gown made as well. Mrs. Talmadge, taken momentarily aback, brought forth a rich satin brocade in a bright purple shade.

"I would prefer, actually, to have something a bit more serviceable," Julia said a little timidly. "Rosie, will you bring the robe for Mrs. Talmadge to see?"

The rose-colored dressing gown was produced; Mrs. Talmadge fingered the material, said she thought something of that weight might be found and asked what color Miss Townes wished to have.

"I rather think I would like a blue one," Julia

replied. "I had such a robe before, and I always felt comfortable in it."

"Yes," Mrs. Talmadge remarked. "Blue is a most becoming color for you, Miss Townes. I will see what I can do." She smiled, for despite the trappings of her profession, Mrs. Talmadge had such a cozy robe of her own in which she retreated of an evening.

The next morning Julia was conveyed to Miss Flagg's academy, where she would remain for the next several days. She made the trip in gloomy apprehension, certain she would prove a disappointment and wishing she had been more diligent at her books. But as they drew near the street where the academy was located, her gloom was replaced with wonder and astonishment.

"You see there, Julia?" her father asked. "That building is the new railway station."

"Oh!" Julia strained her eyes in the direction of this marvel of modern times. "It is a handsome building, indeed. But where is the train?"

"A pity that we missed it. I hear they now run every half-hour. One day, it is said, the tracks will reach into all parts of the kingdom."

"Even to York? How splendid!"

Uncertain at first as to what her exact status might be, Julia soon found that she was not to be treated as a mere student. She was shown to the sitting room which Miss Flagg kept for her guests, though there was a disappointment there. Julia had long looked forward to meeting the mother who had produced this astonishing woman, but Mrs. Flagg was, alas, in Bath and would remain there several more weeks.

Julia dined and took tea with the staff and was treated with respectful cordiality by all of them. Even so, she was subjected by one or two of them, as well as by Miss Flagg, to rigorous and difficult written examinations. All day, every day, for four intense and exhausting days, Julia labored with pen and paper under the pleasant eyes and benign smiles of these academic ladies. And with one of the younger teachers, a Miss Virginia Hathaway, she struck up something of an acquaintance.

"This seems, on the whole," Julia said to Miss Hathaway, "quite a pleasant situation. I often wondered, when at Mrs. Grayson's academy, what sort of life our teachers lived. I confess I rather thought their lot a dreary one, existing on tea and grave discussions about the next day's lessons."

"Ours *is* a pleasant life," Miss Hathaway replied, laughing. "I don't say that it would be to the liking of every woman. Indeed, I am certain it is not entirely to the liking of every woman here. For me, however, it is an employment I have found most agreeable."

"Miss Flagg, too, certainly seems to enjoy it."

"Miss Flagg, more than any of us, remains in this life by choice and not by any necessity. She has had any number of opportunities to marry, and to marry very well indeed."

Julia was not at all surprised by this bit of information, and she took the opportunity that evening, when sitting alone with Miss Flagg in the private sitting room, to ask about the rewards of educating young women.

"Miss Townes," Miss Flagg said with a kind of grave excitement, "it is the greatest satisfaction to do it well. To see the gleam of understanding that comes to a student's face when a particularly troublesome subject has at last made sense is the most exciting sight in all the world." Miss Flagg smiled. "But the life of a teacher has other rewards, too. The company of other educated and serious-thinking women, and sometimes men as well. The opportunity to pursue one's particular interests in a course of study or writing. The leisure and the means to travel to interesting places with agreeable companions. And . . ." Miss Flagg hesitated for a moment, ". . . and one's life is one's own. One's employer must be satisfied, of course, and the proprieties observed, naturally, but, Miss Townes" —she turned glowing eyes to Julia—"it is the greatest joy to know that my soul belongs only to me!"

Julia hesitated, then said, "Forgive me if I inquire where I have no business, but do you not wish to marry some day?"

"Oh, I intend to marry!" came the prompt and emphatic reply. "But I do not intend to do it in haste or with the abandonment with which far too many women approach marriage. Being a wife is a job, after all, and I would be the greatest fool to exchange the job I have now for one less stimulating and interesting. I would be more foolish still to attach myself to a husband whose company would not be as pleasant day after day as the companions I now enjoy, or who would require that I abandon my own interests and devote myself entirely to his."

Miss Flagg snipped an offending thread from her lacework and draped it over the arm of her chair to look at it. Julia saw that she had made an exquisite and distinctly oversized and therefore practical handkerchief.

"And, of course, there is the question of security. I make a very good living. I would not exchange it for a life of less comfort and prosperity. You may think it callous of me, but I believe that any woman who would do so is not merely a fool, but entirely demented."

Despite its rigors, Julia found that she was rather sorry to see her stay with Miss Flagg come to an end. As she and Miss Flagg drove away from the academy, she reflected that again she had had no time to dwell on the question of Philip Sommerville and her father. Of Mr. Sommerville and her mother. Of Mr. Sommerville and Mimmie.

When they arrived at the hotel, Julia found a surprise.

"Julia," said Charles, coming forward, "here are some people you will be glad to see."

"Sir William! Mr. Woodland!" Julia shook hands happily with the both of them. "How surprised I am to see you."

Sir William said, "Our business has taken much longer than we wished or expected. Indeed, Mr. Woodland had to leave me here a fortnight while he saw to affairs in York. He has just this moment returned."

Julia exchanged an understanding smile with Robert.

"And I must credit the excellent Mrs. Carlyle with bringing us to this hotel," Sir William said, "though I never thought to find all of you here."

"I happened to see Mr. Woodland as he arrived

just now," said Charles. "Odd that I did not see Sir William in all our days together here."

Sir William agreed that it did seem strange, but then, his days had been full of business and sight-seeing, and his evenings had taken him once or twice to dine with a former colleague in the clergy.

"Well, as to dining," Charles said, "it is settled that you are to be my guests this evening. It is to be a bit of a celebration of Julia's success at her studies. I have invited Lawrence and Mary, too, Julia."

It was a cheerful group that assembled in the dining room engaged by Charles for the occasion. From her seat next to her father, Julia noticed that Sir William took a lively interest in Miss Flagg. He had received the introduction rather stiffly, but as the dinner progressed, his interest grew. He seemed not to know what to make of such a woman. Miss Flagg clearly was a more widely read and more intelligent creature than he, but once she had established these facts, she somehow injected a note of flattery in her voice and manner, and Sir William acted as if he were in the company of a most remarkable woman. Julia shook her head and marveled again at how this dainty and helpless-looking beauty could disguise such tenacious and formidable intellect and personality.

But if Sir William appeared to be smitten by Miss Flagg, it was another matter that most inter-ested Julia—her father's behavior toward Mary Belleville.

"I hope, Mary," Charles was saying, "that when you come for Christmas, you will stay on for several weeks."

"I should like that very much, indeed," Mary replied with a little flush of pleasure. "But Lawrence talked of remaining only a fortnight."

"Why, yes," Lawrence put in. "I must return to London very soon after the New Year. I will stay through my birthday, but—"

"Oh, Lawrence," Mary interrupted with an affectionate laugh, "you needn't hint! None of us is likely to forget your birthday. And I have a very good idea of the gift you want from me."

"I didn't mean—" Lawrence began a little sheepishly.

"Very well," Charles said quickly. "It is a pity, but Mary may stay, surely, without you. I think it would be pleasant for Julia to have another person in the house." He turned to Julia. "I fear that I may be away myself for some days in January, with Philip Sommerville. It will be best if you have some company."

Julia's heart sank as the old anxieties rose. What were her father's dealings with Mr. Sommerville? It was not a situation to give one ease. Wishing these unwelcome suspicions away, she turned to speak to Lawrence and saw that he was gazing at the end of the table where Mary and her father sat. Lawrence's face was thoughtful and, she thought, a little surprised. It was then that a sudden cold wave of alarm washed over her as she realized that her father was in love with Mary Belleville! And now . . . now that Frances Townes was surely dead, rather than just thought to be dead, he might marry with clear and complete sanction. Julia held a napkin to her lips as the wine she was sipping caught in her throat.

Suppose it were not revenge, but a wish to be free that had led him to an evil association with Philip Sommerville? They "do things for each other"! *Had* Mr. Sommerville done the ultimate favor for his friend and neighbor in order that Charles might be free to marry? Try as she might, she could not force this new suspicion away.

It did not go away through the fittings the next morning, and the triumphant display by Mrs. Talmadge of a new collection of materials. Julia was too distracted to pay proper attention.

"Julia, dear, Mrs. Talmadge has asked you which of these patterns you prefer for the winter cloak?"

"I beg your pardon, ma'am," said the startled Julia. "And yours especially, Mrs. Talmadge. They are both very nice." She forced herself to concentrate as she fingered the soft wool. "I do not believe I have a preference between the two. Which do you prefer, Aunt?"

Aunt Julia held up first one then the other of the swatches, declared herself equally uncertain, left the matter to Mrs. Talmadge, who settled it promptly by selecting the more expensive one.

Next came the fitting of a ball gown, which was to be required the very next evening, for Julia was invited to the first real ball of her life. The gown was red, truly red, with long gloves to match. Its neckline was quite shockingly low and its lines closely fitted. When she saw herself in the looking glass, with so much shoulder exposed, Julia protested. "This is not the same gown, surely, as the sketch I was shown!" She turned in distress to her aunt.

"Of course it is the same gown. What can you

mean? It is quite becoming, too. You will be much admired when your father presents you to the company tomorrow evening."

"But it is so bare! I cannot be at ease in such a gown."

"Oh, well, you must have some jewelry, to be sure. I'm certain I have pearls among my things that will do nicely for now. When there is time, we will speak to Charles about some jewelry of your own."

"Forgive me, ma'am, I do not think that pearls will provide sufficient coverage in this instance." Frowning, Julia turned back to the looking glass.

"You mustn't say so until you have seen the effect, my dear." Aunt Julia sent her maid for the jewel case.

The pearls were tried and found to be perfection by her aunt and Mrs. Talmadge. Even the maid offered her own admiring comments. Julia remained unhappy, however, until Mrs. Talmadge produced a fringed shawl of a complementing design, which Julia wrapped with relief over her shoulders.

"Much better. I shouldn't wonder if London women who dress this way are constantly in bed with terrible colds."

"You will get used to it in time," was her aunt's prediction. "I rather think these earrings will complete the ensemble."

So Julia was attired for the important evening, even found that she grew a little more comfortable with her own dress when she saw the necklines of the other women. Even her hostess, one Mrs. Prentiss, wore a very décolleté gown, though she compensated by filling the ample space bared on her chest with a good many diamonds.

It turned out to be a rather large gathering in a private house. Aunt Julia had prevailed on her friend to find room for Sir William and Robert, so Julia could be confident of having at least one, possibly two, partners besides Lawrence. Then it occurred to her that she had no idea whether either of them could dance. Indeed, she was not certain of her own abilities in this area, for she had only danced with the dancing master at Mrs. Grayson's academy, and that was a long time ago.

But Lawrence led her out among the other couples, and, after a beginning awkwardness, she did quite well. She had a natural grace and rhythm, and Lawrence was an excellent partner. When the dance was over, she was warm enough to dispense with her shawl.

"Your father will not say it to you," Lawrence remarked as they strolled from the dance floor, "for he considers such praise imprudent and despoiling to a young mind, but he is very proud of how beautiful you are."

"What?" said the astonished Julia. "It is kind of you to say it, sir, but I think it unlikely that he considers me beautiful. My mother was beautiful. If he thinks anything of my appearance at all, I should think it is only because it is so like his own."

"Not at all," Lawrence insisted. "Look at him, even now. He is watching us and admiring. And you see that Sir William is speaking to him? He is saying what a handsome couple we are. There! You see that your father is nodding his agreement. Ah, but I believe Mr. Woodland does not share the enthusiasm of the others. How can you account for that, Cousin Julia?"

"Indeed, Mr. Christian, I can only account for it by saying that you are mistaken in every particular."

"Oh please! Can we not have done with 'Mr. Christian' and 'Miss Townes'? Can I not be 'Lawrence,' or at least 'Cousin Lawrence'? You must eventually accept the fact that we are family, you know, disagreeable as the notion may be."

Julia gave him her gravest look. "You mistake me, sir. I am only too pleased to have any family at all, to make frivolous objections as to whom they might be."

It took him a moment to realize that she was teasing. He laughed, his eyes dancing with merriment.

"Well done, Cousin Julia. Never have I been more effectively silenced in my fishing for compliments. I shall retire from the field, but I must conclude by repeating that your father thinks you very beautiful, and a great many people in this room agree with him."

"Thank you . . . Cousin Lawrence."

He stopped to turn and smile into her eyes. "I will be satisfied with that. For now."

They joined their party.

Julia danced with Robert, who did not dance very well, and with Sir William, who was a surprisingly graceful partner, though he seemed rather pensive and sighed a great deal. Julia felt that he was thinking of Frances, imagining how lovely she would look among these elegant people.

Julia found to her surprise that introductions were sought by a number of young men; she had a great many more partners than she could ever have expected, and she was thinking to herself that she had, for most of this evening, put aside the cares and questions that deviled her days. She was very close to admitting that she was enjoying herself.

When a particularly earnest young man returned her from the dance floor to her party, Aunt Julia was speaking to her nephew. "Look, Charles. There is Philip Sommerville."

"So it is," Charles replied. "Lawrence, go and fetch him, will you?"

"Fetch him, sir?"

"Why, yes. You will think it odd, I daresay, but he has not yet been introduced to Julia."

Lawrence departed without much enthusiasm, and Charles beamed at his daughter. "Philip is Mr. Parke's nephew, as I am sure you must have learned, and the next heir of Winterhall. I have been most remiss in not seeing that you meet such a close neighbor. I am certain you will find him agreeable."

"*All* ladies find Mr. Sommerville agreeable," teased Mary.

Julia forced her voice to be calm as she said that she looked forward to meeting Mr. Sommerville at last.

"Ah, here he is!"

Charles smiled as Julia raised reluctant eyes to meet those of Philip Sommerville.

"Julia, may I present our neighbor and good friend, Mr. Philip Sommerville? My daughter, Julia Townes."

Julia could do nothing but grit her teeth and extend her hand. "How do you do, Mr. Sommerville?"

"This is a very great pleasure, Miss Townes." There was that silky, caressing voice, reflecting, almost, the look in his eyes. "My uncle has written and spoken of you in the terms of greatest praise since he had the pleasure of making your acquaintance."

"Mr. Parke is very kind." Julia's voice was as icy as her eyes.

A little frown creased Philip's forehead, then was quickly gone.

"Perhaps you will give me the very great pleasure of dancing with you, Miss Townes, if you are not otherwise engaged for this waltz."

Charles beamed approval, in stark contrast to the scowl that had come to Lawrence's face, then Charles held out his arm to Mary.

"Come, Mary. Do you not think we might take a turn around the floor ourselves?"

They walked, the four of them together, onto the dance floor and stood waiting for the music to begin. Julia was entirely silent, refusing to look at Philip, but intently aware of his green eyes gazing down at her. The dance began and he took her firmly into his arms and led her smoothly away from the other couple.

When he spoke, it was softly, his tone mellow and enfolding. "Miss Townes?"

"Yes?" And without quite meaning to, she did look up at him; he was studying her face thoughtfully.

"I have some news to give you, but I must have your assurance that it will reach no other ears. Not even those of your father."

A frown drew her brows together. "You are a man much given to secrecy, Mr. Sommerville. This is the second time you have demanded silence from me."

"And again this time I have something to offer in exchange."

"What sort of news is it, Mr. Sommerville, to be worth such a promise? The only news I wish to hear is that the man who murdered my mother has been brought to account."

"It does not concern the man called Bellwether. It is not, perhaps, exactly news. Let us call it information."

"Very well. What is this information?"

"I am waiting to hear your promise of silence."

"Mr. Sommerville," came Julia's exasperated reply, "have you no fear that I might give my promise and then break it?"

"I am an excellent judge of character, Miss Townes."

They danced many steps in silence while Julia looked hard into his face.

"Very well. I give you my word that I will tell no one."

He did not speak until he had danced her to the edge of the crowd on the floor.

"I have brought you a letter from the friend who delivered you to your father. Do not cry out!"

"Mimmie?" Julia breathed, obeying the urgent gaze and the firm pressure of his hand.

"Yes. Mimmie, as you call her. She is safe and she is well."

"How can she be safe and well," Julia demanded with flashing eyes, "when she is in the hands of . . ." Her voice died out suddenly when she realized she did not know how to finish the sentence.

He glanced beyond her, looking around at the other dancers, then shook his head, unsmiling, as he looked down at her. "I will give you the letter at the end of this dance. You must not read it until you are safe in your room and quite alone. And when you have read it, you must destroy it."

He waited, still looking down intently into her face, until she nodded slowly. "Yes. Very well. I agree."

Now he sighed. It surprised her, and she saw his green eyes narrow in a tiny frown.

"Perhaps," he said slowly, "when we are all at home again at Christmastime, there will be an opportunity for us to speak at length and privately. It would be well to come to an understanding, you and I."

Julia was not entirely certain what he meant, but she had a good idea. Her eyes flashed hot blue anger, and she felt a flush burn her face.

"And are you planning to sneak into my bedroom once again so that we might reach this understanding?"

He gave a tiny laugh, startled by her words and heated tone. "What a tempting invitation you extend, Miss Townes, but I was thinking of a quiet ride along the river."

Julia, confounded by the range of emotions this man could provoke in her, was struggling to answer calmly when her father and Mary danced near them again. She turned to nod at them, hoping that the flush in her cheeks would be put down to the vigor of the waltz.

The music ended and Julia and Philip followed Charles and Mary from the floor. And swiftly, neatly, unobserved by anyone, Julia felt the message being slipped into the top of her glove. Then came an electric thrill coursing though her as he . . . yes, he most certainly pressed her hand in both of his. When she glanced up at him, the pressure of his hands continued, and his eyes seemed to be sending her a message. It was not of flirtation or anything like it; Julia almost thought it was a warning. Then he made a bow and drifted away into the crowd; Julia saw him no more that evening.

Late that night, alone in her bedroom, Julia read the letter by her bedside lamp. It was very brief.

> *"My dearest Julia,*
>
> *How I wish I could be with you to give these assurances of my well-being. I pray that day may not be long in coming. In the meantime, you must trust, as I do, that the terrible affair that has separated us will be swiftly and justly settled. You are ever in my thoughts and prayers. Please, above all, do as Mr. Sommerville asks of you.*
>
> *Mimmie"*

Julia's first thought was that she had been cheated! Her promise of silence for this—this nothing? Well, not nothing, of course. Mimmie was truly safe, and that was the main thing. But . . .

Why had Mimmie not told her how she might send word?

But the answer came in the next instant.

Of course *he* would not permit it!

Fainway decorated for Christmas was quite lovely. Fragrant boughs festooned mantels in the drawing room and in the two family sitting rooms, and a huge tree stood proudly in the entry hall, its top extending above the railing of the gallery. Most of these preparations had been carried out by Mrs. Holmes's zealous staff prior to the family's return from London, but each day Julia noticed additional candles and more ornaments appearing throughout the house.

She had done her Christmas shopping with her aunt's aid, and had presents under the tree for each of the household servants as well as for the family. She had also bought a birthday gift for Lawrence—a noncommittal book of travel descriptions. And there was a gift for Mimmie, a pretty silver brooch. She had not decided whether to keep it, hoping for the day that she might present it herself, or hand it pointedly over to Mr. Sommerville for delivery.

There was excitement out of doors, too. A few days before Christmas came word that the Druids were gathering at Winterhall's circle of standing stones. Some were staying at the inn in the village; one or two had taken rooms with cottagers. Each day a few more visited in the meadow where they would observe the winter solstice. Julia saw them when she rode out one morning with her father and Mary to the edge of the woods where they could look down on the Druid's Circle.

"Well, Julia, what did you think of the Druids?" Aunt Julia asked when the party had returned to the house.

"How ordinary they look!" Julia replied. "I confess I am a bit disappointed."

"But you haven't seen their leader," Charles said.

"He is an awesome sight, even in ordinary clothing, with that beard of his and those fierce black eyes."

"Yes, Julia," Mary agreed. "And when they gather around their fires in those sinister costumes, really, it is not at all ordinary. It is quite appalling."

Ah, well." Charles smiled from Mary to Julia. "I shouldn't wonder if those who practice the more vigorous religions of the world, perhaps those of Africa or the Indians of the New World, would say the same of our own church services, as subdued and solemn as they often are."

"Except for old Dr. Thornedyke's sermons," Aunt Julia remarked. "You recall, don't you, Charles? Before Mr. Witherspoon came. There was nothing solemn or subdued about a Sunday sermon from Dr. Thornedyke."

"No, indeed!" said Charles. "I recall the time . . ." He stopped, then glanced at Julia. "But then, it was many years ago, and Mr. Witherspoon is a sound man in his way."

He went on then to speak of other things. Julia was certain he had been on the point of recalling an event in which Mama was concerned. It was even likely that Dr. Thornedyke had been the one to perform the marriage service that had united them.

Was it guilt? she wondered. And if not, would they one day speak of Frances in each other's presence without pain or embarrassment?

On midwinter eve the gentlemen of Winterhall were to dine at Fainway, along with a few other neighbors, and go in a group to observe the ceremony at the Druid's Circle from the safety of the rise at the edge of Fainway's woods. Charles had the men from the stable construct a kind of rude shelter which would protect the ladies from the elements on what promised to be a clear and chilly evening.

Philip did not sit near Julia at dinner; he was placed next to Miss Merryweather, a pale and pouty girl with an annoying giggle. She pretended to ignore him while inquiring pointedly of Mary when her brother, Mr. Christian, might arrive and remarked how unfortunate that he would miss the excitement of the evening. Julia, doing full justice to her now permanent duty as hostess, divided her attention between Mr. Parke and Mr. Witherspoon.

After dinner the group set out, leaving only Mary, Aunt Julia and Mrs. Merryweather behind in the warmth and comfort of the drawing room. The men rode on horseback, but a carriage took Julia and Miss Merryweather to the edge of the woods. There they too mounted horses and followed by torchlight the servants who led them along the trail through the trees to the shelter above the meadow.

"It looks as though we shall be very snug here, Miss Townes," said Miss Merryweather. "Here is a sturdy bench to sit upon and they have built us quite a nice fire."

"Yes. But I wonder if we shall really need it," Julia replied. "My father says that the ceremony will be well under way by midnight, and it is half past eleven now. We shall not have long to wait."

"I hope you will not be shocked by what you see, Miss Townes," Miss Merryweather said with a superior old-hand air. "Many do find it shocking. Indeed, I am surprised that Mr. Witherspoon has come at all."

Philip had strolled into the shelter in time to hear this. "Perhaps he means to pray at close range for

174

their salvation." He looked around the shelter. "You have a comfortable nook here, ladies, but not a very good view. They have assembled and seem to be beginning."

Julia was out of her seat and following him to the very edge of the rise where she could look down on the scene below her.

"Why, there must be nearly a hundred of them!" she gasped in astonishment.

"More than last year, it seems to me, Philip," growled Mr. Parke, who stood near them.

"Poor wretched souls," was Mr. Witherspoon's remark, but he stared at them as intently as anyone.

Illuminated by many bonfires and by a bright half-moon, was a large group of otherworldly figures. Some wore long white robes; others were dressed in what looked to be animal skins. Many wore white peaked hats, and Julia could even see that several had long, pointed beards. She wondered fleetingly if any in the crowd might be women. They stood just inside the circle, keeping near the fires, which must offer much-needed warmth. What *were* they wearing under those robes? They had seemed to be talking among themselves, but now they fell silent as the notes of a flute, haunting and eerie, floated on the cold winter air.

Its song was brief; it seemed a call to order as much as anything, and then there came chanting, voices raised in unison, and the figures below began to sway in the firelight. It began as a murmur, then grew stronger, bolder, more and more disquieting, until it reached a hair-raising, climactic throbbing, then fell away into silence as the leader walked into the center of the circle.

To the sound of the flute, he began to chant, holding up a torch and something of shiny metal in the shape of a crescent moon. His voice came faintly to Julia's ears, drowned out completely now and then by the ghostly, disembodied music.

Now the chanting voices rose again, joined and mingled with the flute, and though the words were unintelligible, Julia understood. These supplicants were calling on the unseen, unfathomable forces that governed the rhythms and circuits of the earth and the heavens. Julia felt herself suspended, as though out of all time and reality, looking down on a ritual as bizarre as it was compelling, as barbaric as it was oddly beautiful. It was a strange, gaudy, disturbing sight. One wanted almost to turn away —to run away—from the fearful possibility of being touched in a secret core of one's being by an ancient, mystical power that surely had no place in a civilized soul.

She felt Philip move behind her and knew that she had gasped or even cried out without knowing it. Indeed, she feared that she might have swayed against him, for his arm had caught her and held her now, unnoticed by those who had eyes only for what lay below them.

"Julia," he whispered, "don't be frightened. I am here." And his arm drew her close against him— protectively. Possessively?

For the briefest moment she let her head remain on his chest as she both fought and savored the idea of being held by him, of lying in his arms.

"Thank you, Mr. Sommerville." She drew away from him. "I'm afraid I was overcome for a moment."

"So is everyone the first time they see this.

Everyone, that is, with imagination and . . . and instinct. I still find it troubling myself."

But the spell was lifted now. The chanting had ended, the flute fell silent, even the fires seemed to burn lower.

"That is all of interest we shall see," Mr. Parke was saying. "We needn't stay here in the cold until dawn like those poor fools."

The party broke up. They rode back by torchlight through the woods. When they reached the waiting carriage, Mr. Parke and his nephew left them to ride home to Winterhall, neither of them speaking more than courteous good nights.

Julia rode in the carriage with Miss Merryweather, who fretted and shuffled her feet for several minutes before saying what was on her mind. "Miss Townes, I observed you with Mr. Sommerville this evening, and—"

"How very lucky that he was nearby. I found myself quite overcome."

"Yes. But . . . but, as you are new in the neighborhood, you cannot have been aware of his . . . reputation, and I . . . My conscience compels me to give you a warning in that area."

"Indeed?" Julia hoped her voice conveyed astonished gratitude. "Miss Merryweather, do you mean to say that a young lady might be in danger from this gentleman?"

"That is exactly what I mean to say. He is . . . I have been told on good authority by a lady who was dreadfully deceived as to his intentions that he is most certainly not to be trusted."

"I confess I am most surprised. My father seems to regard him very highly."

"Women are another matter entirely, Miss

177

Townes!" Miss Merryweather's prose might be obscure, but her voice rang with the authority of being two years older, and, Julia rather thought, perhaps with personal experience as well. "Why, he will tell a lady *anything* to . . ." Here Miss Merryweather stopped, hesitated, then judging that she had said enough to make her point, sank back into the cushions. "Well, I mustn't repeat gossip, but I did feel that I must say a word to you."

Julia expressed gratitude for Miss Merryweather's kind concern and assured her companion, "I will be most cautious where Mr. Sommerville is concerned."

And she meant it. She did not belong with a man like that; there could be no contentment, no real happiness in such a union. Her proper life was with a man of a very different sort. A man like Lawrence.

Lawrence soon arrived from London, and the Christmas season brought a round of visits and parties in the neighborhood. Julia was introduced to a number of the families nearby, and she was to have a general introduction to all of the local society at a dance to be given on New Year's Eve at Fainway. These distractions, though they could not entirely overcome the sorrow of memories of Christmases past, did keep Julia from brooding overmuch. And a day or two before the dance, Robert and Sir William, who had spent Christmas in Bath with Miss Sennett, arrived again at Fainway.

"It is kind of you, sir," Julia said to her father, "to include my friends in this way."

"I am sure it will be more comfortable for you to have a more familiar face or two among the party," Charles replied. "I find them agreeable company, and it is a convenient break for them on their return journey north. It is hard to know, also, when you might see them again."

"Perhaps Sir William will fetch his cousin from Bath when her stay is concluded."

"So he might. I shall invite him then, of course. Both of them." He smiled at his daughter. "But I rather think it is Mr. Woodland who has the greater interest in *this* visit."

Julia blushed, and Lawrence, who was sitting nearby (she thought he had dozed off), now looked up suddenly, and pointedly turned the page of his newspaper.

"Mr. Woodland seems a sensible and prosperous gentleman," Charles continued. "He appears to have done quite well with the bank."

"Yes," Julia replied softly. "He is generally reckoned to be quite well off."

"But, by his description, I would say that he lives very quietly." This was almost addressed to Lawrence, who raised innocent eyes over the pages that draped over his long fingers.

Julia smiled. "Indeed, we all lived very quietly in our particular circle in York. Even now, it is hard to imagine Sir William in the splendor and gaity of Winderfields." She gave a tiny laugh. "I fear that Mr. Woodland does not entirely approve of this new frivolity."

"As I said, a sensible young man," was Charles's approving reply.

Later, as Lawrence walked upstairs with her to

dress for dinner, he said with a smile, "You must not think I am such a gay and frivolous individual as your father would describe me."

"How frivolous *are* you, Cousin Lawrence?"

"A little, I confess." He took her arm to steer her around the turn of the staircase. "But I do not think it such a bad thing. There is no graven rule that says mankind must be forever serious and working. Why, even Mr. Townes enjoys a party now and then. And you, if you will forgive me, Cousin Julia, could do with a bit of frivolity. You are a very earnest girl. You must let me teach you the proper way to frivol."

They stopped at the door to Julia's room.

"I will think about it. But perhaps you should tell me what sort of frivolous things you do of which my father does not approve. It is best that I know, so that I may avoid their mention in conversation. I would not wish to make matters worse for you."

"Oh, it is hardly as serious as that! My cousin, Mr. Townes, likes me very much, I assure you. He would only wish to see me live a life more settled and productive, for he is very keen on productiveness."

"So he is."

"It is quite a natural thing for the older generation to wish the younger to be more like themselves. But poor old Mr. Parke has even more to complain of in his heir."

"I have heard this to be so, but my father does not seem to agree. How do you account for this peculiar fact?"

"Indeed, I cannot. I think it *more* than odd that your father and Philip Sommerville should be actually close associates and friends. They have some little business together, I know, but even so . . ."

"Well, we know one thing," Julia said teasingly. "My father approves very much of Mr. Woodland."

Lawrence gave her a wounded look and went to dress for dinner.

The New Year's Eve party was to be a large one. Julia stole downstairs in the middle of the preparations to watch the panels between the ballroom and the drawing room being removed and carried for storage into the small reception room. This provided a very large area for dancing, once the drawing room furniture was moved aside and the carpets taken up. Julia was impressed with the effect and marveled again at the ingeniousness of the ancestor who had conceived the idea.

The dining-room panels were removed as well, to make room for the large number who would enjoy the sumptuous supper being prepared. At least it *smelled* sumptuous whenever she passed the back staircase in the family wing of the house. Early on she had been taken below to the kitchen to be introduced to the under staff; now she could picture cozy bustling as the various dishes were under preparation. It made her think of the days when she was little and took a cup of cocoa sometimes in the kitchen with Polly. She turned away from the stairs and wondered with a pang of grief what Mimmie was doing this night.

But these concerns were put aside and the matter of dressing for the party considered. There was the red gown, of course, but somehow she did not want to be seen in the same dress again by, well, by

Robert and Lawrence, of course. She would wear another new gown, one that had arrived only yesterday from London, along with all the other articles which Mrs. Talmadge had promised but failed to deliver before Christmas. It was blue, though not the icy-blue of the dress made of the fabric Mimmie had given her; that was now damaged beyond repair except for the lace from the sleeves which had been among the things brought by Robert on his last visit. This gown was a rich satin of midnight blue, trimmed in a shimmering silver brocade. She had some jewelry, too, that would be a great compliment to the gown—fiery opals purchased in London to Julia's astonished delight. She had never thought to own anything so fine, even as Robert's wife.

As to Robert, Julia was now pretty sure that he did not intend to propose marriage to her, at least not any time soon. This made her both relieved and a little sad. She was, she found, more and more gently fond of him. She hoped, truly hoped, that they would always be friends. She smoothed her skirts, then she frowned into the mirror of her dressing table, wondering how Miss Pierce would view such a friendship.

The guests began to arrive, in carriages and curricles, a few of the gentlemen on horseback. Mr. Parke and his nephew arrived in company with the Merryweathers. Philip was dressed in a coat of a deep green and had actually a sprig of holly pinned on it, which he explained had been Miss Merryweather's fancy. That was true, for she had brought one for Lawrence, too.

As Robert led Julia staidly, a little sadly, through

the steps of the first dance, she saw that her father had a radiant Mary for a partner. Julia told herself silently, *I am certain that he loves her. Others in the room must be thinking the same thing. If only I could be sure. . . .*

And quite suddenly she *was* sure. It was . . . Why, it was almost as though it was her mother's voice there in her brain, telling her that there was nothing to be feared, there was nothing sinister in the person of Charles Townes. In this instant he was, quite obviously, everything opposite of what Julia had thought of him. He was a decent, prosperous, respectable man who had taken an unknown daughter into his home, treated her kindly and less distantly as every day passed. No. If there was anything nefarious in his association with Philip Sommerville, the evil would be all on Mr. Sommerville's side, and her father an unwitting participant. Julia made up her mind then and there to put aside her suspicions of him once and for all and to speak to him about a plan that had been forming in her mind for some time now.

Julia did not speak to Philip the entire evening, from their first greetings to their final farewells. In fact, Philip had little conversation with anyone except Robert and Sir William, spending most all of the evening in the company of one or both of them. It puzzled Julia, for she could see that his interest was not returned by either of the gentlemen. Philip was at his most trivial this evening; neither the conservative banker nor the clergyman turned baronet could find much to approve in this fashionable and indolent young man.

Julia told herself that she did not regret having so

little of Philip's company herself, except that it meant she could learn nothing new of Mimmie and she would have no use for the haughty remarks she had prepared to deliver when he asked her to dance.

Julia awoke the next morning feeling almost happy. Mimmie's fate notwithstanding, her suspicions of her father were now firmly behind her and she felt a great weight had been lifted from her soul.

This would be the last full day of Sir William's and Robert's visit. A few days more and Lawrence, too, would be gone, then even her father, on this mysterious business with Philip Sommerville. She must try to learn something of what that business might be.

As there were guests, a breakfast was served in a portion of the still-expanded dining room. The members of the household wandered in as they awakened from the late night of activity, lingered to converse, or went away on their own business, as it pleased them. Julia, who found herself awake surprisingly early, ate breakfast in the early shift with Robert and her father. Mary did not appear at all; neither did Sir William, and Robert reported that MacKenzie had been up all night attending to his master, for whom the gaities of the evening appeared to have been too much.

After breakfast, Julia took Robert to the drawing room to view the replacing of the panels which divided the room back into its customary proportions. But after waiting half an hour for the servants to begin, and nothing having happened, Julia went into the hall to see whether they might be removing the Christmas tree first instead.

As she stepped into the hall, she saw a little knot of people gathered at the doorway of the reception room. Her father was just coming to join them, being led from his library by the butler. The look on the faces of both men was of subdued alarm. Something had happened.

Julia and Robert walked behind Charles to see what it might be. Once inside the room, it was clear that there was trouble. All the panels which had been positioned upright, leaning at a safe angle against the sturdy exterior wall, had fallen, or perhaps slid, onto the floor. At first, sliding was the preferred opinion, for there had been no loud noise such as a fall would produce. But then, of course, there was no one sleeping in the bedrooms just above, and below was only the kitchen, vacant from midnight until five in the morning. The panels could have fallen without the noise alerting anyone.

"But just look, sir," said the sturdiest of the servants. "They have all tumbled down on each other, seemingly. They aren't flat on the floor as they would be if they had all fallen together. Someone must have been in here last night, for we stood them up proper, just as we always do, sir."

"Well, the best thing will be to have them up and see if any have been damaged. Just begin as you had planned, Jenkins."

"Yes, sir."

But when the first panel was raised, it became clear that someone had indeed been in the room. The sight of the rose-colored dressing gown that appeared as the panel was lifted almost made the men drop it again. Then, after the first astonishment and horror, the panels were lifted one by one as quickly as it could be safely done.

It was too late. Looking almost peaceful in her sleeping cap and pretty robe, Mary lay crushed and lifeless at the bottom of the pile of heavy panels.

Chapter Ten

Colonel Horton, who served this and the neighboring parish as magistrate, arrived at Charles's urgent summons within an hour of the discovery of Mary Belleville. He was a heavy, florid, balding man of fifty-odd years, smelling of whiskey and dogs.

"And so, Cobb," Colonel Horton said to the butler, "you inspected the placement of the panels after the men had taken them there?"

"Yes, sir." Cobb's normally passive face was strained and gray. "Everything was done in the customary way, sir. The panels were placed, leaning at the usual angle against the far wall, from which the paintings had been removed."

"And were they placed upright or lengthwise on the floor?"

"Upright, sir, on a mat of carpeting laid down to protect the flooring. There would not be room for all of them to be placed lengthwise, sir, without a great shifting of furniture. And it is easier for the men not having to lift them from the floor when it is time to replace them. This is the way it has always been done, sir, for a very great many years, now."

"And were they braced at all?"

"Yes, of course, sir. With the large captain's chest, which was pushed against them, just as is always done, sir."

"I see."

Colonel Horton now departed the library with Cobb and Charles to view the reception room where the tragedy had occurred. When they had gone, Sir William and Robert sat together, speaking to each other in low tones. Julia could not have caught any of their words, even had she been listening. She sat staring at nothing, twisting and turning her hands in her lap, her usual composure vanished, replaced by something very close to cold, black fear.

Lawrence watched her for some moments. When she raised anguished eyes to him, he said firmly, "I know what you are thinking, Julia. You must tell him."

"Tell him what?" Aunt Julia looked up sharply.

"The dressing gown," Julia said softly.

"Yes? What of the dressing gown?"

Julia saw that Sir William and Robert had stopped speaking. They turned troubled faces to the group at the fireplace.

"Miss Belleville was wearing the dressing gown she had lent to me," Julia said, her voice still faint. "I returned it only yesterday, when my new one arrived."

"My God!" Aunt Julia breathed, and it was soon

echoed by Robert. Sir William only continued to look puzzled.

"And was Mary wearing her sleeping cap as usual?" Aunt Julia now asked, her brows drawn together in a frown.

"Yes, Aunt Julia."

"So that her brown hair could not be seen," Lawrence said grimly, a little too loudly.

In the silence that followed, Sir William's look of confusion intensified, then changed suddenly to horrified astonishment.

"Bellwether," was the word Robert had whispered.

"No!" Sir William declared a little wildly. "How can it be?"

"I pray you are right, Sir William," Lawrence said. "I pray this was in truth a tragic accident. But I fear we must consider the question of whether my sister might have been deliberately killed by this fiend, thinking it was Miss Townes. They are much the same height, and . . . and I see that Miss Townes herself is quite anxious that such a thing might have occurred."

But Aunt Julia, after the first rush of feelings, had returned to a more reasoning calm. "But wait, Lawrence. How could such a person gain entry to the house? How, for that matter, could he know that Julia wore such a robe?"

Julia could not prevent a visible start as she heard her own questioning dread put into words. One person had *seen* her in that robe, and he had had no difficulty gaining entry to the house.

"I cannot say, ma'am," Lawrence replied. "Perhaps he had information and assistance from a servant."

"One of *our* servants?" Aunt Julia's eyes snapped.

"It is not entirely impossible, ma'am. Bellwether is known to be a clever and resourceful man."

Sir William was very skeptical. "Anyone may be a victim of a wicked or unfaithful servant, to be sure," he said. "But this man Bellwether, if he existed at all, is, in my judgment, surely dead. And why are we supposing that this is *not* a most unfortunate accident? Mr. Townes thinks it is. That is what he said to me. 'There has been an accident.'"

"Which means just exactly nothing, Sir William," Robert exclaimed, with an uncharacteristic lack of tact. "Miss Forrest . . . oh, I beg your pardon, Miss Townes, I urge you to do as your cousin suggests. This is not a matter to be taken lightly."

"I intend to do so, Mr. Woodland," Julia said quietly. "I shall speak to Colonel Horton about it when he returns."

Lawrence rose urgently from his chair and stood at the fireplace. "I must urge—no, insist," he said, "for I believe I have that privilege as a cousin." He saw Robert bristle but paid no mind. "Yes, I *insist* that this question of Bellwether be viewed more seriously by all of us. Steps must be taken to insure Julia's safety! Mr. Woodland"—he turned fiercely— "you *must,* if Sir William will not, help me to prevail upon Mr. Townes to see that care is taken. To lose my sister is bad enough, but—"

At that moment Charles and the magistrate returned, their faces still grave but reflecting a strong hint of relief.

"We have found the answer, I believe," Colonel Horton said importantly, "to a question that had puzzled and distressed my friend, Mr. Townes. The question which prompted him to seek my advice in this matter."

"I could not fathom, you see," Charles interrupted with an anxious glance at Lawrence's strained face, "why Mary would have gone into that room in the middle of the night."

"Yes!" Lawrence exclaimed. "This is the very thing that has disturbed me so greatly. It makes no sense that she would come to be there at all!"

Charles hesitated, wishing he could avert his eyes from Lawrence's face, that he need not watch as Colonel Horton produced a long narrow box, gaily wrapped and beribboned, but now crumpled, flattened and torn.

"It appears that she had hidden a gift there, apparently in the space on the floor behind the panels." Colonel Horton turned to Lawrence. "I am told, sir, that tomorrow is your birthday."

"My God! This cannot be true!" But Lawrence's face, despite his words, showed plainly his own certainty.

"It is the riding crop," Aunt Julia said, her voice sounding rather absent and somehow normal. "It can be nothing else."

Lawrence stood very still, frowning, his eyes fixed on the leaping flames in the fireplace. Julia, still reeling from this new idea, felt her heart go out to him in this new anguish.

When Lawrence spoke at last, his voice came hushed and rasping. "Yesterday afternoon I followed her into that very room. I had seen her as I came into the hall from the family wing. She was just turning from the front door. I called to her, but she didn't hear, or pretended not to hear. She hurried into the reception room. And I followed. I . . ." His face contorted with an expression of painful remembrance. "I thought she seemed awkward when I came to fetch her for . . . for something so foolish as an opinion as to which coat I should wear last evening."

Lawrence now looked up to meet Charles's eyes, then shifted his gaze to Colonel Horton, who still dangled the package in his hands. With a muffled sound that might have been an anguished sob, he moved away from the mantel.

"I fear I must ask you to excuse me." He hurried from the room.

When the door had closed behind him, a great oppression sat on those who remained together, yet separated by their own feelings as each absorbed and reacted to the events of the last hour.

Only Colonel Horton was unaffected. "Poor young man," he said gruffly. "It is a bitter knowledge he must bear, to be sure."

No one answered him.

"Well, I guess I must be going." Glancing from face to face as though expecting a protest, Colonel Horton finally realized that none was to come, even from his good friend, Mr. Townes. Then, observing that he still held the crumpled package, he placed it absently on the table next to Julia's chair and went away.

Julia was surprised at first when she heard Lawrence ask that Mary be buried in the village churchyard rather than in her own parish in London.

"Mr. Witherspoon has no objection, sir," he said to Charles, "as she was really as much a part of this society as that of London. I believe she would wish it, and . . . and I would like to have her here."

"Yes, yes. I quite understand. It will be a comfort to you in later years to have her nearby. I confess, I was going to suggest it myself."

And so on a day of bitter cold and leaden skies, Mary Belleville was laid to rest in the church cemetery, some distance, Julia was relieved to note, from her mother's grave. She supposed that Mr. Witherspoon should be given high marks for tact.

Despite the weather, the ceremony was well attended, for Mary had made a good many friends in the neighborhood on her frequent visits over a period of many years. Mr. Parke and Philip arrived in the Winterhall carriage, and Julia saw Philip draw her father aside and speak to him in a brief whisper. Charles answered with a nod, and Julia heard the word "tomorrow," before Philip moved on to offer condolences to Lawrence. Philip glanced at her, but did not come near where she stood with Sir William and Robert, who had delayed their departure to see Miss Belleville laid to rest.

As the service began, Julia saw the droop of her father's shoulders, the new lines of care in his face, the wounded look in his eyes, and in that moment felt irresistibly drawn to him. Without quite knowing that she did so, she moved close to him, slipped her arm into his, and stood silent by his side.

The next morning, despite the chill, Julia strolled outdoors with Robert to say a private good-bye. Sir William had actually set out with them, but he had been found by MacKenzie and taken away to the stables to see firsthand some problem with the carriage which now threatened to delay their departure to the next morning.

Julia was surprised when Robert took her hand in both of his and pressed it urgently. "Are you sure, Miss Townes, truly sure, that you do not fear for your safety?"

"I was apprehensive for a time," Julia admitted with a little frown, "but it seems clear now that what happened to Miss Belleville was a most tragic accident. It can have no bearing on my situation."

"No. No, I suppose not."

His sigh was so heavy and his face so concerned that Julia was compelled to lighten the moment.

"As to Bellwether," she said, "my father believes he must see that I can pose no danger to him now." She turned to glance in the direction of the stables, where the baronet stood in intense consultation with his servant. "And Sir William does not believe in him at all! I do think I may consider myself quite safe."

"All the same, Miss . . . Julia . . . do promise me that you will take care."

"Yes, Robert. I promise."

He lifted her hand slowly, a little sadly, to his lips. Julia felt a warm glow of affection and regard for this faithful friend, and she realized there was a little sting of tears in her eyes as they turned back toward the house. When they reached the front door, she uttered a request that, when he got home, she be remembered especially to Miss Pierce.

When Robert had left her, to offer what help he could at the stables, Julia wandered back into the house where the occupants were going about their own affairs. Charles was in his library; Aunt Julia had gone to the small sitting room with letters to write; and Lawrence had stayed in his room. Julia had one important affair of her own to see to, and in the next instant she had come to a decision. She turned and walked to her father's library and tapped on the door.

"Oh, Julia." Charles appeared to be on his way out the door as Julia opened it.

"Do you have a moment, sir?"

"Of course. I am expected at Winterhall, but I needn't leave just yet. Sit down. I was just thinking of you, actually, remembering the first night we sat together in this room. It was not so very long ago, but it often seems to me that you have always been with us."

"Thank you, Father." Julia sat in a chair near him and recognized with some surprise that she had just called him "Father" for the first time. "There is something I have been wishing to speak to you about. It concerns my mother's death."

"Yes?"

"It has been some months now since she died, and it does not seem that Bellwether, or whoever is responsible for the deed, is near to being apprehended."

Charles looked into her troubled blue eyes. "I feel certain every prudent possible measure is being taken by the authorities, Julia."

"Yes, sir. I am sure that is so. But with every day that passes, I fear that bringing Bellwether to justice grows less likely. I think the time has come for action that is, perhaps, not entirely prudent, but very likely of success."

"What do you mean, child?" Charles's brows drew together.

"I think it should be known, or perhaps only

rumored, that I *do* know something that is of danger to Bellwether. Then, I believe, he will have to come and find me. If we are clever and plan well, it should be possible to catch him before . . . before he does harm."

Charles sat silent for a long time; the only sound in the room was the deep tick tock of the library clock.

"It is a brave thing you are suggesting, Julia," Charles said finally. "Does it mean this much to you?"

"It does. I will never be easy or satisfied until the man who killed my mother is caught and punished."

"I see." Charles fell silent again, then rose and went to stir the fire. Turning back to her, he said, "Will you give me some time to think about this? To ponder how it might be done?"

Julia, surprised at not having to plead for her proposal, nodded gratefully and said, "Of course, Father." She stood up, hesitated uncertainly, but did not yet feel that she could embrace him spontaneously. "I will speak to you of this again in a few days' time."

She came out of the library and stood in the entrance hallway for several moments, watching and listening as the maids went about the business of erasing the final traces of its recent holiday trappings. Presently she turned and walked to the small reception room.

Julia had not entered the room since the discovery of Mary's accident, nor, so far as she knew, had any other person, except, perhaps, a maid intent on dusting. And, of course, the men servants who had at length completed the removal of the panels and replacing them in the drawing room. The reception room wore its ordinary face. The paintings had been rehung on the wall, and the chest which had braced the panels (inadequately, it seemed) was back in its accustomed position near the door. The several chairs that had been moved here from the drawing room to make room for dancers were gone. There was no suggestion that anything shocking, dreadful, tragic had occurred here; it was just a room. But what had happened had dashed the hopes of her father, devastated her cousin Lawrence, and even left a vacant spot in Julia's own heart, for she had come to appreciate Mary's goodness. One could not help it.

And now the kind Mary was buried in the village churchyard, where she would be near the man who had loved her, and, later, near the brother who would one day be master of Fainway. An accident had taken her from them. Of course it was an accident. It could be nothing else.

Misfortune does seem to dog my father's heels where women are concerned, she thought as she wandered to the window to look out on the front drive. *It is true, even of me. How unhappy he would be if he knew the ugly suspicions that once haunted my heart. He deserves better from this life. And so does Lawrence.*

Turning from the window, Julia's eye fell on something on the table beside the settee. It was the package that Mary had come into this room to fetch on that fateful night. She picked it up, wondering how it came to be there. Someone must have brought it here to keep it out of Lawrence's sight, knowing this was the one room he would not be likely to enter.

She debated silently for several minutes, then began a deliberate unwrapping of the package. When the riding crop was in her hands, unharmed by its trauma, she stroked the leather thoughtfully, then she walked deliberately from the room with the crop in her hands.

She mounted the main staircase, nodding to a maid who curtsied to her as she reached the gallery and opened the door into the family bedroom wing. A few moments later she was standing before Lawrence's room and tapping softly on the door.

"Come in."

After a moment's hesitation, for she had never entered a man's bedroom before, Julia opened the door.

"Oh, Julia." Lawrence rose from the chair near the fireside and straightened his coat as he came to meet her.

"I have brought something, Lawrence." She held out the crop to him, but he seemed quite visibly to shrink from it. "You must take it and you must use it. You must use it every time you ride. If you do not, you will never stop blaming yourself for something over which you had absolutely no control. Mary bought this for you in love. You must honor her memory by accepting it in the same spirit. Please, for my sake, will you try?"

His face and voice were very grave as slowly, hesitantly, he took the riding crop from her. "For your sake, I will."

She extended her hand. He took it and kissed it gently, his eyes downcast at first, then raised, holding an expression of gratitude and fondness. Julia, sensing that more conversation would be awkward now, left him and went to see that Mary's belongings were packed for distribution to the poor.

That afternoon Philip Sommerville and his uncle arrived just at teatime. They accepted some refreshment and contributed their share of commentary about the weather, which threatened to turn from dull gray cold to wet and stormy.

"We called to tell you, sir," Philip said to Charles, "that the gypsies have returned, and we fear they have strayed upon your land."

"Strayed, my foot," Mr. Parke snorted. "They have deliberately trespassed, and Philip thinks they have even cut down several of your trees for firewood."

"Indeed?" Charles raised questioning eyebrows.

"Shocking!" Aunt Julia's nose quivered indignantly. "Truly, this is most outrageous. This is what comes of indulging these heathens as you do, Mr. Parke. Next they will be stealing chickens and begging coins in the village!"

"You say several trees have been cut," Lawrence said. "How did you happen to notice that this had been done?"

"I rode down to the circle where they were encamped this afternoon," Philip replied, "and saw that they had a good many sizeable logs in the camp. I made a tour of our own woods and found nothing cut of the size I had seen. Being a suspicious sort of fellow, I rode up onto the rise and discovered three or four freshly cut stumps just inside the boundary of Fainway's woods."

Aunt Julia muttered something unintelligible over her teacup, but Charles only clucked a mild disappointment.

"Did you challenge these ruffians about the trees, Mr. Sommerville?" Robert asked.

"I did not. I thought, since it is not my property in question, that I should inform Mr. Townes and offer to go along if he should care to go and talk with them."

"That is an excellent suggestion." Charles put down his napkin with an air of decision. "Yes. I think it would be best to go and warn them that this will not be tolerated."

"*I* would propose having the lot of them arrested on the spot!" was Aunt Julia's firm declaration.

"Oh, I hope it will not come to that, Aunt. This is, after all, the first time we have had any trouble with them, and it is not as though we cannot spare a tree or two."

"All the same, sir," said Sir William, with the wisdom of a fellow landowner, "I believe it would be best to take a firm stand right now. It must be clear that such behavior will not be tolerated, otherwise, you will have nothing but trouble from these pesky squatters."

"I daresay you are right, Sir William," Charles replied. "Perhaps you and Mr. Woodland will be good enough to bear me company." He rang the bell. "I will have horses brought for us all."

"Do you think it wise to go now?" Mr. Parke asked querulously. "It will be dark before you return."

"Oh, I think it will not take long," Charles replied. "I would be obliged if you would remain and keep my aunt company until we return. Lawrence will wish to go along, of course, and," turning to his daughter, "perhaps Julia as well."

"What?" Now Aunt Julia was truly scandalized.

"Oh, not down into the gypsy camp, of course, Aunt. I thought she might like to see it from the rise. Lawrence can stay with her while the rest of us ride down to attend to this business."

"Yes, certainly," said Lawrence. "I think it would do us all good to get out into the air for a bit."

Julia held her breath while her aunt considered this unwelcome notion. But at length the old woman relented, and Julia went to her room to don her riding dress.

As they rode past the stable and outbuildings, past the near farms, so quiet at their winter rest, beyond the pastures, where cattle and horses had already been taken into the barns as a precaution against the whim of the January night, Julia thought their band looked impressive, even intimidating enough to bring any wayward gypsy to his senses. Besides her father and Philip, who were both large, commanding men, there was Lawrence, and though he was more slightly built, his height alone would catch any eye. Robert was also rather tall, and, though Sir William was not, he could not, certainly, be considered undersized. And the largest of all the party was Philip's servant, Thomas, a giant of a man, who must be near seven feet tall, with the broadest shoulders and fiercest eyes Julia had ever seen. Thomas rode in front of the party with his master and her father, followed by Sir William and Robert. Next came Julia and Lawrence, separate and a little behind.

As they rode, Julia found herself straining to hear

the conversation of the leaders. Now and then she could hear Philip's voice, mellow, low, almost musical. It had a mesmerizing effect on her, even though, or perhaps because, she could not quite make out what he was saying. He wore a brown coat, though it was not the same coat he had worn on that night when she had first seen him. This was of a heavier, warmer material, but it looked as though it would be soft to the touch, even if one were to lay one's face against it.

With a guilty start she realized that Lawrence had broken the long silence that had existed between them almost since setting out.

"I beg your pardon, Lawrence. What did you say?"

"I said that I must go on the day after tomorrow."

"Must you? Do you not think it better to remain a little longer with us? It has been such a few days since . . . since we lost your sister. You must take time to recover, as must we all."

"I know I will find little comfort in London, but now I must see to Mary's affairs as well as my own. It would be foolish to delay what must be done at some time. If I take matters in hand now, it will make little increase to the pain I am feeling. Later, I fear, that will not be so. It would be even harder then."

"I understand. You are right, of course."

Julia tried to listen with full attention as Lawrence's voice went on about the need to attend to some business promptly that, if left undone, could be costly, but it was hard to concentrate on his words while her ears still strained to catch that other voice and her eyes seemed intent on fixing themselves on the brown-clad figure on the big brown horse.

Where the woods began, they separated. Her father and his party moved along the trail which would take them around the woods and onto the grounds of Winterhall. Julia and Lawrence rode, as they had done on their first ride, through the timber which led to the rise overlooking the Druid's Circle.

The day had been foggy, but clouds were beginning to gather now, obscuring the filtered sunlight and making the woods seem darker still. They rode almost silently, each lost in private thoughts. Julia's thoughts centered on her irritation with herself that she could still be oddly, inexplicably drawn to Philip Sommerville. For a few moments this afternoon, as he talked in an ordinary way, he seemed, well, not ordinary, certainly, but normal, charming, delightful. She had almost forgotten that he was the man who held some dark sway over her father, who held Mimmie, if not a prisoner, at least—and here again, she did not know how to finish the thought.

"You are very silent, Julia. I would like to think it is because you are considering how very much you will miss me." Lawrence, when she turned to him, seemed to be trying to show her a tiny smile on his sad face.

"I shall miss you very much indeed, Lawrence, but I was thinking of the gypsies. I confess I am quite intrigued to see them."

"I suppose some might think it a mysterious and romantic life they lead. I rather think it would be tedious and uncomfortable and most unsanitary."

"I do not mean to suggest that I would wish such a life for myself," Julia said quickly. "But it is very interesting, even quite exciting to look for myself upon those who have chosen this life. I suppose it *is* a life that they choose. Or are they simply born into it?"

"I suspect it is a bit of both."

Now they had reached the end of the woods. A sudden gust of chilly breeze made Julia shiver. They urged their horses to the edge of the rise, and there below they could see the gypsy encampment.

"I believe you are right, Lawrence," Julia said after studying the scene below her for a few moments. "This does not look at all a pleasant life."

Below her was a band of four ragged-looking wagons drawn into an untidy circle. In the openings of a couple of the wagons, dark, heavy women huddled silently. In the center of the wagon circle, a couple of campfires burned cheerlessly and for no apparent reason. No one stood near them for warmth, and there were no signs of cooking. The few men she could see were gathered around one particular wagon, close together in what appeared to be urgent conversation, interrupted now and then by spitting on the ground. The scene was an ugly contrast to the stark and splendid stones that stood in noble simplicity beside the wagons.

Now Julia saw her father's party approaching. They rode slowly, deliberately to the wagon where the men were gathered. As they approached, the men drew apart, some shifted their feet, others thrust their hands belligerently into their pockets.

Julia shivered again in the ever-freshening breeze

and dismounted, thinking that the animal might serve as a windbreak. Lawrence stood with her as they watched a conversation they could not hear but could understand by the gestures and posturing of those on the two sides of the question.

With no warning sound, with no warning at all, Julia suddenly felt herself seized from behind! A large and rather sweaty hand was clapped over her mouth, and her legs tripped from under her. Frantically struggling, she saw that Lawrence had been seized in the same instant. He was in the hands of three men who were thrusting a dirty-looking rag into his mouth, silencing him effectively. Julia watched in horror as he was bound hand and foot and hauled like a struggling animal to the shelter, where he was tied to the massive bench with much looping of a sturdy rope. When his assailants were satisfied that he was well secured, a black hood was placed over his head.

Now it was Julia's turn. Her hands were bound and her mouth gagged with a handkerchief tied tightly and uncomfortably against her braid. Then, despite her most energetic resistance, she was placed astraddle a horse, in front of one of the men who held her fast from behind. In the gathering dusk and first raindrops of the imminent storm, they rode away.

Chapter Eleven

By the time he was discovered, Lawrence had managed to dislodge the vile rag that had threatened to choke him, and was calling out from time to time to assist the searchers he knew would come eventually. He had also, by painful straining and twisting, released his hand, but to no good purpose, as his arm was still held fast.

The rain had begun to fall in earnest, drumming on the roof of the shelter and blown inside it by a sturdy wind from just the right direction. The hood became clammy, and his wet clothing chilled him quickly and thoroughly; he shivered whenever he rested from his struggles.

Lawrence had a keen sense of time and had gauged the interval at about the two hours it actually did take for him to be found and released.

It was Philip's voice he heard first.

"I have found him! Come this way!"

There was a sound of horses and shuffling feet, and then the hood was blessedly removed. Taking a deep and gasping breath of the fresh, unfiltered air, Lawrence saw at first only torches and lanterns, then slowly the figures appeared—Philip Sommerville, Mr. Townes, Mr. Woodland and Sir William.

"We must go after them!" Lawrence cried, frantically twisting and straining in an effort to be free more quickly. "They have taken her! They have taken Julia!"

"What?" It was Mr. Townes who spoke.

"Which way did they go?" was Philip's question.

To this, Lawrence could not answer. His eyes had been covered. He had listened to the retreating hoofbeats, but they had faded so quickly he could not tell which direction they had taken through the woods.

After a moment of consideration, Philip said, "Sir William, can you manage to get Christian home to Fainway? Send all of Fainway's men to help us search. Ask my uncle to return to Winterhall and do the same."

"It's the gypsies will have taken her, sir," Philip's servant growled. "That's where we'd best begin. With the gypsies."

"No!" Lawrence shouted. "They were no gypsies! I saw them just briefly before my eyes were covered. They were Englishmen."

"Englishmen of what sort?" Philip demanded.

"Not gentlemen, certainly." Lawrence pressed fingers to his eyes as he remembered. "But . . . but respectable-looking. Perhaps like, oh, like innkeepers or . . . or servants of a good family."

"Servants? Did you recognize them?"

"No, Sommerville, I did not! They wore a covering—handkerchiefs or something of that sort which concealed the lower half of their faces. They were tall, big men—all of them."

"How many?"

"At least six. Perhaps one or two more. Though I think not. And—"

"What?"

"I seem to think there *was* something familiar about one of them—the one who first seized Miss Townes."

"His voice, perhaps?"

"No, he did not speak. None of them spoke. It must have been the way he moved or stood. I cannot say just now."

"Can you tell us anything more, Christian?" Philip asked as he turned to mount his horse. "If not, we must be off without delay."

"I must come with you."

"You are in no fit condition, sir. Return with Sir William to Fainway. We will see what, if anything, can be discovered of them in the darkness. Someone will bring word to Fainway as soon as there is any news to deliver."

So Lawrence allowed himself to be wrapped in a blanket and put on his horse, which, along with Julia's mount, had been left where it was tied. The party of searchers departed at a fast trot, the servant, Thomas, calling out that he saw signs of the abductors' horses.

Huddled and shivering, Lawrence listened on the way home to Sir William describe his party's arriving at the rendezvous point where they had separated earlier from Lawrence and Julia, and when Lawrence and Julia were not there, they assumed quite naturally that the two of them had returned ahead to Fainway. It had grown cold and wet, after all, and Miss Townes most likely was uncomfortable, perhaps even bored or weary of waiting on the rise during the long discussion which took place in the camp below. When the party had returned to Fainway and learned that Lawrence and Julia had not come home, they hurried at once back to the woods to search.

Lawrence had a bath and a brandy, but he refused dinner. He sat with Sir William in the drawing room listening to Aunt Julia alternate between weeping despair and heated words on the folly and danger of Charles's encouraging or even permitting Julia to have gone along in the first place.

When she paused for breath, Lawrence, hoarse from his shouting, croaked, "Bellwether. He is alive. At work again. I say he has returned to lead this new band of anarchists."

Sir William did not answer, just stared into the fire as he nudged a log with the toe of his boot.

"I fear you are right, Lawrence. And this is his warning to us all!" Aunt Julia wiped frustrated and frightened tears. "That poor, dear girl. We have had her so brief a time, and now . . . Oh, I cannot bear to think of it!"

Sir William turned abruptly from the fireplace. "I will step outside to see if anyone is returning with word."

When he was gone, Lawrence and Aunt Julia moved their chairs a little closer to the fire and to each other to wait and to offer each other what comfort and hope they could command.

But word did not come. Not at seven o'clock or at

209

nine or eleven. Just before midnight, Charles's own servants arrived, in a state of hunger and exhausted frustration. The senior man was taken to the party in the drawing room.

"Mr. Townes sent us home, sir," he addressed his comments to Sir William, "as we'd had no dinner, nor any luck either. There is no trace of them sir, and we asked at every house in the village. We inquired, just as Mr. Sommerville instructed us, sir, to ask if anyone had seen horses or even a carriage, thinking they might have transferred the young lady to a coach. Nothing, sir, though all the village is most concerned. We could have any number of volunteers we wish, sir, to continue the search in the daylight."

"What has Mr. Sommerville proposed for the morning?" asked Aunt Julia.

"He has sent a man to the garrison, madam, to inform the commander of what has happened, and a message to London as well. He thinks we might discover something by covering the same ground by daylight, but it is his opinion, madam, that they may have managed to take her some distance by now. I am to meet him with the men again at daybreak."

"I see." Aunt Julia turned haunted eyes to Lawrence, then turned back to the servant. "Thank you, Potts. You had best get some food and what sleep you can. Please thank the men for us."

"Yes, madam. And, madam, we all think kindly on Miss Townes. My wife will be praying for her, and her prayers have been mighty helpful from time to time."

"Yes. Thank you, Potts. And Mrs. Potts, too, of course."

"Yes, madam. Good night, madam. Good night, sir."

It was only after another hour of almost silent waiting that Charles and Robert themselves returned. But they brought no fresh news. Then, as there was nothing more to be done, and as talk of the situation was dangerous, the household went to bed.

By the light of the small candle that had been left with her, Julia tried the door again. It was still locked fast. So was the single window, and the shutters were also fastened, apparently from the outside, for she could see no means of opening them, even had she been able to force the window open.

It was a small room, and judging by the number of flights she had been forced to climb on arriving, it was at the top of a house. She was fairly certain that she had been carried through a kitchen when she had arrived with her captors. The savory odors of roasting meats had assailed her nostrils to confide what her blindfolded eyes could not see. The spartan furnishings of her prison suggested that this was a servant's room. Julia was fairly sure what house she was in; the length of the ride from the point of her capture left little doubt of it. She had almost certainly been carried to Winterhall.

As Miss Flagg had observed, Julia was not a flighty girl. She did not scream or kick at the door or the furniture or tear her hair or garments in anguish at her predicament. After satisfying herself yet again that there was no immediate means of leaving this room, she sat down on the narrow bed to think what was best to be done. She was not in immediate fear of her life. If it was merely her death that was wished for, the men who had taken her had had plenty of opportunity to do away with her on the spot, rather than burden themselves with the difficult struggle of transporting her here.

Muffled sounds at the door—a key turning in the lock, a rattling of crockery—and one of the men who had taken her entered with a tray of food and a supply of candles. Julia did not speak and remained motionless on the bed as he silently deposited his burden without looking directly at her. In only a moment he was gone, and she heard the lock being turned again.

Julia lit a fresh candle and inspected the offerings on the tray. She had little appetite, but, uncertain what her fate might be or when she might again be offered food, very sensibly ate what she could. Then, since there was nothing else to do, and as the room was growing very cold, she removed her dress and slipped into bed, leaving the candle burning for comfort and company.

As she lay watching the flickering light play about the walls of the room, Julia wondered what her mother would do in a situation like this.

She would somehow escape, of course. Yes, but how? Seduction of her jailer? Yes, if necessary. Mama always did what was necessary. But Julia was not her mother, and she was very unsure that Philip Sommerville would be easy to seduce, even if she'd had the faintest idea how to go about it. And anyway, he always made her so . . . Well, seduction was not a solution.

She would have to outsmart him then. But this would not be easy, either. Philip, for all his air of idle triviality, was, she felt somehow sure, a very shrewd and cautious man. One thing was certain: She must keep her head.

Julia realized that she must have been dozing when she heard sounds at the door again. The lock was turned, and in the dim light from the hallway, she saw a tall figure silhouetted in the doorway. There could be no mistaking that figure; Julia knew at once who her visitor was.

"Were you sleeping?" Philip asked, advancing with a candle to light the one that had gone out at her bedside.

"No." Julia forced her voice to remain calm as she sat up and drew the bedcovers up to her chin.

He drew up the single chair in the room and sat down near the bed. With what she hoped was calm contempt, Julia gazed at the strong, dark features of his face, the little frown that creased his forehead.

At length Philip moved his feet restlessly on the bare wooden floor and said, "I thought you might be frightened, not knowing that you were with me. That is why I have come."

"Is my cousin safe?" Julia asked coldly.

The frown between his brows deepened. "He is safe. I released him myself when I returned with the others to search for the two of you."

She nodded and again sat silent.

"You are at Winterhall."

"So I had supposed."

"You will remain here for a few days. I regret the accommodations are not what you are accustomed to, but it is only for this night. Tomorrow my uncle will depart for London, and you may then be moved to a room on the main floor of the house."

"I see. And since you are so good as to have come to reassure me, perhaps you will tell me why I have been brought here at all."

This, of course, was the question he had been expecting. It was asked in a cool, almost impersonal tone, but he could tell that she was very angry.

"Why do you think you are here, Miss Townes?" He asked it softly, hoping to blunt her resentment.

She flushed deeply and had to take a deep breath before she answered again in that icy voice that matched her eyes. "I can only suppose that you no longer trust my silence."

He rested his arms on his knees, leaning closer to the bed, watching her intently.

"Would you believe me if I told you that you have been brought here in the interests of safety?"

"In the interest of *whose* safety, pray?"

"Why, your own safety, Miss Townes."

Julia's expression of skeptical disdain was eloquent. "And from what or whom am I to be safe *here,* Mr. Sommerville?"

He did not answer right away but continued to look into her face. She forced herself to meet his eyes. The silence between them seemed to change, grow ominous with the anger and the other indefinable emotions Julia felt in this moment.

Finally, Philip leaned back, away from her. "I have come to the opinion that it would not be wise to talk of this just now." He rose from the chair with a sharp scrape on the wooden floor. "You are angry and in no humor to believe what I would tell you. And on points on which you have no information, I need not trust your silence. Good night, Miss Townes."

His boots sounded far louder on the floor than

they had when he had entered the room, and the door, it seemed, closed with unnecessary authority. And now, though her light had been restored, Julia somehow felt very much alone.

Just as promised, Julia was given new quarters the next day. As she was finishing her breakfast, a maidservant came to tell her that she was to be taken to her new bedroom. As she had nothing of possessions to take with her, Julia followed at once out of the room and down a hallway covered by a carpet in a dull shade of gray. It was anything but cheerful, but she supposed that no one actually lived in this area of the house anyway. She had heard no signs of habitation in the hours she had spent there.

They arrived at the next lower floor but did not stop there. They continued on to a larger staircase which led down to a heavy door. The maid opened it and indicated that Julia should enter. Now they were in what appeared to be the main living area, for the hallway was wide and carpeted with a sumptuous and colorful runner. Paintings and ornate mirrors hung from the walls, and the wood of the doors leading into the bedrooms on this floor was finely carved and highly polished.

The maid paused before one of the doors. "This is to be your room, madam."

Julia found herself in a prettily furnished bedroom with windows unshuttered and a fire burning cheerily on the hearth. A few books and a paper had been placed on the table that sat between a comfortable looking chair and the high, four-poster bed. Julia went to stand at a window, relishing for a moment the natural daylight, feeble though it was, and reflecting how precious commonplace things like the view from a window become when one was denied them.

"There are a few items of clothing in the wardrobe, madam, which are for your use, and there are some articles on the dressing table as well. I fear you will not be able to ring for anything you need, madam, for some of the servants do not know that you are here. However, Tulley will be outside in the hallway. If you just knock on the door, he will open it and ask what you need. You may send for me at any time. My name is Becky."

Julia nodded expressionlessly. Becky curtsied and departed. A moment later Julia heard the door being locked.

She could not help being reminded of the first day in her father's house, when her horizons had also been confined to one room. She was no less confused and apprehensive now than she had been then. She felt tears of frustration sting her eyes, forced them aside (Mama would not have wasted time crying), made a tour of the room, inspected the clothing and toilet articles left for her, and stood again at the window. It was not raining, but the wind was still blowing with some vigor, and it looked as though another storm might be coming. She thought of Mr. Parke, presumably on his way to London. Would he have to take refuge at an inn? Perhaps he would abandon the journey and return to Winterhall. *That* would give the arrogant Mr. Philip Sommerville some difficulty. How could he explain her presence to the owner of this house?

She sighed. He obviously had little interest in her reputation, so he might well say that she had come of her own volition to keep an amorous engagement.

And she could not help sitting down in the chair to think about the idea of such a thing. No doubt Philip Sommerville had plenty of women. Miss Merryweather and even Mary had as much as said so, and, handsome as he was, it was inevitable in any case. Was there one particular woman? He must be something of a catch for he would inherit this estate one day from his uncle.

But this sort of thinking would do her no good. She must somehow get away from him and from this house. She returned to the window and gave a disappointed sigh as she verified that she was at least two floors from the ground, and a very hard ground at that, for a wide flagstone path ran just below her windows. There was no escape this way, even if she broke the window, which appeared to be nailed closed from the outside.

Perhaps she could sit here at the window and signal with a candle or by tapping to anyone passing below.

But, of course, he would have thought of that. No one would pass below, or she would not have been put into this room. All the same, there *must be a way*. If her mother were here, what would she do? The answer, of course, was whatever it took.

Julia spent a few minutes wondering what sort of bribe or threat might corrupt Becky or—what was his name?—Tulley.

But she could hardly hand over money since she had none. Perhaps one of them would take a message to her father. . . .

Oh, dear—her father. For the briefest of

instants, the old suspicions rose in her mind. She dismissed them without a thought, knowing instinctively, certainly now, that her father would never harm her.

How frightened he must be. And her poor Aunt Julia. And her anger for Philip Sommerville grew hotter.

She was staring down again at the flagstone path when there was a bustle at the door. It was unlocked by Tulley, and the maid came in with a tray.

"Well, Becky, it seems you do not mean to starve me."

Becky's expression did not change as she put down the tray. "Mr. Sommerville asked me to say, madam, that he will be in to dinner. I will come at six o'clock to take you to the drawing room."

"I would like to have a bath, Becky."

Julia expected to be refused, since the preparation and bringing of a tub and water could hardly escape notice of a good many servants, but Becky only curtsied.

"Certainly, madam."

After bathing and putting on the dress of soft gray wool which hung in the wardrobe, she found herself dressing her hair, not in its usual braid, but in the soft twisted bun she had worn at the New Year's ball. She stopped and quickly began to braid the long heavy hair into its usual style. After all, she had dismissed the idea of seduction.

"Ah, Miss Townes."

Philip rose from his chair as she entered the drawing room, and came with great formality to take her arm and lead her to a seat by the fire.

"I hope you will take a glass of sherry."

His eyes held a mocking challenge, so she answered, "Yes, certainly."

"The dress becomes you," he said as he handed her a glass of wine. "It belonged to my late aunt—one she had near the end of her life when she had grown rather frail. She was a woman of comfortable size before that time."

"I am grateful to have clothing that is dry and clean, whomever it may have belonged to previously."

He lifted an eyebrow, then raised his glass in salute. Julia ignored it and placed her own glass on the table beside her. He shrugged and took a sip.

"I have been some hours at Fainway today. Your father and aunt keep well—bearing up under the strain of your absence."

"You can hardly expect me to be amused by such remarks, Mr. Sommerville."

"I seek merely to inform, Miss Townes. When I wish to amuse, you will know it."

Julia took a sip from her glass, after all.

"You will be interested to know," he went on, "that a search has been conducted throughout the county and even beyond. The commander of our nearby garrison has even placed troops upon the road to stop and investigate any suspicious carriages which might pass."

"Very thorough."

"Your abduction is quite a major sensation. Your friends will have much of wonderment to tell when they return to York."

"They are indeed my friends, and they must rue the day they heard of Fainway. They have had much to distress them while visiting there."

"Both are most alarmed at the evil that has befallen you. I wonder if they will remain to assist in the search for you."

"Mr. Woodland might do so," Julia said thoughtfully, "but I rather expect Sir William will go straight home to Winderfields and behave as though he has no concern at all in such an unsavory sensation."

"I see that you, too, are something of a judge of character, madam."

She met the mischief in his eyes with a pointed look. "I hope neither will remain. They can be of no help to my father, and perhaps they would be a distraction that would prevent him from discovering what has really happened to me. But one day, Mr. Sommerville, my father will see the truth about you."

Once again Philip seemed to be making up his mind about something, but his deliberations were interrupted by the entrance of dinner.

"I thought we would dine in this room," he said as he stood. "The dining room is a little too public for our purposes tonight."

"Meaning," Julia said, keeping her seat, "that not *all* your uncle's servants help to do your mischief?"

"But you must come and dine properly one of these days, Miss Townes." He held out a hand to her.

Julia ignored the hand and rose without assistance. "Your words suggest that there may be a normal future in which I might do such things. What of Mimmie, Mr. Sommerville? Where is she dining tonight?"

"Come, Miss Townes. Our dinner is getting cold."

She was seated with ceremony and served with skill and deference by the single servant who attended them. And the dinner conversation was not permitted by Philip to settle on contentious matters; he spoke of music, books and plays. Julia at first maintained a frosty silence, but that odd feeling that he was just a witty, intelligent, delightful man crept steadily, stealthfully back, and when he came to speak of a performance that Julia had seen on her visit to London and particularly enjoyed, she could not help responding to offer her own opinion.

"How pleasant it is to discover," he said when the servant had left them alone with coffee, "how similar our tastes seem to be. Don't you agree, Miss Townes?"

His words startled her back to a manner more befitting her circumstances. "I cannot say, sir, for I have no certainty as to what your tastes or opinions might be. I think you capable of expressing any view that might further your own ends."

"Do you, indeed?" He handed her into the same chair by the fireplace. "And what ends do you think I might further by such means this evening?"

His smile was teasing, but his eyes held a gaze of intensity, of something else. She found herself blushing. "You want me to trust you, to believe that you are not an evil man, that you do bizarre things such as kidnapping for some unknown, unselfish interest, even in my own interest."

"That is true. And do you believe it?"

"I do not! No sensible person could believe anything of the sort."

"I am sorry to hear you say so." His eyes were only half teasing now. A look that could only be described as grimness had come to his face. "I realize that on the surface, things do not appear to my advantage. I had hoped, however, that you and I might have an understanding that went deeper than the surface."

His words, so heavy with meaning, took her aback. Her blush deepened and she stood up suddenly, anxious to be gone, away from that green gaze which threatened her resolve, even her sanity. "With your permission, sir, I will retire now."

He rose from his chair as she was turning toward the door; he caught her arm and drew her to him. For an instant they stood, separated by only a modest space, and that space became somehow less and less until, without knowing how she came to be in his arms, his green eyes were closing as his lips met hers. Anger, fear, even reason dissolved and were replaced by a single, enveloping sensation, a longing so intense to be at one with this man, to surrender to the desire that had grown from a flicker with that first kiss, so many weeks ago, to this searing, scorching, craving that seemed always to be with her and threatened always to be with her unless it were satisfied in the only way possible.

And that, of course, was unthinkable.

"I am not my mother!" she cried as she tore her lips from his and wrenched herself free of his embrace.

"Julia, you—"

"No! No words." She had run to the door, where she stood gasping for breath as she looked at him through tears that were beginning to sting her eyes. "I understand, Mr. Sommerville, that you have this effect on all women, so I suppose I should not be astonished at myself." She took a breath to steady her voice. "But I am not so weak or so headstrong as to abandon all reason and control for a passion that can only lead to . . . It would be madness!" She turned to open the door. "I will not permit myself to be this foolish again if we have any futher meetings during my remaining days here. Good night, Mr. Sommerville."

She opened the door without interference, and as she stood in the hallway, she debated which way she might run to escape from the house. But she did not wonder long. The man who had served their dinner was nearby.

"I will show you to your room, madam."

Too distressed and distracted to resist, she followed him up the stairs.

The maid was in her bedroom when Julia arrived, turning down the bed, remaining to help madam undress. When she was once more alone, Julia sat numbly on the side of the bed, her mind screaming only one thought, *I must get away from this house!*

By candlelight she made yet another tour of the room, trying each window again, growing ever more frustrated as she verified that each was secure. She could break a window, of course, but then what? It was still a very long way down to the stones below. With a sigh, she returned to the softness of her featherbed.

Softness. Yes. If she had something soft to land on. No, it was still to far. She would be injured, certainly, and would not be able to run. Still . . . Julia sat back against her pillows to think about it.

An hour later she knocked on the door of her

bedroom, and when it was opened, she told the servant that she needed another pillow or two and more blankets as well. When the maid appeared with these items, Julia meekly allowed the woman to settle her down in the bed again, expressing thanks for the additional comforts.

"You are welcome, I am sure, madam. It does look to be a cold and rainy night."

Alone again, Julia got hurriedly out of bed and dressed, choosing the gray dress rather than her own lighter colored frock, which could be seen more easily. Lighting a second candle for better illumination, she began to take the sheets and pillowcases from the bed and tie them together. It was slow work. She was not at first satisfied with the strength of her knots, but after some trial and error, she had achieved a satisfactory product: a sturdy rope, knotted at intervals for gripping, with which she would lower herself from the window. It was still not long enough to take her all the way to the ground, but with something soft to land on . . . And that was the next step.

She gathered together on the floor by the window all the pillows and blankets from her bed. Last of all, she brought the featherbed itself. It was large, thick, awkward to handle, but she thought that it might just be maneuvered through the window.

She waited there by the window until her watch said that it was two hours past midnight. Now was the hour she had chosen as the most likely that all the household would be asleep. She rose stiffly from her cramped position. Now was the time; she must act or remain a prisoner.

She had chosen the featherbed to use in breaking

the window. Holding it as close to the glass as possible to muffle the sound, she gave a sharp rap on the pane and had the great satisfaction of hearing only a faint tinkle as it broke. Still protecting herself with the thick bedding, she removed the remainder of the glass shards carefully from the window. When the window was cleared to the wooden frame, she began to force the featherbed, by wadding and squeezing, through the window. It grew very heavy when most of its weight was hanging outside, but Julia clung to it fiercely until she could see that it would drop properly onto the spot she had chosen just below the window. With a whispered prayer, she let it go; it fell with a soft thump just as she had hoped.

Now for the blankets and pillows. She stood for a moment debating which should form the next layer, but she froze in despairing anger as she heard, unquestionably, the key being turned in the lock of her bedroom door.

A moment later Philip was silhouetted in the light from the hallway, holding a candle of his own.

"Ah, Miss Townes, I see you are dressed. That will save us a great deal of time. Come along, please. We are leaving the house rather sooner than expected."

Julia stood only a brief moment with the pillow still in her hand, then, recognizing defeat with her usual clarity of mind, she put down the pillow, picked up her cloak and followed Philip into the hallway.

Within a few minutes, she was sharing a horse with Philip as they galloped through the night, led by Philip's fierce servant who rode just ahead of them. She sat in front of Philip, his arms around her tightly as his hands held the reins. The wind blew strong and cold, and sudden blusters of rain fell intermittently from the clouds that moved swiftly across the face of the moon. Julia was quickly chilled, making her treacherously grateful for the warmth of his nearness. They remained in silence after his one inquiry, "Can you ride astride?"

Julia tried to take note of her surroundings, discern in which direction they rode, but it was futile in the wind and confusion and lack of any even vaguely familiar landmark. At length, however, just as the rain was beginning in earnest, they came to a roadway, crossed it, and after a few minutes more, Julia heard the servant call out softly.

"I see them, sir. They are just ahead."

They rode slowly now, quietly. Julia heard the whinney of horses nearby as they drew near the shadowy shapes that stood silent in the night. Julia drew in her breath as she recognized the gypsy wagons.

"Jacob," Philip was calling softly. "Are you awake, you old beggar? We are here."

"Awake is it?" came a heavily accented boom that was intended as a whisper. "Of course I'm awake. And dry and warm, too, which I cannot say for you. Come into the wagon."

Julia found herself being taken from the horse, led up a rickety set of steps and wrapped in a blanket as she settled onto a pile of what she supposed must be cushions.

"You are a little earlier than we expected you," came the booming whisper again.

"Ah, well, Miss Townes was eager to be gone from Winterhall, so I thought it best to come a few days early."

"I'd best get back, sir," Philip's servant said as he took a long drink from the cup that was offered to him. "I will see you in . . ." He stopped just in time at Philip's sudden glance. "I will see you when you arrive."

"Yes. Thank you, Thomas."

Philip poured some liquid into a cup for Julia and held it out to her. After a moment's hesitation, she took it and drank.

It was whiskey and she sputtered and gasped. But it was warming to her shivering flesh, and she drank it all.

Philip's servant, his cloak dripping, nodded to the two men, then politely to Julia, and without knowing why, she nodded in return. Then she sat holding the cup from which she had drunk as she watched him tie Philip's horse to the wagon, then mount his own horse and ride away.

Chapter Twelve

"What will happen now?" Julia realized with a start that she had spoken the question softly, but neither of the two men seemed to have noticed. Philip, still crouched at the wagon's opening, stared into the darkness after his servant, and the gypsy man—"Jacob," Philip had called him—noisily yawned and stretched.

Philip turned and moved back into the center of the wagon, sinking with what seemed like weariness into his own pile of cushions. Lifting the cup to his lips again, his eyes gazed into Julia's above its rim. Her own gaze wavered under his and she looked away.

"Jacob," Philip said, "is there any sort of curtain we can give Miss Townes in *that* area of the wagon?"

Julia followed his glance, then blushed as she saw

a chamber pot standing starkly next to a makeshift washstand.

Jacob, who was just settling himself as though for a comfortable chat, rose to his feet. He was a short man and could stand upright in the wagon, while Philip and even Julia had to crouch to move about. Jacob extracted a blanket from the pile beneath him and strung it from some hooks that had been placed, apparently for just this purpose, in the boards of the ceiling. The privy area was now concealed.

Julia supposed she should be grateful for this display of delicacy on her behalf, but her eyes were growing heavy from her exertions and the whiskey. Hoping faintly that this might be another of those dreams from which she would soon awake, she lay down on the pile of cushions, wondered briefly how clean they might be, then felt Philip draw a thick blanket over her and tuck it beneath her chin.

She awoke to a sensation of motion. It was pleasant, comforting, and so was the warmth of the arm that encircled her and the body that lay so close to her. In that enchanted state between sleep and wakefulness, she savored the sensation, nestling more closely to the safety of the form beside her. With a soft little moan, he drew her even nearer; his hand found the softness of her breast and caressed it gently. It was a lovely feeling—warm, contented, with a promise of coming delight. And the lips that brushed her neck sent a little shiver of pleasure through her langorous body. She sighed, but it was not entirely a sigh of happiness, for the spell was lifting slowly. She opened her eyes.

In the gray light of the winter morning, the wagon was a shabby place. What the candle of the night before had shown as exotic and colorful now seemed garish and ugly. She blinked once or twice to bring it into better focus. Then there was the matter of the hand on her breast. She sat up, suddenly wide awake.

Her abrupt movement brought Philip to full wakefulness from a dream he was finding especially pleasant. He raised himself onto his elbows and found himself looking into blue and angry eyes.

"Good morning, Miss Townes," he said very soberly.

Not trusting herself to answer, Julia rose in silent fury, went to the privy corner and hooked the curtain closed.

Her intention had been to remain there, separated, if only by a curtain, from her captors. But it was not a pleasant place to be, after all, and when she did emerge, she found that she had the wagon's main compartment to herself. Philip had gone to sit with Jacob, who was at the reins in the front of the wagon. She found her shoes, which someone had thoughtfully removed for her, and stole quietly to the rear opening, thinking of her chances of escaping and running . . . running somewhere. Away. Perhaps there would be a farmhouse.

But there was another wagon just behind. In the driver's seat was a young man who was dark and certainly taller than Jacob. He flashed a white smile as he saw her, and raised a hand in greeting. Julia, without knowing why, began to raise her own hand as though by instinct, then drew it back and closed the curtain flap quickly.

She went dejectedly back to the pile of cushions

where she had slept. She was hungry and she was cold. As she sat down and wrapped herself in a couple of blankets against the chill, a stray and treacherous thought of the strong and sensuous body that had warmed her through the night brought the heat of a flush to her cheeks. She settled herself as comfortably as she could and wondered what would be the next occurrence in this dumbfounding series of events that her life had become.

In fact, nothing happened all that entire day. The wagon moved along a road which seemed, when Julia observed it from time to time, to be a part of a farm track and not a proper road at all. She neither heard nor saw any other travelers to whom she might have signaled or called for assistance. Only when the early winter dusk had settled and Julia was ravenous with hunger, did the wagons draw themselves into the familiar circle, and Jacob came to tell her that she could step out to stretch her legs.

"You will have to get up with the rest of us tomorrow, Miss," he said as he paced up and down with her outside the wagon, "if you want to eat breakfast. There is so little daylight at this time of year that we do not stop during the day. There will be food for all of us in an hour or so. Nice and hot."

Julia's heart gave a leap of relief, but she only nodded as though in the greatest indifference. "I see."

"Ah, here is Milus, coming to meet you."

It was the young man who had greeted her from his wagon that morning. He was tall, as tall as Julia, anyway, and quite handsome, too. Julia judged that

231

he must be about twenty years of age, with dark eyes that reflected good humor and friendliness.

"Miss Townes," Jacob was saying, as though he were presenting the greatest personage of the age, "this is Milus, my son. He also speaks English!"

Julia would never understand why she should offer her hand to this dusty and, no doubt, disreputable individual. It must have been the eager pleasure he seemed to exude, or the twinkle of innate charm that danced in his eyes. In any case, she saw him grin with delight as he took her hand in his and made quite a proper bow before releasing it.

"It is Philip who taught me the right way of introduction," he said with less accent than his father, and with the grin growing wider.

Julia could not help smiling a little in return. "You did it very well."

"Perhaps you will ride with me one day before you leave us, and tell me something of English society."

"I'm afraid I've not been a member of English society very long myself. I know little of it, quite honestly."

"A pity." His forehead creased in consternation, then cleared. "Ah. Perhaps Philip will instruct us both!"

Julia was rummaging for a kind, but firm, refusal of this service, when a girl appeared from out of the gloom. She was dark, of course, and she was also exotically beautiful, though Julia thought she could not be more than fifteen. She had large black eyes and thick black hair that cascaded in tumbling waves and curls from a brightly colored band that held it back from her face. Her budding figure was ripe in a way that belied her youth; here must surely be the jewel of this gypsy band.

"Miss Townes," Milus said, "this is my sister, Jonetta. Make your curtsy and say 'how do you do' to Miss Townes as Philip taught you, Jonetta."

Eyeing Julia closely, Jonetta made a brief curtsy, and Julia nodded pleasantly in return.

"Papa," the girl said to Jacob, though her sultry eyes still studied Julia, "Dakar asks that you come to his wagon."

"What? Is it another of his spells?"

"I do not think so."

With a grumble and a mutter, Jacob moved away in the direction of another of the wagons. Julia heard Milus chuckle.

"Dakar only wants help in deciding which chicken is to be killed for tomorrow." Milus leaned easily on the wheel of the wagon. "He grows fond of every bird he keeps."

Julia could think of no suitable comment by way of reply, and, still feeling the hot eyes trained on her, she turned to the girl.

Jonetta met her eyes boldly. "I have never seen hair of such a color, except on an old woman," she said tauntingly.

A peal of laughter at the unexpected remark welled up in Julia, and it left her feeling relieved at the expression of some natural emotion. Milus was laughing too, after a sharp intake of breath which Julia supposed was preparatory to correcting his sister's behavior.

"And I, Miss Jonetta," Julia said with a smile, "have never seen curls as nice as yours. Except . . . except my mother's."

"I am the most beautiful of all the girls in any group we meet in our travels," Jonetta replied matter of factly. "I will have a very fine husband."

"I am sure you will," Julia replied.

Milus said, "Jonetta is very pleased with herself since she learned to speak English. She thinks she will become a fortuneteller, but I believe it is Fellie who has the gift instead."

"No!" Jonetta spat the word at her brother. "You will see, Milus. Fellie is a fool, and she isn't even pretty. The English will not pay to have their fortunes told by such a girl!" She stalked away, then turned back to say again, "You will see."

A wonderful aroma now found its way to Julia's nostrils. The smell of roasting meat and, yes, it must be potatoes and onions, perhaps carrots. Her stomach gave an anticipatory growl.

"Come, Miss Townes," Milus said. "Philip has told us that we must call you 'Miss Townes,' though I know your name is Julia. I will walk with you a little around the wagons until dinner is ready. It is best to take our exercise as we can. You probably find this sort of travel uncomfortable."

After dinner, of which Julia was sure she ate more than her fair share, the encampment settled down to evening occupations. Preparations for the morning meal were begun and the selected chicken which would figure prominently in tomorrow's dinner was dispatched and plucked by the light of one of the fires. And there was music. The girl whom Milus identified as Fellie played a series of songs on a violin of rich and mellow tone. If Julia had not been so lonely, so uncertain, so anxious of her own fate and that of those she cared most for, it would have been an evening of great interest and enlightenment.

234

The moon had not yet risen; it was one of those clear, cold winter nights, with a sky full of brilliant stars that one could see when away from the brightness of the fires. Julia wondered very much what had become of Philip; she hadn't seen him at dinner, indeed for several hours. Well, she certainly wasn't about to ask.

When Jacob escorted her to her wagon, she found a fat gypsy lady there ahead of her. This, it seemed, would be her companion for the night.

Indeed, Julia was very well guarded; there could be no thoughts of escape. Jacob slept at the rear opening of the wagon, and the fat lady slept at the front end. Julia was left alone to keep warm as best she could throughout the hours she lay wakeful with distressful and unproductive calculations as to how she might escape from this bizarre, really quite incredible situation in which Philip Sommerville had placed her.

But, *why* had he done so? Why on earth was she there? Try as she might, she could make no sense of it.

After finally falling into a restless and dream-tormented sleep, Julia was instantly awake when she became aware of rustlings and movement about the wagon. She opened her eyes just in time to have them blinded by the fat woman lighting a stub of candle.

Julia now was to learn of the morning rituals of the gypsy encampment. When she stepped outside with Jacob, she saw that a single fire had been lit; a cauldron strung over it was cooking a meal. And in the dank and foggy morning chill, there was the smell of coffee.

How on earth, Julia wondered, had these people

come to have coffee?

Breakfast was not a leisurely meal. Everything was done with great hurry, and in less than an hour of opening her eyes, Julia was rocking along on her pallet of cushions in the back of the wagon. She was alone, the fat woman having gone back to wherever she belonged, and Jacob was again at the reins.

Julia wondered more than once during that tedious and uneventful day, what had become of Philip Sommerville. He had not been seen at breakfast, nor did he appear for the evening meal, which consisted of a spicy stew made of yesterday's unfortunate chicken. The evening, too, was unremarkable with only a few words of conversation with Milus, and at bedtime, the reappearance of the fat woman, who Julia learned was called Cossie.

Another day, another night. And another and another. They camped every evening in a place that afforded access to a stream or some other water source; each morning they departed, leaving their litter of the night's encampment wherever it happened to land when it was flung or dropped. It was no wonder, Julia thought, that gypsies were not entirely welcome visitors by the owners of the lands they used.

By the morning of her fifth day with the gypsies, Julia could bear not another instant spent inside the wagon. For all her placid demeanor, Julia was an active person. She had been accustomed in York to take at least one and usually two long walks each day on errands for her mother or in her visits and efforts on behalf of the poor or the orphans. And at Fainway, too, there had been almost daily exercise. To be confined day after day in a musty wagon was becoming unbearable. She requested and received

Jacob's assent that she walk beside the wagon.

So with her blond hair safely covered against the weather and the glances of any stranger who might happen by, she walked the better part of that day and felt she had achieved a great victory when she determined that, at least right now, they were headed in a northwesterly direction. When supper was over that evening, she fell asleep at once under the haunting melody of Fellie's violin.

Julia awoke wishing more than anything for a bath. She had tried to keep herself reasonably clean with the scant water and sliver of soap provided at the washstand, but her clothing was soiled and disheveled and she longed to wash her hair. It was much too cold for bathing in any outdoor stream, even had the ones the band had come across been deep enough. With a sigh, she washed her face and hands and made ready for breakfast.

"Ah, Miss Townes," Milus said as he strolled with his tin of coffee to stand beside her. "You will be glad to be off the road, too?"

"Off the road, Milus? Do you mean that we have a destination, after all?"

"It will be a long day of travel today, but if the rain holds off, we should make it just after dark."

"Make it where?"

"It has no name," he said suddenly cautious. "It is merely a place that we go for a time in the winter."

"I see."

"There is shelter," he said proudly. "It is more comfortable for the colder weather."

"Yes. Yes, it would be, of course."

"It is better for the animals not to have to travel in this weather. All of us will get a little rest."

237

"Milus!" Jacob called from the wagon. "Do not keep the lady. We must be off. There can be no slacking today."

So Julia climbed once more into the wagon, glad enough to ride this morning, for her legs were sore and reluctant from the previous day's exertions.

As Milus promised, it was a long, uncomfortable day. It was very dark, and a cold, dreary rain had begun to fall as they arrived at a building that loomed out of the shadows. It looked to Julia exactly like a barn, and, indeed, when the animals had been unhitched from the wagons, they were the first to be taken inside.

And inside there was room for all. It was lofty and even fairly clean, with two large fireplaces which the women hastened to light. Julia was shown by Jacob to a spot in the loft that would be her sleeping quarters; he gave her blankets to cover the straw.

"It will be a cold supper tonight," he said. "Tomorrow we will settle in."

After eating the portion of bread and cheese brought to her by Milus, she fell onto the blanket and soon was fast asleep.

Morning brought a flurry of activity. After breakfast all the men disappeared and the women began a furious round of work. One activity that Julia was especially glad to see was laundry being done. She received accepting looks from the other women as, wrapped in the blankets from her bed, she brought her clothes to the community tub, scrubbed them *very* thoroughly, and hung them with the other items near the fire to dry.

And next, to Julia's great joy, there was bathing. A single tub of hot water, to be sure, but the other women politely insisted that she bathe first which she did. Then she retired to her loft to comb her wet hair dry and to wait for her clothing to be ready.

When she was dressed again, she went down to help the other women with the remaining chores. She swept and arranged, she gathered and stored the provisions which were carried about in the wagons. It was a cheerful group of women, and if Julia was not so carefree as they, she was at least as glad to be off the road.

At dusk the men returned with two of the wagons laden with firewood, and preparations for yet another meal were begun.

"I will be happy to help with the work," Julia said to the fat woman.

Cossie, who did not speak English, appealed to Jonetta, who translated. "Cossie wants to know if you are accustomed to cooking."

"Well, no. But I don't see that it would be beyond my powers to slice a potato or stir a pot or do whatever is required."

After another exchange with Cossie, Jonetta turned to Julia and said, "You may cut the bird."

And Julia was handed the chicken which Cossie had just finished plucking, along with a board and an enormous cleaver. Cossie moved away to inspect the store of seasonings, leaving Julia alone with her task.

This was not the sort of job she had expected to be given, and she had no idea how to proceed. Julia closed her eyes and pictured the dishes of chicken and vegetables she had eaten in her time. Polly had made such a dish in York. Then, with a mental picture of the pieces of chicken that had found their way onto her plate, she began on the legs.

Cautiously, methodically, and of course very slowly, she made a respectable job of disjointing the bird, though there were one or two strange and rather bloody items from inside the creature that Julia could not hope to identify. Cossie returned in time to give a sniff of faint approval and hand her several carrots to cut. Later, when the meal was cleared and Fellie was playing her violin, Julia was accepted without comment among the other women, who sat talking among themselves. Though she could not understand them, their voices sounded satisfied, untroubled.

It seemed almost as if they had come home, Julia mused, even though one never thought of gypsies having a home to go to. Perhaps the women were talking of the places they had seen on their journeys since their last stay in this place, and it was probably pleasant for them to remember those sights without the hardship and discomfort of seeing them. She wondered very much if the women might grow complacent here—perhaps enough so that she could slip away unnoticed. She went to bed with vague plans forming.

The next day began in a very different manner, especially different from life on the road. Julia, along with the rest of the inhabitants of the barn, slept until the sun was well up and beaming a friendly and unaccustomed warmth into the solitary window of the structure. Julia went outside to take stock of her surroundings.

The barn seemed to sit in complete isolation from the rest of whatever farm it was part of. There were gentle hills covered with woods in the direction she judged must be west. This must be where the woodcutters had been at work the previous day. She set out to stroll in that direction.

"Are you thinking of taking a walk, Miss Townes?"

Julia turned to see Milus, hurrying toward her from whatever work he had been doing.

"Yes. Cossie has nothing for me to do, and I feel I must have a little air and exercise."

He stood thinking about it for a long moment. "No harm, I guess. I will come with you."

This was only to be expected, but Julia, who was very tired of never being alone, was disappointed. Still, Milus was a better companion than most, and they set off at a brisk walk.

For the most part they walked in silence. Julia could tell the young man was eager for conversation—all these people seemed to talk incessantly, when one came to think of it—but she made only brief replies to his questions and he soon fell quiet.

When they reached the hillside where the timber began, Julia turned around and surveyed the country from this point of elevation. It looked, unfortunately, like most everywhere else. Large meadows separated by a small river. A rutted track, a solitary barn. She could be anywhere in England.

"Do you like this life, Milus?" she asked suddenly.

He was startled by the question. "I will be the leader after my father."

"But do you ever wish for a more settled life, perhaps on a farm or in a village?"

"There I must keep other men's hours."

241

"So you must, though the hours we have kept these days I have been with you are not easy."

"That is different."

"Why?"

He would not answer, shook his head and looked away toward the river.

"But how are your people educated, Milus? Can you read, for example?"

He drew himself up. "There must always be someone who can read. I have learned from my mother. And my sister has also learned. And Fellie. She reads best of all."

"Ah. Fellie. She is a girl of many gifts."

"I will marry her, probably."

Julia fell silent to consider the picture of Milus and Fellie, and perhaps their children, traveling year after year, mile after mile throughout their lives. She was uncertain whether to be sad.

"You do not like to stay with us?" Milus was asking.

Julia gave a long sigh. "No, Milus, I do not. It is not a life I could become accustomed to. And I am anxious about the friends and family who do not know what has become of me. I want to go home." And it surprised her that for the first time she actually thought of Fainway as home. She missed, desperately missed, her father and her aunt and her cousin Lawrence, too.

"Do you spend the winters in this place?"

"Now we do." His voice held a note of caution.

"And before?"

But again came the shake of the head; he would not answer.

"Is it Mr. Sommerville who has told you not to tell me anything?"

"Philip would not be pleased if you were to learn something you should not know."

"So it is better to err on the side of caution and tell me nothing?"

He shrugged. "Philip is a wise man. And a good one."

Irritated, Julia was wondering how much store she could put in the praise given by a gypsy, whose reputation was one of stealing and idleness, when she felt Milus stir beside her. By mutual and silent consent, they now moved back down the hillside. As they drew near the barn, Fellie came outside, on her way to one of the wagons. When she saw them, she stood still as a statue, watching intently as they passed her, then parted at the doorway of the barn. Julia could still feel the black eyes burning into her back after she had gone inside.

A little later, Julia decided to test her freedom again. She took a pail and strolled down to the river to fill it. As she passed the men at work on the wagons or stacking the firewood, she could feel them turn to watch her. But no one challenged her. She carried the water back to the barn, heated it over the fire, took it with her to her own sleeping quarters, undressed and washed herself thoroughly. Tomorrow, she vowed, she would launder her blankets, even if it meant sleeping under straw for a night or two.

And she knew that she might go as far as the river.

Julia came back down into the main part of the barn just as dusk descended. She could hear a noise and clamor outside, and the women were looking up from their pursuits to see what it was all about.

Jonetta ran inside excitedly, announcing something in her native tongue, then she turned to Julia, her lovely eyes dancing with eagerness. "He's here! They have come!"

"Oh!" cried Fellie, peering from the window. "You should see what they have brought!"

There was now a great movement toward the door. Julia went to the window, wiped away the dusty film and looked out into the evening dusk.

There was a great knot of people surrounding two horses and the men upon them. One was a man of giant hulking size, and the second was a figure she could have identified out of a thousand others. Philip Sommerville had returned.

Chapter Thirteen

He came inside surrounded by the excited, chattering gypsies. So tall among them, he towered over all. Only Milus reached Philip's shoulders. And Philip was himself towered over by Thomas, who walked behind, never far from his side. In the gathering gloom of evening, Philip's eyes seemed to search the space of the barn's main area for her, to confirm that she was still under his control.

When he saw her at her place by the window, he nodded in satisfaction. Their eyes met briefly and he almost, it seemed, wished to smile at her. She met his eyes with a steady gaze, then turned and moved back to stand by the fire.

There was much excitement in the room, for Philip had not come empty-handed. There was a great quantity of meat and other provisions, including more coffee. Cossie, who seemed to be the main chef, fell upon the offerings with expressions of delight and surprise. And when Thomas had returned from settling his own and his master's horse, he came directly to Julia and put a package into her hands.

"What is this?"

"It is yours," he replied, and moved quickly away.

She was uncertain at first just what to do, then seeing that Philip was very much engaged with the excited women, or so, perhaps, he would have it appear, she took the package and went up into her loft quarters.

The package contained a gown of a vivid lavender color and a complete set of undergarments. There was a smaller package inside which contained a comb, several ribbons and best of all, a tablet of soap, richly scented. She inhaled the fragrance with delight.

I suppose, she said to herself, *a proper English lady would throw these things in his face and suffer in discomfort and dignity.* But that would be foolish. She had not asked to be traveling with a band of gypsies, and she saw no reason why Mr. Philip Sommerville, whose idea it *had* been, should not make her as comfortable as possible. She placed her new belongings in the rough wooden box that served as a table beside her pallet. All the same though, she supposed she would have to thank him.

She decided to do it at once, so there would be no long dreading of the moment. She went down into the main room and stood where he would see her when he looked up from the chattering group around him. It did not take long. He lifted his head, which had been cocked in attention to something that Jonetta was saying to him. His green eyes, even in the dim light of the fireside and candles, glinted brightly before they narrowed as they looked at her. Slowly, with that elegant grace, he moved out of the circle of women and walked to where she stood.

"Mr. Sommerville," she began, "I wish to tell you that I appreciate the things you have brought me."

"But curse me, nonetheless, for having left you for a week without a change of clothes. I would not have done so had it not been most necessary."

With a nod in the direction of the women and their treasures, Julia asked, "And have you also brought payment to these people for keeping me?"

He laughed out loud, and several of the group, still admiring the food, turned to look at them. He took her arm and steered her away, toward the other fireplace.

"You have an inquisitive mind, Miss Townes. That is not always a safe thing to possess."

"What do you plan to do with me, Mr. Sommerville?"

He sighed, and a little smile played around his green eyes. "Inconvenient as it is for the both of us, I fear that we must keep you with us for a little longer. Matters are not proceeding quite so quickly as I had hoped. There have been . . . disappointments."

"I see. Have you any recent news of my family? Of Mimmie?"

"All are well."

"All are well? Is that all?"

"That is all for now."

"Very well."

She left him abruptly and went to speak to Milus, who was just coming in with another armload of firewood.

"Ah, Miss Townes. It will be quite a feast tonight. Do you see the good things your friend has brought us?"

"Mr. Sommerville is not my friend, Milus. But I do agree that I am looking forward to dinner. Milus, are there any books that I might read?"

"Books?"

"Books. I should like to have something to read. I would read to any who might like to listen. Or I shall be glad to teach any who wish to learn."

"We have several already who can read, Miss Townes. And I don't know where we might find books. There are none here."

"Not even a Bible?"

He shook his head.

"And what will you do when it is time to teach someone to read? How do those of you who do read manage to keep the skill?"

"When we need a book, we go and get one, Miss Townes." He spoke abruptly, almost unkindly.

"I see. Well, if there are those who care to learn, and if you come across a book or two, I shall be happy to make use of them."

He nodded, then turned to take up the poker and stir the fire. Julia sighed and moved away.

She could feel Philip's eyes on her as she moved and Julia suddenly felt entirely, hopelessly alone. Unlike Philip Sommerville and even his servant, she was an outsider here among these chattering, busy, noisy people. Their exuberance and their earthiness were foreign, unwanted, oppressive. She went up again into her loft and did not come down until Cossie called loudly from below the message she had come to know meant that the evening meal was ready.

When the feast had been eaten and cleared, Fellie began at once to play. A circle formed, and Jonetta, with very little encouragement, began to dance.

Her movements were graceful, sensuous, riveting. Her black eyes glinted with some secret hunger as she swayed and twirled and cavorted to the clapping hands of her audience and the haunting melody from the instrument of the thin, intense young Fellie. Julia wondered which of the two was more swept away.

When the dance ended to enthusiastic applause and calls for more, Julia turned curiously to see Philip's reaction to it all. She found to her astonishment that his eyes were not on the dancer or the musician, but on her. Was he measuring her reaction to this hedonistic display? She determined angrily that he would not have the satisfaction of seeing her show any emotion whatever. Again her steady blue gaze answered his green, and Julia carried the point. He rose and came to sit beside her.

"What *did* you think of the entertainment?" he asked, as the voices around them debated what song would be played next.

"Fellie is a fine musician. I should like to see her have proper instruction."

"Why?"

"Does it not seem wrong to you, Mr. Sommerville, that such a gift should go unnurtured?"

"To our way of thinking, perhaps. But Fellie's life is here, and her companions are more than satisfied

249

with her skills. Look. You can see how proud Milus is of her."

"Perhaps his smile is one of admiration for his sister's dancing."

, "Jonetta receives admiration enough from all the others. She can spare some praise for the one who is truly accomplished."

"If you mean to suggest that the two girls are jealous of each other, I will tell you that I have seen no signs of it."

"Of each other, no."

"Of what or whom, then?"

He only shook his head in answer, then said, "Another time, perhaps. Fellie is about to play again."

This was a slower, more exotic melody, to Julia's ears almost haunted. Jonetta, her silver earrings flashing, her eyes nearly closed, her hair tumbling softly with the undulating motions of the dance, moved nearly silently within the circle of rapt observers. So, Julia thought, must ancient peoples have expressed themselves in an effort to release and relate emotions they could not express in words or in any other deed. It reminded her of the Druids and the strange, intense sensations their ceremonies had roused in her. Though not as, well, as frightening, it was a primitive, compelling, mesmerizing sensation to observe this performance.

"This must be quite something to see if it is done outside in the summertime," she whispered, more to herself than to Philip beside her.

"Yes," he whispered in return, and his sleeve brushed her arm as he leaned a little nearer. "I saw this same dance at Winterhall last summer. Just before I went north."

She drew in her breath sharply and turned to him without meaning to.

"And there, I found *myself* dancing." He smiled at her. "On the last summer night."

For a moment their eyes held each other, and Julia found herself remembering, with instantly flaming cheeks, the dream that had haunted her slumber at the end of that night. That force she did not understand was between them again. The expression on his face was as intense as the music which was just ending in a sudden crescendo, then Jonetta fell into a dramatic heap just where they were sitting. Julia drew herself back from a great distance and joined in the applause. Philip unwound himself and helped the girl to her feet.

"That was very entertaining, Jonetta," he told her. "Quite beautiful. You are dancing better than ever."

Jonetta, already flushed from the fire and her exertion of the dance, accepted the praise with silent satisfaction, turning to Julia, who hurried to add her own compliments.

"You have a unique way of moving with the music, Jonetta. I daresay the finest ballerina could not have been more expressive in this particular dance."

Jonetta did not acknowledge the accolade. She gazed at Julia through narrowed eyes for a moment, as though trying to decide what merit her words ought to carry. Then she shrugged. "I do not dance more. I am tired."

When Jonetta had moved away from the circle, the party atmosphere seemed to wither. One by one, with yawns and stretches and forms somehow drooping with weariness, the group drifted away.

Julia found herself thinking that this was the first time since their arrival at this place safe from persecution and scorn that all the little band, the men included, had seemed to relax. She was surprised to find that she felt happy for them to have this respite and wondered how long it might last.

Philip had turned away from her and fallen into conversation with Jacob. Julia rose, noting that Philip's eyes followed her as she went up the steep ladder to her loft. She wondered where he would sleep tonight.

The feeling of a more leisured life continued the next morning. Philip and his servant were nowhere to be seen when Julia came down from her loft. The women worked in quiet groups, the men, outdoors in the bright winter sunlight, moved cheerfully yet more slowly as they mended wagons and tools. Julia went to Magda, who also spoke some English.

"Magda, where is Milus?"

"He is not here. He has gone into the village."

"Will he be back soon?"

Magda tossed the carrot she had been chopping into a pot that must contain the beginnings of the midday meal.

"Not until evening. He is the best of the sharpeners. He will make much money in the village today. Everyone waits for Milus to return to have their scissors and knives sharpened."

Julia was disappointed but decided she would speak directly to Fellie. She looked around, then asked where the girl might be found.

"She is gone with Milus," Magda replied. "And Jonetta, too. They will help him, and they will play and dance." Her wrinkled face took on a naughty, knowing look. "More money will be made, you see. A young man whose knife might not need sharpening will bring it anyway."

Julia returned the smile as best she could, then, dismissing her plan for the morning to discuss Fellie's musical future with her, drew a shawl over her shoulders and went outside to walk to the river.

There were a few glances from the men as she passed them, but Julia knew she would be permitted to go without challenge. She walked up and down along the river bank, asking herself how she might turn this liberty to her advantage.

She knew now that there was a village nearby and if she watched carefully this evening for Milus and the others to return, she would know in which direction it lay.

Strolling slowly, bending now and then as though to examine a plant along the bank or to stare into the water, a plan began to form.

If she came here a few times in the afternoon, perhaps to fetch water for washing or bathing, she might arrange to go out as it grew dark. By going in and out several times, the gypsies would grow accustomed to it. They would not miss her, perhaps, for several minutes. There was no moon now, and if she kept to the river, she might, she just might be able to make her way into the village. In any case, it seemed worth trying.

On her way back to the midday meal, Julia almost stopped to ask one of the men when Milus might be expected to return. She thought better of it. These people were clever in their own way; it was best to give no hint of what she might be thinking.

Julia ate her stew thoughtfully, and when the meal had been cleared and the group went about its

253

tasks or withdrew to rest, she went to her loft to think quietly. In an hour or so she had devised a plan. She decided to implement it at once.

When the time seemed right, she again put on her shawl and, taking a small pail, walked down to the river. Within the view of the two or three men who were at work, she began to gather stones from the icy water. When she had half-filled the pail, she returned to the barn, but she left the shawl behind, hidden in a bush where it would stay dry.

"Look, Magda, at the pretty stones from the river," Julia said, pouring out her gatherings onto a cloth. "See how smooth the water has made them?"

Magda fingered a couple of the stones. "They are smooth, yes. But they look like all the other pebbles from all the other rivers I have seen."

"You are lucky to have seen so many pretty streams and rivers," Julia replied, her eyes riveted on the rocks. "I was raised in a city and have never traveled before now. I think they are quite lovely, almost like jewels."

Magda turned away with a sniff and a shrug and went on with scrubbing the carving board. Julia sat beside her, seemingly engrossed as she sorted through her treasures.

"I rather think these stones could be arranged into a design. You can see that there are many of the same colors. Yes. Perhaps even a picture. Or a table top."

Magda came to look, said, "Mmm," and had no further thoughts for the useless pursuits of idle English ladies.

Julia worked in silence or hummed a little tune under her breath. She grew absorbed in the task for its own sake as she made separate piles of the different colors, then began to arrange them into a mosaic on a board she had acquired from Jacob.

"I only wish I had some sort of adhesive," she remarked to the stolid Magda. "Is there any, do you know?"

"You must ask the men. There may be a bit of glue left from the last horse that died, but they've better uses for it, I'm sure."

Even so, Julia went to ask about glue; this would give her comings and goings even more authenticity. She was unsure whether to be pleased when Jacob obligingly produced a small pot of a thick and foul-smelling substance.

After working half an hour at the design, which was beginning to look quite decorative, Julia again took the pail and made a very hurried visit to the river. She shivered in the absence of her shawl, for it was beginning to grow cloudy again and a blustery little wind had sprung up. She whispered a prayer that there would be no rain before she had a chance to try her plan. And on the way back into the barn, she reminded herself that in another hour or so, she must begin to watch in earnest for the ones on whose return from the village the success of the plan depended.

But it was not to be. She had just finished sorting the new batch of stones and was holding the pot of glue in her hand when Milus burst through the door, holding a weeping, nearly hysterical Jonetta by the arm.

"Where is my father?" he demanded of Julia, pushing Jonetta away from him.

The girl cried out and ran to throw herself into the arms of Magda, who was just coming from the curtained area that served as a storeroom. In the confusion, Julia saw Fellie creep in, holding her violin closely.

"I don't know where he is, Milus," Julia told him as she watched Fellie disappear into the area where she slept. "Perhaps he is outside with the others."

"What is the noise?" Jacob came from the stables at the back of the building, emerging from the gloom into the fire and candlelight.

Milus said something to his father in his native tongue, then drew Jacob back toward the stables. As they went past her, Julia heard Milus say Philip's name.

The two men stood talking too softly for Julia to catch more than an occasional word, even had she been able to understand them. But she saw very plainly when Milus held out his hand and Jacob took a golden chain and pendant from it. That is when she caught a stream of words barked angrily by Jacob. It was followed by a solemn nodding of Milus's head.

Their voices dropped again, and Julia heard nothing more until they moved back into the main living area. After a moment of hesitation, Julia got up from her seat and approached them.

"Jacob, Milus, what has happened? Can I do something to help?"

"No," Jacob replied shortly. "You can do nothing!" The look in his eyes was not precisely anger at her, but something very near it. Julia turned away, only to see Milus looking at her with something of the same expression.

Jacob now went forward to deal with the unhappy Jonetta. Not wishing to be a witness to this scene, and knowing that she might as well retrieve her shawl, she took her pail and went again to the river.

Julia's intention was to stay outside until the business with Jonetta, whatever form it might take, was over. It was strange. Gypsies were generally supposed to be a thieving lot, but if Jonetta had stolen that pendant in the village, her deed had aroused great anger in her father and her brother, and, judging by the grave expressions on the faces of the others, what she had done was not approved by any. Then Julia stood suddenly still as she realized that very likely this act would bring a visit from the townspeople. They might be on their way now!

No, she decided after a moment's reflection. It would be dark soon and it would be more sensible for them to wait until daylight. But whenever they arrived, she would make certain that they saw her.

She was shivering with cold, and a few drops of rain had begun to fall when she judged it safe to return indoors. She had just reached the door when she heard hoofbeats. Her heart sank as, in the gathering gloom, she saw that Philip and his servant were returning. Jacob came hurrying outside, not noticing her. She withdrew a little toward one of the wagons.

"Philip!" Jacob was calling. "You have come none too soon."

"What has happened?" Philip dismounted and handed the reins to Thomas, who disappeared with the animals toward the back of the barn.

"It is that foolish girl, Jonetta. She has stolen a trinket from the village. We can expect a visit from them by morning."

Philip stood silent, his hands in the pockets of his coat, his eyes fixed on the stony barnyard as he listened.

"I am sorry, Philip. I cannot account for Fellie's part of it, but you must know why Jonetta has done this thing."

"I can guess."

"She admitted to me that she wanted your lady to be found and taken away. She could not think beyond that wish."

"Where is Miss Townes?"

Jacob looked around blankly.

"Find her," Philip commanded. "We must leave as soon as it is entirely dark."

Jacob nodded, and Philip went inside.

Julia stood breathless, motionless in the concealment of the wagon, mourning the loss of her beautiful plans and elaborate preparations, uncertain what to do. Run? She would surely be caught at once. Everyone would be searching for her if she did not make an appearance right away. With a sigh, she realized that her best option was to pretend that all was well. She left the safety of the wagon and went inside the barn.

Philip saw her at once. He took her pail of stones and herded her toward the ladder, even followed her up into the loft.

"You must gather everything. Clothing, soap, nothing of yours may be left behind."

Julia stood looking at him steadily in the dim light. His eyes glittered green and hard, close to anger; it would be useless for her to refuse or resist. She began without a word to gather her belongings together into a blanket. When she was finished, he

258

looked carefully around the small area that had been her private sanctuary, looking under the straw, in shadowy corners, to be sure she had left nothing. Then he picked up her bundle and took her below.

The servant came forward. "The horses have been fed," he told Philip.

"Saddle them as soon as it is completely dark."

"They need more rest."

"We all need more rest. It must wait a few more hours."

Julia was left to sit at her rock design while Philip had a prolonged conversation with Jacob. Neither Jonetta nor Fellie was anywhere to be seen. The men were coming one by one into the barn for the night; they spoke little, and then in low voices. The women went about their work in a silence that seemed both sullen and embarrassed. It had begun to rain; Julia could hear large drops falling on the roof.

It was still raining, a steady, dreary, icy pelting, when she was taken outside and hoisted by Thomas onto a horse behind Philip. With no ceremony, without even a word of farewell, they rode off into the darkness, followed by Thomas.

They rode silently, steadily, carefully in the dark and threatening night. Julia clung to the man ahead of her, for warmth as well as to keep her balance. Never in all her days in York, or even less her days at Fainway, could she have imagined herself in such a condition. Wet, frightened, angry, desperate, it took all her strength to keep from screaming in frustration.

She tried to calculate how long they rode, as

directions of course were impossible. By her best estimate, it seemed they must have been on the road three hours or more before they drew up, wet, cold and bedraggled, before a large and shadowy house.

The place looked quite deserted to Julia, peering from behind Philip as they traversed the overgrown drive, but then as they made a final turn, she saw a single light gleaming in a window. It shone on what must be the main floor of the house, just above the front door. Philip reined his horse a good way from the steps and turned to his servant.

"You must stay with her until I have announced us. See if you can find a bit of shelter in the stables."

So Julia, still on the horse, was led in silence to the back of the house while Philip pounded loudly on the door.

The stable was dark but certainly dry, and Julia slipped gratefully from the animal's back and sank into a welcoming pile of hay. Thomas found a lantern and, with its light, led the horses away to be settled for the night. For long, weary minutes Julia listened to the sounds of saddles being removed and hay distributed and the soft movement of a brush on the horses' coats. These rustlings had just ceased and Thomas had returned to the stable entry when the stable door opened and a kindly looking man stood in the doorway, holding a lantern and an umbrella.

"It is quite safe to go in now. Through the front. Everyone is in the kitchen."

Thomas nodded and held out a hand to help Julia rise from the hay. As though in a dream, she gave him her hand and went out again into the night, vaguely amused at the new man's care to shelter her dripping form with the umbrella. At the door, the umbrella was handed to Thomas while the other man took a key from his pocket to admit them.

"Quickly now, miss," he said when the door had been locked again behind them, "up the stairs. Thomas, I will see you in a moment in the kitchen."

Julia was hurried up the flight of stairs and then up another and into a bedroom where a fire was blessedly burning. Philip was there already, his clothes in a pile and himself wrapped in a couple of blankets.

"There is a tub of water, good and hot, in the next room. Dinner will be ready by the time we have bathed."

The door of the room he had indicated with a nod of his head now opened, and a serving woman of middle age smiled at her.

"This way, miss. I'll help you with your wet things and see that they are dried. We have found something for you to wear tonight."

Unprotesting, Julia was undressed and got into the tub. The water was uncomfortably hot at first to her icy skin, but after the first shock, she sank deeply into the soothing water, leaning back to let the warmth flow through her hair. Left alone as the woman departed with her sodden bundle, she wished that she might just be left here undisturbed for eternity. Here was peace, quiet, solitude after so many days of unremitting observation and the company of strangers. Yes, if only she could stay here, safe from whatever lay waiting for her beyond that door. . . .

Julia was aroused with a start when the woman returned with a large towel and some clothing. With a sense of dread, she allowed herself to be toweled dry and dressed in garments that must have been warmed before the fire. Then she was taken to the next room and settled in an armchair by the fire. Near the door, Philip was just dismissing his servant.

"I've brought a fresh kettle, sir," the woman told Philip when Thomas was gone. "I'll just heat the tub up for you."

"Thank you, Tillie. I'll do that myself. You'd be doing us both great good if you could hurry dinner along."

"Yes, sir."

Philip disappeared into the other room with the kettle. Tillie slipped a pair of heavy woolen bedsocks onto Julia's feet and left the room.

Alone again. But not for long, she was sure. Julia wriggled her toes in the warmth of the wool and thought of another night when she had come to a strange place to be bathed and dressed by unfamiliar hands. A great wave of weariness and futility tugged teardrops to the edges of her lashes. She lay her head back and let them fall in unheeding silence.

"Oh, my dear girl, whatever is the matter?"

Julia's eyes flew open to behold an elderly gentleman. He was tall, exquisitely lean, white-haired, and looking for all the world like a kindly, bewhiskered vicar.

"Oh! I did not hear you come into the room, sir.

Are you—" Julia was not sure just what to ask him.

"I am Lord Wrayburn. I am your host. I apologize, as I am sure my cousin must have done, that we cannot give you your own room. It seems the servants, except for Tillie and Bobbit, must not know that you are here." He gazed absently toward the bed, which was an overlarge one. "I daresay you and Philip will manage."

Too astonished and confused to reply, Julia blew her nose with the handkerchief he had handed her.

"I have not been told your name, myself. Perhaps you do not wish—"

"Julia. I am Julia Townes."

"Well, Miss Townes. I bid you welcome. I regret that I cannot join you and my cousin at dinner, but I have just begun a most interesting experiment and I cannot leave it long."

"Experiment?" Julia snatched at this thread of implausible conversation.

"It's glass, you see. The trouble with glass is that it breaks so easily. If it could be made harder, less brittle . . . Oh, Philip, there you are. I am sorry I was not at liberty when you arrived. I hope you are comfortable. I rather fear Miss Townes is not."

An expression Julia could not read flickered across Philip's face. Perhaps annoyance that Lord —what was it—Wrayburn knew her name? All trace of it was gone in a moment, and a smile of what appeared to be affection replaced it.

"We are certainly more comfortable than we have been in some days, sir, and truly grateful for your hospitality. Miss Townes is weary, and with good cause."

"Indeed, Philip, it seems that on the rare occasions you honor me with a visit, you are always weary, harried and in a hurry to be off again. You must come here properly one day so we can have a long and much overdue talk. And I should like to see Miss Townes return as well." He made a courtly little bow. "She is a great improvement over—"

"Well, cousin," Philip interrupted, "I thank you, and I am sure Miss Townes does, too. We shall try to accept your kind invitation when times are more leisured. Won't we, Miss Townes?"

Julia removed her hostile stare from Philip to smile warmly at Lord Wrayburn. "Thank you, sir. You are very kind, indeed."

There came a clatter at the door, and Tillie and Bobbit brought in a laden tray.

"Your lordship," Bobbit said anxiously, "Myers asked me to say that—"

"Oh, my," exclaimed the old gentleman. "I declare it had quite slipped my mind. I must hurry back to the laboratory." He bowed again to Julia and took the hand she could not help offering. "I hope we will meet again soon, my dear. Good night."

Dinner was placed on a table drawn up to Julia's chair, and she and Philip were left alone.

"You must forgive the scanty crockery," he said as he took a chair opposite.

"I suppose it is intended to convey the notion that there is but one person in this room."

"Precisely. Tillie and Bobbit are entirely trustworthy, but the other servants may not be. Ah!" He smiled into the still stormy blue eyes. "You must have made a most favorable impression on old Bobbitt. He's given us a bottle of his lordship's very best claret. And two glasses as well."

"How kind."

He poured wine for both of them, then inspected the dishes. "Roast duck! A welcome change from the fare you have been used to these past days, Miss Townes. You must have been wishing for something akin to roast duck."

"You are wrong, sir. I have been wishing for the life I once knew, a life that was tranquil and simple before I ever set eyes on you. I have been wishing that I might never have—"

"Never have come to know your father?"

"That is not fair! One cannot weigh the loss of a mother against the gaining of a father. A life is a life. Hers is lost."

"I understand better than you might think, Miss Townes," he said softly. "Though my own mother died when I was seven, I still miss her. I even dream about her now and then."

Her expression made it clear that she thought it unlikely he ever *had* a mother, but he only smiled at her with the manner of calming a wrathful child.

"It would be best, I think, to keep to less personal topics for our dinner conversation." He handed her a plate of duck and cabbage and passed the only fork, keeping the large serving fork for his own utensil. "Shall I tell you about my cousin, Lord Wrayburn?"

Julia did not answer, but she did take a bite of the duck.

"He is a cousin on my father's side. Most anyone will tell you that side of the family tends to eccentricity. He has little use for his title and properties. Indeed, the estate is in a shocking state of neglect. He is an inventor, you see. In fact, I think he's rather brilliant in his own way, but up to this point, none of his inventions or ideas has been at all successful."

Julia chewed in noncommittal silence.

"I'm rather fearful of this scheme he's working on tonight. It would be most unfortunate if there were to be another fire."

She looked up to see if he was speaking seriously, but found it impossible to tell from his expression of concentration at carving the duck.

"I can see how that would be inconvenient for you," she said. "It would be difficult to explain my presence, even in the confusion of a fire. Unless, of course, you intend to lock me in and leave me to my fate."

"My cousin, though vague of mind, would not permit it." His eyes now seemed to hold a gleam of humor, and he refilled her wine glass which had seemed to empty itself very quickly.

"Lord Wrayburn is a kind gentleman and a most obliging relative. Does he not find these . . . these occasional visits from you at all peculiar?"

"As I said, Miss Townes, the family is known to be eccentric."

"Those gypsies work for you, don't they?"

He took a long moment to answer. "Let us say that we help each other."

"It is a convenient concealment for your activities, no doubt, to be able to travel unnoticed with a band of gypsies. But what do you do for them, Mr. Sommerville? Besides such things as food and coffee, I mean."

"You ask a great many questions, Miss Townes."

She looked at him thoughtfully. "Let me see. You are a gentleman of means, so you might pay them, but I did not see evidence of much coin of the realm among them." She tore a piece of bread and ate it thoughtfully. "I should think it more likely that you have provided them with the place where it seems they will winter. They seemed to have no fear of being evicted, and it is quite a secure and pleasant spot, though, judging by what I learned at school about the topography of England, I should say it is farther north than they might normally be found at this time of the year."

"You are quite observant, madam."

"And here is another question. What will happen to Jonetta?"

He sighed and pushed his plate away. "Nothing, I hope. At first light, Jacob will go into the village to return the wretched trinket she stole. I hope that will satisfy the villagers. As for her family and the others . . ." He shrugged. "I cannot say, for I do not know their ways well enough."

"She is in love with you."

"Do you find that astonishing?"

His eyes held hers. Did they hold a challenge, too?

"How do you find it, Mr. Sommerville?"

"Most inconvenient at this time."

"I may assume then, that whatever business you are about has been interrupted for the moment?"

He smiled and shook his head. "You may assume that you and I will remain in this room for a day or two, until it is safe to return you to Jacob's care."

Julia closed her eyes against his gaze, against the thought of it.

"Come now, Miss Townes, it is not so bad as that. Have you not been wishing for an opportunity to become better acquainted?"

Her eyes flew open, flashing blue fire. "I have been wishing that I might never have been acquainted with you at all."

"Now that is most unfortunate. I had come to the conclusion that, for all your having the look and manner of a Frost Princess, you are, at the core, a woman of fire and grit. It seems to me that the adventures I have provided you will give you warm memories when you are a well-settled and respectable wife. It should help to lift the tedium of domestic dilemmas and colicky children."

"You are quite mistaken, sir, in thinking that I have any wish for such memories. Nor do I consider the married state to be one of tedium."

"Not tedious? Even if married to your cousin, Mr. Christian?"

"Mr. Christian is a fine gentleman. I regard him very highly and am certain he will be a most agreeable husband. He has shown me kindness and friendship. I refuse to hear him spoken of in this manner by a man who—" She threw her napkin onto the table. "You have been a source of grief and confusion and despair from the very moment I first saw you!"

"I am sorry about your mother, Julia." His voice was soft and flat.

"Sorry? You are sorry?"

Her voice, cold and hissing, seemed to strike him like a blow. He sat very still for a long moment, looking back intently into her angry eyes. Then he pushed back his chair and stood up slowly.

Even as he moved toward her, even before he grasped her arm and lifted her to her feet to hold her to him and enfold the silky, still-damp hair, Julia knew that this night she would surrender to this man. This was what she had dreaded, feared and wished for. It was incomprehensible, treasonous, unthinkable, and yet, somehow, inevitable.

His lips met hers with a soft fierceness that stopped her breath and hurt her eyes and burned a suggestion of passion real and overwhelming. As though her lips and arms and body were independent of her more prudent intentions, she clung to him, helpless and unrestrained, savoring the touch of his hands as they slipped the loose garment from her shoulders. A small sound between a moan and a sigh was heard, but Julia was not sure which of them had uttered it as his lips moved along her throat, then found the taut and welcoming pinkness of her breasts.

Eager and, of course, experienced hands undressed her quickly, then moved persuasively over her silken skin. Julia, lost in a cloud of untried and overpowering passion, savored each stroke, anticipated where his hands might go next, yet was again and again surprised as her desire to be wholly possessed by this dangerous, irresistible man enflamed her.

He did not even carry her to the bed. He lowered her to the hearth rug, making a pillow of her clothing for her head, and there, with an urgency of a desire too long restrained, he took her with a quick, stabbing pain that was instantly forgotten in the rush of sensation that consumed her. With murmured words of delight and desire, he moved over and within her, exciting wonderment, astonishment, and ardor that grew in a rhythmic ascension until, like a thunderclap, they were swept to a crescendo of sensation in which they could only cling to each other, breathless, exultant, wonderstruck.

They remained coupled a long time when it was over, touching each other gently, reluctant to part, to leave the enchantment behind. At length, Julia stirred decisively, and when he had released her, she rose and went into the next room, avoiding the hand that would pull her back.

She got straight into the tub of now tepid water, savoring the coolness on her fevered flesh. With her hair draped and dangling over the back of the tub, she lay still, recovering her breath and reason, until she began to shiver.

As she was soaping herself, the door opened and Philip came in, still naked. Julia averted her eyes from him, noticing before she turned away that he smiled at her embarrassment.

"Come," he said. "You must be getting cold." He held out a hand and raised her from the water, wrapping her in a towel and holding her close to him. His lips found hers and he kissed her deeply, moving his mouth on hers in a gentle, persuasive insistence.

"Now, my beautiful Julia," he whispered, "I am going to make love to you properly."

He swept her, towel and all, into his arms and carried her into the bedroom. There he placed her gently on the bed and lay down beside her. With another long and searing kiss, he moved his hands over every inch of her, and where his hands had been, his lips soon followed. Julia, who had thought her passion squandered irreplaceably, soon found it returned tenfold, for now she knew what delight awaited her. She responded with sighs and burning kisses of her own, and her hands now ventured to touch him, caress him eagerly as he claimed her once again. Blue eyes burned into green, except when a special wave of sensation would cause first one pair, then the other to close, so the feeling might be savored before it retreated only to erupt again in rapture. Time and the world were suspended as they moved together, eyes locked, hands, bodies, even souls joined in an enterprise of ageless, exquisite wonder, until the moment came when the tumult and delirium overtook them again.

At last, released from the delicious torment, they fell asleep still closely wrapped in each other's arms.

Chapter Fourteen

As the feeble winter sunlight made an effort to brighten the room, Julia raised herself on her elbow and studied the man beside her. With his eyes closed, their green light hidden, with the lines of concentration erased by sleep, his face had a placid, almost innocent look. He stirred, as if in response to her gaze, and she lay back softly on her pillow, not wanting to wake him just yet, and contemplated the enormity of what she had done. In fact, it was strange now that she came to think of it, that she had not been awake all night contemplating it!

She had given herself willingly—no, eagerly, to a man she hardly knew and whom she should not trust. He was a notorious flirt and womanizer, and much much more disturbing, he was engaged in some dark enterprise which he would not explain. Something at least discreditable and more likely treasonous. With a silent groan, Julia stared at the white ceiling and reflected that she was not so different from her mother, after all.

But it is not too late for me, she told herself silently, firmly. *In spite of . . . of what has happened, I will not remain with him.*

Even as she resolved it, Philip sighed, opened his eyes and smiled into hers, then he reached to pull her toward him. Her determination evaporated as he kissed her deeply, as eagerly as the night before. He was murmuring her name softly and clasping the silky, silvery hair when the loud knock sounded on the bedroom door.

"It is Thomas," called a muffled voice. "You must wake up."

"Damn!" Philip swore as he drew away from her and reached for his trousers. Julia, after a moment's debate, snatched up her clothing and ran into the adjoining room.

She left the door open a crack and stayed nearby to hear what was said. She could not catch every word, but she heard Philip say, "You must take her to the house. Tell Mary . . ." Then the word "servants" and "my cousin must contrive it." She heard boot steps, then the closing of the door. When she went again into the bedroom, she found Philip pulling on his boots.

"I must go. And now, without delay."

A knot of apprehension lurched in Julia's stomach. "Why? Where are you going?"

He stood studying her for only an instant, then he shook his head. "Do as Thomas tells you. He will take you to a place where you will be safe. I will explain, truly I will, when I see you. It should not be long."

He hesitated, but did not come to embrace her.

He went through the door, drawing his coat on. Julia was alone.

A few minutes later, Tillie appeared with Julia's clothing but no breakfast. After an hour of speculation and waiting, there was a sudden knock, and Thomas came into the room.

"You must prepare yourself to depart, madam. I will return in ten minutes' time."

And he was gone again.

He returned with a dark, hooded cloak. When Julia had put it on, he led her down what must have been the back stairs, through a series of hallways and toward the door through which she had entered the previous night. They encountered no one from the household as they made their way. Only when they had stepped outside did she see Bobbit, coming down from the carriage he had driven to the steps. Bobbit helped Julia into the carriage, handed her a parcel and closed the door. Thomas, meanwhile, had climbed into the driver's box and in only a moment the carriage began to roll away.

It was dark inside the carriage, which was attired, she had noticed, in mourning draperies. She tried to peer through the black curtains, but they were fastened snugly top and bottom. One could tear them, of course, and she felt no compunction about doing that, when and if it might be useful to try to see where she was being taken.

The parcel proved to contain buttered bread, cheese and thick slices of ham, along with some lukewarm tea. Julia ate and drank and sat back to wonder where Philip might be and how soon she might see him again. If they had not been interrupted that morning . . . Julia found her thoughts wandering to the night before. In some ways, what had happened was all a dizzying blur, yet she could recall very clearly the sensations, the sense of bewitchment that had enveloped her from the moment he had taken her into his arms. In his arms was where she wished to be right now, and always, for better or for worse.

But did he love her? Julia's cautious and sensible nature reasserted itself after an absence of many hours. He had never said so through all those passionate kisses and caresses. He had murmured words, she recalled, but they had been of her beauty, her perfection, his surprise that she could so eagerly meet passion with passion. No. Julia was quite certain that he had not said he loved her. Had she said it? She must have, for she had certainly thought it.

With this to fret and puzzle her, Julia turned her thoughts to the carriage which was comfortable, well-fitted out, suitable for the nobleman whose coach it must be. Julia thought of the other time, not so very long ago, really, though it seemed a lifetime away, when she had ridden in a strange carriage to an unknown destination. What, she wondered, was happening at Fainway today?

Fainway. It had been so easy to picture life at Fainway—married to Lawrence, raising their children. But now, in one disastrous night, she had squandered her chance for that tranquility and gentle happiness. Good sense told her plainly, indisputably, that she must free herself from this dangerous affair which entangled her, while her instincts told her she would never be free of the man who stirred her passion, the madness which even now made her tingle and burn with the memory.

Julia judged that they must have been underway two hours or more when the carriage seemed to leave the road and in time came to a stop. Ducking and stretching to look through the curtains, she saw Thomas appear at the carriage window, and in a moment, the door was opened.

They were in a grassy spot screened by trees from where the road must be. As Julia was permitted to walk around and stretch herself, Thomas unhitched the horses from the front of the carriage, along with the pair which had been drawn along behind, and took them by twos to the stream to drink. Then the fresher horses were hitched to the front and they were ready to go on.

This leg of the journey was longer, three hours easily, perhaps four, and when the carriage stopped again in another secluded field, daylight was nearing an end. It had also become cold, with a freshening wind and threatening clouds gathering in the direction from which the wind was blowing. The horses were refreshed and changed again just as the first drops of rain began to fall, but the carriage remained in place for three quarters of an hour more. Only when darkness was most certainly falling did Julia, who had sought the protection of the carriage, feel the shift of weight as Thomas took his place, and they began to move again.

We must be nearing our destination, she told herself. *He cannot think to drive all night in this weather and in the darkness, too, for there is no moon tonight.* With the thought that this must be so, with the darkness too enveloping to see anything from the windows, and with the uneasy hope that Philip would be wherever she was going, she stretched her feet onto the opposite seat and waited for the journey to end.

It was the greatest surprise to find that she had dozed off. She awoke slowly, reluctantly, trying to snatch at the fragments of the dream she was leaving behind. Something was different, and she knew in an instant that it was the sound of the horses' hooves. It was no longer the soft plod of the road; they were on cobblestones. They must be in a village, perhaps even passing through a town.

Now she did tear at the curtains, and soon had freed a corner so that she could look out. But the darkness of the night was made more intense by the heavy pelting rain, and she was not able to make out much of what they were passing. There were lighted windows of what must be houses, even shops, but it might be any town (too extensive for a village), anywhere.

They clattered on for several minutes until the cobblestone sound gave way again to the soft plod of bare earth. Julia supposed they must be on the road again, but then realized that they had not regained speed. She looked out into the night and saw that they were passing what seemed to be a high wooden fence, glistening whitely in the rain. Now they turned, then stopped, and a moment later Thomas was helping her from the carriage.

They were at the back of a tall and narrow house; Julia forsook the protection of the hood to try to look around her, but she could see nothing helpful as she was hustled up a walk, up a flight of wooden stairs and into a kitchen which offered friendly smells of a dinner in preparation. They paused only briefly as Thomas held a whispered conversation with the tall, husky serving woman who had admitted them. Then Julia was taken by both Thomas and the woman up three flights of stairs and shown into a barren, narrow room.

And there she was left to stand in the darkness, for there was not a single stick of furniture in the room. She was locked in, too. She soon verified that the sound she had heard as the two had left the room was the key turning in the lock. She went to the window, grimy and small, to look out on the back garden, where in the darkness, she could just see the lightest of the four horses, still hitched to the carriage. As she watched, a light emerged from the back of the house and moved toward the animal.

The darkness and the cold were soon relieved. The woman came back with candles and kindling and quickly had a welcome fire blazing in the tiny fireplace. She went away again, locking the door each time she entered and left the room, returning with a brightly colored rug which was unrolled onto the floor, a round and spindly table, and bedclothing which she placed on the table. She then disappeared for a longer time, and when she returned, she was accompanied by Thomas, who brought boards, hammer and nails, which he used to cover the lower portion of the windows. Next he carried in a narrow bed with a feather mattress, a chair and finally a clothes tree. As he finished arranging these items around the room and waited for the woman to unlock the door for him, Julia noticed that his face was etched with weariness; it occurred to her that, while she and his master had dallied last night, Thomas had been on some errand that had kept him from his bed.

The bed was made, the fire replenished, and the woman murmured something about supper and left Julia alone. She took off the cloak and hung it on the chair to dry before the fire. So this, presumably, was to be her quarters for a time. And it looked as though she would not share them, for the bed was too narrow to accommodate even the most passionate and diminutive couple. She went to test it and found it of passing comfort. Next she had a look at the boarding of the windows. Though weary, Thomas had done a journeyman's job; she could not budge a single nail. Upon reflection, though, she decided that the purpose of the boarding was to keep anyone from seeing her rather than to keep her from looking out, for she was pretty certain that by standing on the chair, she would be able to see into the garden below.

"May I know your name?" she asked when the serving woman returned to lay out a meal on the spindly table, which was hardly up to the purpose.

"You may call me Mary, madam."

"Mary. Where am I? Where is Mr. Sommerville?"

"I cannot say, madam," the woman replied, leaving it uncertain whether the answer was to one or both of the two questions.

"How long am I to be here?"

The woman answered only with a shake of her head, then said, "You cannot ring, madam, for there is no bell. I will look in on you often and do what I can to make you comfortable. Those are my orders, madam."

"Perhaps, in that case, you will bring me something to read. A newspaper. I cannot sit here alone and idle, however long I may be required to stay."

"A newspaper will not be possible, madam, but I fancy there are a few books about."

"Books, then." Julia sighed.

"Yes, madam."

Julia washed her face and hands and sat down to the meal. It was tasty enough, but she had little appetite; she felt restless, vague, disoriented. The woman returned with a few books, removed the dinner tray and said "Good night, madam." Julia was left alone, presumably until morning. She had no idea of the time; her watch had been left behind in the haste of leaving Lord Wrayburn's house. She made a mental note to ask tomorrow for a clock.

After a few turns around the tiny room, a look through the books, and sitting for a few unsatisfactory minutes in the chair by the fire, Julia undressed and went to bed.

She woke to the sound of icy rain pelting at her window. What she could see of the sky through the portion of the window that was not boarded was leaden and uncompromising.

Well, if she was to be confined indoors, this was the very day for it.

She got out of bed and, holding the blanket around her for warmth, stood on the chair to look out the window. She was just in time to see Thomas complete the hitching of the horses to the carriage that had brought her. As she stood watching, he climbed aboard and drove off, whether to rendezvous with his master or to return the carriage to Lord Wrayburn, she could only speculate.

The day was spent with the books at her disposal, punctuated by the arrival and consuming of three meals. Julia asked Mary where Thomas went with the carriage but got no satisfaction.

"I cannot say, madam," was the same aggravating reply.

When darkness fell, Julia was forced to admit to herself that she had been hoping, expecting some word of or from Philip. She treated her disappointment by assuring herself that it was too early for such a thing to be practicable. And it was such a wretched day for travel of any sort; poor Thomas must have been quite drenched on his journey, wherever it took him. No doubt she would hear, or very likely even see Philip tomorrow or the next day at the latest.

But she did not. The second and the third day of her confinement were just the same as the first, except for slight differences in the intensity of the rain and the composition of the menu and the heightening of her anxiety and resentment that she had been left so long with no word of Philip's safety, no clue as to what she might expect from the man. When the sixth day had passed, her apprehension was steadily replaced by frustration that was growing into a cold bitter anger.

He had no right to embroil her in—in whatever devious business he was about! No right to keep her there so that she would be handy for whenever he wanted her!

In this solitary place, away from his eyes, his lips and his arms, away from the magic of their night of passion, she could see the entire encounter as the wanton and irrational act it had been. And she could see very clearly that she had, for a certainty, been the worst kind of fool.

* * *

As he closed the door against the windy night, Lawrence inhaled the air of the tavern. It was a little thick from the pipe smoke of the elderly men who sat lingering over nearly empty tankards. This wasn't, he decided, an establishment where the elegant gentlemen of Leeds would be found. Certainly nothing like the strictly private and proper gentlemen's club where he went of an evening in London. Still, it seemed a respectable place, and even a friendly one.

This was where he had been told to come and wait. He looked around for a place to sit and noticed that three young men—students, he expected—were just getting up from a table at the back of the room. He stood waiting while the barmaid cleared the debris from its surface, then sat and ordered a pint of ale.

The man he was especially interested in sat a few tables away, sipping slowly now and then, pretending to listen to the conversation of his table mates, but lost, it seemed, in thoughts of his own. They must have been thoughts of a stimulating nature, for his face wore an expression of quiet excitement, even exultation. Now something was said that made the man laugh out loud, and Lawrence listened carefully to that voice as the man made a loud remark to his companions.

For half an hour Lawrence sat in the tavern, sipping from his tankard, speaking to no one. The man who had drawn him to this place rose, along with his friends, and departed; a couple of other groups of patrons also went out into the wind and darkness, struggling each time the door was opened to keep it from slamming back against the wall.

Lawrence finished his ale, ordered another and continued to sit patiently. When he had been nearly an hour in the smoke and din of the tavern, he heard a soft voice speak behind him.

"Do not show surprise when I sit down with you. Just behave as though you have been expecting me."

Lawrence nodded, and the man came around into his field of vision and sat down across from him.

"Sommerville!" Lawrence caught himself just in time and managed to say the name in a normal tone.

"Good evening, Mr. Christian." Philip's eyes held no expression. "I take it you *are* surprised to see me."

"I confess I am."

"I trust the arrangements have been to your liking?"

"A private carriage, and a very fine one, too. The accommodations are not stellar, but I understand they are the best the city has to offer. I have nothing to complain of."

"Except, of course, the loss of your time. But I hope to keep that to a minimum. You have recognized the gentleman?"

"I have. It is the same man I saw and sketched. Also, I have heard him speak and he is not their leader."

Philip sat back with a sigh. "You have keen eyes and ears, Mr. Christian. I am grateful for your help. Others will be, too."

"Perhaps it was the younger one. The one with the limp."

"Perhaps."

"Who is he?" Lawrence asked with a discreet nod in the direction of the table where the loud-voiced man had sat.

"His name is Harkins. He is a minor official at a firm here in the city."

Lawrence nodded thoughtfully. "It *is* very often those in a position of not quite enough authority who become disaffected. And the other one? The one I followed to the lodging house?"

"Ah. Mr. Davis. That one we found without difficulty, thanks to you. He, unfortunately, has a high-pitched and rather grating voice. Not the mellow tones you described." Philip waited until the barmaid had served him a tankard, then said, "I expect you will be leaving in the morning, then?"

"I needn't, if you have further use for me."

"I thank you, but it is doubtful. And I cannot think it right that we keep you away from Fainway. I know you are concerned for your cousin's safety. Had there been any news at the time of your departure?"

"None, sir, I regret to say. But surely your successful conclusion of this business will bring some result."

Philip shook his head. "I regret, Christian, that I cannot say with assurance that these are Bellwether's men."

"What? But then who. . . ."

"Their goal, however, is equally evil and, in my judgment, they are far more dangerous than this mythical old criminal."

"But—but do you mean to say that they do not have Miss Townes? Or know where she is?"

"I fear that may be so. I had thought there would have been a ransom demand made by now. Would her father pay it, do you think?"

Lawrence stood up suddenly. "I *will* be leaving in the morning. Good night, Sommerville. And good luck."

Philip sat alone in the tavern for another quarter of an hour, slumping wearily in the hard chair, sipping slowly from his tankard of ale and thinking of Julia. Then he rose, drew his coat around him and went out into the bluster of the night, to make his way to the house where Mr. Harkins dwelled to keep watch until morning.

By the following afternoon the storm had passed and the weather had brightened. As the late-afternoon show of sunshine was near the point of fading into twilight, Philip hurried along a quiet street of large houses, once grand, now fallen on shabbier times. At a particular house which displayed a sign that there were rooms to be let, he turned and went in the direction of the back kitchen. He tapped softly, and in a moment the door was opened.

"He should be coming soon," he said to the woman who admitted him.

"I'll put the kettle on, then." She hurried toward the scullery. "He will like to have tea brought."

"I think we may see something tonight. Harkins spoke to each of them at some time today. Except, of course, the one in York."

"Perhaps they have written," the woman said hopefully. "He may come, too."

"Perhaps." Philip sat down with a sigh and took

285

the cup of tea she gave him. "Harkins received a couple of letters today." He gave her a weary smile. "It is almost too much to hope for."

Thomas came in from the main part of the house. "Davis has just turned the corner."

Philip took a large gulp of the tea and stood up. "Then we had best have a last look at your preparations."

The two men left the kitchen and went up the stairs, along a bare hallway and into a room that faced the back of the house. Once inside they crossed to the wall which divided the room from its neighbor next door. Thomas lifted the washstand and placed it away from the wall, then removed the mirror which hung above it, revealing a large hole in the plaster and the back of another mirror.

"I have fastened the mirror on his side so that it can't be moved," Thomas whispered, "but it is not so close against the wall that we cannot hear."

"Very good."

The two men leaned their shoulders on the wall on either side of the opening, and in a moment, they heard the key turn in the lock of the room next door, and the sound of the door being opened. Next came the quiet rustlings of an outer coat being removed and hung in the wardrobe, and boots being exchanged for soft shoes. Then another tap on the door.

"Come in," came the call, in a high-pitched voice.

"I'll just get the fire started for you, sir," came the voice of the serving woman.

"Thank you, Lizzie. The service has improved very much since you came."

"Thank you, sir. If you are pleased, perhaps you would say a word to Mrs. Allen. And for my boy, too."

"I will do that. Ah, tea. Thank you again."

Soon there was a cheerful crackling of the kindled fire.

"Oh, Lizzie."

"Yes, sir."

"Some gentlemen will be coming here again tonight. There will be three at least. Perhaps four. Will you be good enough to have your son fetch some ale?"

"Yes, sir. Will you be wanting it at the usual time?"

"Around nine."

"Yes, sir. Supper will be ready in half an hour. You will be alone, I fear, except for Mrs. Allen. Mr. Dobbs has not come back from York."

"Ah, well. More supper for me, less work for you, Lizzie. We must take advantage of it while we can. I doubt the other rooms will be vacant much longer."

"No, sir. I understand from Mrs. Allen that two already are rented, but the people are not expected until next week."

"I hope they will be agreeable tenants, Lizzie. I've seen a number of undesirable people come and go in my three years here."

"Yes, sir. I hope so, I'm sure."

The door opened and closed again. Philip and Thomas stood up but did not speak or move away from the wall until they heard the man in the room leave to go down to his supper.

"I will bring them, Thomas. It will be up to you

to delay him if he shows any wish to hurry back here before we are ready."

"Yes, sir."

The magistrate was a portly man, and with a tendency to wheeze; Philip had grave second thoughts as he showed him hurriedly, as quietly as possible, into the room. The third man in the party, Mr. Porter, a respected manufacturer, was lean and sound of wind. Philip wished again that he could have done this with the help of only Mr. Porter, whom he had long known and trusted, but, of course, some local official must be present, and London thought the magistrate reliable.

Inside the room, shuttered and illuminated by a single candle in the most distant corner, Philip showed them where they would stand at the opening in the wall.

"Unless the fifth man comes," he told them, "it is not likely that we will hear precisely what they plan."

"And if he does come?" Mr. Porter asked.

"If we hear absolutely that they plan an attempt on the queen, and if all of them are present, we shall arrest them without delay."

"We should have brought constables," said the magistrate.

"We cannot risk having them seen here, sir," Philip told him. "This may be just another ordinary meeting where our friends rail to each other of the injustices they have suffered." Then, with another warning that absolute silence must be observed, Philip took his place between his companions, and they settled down to wait.

Twenty minutes had passed when the door of the

adjoining room was opened. There was a scuffling as a table was dragged away from the wall, chairs put in place. Then there was silence for nearly half an hour, except for the turning of the pages of a newspaper. Philip watched the faces of his companions as best he could in the dim flickering light, fearing any sound from them might end his most elaborate plan.

Finally they heard a long awaited tap on the door; it opened. Thomas's voice came to them faintly, "Two gentlemen, sir."

"Come in, come in. Thank you, Samuel."

"Yes, sir," Thomas was heard to say, then the door closed again.

"Who *is* that fellow, Davis?" came a gruff voice.

"Son of the new serving woman."

"Enormous beggar, isn't he?" said another voice, a flat tenor.

"And not especially intelligent, I fancy," Davis said, "but a handy one if there's a bit of lifting to be done. My gracious landlady takes full advantage of that, I can tell you."

Now there came a second tap on the door; Thomas was again heard to announce, "A gentleman, sir."

The door closed again, and there was no sound from the room until long moments had passed.

"Is he coming?" It was Davis's voice.

"No," came the voice Lawrence had heard in the tavern, rather louder than any of the others who had spoken. "He dare not risk it now."

Philip and his companions exchanged glances in the dim light.

"But. . . ." came the tenor.

"It does not signify," Harkins spoke again. "The

plan is settled. He will do it alone."

"Impossible!" Davis cried. "It will take all of us. She is very well guarded."

"Do not say so until you have heard the plan," Harkins said. "All of us are willing to die in this cause, but if it takes only one death, so much the better. The rest of us will be left to continue the struggle, to savor that day when the yoke of the monarchy is lifted from the necks of the people!"

Harkins's voice had risen in excitement; it held a note of hysteria, even of madness, and the three men who listened in the darkness shook their heads at each other in silence. Then came the urgings of Harkins's companions that he speak more softly.

"He has determined that it is to be done at the coronation," Harkins went on in a quieter tone. "It is a splendid plan—elegant and simple. And since it will need only a single shot, he may even manage to escape in the confusion."

Amid the murmurs that greeted this statement, Philip saw to his horror that Mr. Porter was struggling to stifle a cough. He put a hand out to touch the man, who had covered his mouth and was shaking all over with his efforts. Philip, signaling quiet, began to lead him on tiptoe to the far corner of the room.

But luck was not with him. As they crept in the flickering dimness of the room, Mr. Porter's foot struck the frame of the iron bed. To his credit, he did not cry out, but the sound of the impact resounded in the silence.

"What was that?" the magistrate, still at his post, heard the cry and the unmistakable scufflings in the next room, footsteps stomping, the door jerked hurriedly open.

In the next instant, Harkins stood in the doorway, the candle in his one hand illuminating the room. The first thing Harkins saw was the magistrate at the listening post. With a shouted oath, he raised the pistol in his other hand to fire.

Leaping from the darkness into the candlelight, Philip caught Harkins's arm, wrenching it in a quick twist, releasing the pistol and sending it clattering to the floor. The magistrate and Davis flung themselves toward it in the same instant.

A clatter of boots announced Thomas's arrival from his post on the stairs just as Philip, with one fierce and well-placed blow, sent Harkins to the floor. He landed with a heavy crash and lay still.

Mr. Porter, coming to his senses, seemed uncertain where to pit his efforts, then moved to assist Thomas, who had just seized the other two men together in his enormous arms. Philip had already moved in the same direction. The magistrate, left to struggle alone with Davis, found his quarry wriggling out of his grasp. He called out.

But it was too late. Davis had recovered the pistol; without rising from the floor where he knelt, he fired a shot into the heart of the prostrate Harkins. In a flash, Philip and Thomas were lunging toward Davis. Another shot rang deafeningly, this time from behind them. Philip felt a searing pain as the bullet tore his flesh. He and his servant fell together onto the bare wooden floor, and fresh blood soon mingled with the pool spreading from Harkins's body.

I must simply face the truth, Julia told herself again. *Philip Sommerville views me only as another of his conquests. Otherwise he would not leave me*

*here day after day with no idea why or for how long.
Without explanation, without assurance of his—his
intentions. With barely a word of good-bye. The
more I think on it, the more implausable, the more
insane the entire business becomes. And this foolish
woman who is my jailer will not have sense enough
to judge for herself when I have been kept beyond
reason, even should it take a year. Or ten. "I cannot
say, madam!" She will go on bleating those words at
me until kingdom come, unless Philip comes first.
Or Thomas.*

But there had been no sign of Thomas since he
had disappeared with the carriage many days ago.
Julia dragged the chair once more to the window
and looked out into the world that was denied her.
It was an unpromising sight, as always. A dreary
back garden led to a stable. A fence and trees
bounded what seemed to be the property line and
beyond, more trees, and, she thought, a rooftop.
Another house. Humanity. Rescue? Julia stared
thoughtfully at several ravens sitting in the tree
near her window, including one perched, hawklike,
in the very top. In that moment came the final
resolve that she must find a way to escape.

I must get home! she vowed. And again when she
said "home," she meant Fainway.

Julia was staring into the fire when Mary came
into the room with the midday meal.

"Mary, I must have employment of some sort.
You must bring me materials for needlework."

Mary looked doubtful. "What sort of needlework
would you be meaning, madam?"

"Anything! Petit point. Tapestry. Knitting. I will
even mend the kitchen towels! Please, Mary, I shall

go quite mad if I have another day of nothing to do."

"Yes, madam. I will see what might be done about it."

That very afternoon Mary brought a sewing basket, quite a large one. It was well-fitted out with needles, pins, threads of many colors, patterns to embroider and a tiny pair of silver scissors. Julia fingered the scissors thoughtfully. As a weapon they held little promise, but Julia, who had had the entire day to think about it, was beginning to see the glimmerings of a plan.

She had usually been up and even dressed when Mary brought breakfast, but the next morning she remained in bed, only lifting her face from the pillow where it was buried when she heard the door open. Mary stood as usual, cautiously, in the doorway, peering in to be sure that all was in order before lifting the breakfast tray from the table just outside the door and carrying it in, locking the door behind her.

"Are you not feeling well, madam?"

"I cannot say that I am ill, precisely," Julia replied. "But there is precious little to draw one out of bed."

"Just so, madam. I have found another book, madam."

"Thank you. I rather think I should like to have the tray brought to bed, Mary. It will be more comfortable to remain here until the room is warmer."

Mary placed the tray on Julia's knees and went about her morning duties without further conversation. Julia sipped the tea and made a point to sniff once or twice before producing a quite authentic-sounding sneeze for Mary's benefit.

"Oh, are you taking cold, do you think, madam?"

"Certainly not. I never have colds." Julia blew her nose.

"There now. That's very lucky, that is. All the same, I'll build up the fire a little more. It is a perishing cold morning."

"I'm quite all right." Julia's voice was low and grumpy.

"Mmm," was Mary's knowing reply, and she did make it a point to look in on the fire more often than usual during the course of the day. During the first two of those visits, Julia made a great show of being at work on her embroidery near the fire, but when dinner was brought at the end of the day, she had returned to bed, and she asked for a few more handkerchiefs.

"I brought a little whiskey, madam," Mary said when she returned with the requested handkerchiefs. "It will help you to sleep better."

"I cannot understand this." Now Julia's voice was a self-pitying whine. "I have not had a single cold since my childhood." She put a hand to her forehead. "I wonder if I have taken a fever."

Mary placed a hand on Julia's face with an air of great experience. "I don't think so, madam. But you must stay in bed and keep very warm. Perhaps it is just a slight indisposition that will be gone by morning."

"Yes," came the listless reply. "Of course, it must be, for I am never ill."

"I will leave extra water and a bit more whiskey

for the night. And perhaps I'd best bring another blanket, too." Mary hurried off on these errands, almost forgetting to lock the door, then remembering just in time. Julia heard the lock turn and punctuated its sound with another sneeze.

Julia did not drink the whiskey. She would need her wits about her this night more than any of her life. When the dinner tray was collected and the fire made up for the night, Julia tucked the pieces of bread she had hidden under her pillow into one of the handkerchiefs. She would save this nourishment for the morning. She waited until the sounds of all activity in the house had ceased (she still was not certain whether there was anyone else besides the woman, but she thought not) before she left the bed and took the candle to sit by the fire.

She placed the sewing basket on her knees. As she gazed at it, she thought of another sewing basket, so beautifully and lovingly made, so different from this utilitarian object she held. Frances was very much on her mind as she took out the embroidery scissors and, a few strands at a time, began to cut her hair.

It took nearly two hours, and her hands were sore and stiff, but when she finished, she had a thick swatch of pale blond strands about five inches long. She placed it on the table in front of her, lit a fresh candle and began to form a braid. After another hour she had fashioned, by dividing the hair in half and braiding it together lengthwise, a respectable-looking braid which she tied with the large blue ribbon she had worn for the past several days.

Next, by the flickering candlelight, for the fire was quite dead, she spent most of the following hour preparing the bed, rolling, unrolling and rolling again, bunching and twisting the extra blankets Mary had brought. At length she had an arrangement she thought would pass muster. She brought the braid and laid it on the pillow, covering the whole arrangement with an artistic draping of the top blanket. She carried the candle to the bed to study the effect with great care. When she was satisfied, she turned her attention to the clothes tree.

She nudged it very slightly, to be sure that it would be seen first when the door was opened in the morning. The lavender dress was hung in prominent view, the shoes with their stockings also were displayed on the floor below where the dress hung. This left only the shawl to be placed with the other things at the last minute. Julia went next to the washstand, lifted the water pitcher, stood as though judging its heft, then carried it to place it in just the right spot by the door.

The clock she had been provided now said that it was half past four in the morning. It would be half past eight before Mary would reappear with breakfast. With only the shawl for warmth, Julia sat down in the chair and remained shivering to wait for the hours to pass.

When her head jerked back with a painful snap, Julia knew that she had fallen asleep. Blinking and rubbing her shoulder, she looked at the top portion of the windows and was elated and a little frightened to see that the late winter morning was arriving. Now there could be no hesitation, no second guesses, no regrets. The clock said a quarter to eight. She had best get ready.

After flicking a little of the icy water in the wash basin on her face, she ate the bread she had saved from last night's dinner, then checked her preparations a final time. Finally, reluctantly, she removed the shawl, placed her slippers by the bed and went to stand by the door where she had placed the water pitcher.

She was none too soon. She had not had more than five minutes to shiver when she heard Mary's heavy tread on the stair. There was a rattle of crockery as the tray was placed on the table outside the door. Quietly, stealthily, Julia lifted the pitcher. The key was placed in the lock. The door opened, and it seemed to be a less cautious operation than usual. Standing unseen behind the open door, Julia knew that Mary was looking round the room, insuring that nothing was amiss before she entered. Julia kept her own eyes trained on the edge of the door, not allowing herself to turn for a reassuring glance at the deception on the bed. It seemed to Julia that she stood for an eternity, waiting, gripping the pitcher, forcing herself not to breathe or shiver, not permitting her teeth to chatter with the cold and the sheer intensity of this frozen instant in time. On the other side of the door was the sound of Mary's labored breath and, to Julia's dismay, a little cluck of sympathy for the sick young woman who was too unwell to rise from her bed.

The tray was settled on the table just inside the door; Julia heard it placed there with a reassuring rattle, and then, at last, Mary's large and solid form moved into the room.

Julia had to move fast, for the first thing Mary would do was to turn to the door to lock it as usual.

In fact, the movement had already started, when Julia struck with all her strength, bringing the pitcher down on Mary's head. Without even a cry of surprise, Mary went sprawling in an unseemly heap onto the floor. In an instant, Julia was out of the room and running heedlessly down the stairs. She had dismissed any thought of trying to escape unnoticed; if there was another person in the household, especially if it were a man, she would face certain capture. She must simply take her chances.

But no one stirred or called out as she clattered down the stairs, first one flight, then the next. She went directly to the back of the house, the way she had come in, the way she knew there was at least one more dwelling where she might go for assistance. She flew past the kitchen, not even turning to see if it was occupied.

The back door was locked! It would be. But the key was in the lock, hidden beneath the white curtain that hung over it. Julia turned it frantically, ineffectually, until she paused, took a breath and reversed the direction. A moment later she was out the door and running to the fence beyond the stable. From the corner of her eye she could see now that there were houses on both sides which had not been visible from her vantage point.

Now she was again in the alley; she had already decided that she would run in the direction from which she had come to this house. She knew that houses and stores lay in that direction. She cried out in pain as her bare toe struck a rock in the alleyway, but still she did not stop. She could see the point now where the alley crossed with a street;

even as she ran she saw a roughly dressed man hurrying to his work. Perhaps as a gardener, for there were, indeed, houses all around.

She came into the street. Here, of course, she must turn in the direction away from the street on which the house where she had been confined must front. She had already made the turn and was searching with her eyes for the most likely place to appeal for help. And then she slowed her pace, and looked around more closely.

This . . . Surely there was something familiar about the house on this corner. About the two houses that faced each other. It was impossible, of course, but—no! It was not impossible! There was the milliner's shop. And the bakery with its wonderful smell of fresh bread and buns. And there, too, was the fishmonger.

My God! Julia came to an abrupt halt in the street. She was in York!

There was no question now as to where she would go. She began to run again, barefoot and barely clad, to the astonishment of those merchants opening their shops. She flew past the church which still sat, as she had always thought, in silent disapproval of the ale house just opposite. There were a few more people on the street now, some turned to stare, some started toward her, as though to offer their help; others, too occupied with their own concerns or perhaps still too recently awake to comprehend fully, did not see her until she had galloped by them.

On now, past Mrs. Tuttle's store. A final corner to be turned, only a few yards more. She rushed up the familiar steps, pushed open the heavy oak doors, thundered gasping past a group of gentlemen in animated discussion of some news in their paper. She dashed past the counter, through a gate, another door, and straight into the arms of the astonished Robert Woodland.

Chapter Fifteen

"I'm sorry to say, Miss Townes, that there was no sign of the woman, this Mary, when the constables arrived at the house."

"I don't understand! It seemed as I was running away that it must have been the house across the street from Mrs. Ponder where I was held. I am sorry if I have misdirected the officers."

"Not at all." Robert smiled down at her as he held out his hand. "This was found in the garret room where you most certainly were imprisoned."

Julia took the braid of silvery hair, still tied with the blue ribbon. "You mean, then, that the woman had simply left the house?"

"And in quite a hurry, too. A pie was found in the oven, not even much overcooked."

Julia rested her head on the high back of the deep leather chair and sighed as she looked at Robert. His honest, kindly face invited her to tell him everything, tempted her to name names, to give clarity and sense to events that must seem little short of incredible. But she could not. Some latent sense of self-preservation, of caution, of some instinct she could not even quite identify, held her back. She wriggled her bruised and bleeding feet in the pan of soothing warm water that sat on the expensive carpet of Robert's office, and huddled more deeply into his overcoat which had been provided to cover the thin nightgown which she wore.

"But you must not despair, Miss Townes. I have good reason to believe that she will soon be apprehended. There is very welcome news in this morning's paper, you see." He handed her a folded newspaper. "When you are feeling more yourself, you may read the entire account. For now I will simply tell you that a band of traitors, no doubt the very persons responsible for your abduction, have been captured."

"What?" Julia sat up straight, her mouth open in surprise, and feeling a strange sense of panic. "Captured when? Where?"

"Not very far from here, which is reasonable, in light of what has happened to you. They were apprehended the day before yesterday in Leeds. They are being taken to London for trial."

"Leeds. Yes, I see." Julia was every bit as surprised as Robert to discover that tears had begun coursing down her cheeks. Robert handed her a handkerchief.

"I am not at all surprised to see your relief manifested in this way," he said kindly. "What a dreadful ordeal you have been through."

Julia managed to thank him, but she could say no

more for several minutes as she struggled against the pain and horror that had gripped her heart. Philip had been captured! That was why he had not come for her.

She sat huddled in the chair, now and then wiping at tears that refused to stop, until Mrs. Woodland and Miss Pierce arrived. Julia had to sit up and respond suitably to their unremitting exclamations of shock and distress at her appearance, her shortened and untidy hair, her scanty attire, the very idea of her progress through the streets of the city in such a state! At length, however, their gasps and clucks faltered, and Julia was taken in a hired carriage to the Woodland home, still clutching the newspaper and the poor pitiful braid that Robert had handed to her.

Julia was given breakfast and a bath and clean clothing, including a pair of slippers to warm her aching feet. When she had dried and even managed to arrange her hair into some sort of coiffure, she presented herself to the justice of the peace, who waited for her in the Woodland drawing room.

"You must forgive me, ma'am," said Major Forbisher, "if I sometimes forget myself and call you Miss Forrest. Dear me, such a lot of things have happened since, well, since last we met."

"I understand, sir, and there is no call for forgiveness. Indeed, I recall with fondness the days I bore that name."

"Yes, well. You must not fear, my dear Miss, er, Townes. Your good father shall be informed without delay of your safety. Then we must see about getting you home to him, now that this dreadful gang is at last in custody."

Julia, wishing to avoid as many questions as

possible, asked, "Major Forbisher, were you present at the capture?"

"Well, no. Not present. Certainly not, though there *was* a magistrate who figured prominently in the actual arrest." He stood a little straighter in this reflected glory of his office. "It seems there had been quite a lengthy investigation of these persons by a certain gentleman, empowered by the government and with the sanction of Her Majesty when she ascended to the crown."

"Indeed?"

"It seems he was assisted by his own servant and by a woman, too, according to the papers. Most extraordinary. One of them, unfortunately, is dead. Killed by one of the villains."

"Oh!" Julia barely stifled the scream that almost escaped. Had Philip done this, too? Had he killed a man?

"Not many details are known just yet, but I daresay all will be revealed in good time."

"Have the persons who were arrested been identified?" Julia could barely manage to whisper the question.

"Not yet. When they are brought to court in London, no doubt all will be known. Now, Miss Townes, I know that you are very tired, but if you can just tell me, as best you can, how you came to be taken and brought to this place? I must report with some detail, you see."

Julia put her wrist to her head in a gesture of weakness she did not feel, and said faintly, "I believe I have lost track of time, Major Forbisher, but I calculate that I have been here, without knowing where, for some ten days."

"Ten days. Only fancy," said Mrs. Woodland, who was sitting nearby as chaperone.

"And did you see no one but the woman in that time?"

"Just the woman. Except for the man who brought me here. And I saw little of him." Julia looked very seriously at the justice, then glanced meaningfully at Mrs. Woodland. "There were others as well, but I cannot describe them to you either."

Both Julia and the major heard the disappointed tsking from Mrs. Woodland. He looked at Julia with perfect understanding and said that he was satisfied. "But if anything does occur to you, perhaps you will be good enough to send for me, or make note of it for the authorities in London."

"Yes, certainly."

Robert now came into the room, carrying the day's newspaper. "Major Forbisher, I have decided, with your consent, of course, to take Miss Townes to Winderfields. There is now said to be one other of these traitors who was not captured, and who is believed to be here in York. I do not feel I can rightfully leave her here in these circumstances."

"Hmm," said the justice doubtfully.

"By a previous arrangement, Sir William's carriage will arrive this very evening to take me to Winderfields tomorrow. I am required to spend ten days, perhaps a fortnight there." He looked at Julia. "I trust for the final time. I propose that Miss Townes accompany me"—he cast a look at Mrs. Woodland—"and my mother. Sir William will have no objection, I can assure you."

After a long and thoughtful pause, Major

Forbisher inquired, "What do you say to this, Miss Townes?"

"Oh, yes! I should like to go to Sir William's. Please!"

So it was done. A special messenger was dispatched by Robert to inform Charles that his daughter might be claimed from Winderfields, and, if it was inconvenient to come or to send for her, Robert and Mrs. Woodland, of course would be honored to bring her home to Fainway themselves as soon as the business with Sir William was concluded.

Major Forbisher departed and was replaced by Mrs. Carter and two of her best seamstresses, summoned and paid for by Robert, to fashion garments for Julia. The lavender dress brought from the house where she had been held Julia could not bear to put on. The curate who assisted the Reverend Mr. Simmons (Mr. Simmons being indisposed or he would, Julia had no doubt, have paid his respects to the newly prosperous Miss Townes) had obligingly taken it away for donation to the poor. By dinner time Julia had been supplied with a plain, but serviceable, warm green dress, with another of deep blue-black promised for delivery before the departure on the morrow for Winderfields.

Julia went to bed in the ornately furnished guest room of the Woodland house as soon as she could excuse herself without overt rudeness. Huddling beneath the covers, she gave way to the tension and terrors that had stung and prodded her all through this incredible day.

Philip was captured! He had not come for her, had sent no word because he could not. He was on his way to imprisonment in London, to await whatever fate the justice of the kingdom might deliver to him. And, of course, it must be death. Treason was punishable by death, even if he had not been the one who had killed one of his captors.

An audible sob of desperation escaped her as she thought of never seeing him again. That tall, graceful, heartbreakingly handsome man—never to move again through the rooms or grounds of Winterhall or Fainway, or, for that matter, through the streets of London or the camps of the gypsies. To think that those green, mysterious eyes would never blaze into hers with the fires of passion that had so engulfed her, that she would never again be held by those arms, caressed by those strong, possessive, knowing hands . . . She buried her face in her pillow and lay awake, in dry-eyed and bitter hopelessness through the long, unfriendly night.

Julia was already waiting in the entry hall when the carriage was brought to the front door. The second new dress and the few personal things she had acquired the previous day from the nearby shops were packed in the small portmanteau that sat at her feet.

"How could I ever have imagined myself living in this house?" she whispered to her reflection in the mirror that hung by the door. But there was no reply from the pale, sad girl looking back as she straightened the rather becoming and fashionable hat which Mrs. Woodland had insisted she accept as a gift.

Poor Mrs. Woodland. She still did not like Julia, still would prefer that her son marry Miss Pierce, but Julia was presumably a woman of some wealth now which certainly created a puzzling dilemma for Mrs. Woodland.

Robert came down the stairs. "Good morning, Julia. I hope you have slept well."

"Good morning, Robert. Thank you. I was most comfortable, indeed."

His kind gray eyes were concerned as he observed her drawn and weary face. Julia was only saved from further inquiries about her welfare by the arrival of her hostess, who was followed by a maid and two stout serving men laden with trunks.

Robert exchanged an amused look with Julia, then led both ladies out to the carriage.

"Good morning . . . Chester, isn't it?" Robert called to the coachman.

"Yes, sir. Good morning. Good morning, madam." He bowed to both ladies.

"But where is MacKenzie? Not ill, I hope?"

Chester adopted an attitude of reverent sadness. "Died this Wednesday fortnight, sir."

"What! Died, you say? You do surprise me, for I declare I have never seen a heartier man."

"Died in his sleep, sir," Chester said with relish for his role of conveyer of important bad news. "Found him myself, looking just as peaceful as a sleeping man can. Must have been his heart, sir, attacking sudden-like, for, as you observe, sir, he was a healthy one." The coachman cast a respectful look at the ladies to be certain he had not unduly shocked these sensitive creatures, then said cheerfully, "God rest his soul, I'm sure."

"Yes." Robert held out his arm to his mother. "Well, as I trust you were informed last evening, the ladies will be accompanying me to Winderfields."

"Yes, sir. Mr. Crowe told me, sir. I've taken it upon myself to hire a pair of extra horses." Chester cast an unsubtle glance at the girth of Mrs. Woodland, then, under her outraged eye, explained hastily, "It will be a quicker trip that way, sir, and not so tiring for the ladies."

"Well done, Chester. Let us be off."

The journey began, and a tedious one it was. Outside was a dull late January drizzle and fog, and inside, the intruding presence of Mrs. Woodland stifled whatever spontaneous and comforting conversation Julia might otherwise have enjoyed with the kind friend who now sat quietly beside her. But the inevitable exhaustion of two sleepless nights took its toll, and Julia dozed restlessly from time to time, lulled by the motion of the carriage, then awakened by the beginning of a dream too disturbing to examine. Once she was aware that she had actually cried out, for Robert was holding her hand and speaking to her soothingly when she opened her eyes. Even Mrs. Woodland's face took on a look of concern.

But on they rode, away from York, whose familiar streets and neighborhoods Julia had barely glimpsed on this very peculiar return to what had so long been her home. Toward safety, friendship, shelter, and then, soon she hoped, she would be going home to Fainway.

There were a few minutes of daylight remaining when the carriage rumbled through the gates of Winderfields. Julia was able to observe something of the drive and the park of this fabled place that had been so much on the minds of all her connections less than a year ago. From what she could see of the grounds and the house, Winderfields was not so fine a place as Fainway, and certainly nothing to compare with the vastness of Winterhall. Winterhall! With this thought came a pang of something beyond pain, beyond understanding.

The carriage stopped and they alighted. A servant, presumably the butler, hurried down the imposing steps to draw Robert aside. They were entering the massive front door, where Mrs. Woodland, from her experience of one previous visit, was exclaiming to Julia about the elegance and fineness of the house. But she fell silent when her son approached with a shocked and ashen face to announce that he had just been informed that Miss Sennett had died that very morning.

Robert hurried off to find Sir William. The ladies, stunned and quiet, were shown into the drawing room and given tea. Mrs. Woodland detained the housekeeper to explain all the details of the unhappy circumstances.

"She was quite ill all the day yesterday, madam," Mrs. Ferguson said. "The old trouble, of course, that had bothered her off and on since she was a girl, I am told."

"Was her stay in Bath of no benefit to her?" asked Julia, declining the plate of cakes the housekeeper was holding out to her.

"Oh, yes, madam. She returned from her stay in Bath much improved, we all thought. Sir William was most encouraged. But in the last couple of weeks the trouble had returned, slowly at first, and she had some good days when she was not bothered at all. Then yesterday she was taken so badly. The pains in her poor stomach were something fearsome, and she was so pale and shaking all the day. Even the compound she set such store by, given to her by a lady in the south, had no effect. The pains grew worse and worse."

"Poor soul," said Mrs. Woodland, and helped herself to another teacake.

"It *is* so very sad, madam. She was a dear, kind lady, and it seemed that she was finally finding true contentment since Sir William came." At Mrs. Woodland's sudden glance, the housekeeper decided she had, perhaps, been too forthcoming. "You'll be wanting to see her, I expect, madam. We've nearly finished laying her out, and as soon as Sir William has been to see that all is to his satisfaction, I will inform you."

Mrs. Woodland, had she been able to swallow her cake in time, would have said more, but Julia nodded to the housekeeper and said, "Thank you," and the good lady left the room.

"I thought so!" Mrs. Woodland exclaimed as she put down her teacup. "I told Robert weeks ago I felt sure they would soon marry. He did not believe it, of course. Men never see what is plainly before them where such things are concerned."

"I should have said that Mr. Woodland is more perceptive than most men in such matters."

"But he is still a man, my dear. Oh, poor Sir William! To have lost his love so soon again after . . ." Mrs. Woodland shifted awkwardly in her chair. "Poor man. Tragedy *does* so often dog the footsteps of the most worthy of us, Miss Townes."

Robert now rejoined them.

"I have explained to Sir William how I came to arrive with additional guests," he said as he took the tea his mother had poured for him. "He agrees that it was the prudent thing to bring you here, Miss Townes."

"But we must not stay, in view of what has happened, Mr. Woodland," Julia protested. "Perhaps a carriage can be hired to take me on to Fainway. And if Mrs. Woodland will be kind enough to accompany me, I will be most pleased to extend the hospitality of my home."

A great struggle now took place within Mrs. Woodland, but the attraction of a tragic death brought her down on the side of Winderfields. "Oh, we must not leave poor Sir William now, Miss Townes, when he most needs his friends about him. Robert, of course, can see to the business side of things, but it is always a woman who can be of comfort in sad times like these."

Julia turned to Robert. "What are Sir William's wishes in the matter?"

"It is difficult to say, for he is very distressed, understandably so. In any case, it is not possible to depart before morning, so I would suggest that we simply wait and see. Sir William will be more himself by then, and we can judge better what we ought to do."

The housekeeper returned to announce that rooms had been made ready for the unexpected guests, and the party separated.

Julia, for all her having had so little sleep, was too restless to remain quietly in her room, or in any room. After her long confinement, what she most wanted was the freedom and fresh air of the outdoors. Though it was a cloudy evening, it was not actually raining, and the air had turned rather mild for this time of year. She took her shawl from the wardrobe where the maid had hung it and went downstairs to try to find the terrace she had noticed when they had arrived.

In the hallway she found a servant and asked directions. He escorted her to a French window in the dining room which opened onto the terrace.

Julia stepped outside and breathed deeply of the moist, clean air, savoring the sensation she had so sorely missed while a prisoner in her garret room. She walked briskly along the terrace, vaguely glad of the movement, the exercise, even of the cold.

She was safe at last. Among friends. Soon to be rejoined with her family. Yet here, alone with only the breeze and the scuttling clouds that obscured the patchy moonlight, she felt as if she would go mad thinking of Philip.

What was he doing at this moment? Was he frightened? Defiant? Angry with himself or his companions for having been so foolish as to be caught at last? Could her father do anything to help Philip now? A gust of wind caught at her skirts and she pulled the shawl more closely around her. Was it right that anyone should try to help him?

Around and around, these questions swirled in her head, until, turning a corner of the terrace, she stopped short with a small pang of guilt, for there was poor Sir William entering the room of the window she was passing. Julia, so intent on her own grief and confusion, had spared no thoughts for this bereaved man who had so long been her friend.

As she watched, Sir William locked the door he

had closed. Julia, who had been considering tapping on the window and going in to give him her condolences, stopped with her hand upraised. Sir William might wish to be undisturbed. She was about to turn away when she saw him take something from his pocket. As he crossed directly in front of the window, Julia realized that it was something familiar. Why, it was one of the brown bottles which held the mixture Aunt Julia had given poor Miss Sennett!

Julia saw Sir William stride to the fire, and slowly, so as not to extinguish the flames, he poured the mixture that remained in the bottle out into the coals. Julia stood fascinated as he now moved to the desk, unlocked the bottom drawer, placed the bottle at the very back and locked it again, testing the drawer to be sure it had closed securely. Then he sat down in his chair.

He seemed so close to her, separated by only a foot or two beyond the pane of glass. In the lamplight, Julia could see him in profile, the lines of strain around his mouth, the frown that creased his forehead. She could almost hear the heavy sigh as he lowered himself into the deep leather chair. Now she saw him open the middle drawer of his desk and take from it what looked for all the world like a ladies' lace handkerchief. He buried his face in it, as though to catch a breath of any perfume that might linger there. What is more, the lines of his face softened into a gentle smile, the smile of a man in love!

Julia turned away from the window and quickly moved back along the terrace and into the dining room once more. She stood for a few moments, confused and uncertain. She knew she had not just witnessed a man taking comfort from a personal article of a dear departed relative. She had recognized the lace on that oversized and beautifully worked handkerchief. It could have been created only by the skillful hands of Miss Flagg.

She went back into the hall and up the main staircase, then up another flight of stairs, drawn by some force or some instinct that became more and more pronounced with every step. What it was she could not say, could not even guess, she only knew that she must follow it.

As she reached the top of the stairs, she gave a start as the last step creaked, it seemed, very loudly. Julia froze in her tracks.

But there was no one in the hall, no one had heard. Wait! Someone was coming! Footsteps announced the arrival of a housemaid, carrying a large potted plant. Julia waited out of sight in the shadows at the far end of the hallway. In a few moments the maid came out of a bedroom along with another serving girl. She heard one of the women say to the other, "I think the other dress was not nearly so pretty, though I am surprised at the master insisting that she be buried in the blue." The younger girl nodded and said she supposed they might as well start on the poor lady's bedroom now. "No," came the reply. "A death room must be aired overnight."

When they had gone down the stairs, Julia slipped quietly into the room where Miss Sennett lay.

A lamp burned on the small table beside the bed, casting a warm glow on the pinched face of the dead woman. Julia recognized the blue dress as the one Miss Sennett had worn at the ball at the Beatrice. It was a pretty gown, though not especially becoming to the lady, then or now. Studying Miss Sennett's face, Julia thought she looked, above all, disappointed.

And well she must have been, if she had expected to marry Sir William, Julia thought, wondering if Miss Sennett had known or guessed before her death that she had a rival, a most formidable rival, for Sir William's affections.

She was about to sink into the chair that had been provided at the bedside to think about it, when the creaking board at the head of the stairs again announced that someone was coming. Suddenly she recalled that Sir William probably had not yet passed his blessing on the laying-out. Still obeying that unaccountable something that led her, she retreated into the shadows on the far side of the room and slipped into the heavy wardrobe, leaving the door open just a crack.

From her vantage point, Julia could see Sir William, accompanied by the housekeeper, approach the bedside into the lamplight. They exchanged whispered remarks.

"I have had her dress changed, as you ordered, Sir William. It is a pretty dress, too. I think she would be more pleased with this selection."

Sir William nodded sorrowfully. "Even seeing her here, Mrs. Ferguson, I can hardly believe that this has happened."

"It was very sudden, to be sure, sir. I believed myself that she was getting over this affliction."

"Ah, but we must not question the wisdom of the

Almighty. It is our place to accept the burdens He sends to us all."

"Yes, sir."

Sir William took a moment to touch gently the hair that peeked beneath the lace cap on Miss Sennett's head.

"Thank you, Mrs. Ferguson. I am pleased with what you have done."

"Yes, sir. I expect you'd like to be alone with her now. I'll be in my room if you need to ring for me."

"Thank you."

The housekeeper disappeared from the pool of lamplight, and Sir William sat down in the chair, studying carefully the features of his dead cousin. And there in the clear soft glow of the lamp, Julia saw on his face exultation, which turned her blood cold. She could hardly keep from crying out as her brain shouted silently, *He is* glad *that poor woman is dead!*

But she had to keep silent and listen. Sir William was whispering to Miss Sennett's still form. "My poor, ugly, stupid cousin. What have your coy little threats brought you now? You hadn't even sense enough to fear me. Not like . . ." His voice trailed off and he shook his head. "Ah, beautiful Frances."

Julia felt her stomach lurch, and for an instant she was certain that she *had* cried out, had gasped or screamed at the wave of certainty that swept over her, at the ugly, stark, impossible truth that stood unmasked and unmitigated before her. She closed her eyes and waited to be discovered.

But there was no gesture from the man in the chair; he remained still and silent in the lamplight, staring, gloating. Now for the first time it was clear why this man's character had always been such a puzzle. He was not righteous but pompous, not clever but cunning—the same man he had always been, but now his underlying evil stood naked in the cold light of truth.

It seemed an eternity that Julia crouched in the wardrobe, breathless, cramped and horrified. And even when Sir William did rise and disappear from her field of view, even after she had heard the door close softly, she remained frozen in her hiding place, fearing he somehow knew that she had been there. He might be waiting for her on the stairs. Waiting to—to silence her.

At length, very slowly, she pushed the wardrobe door open a wider crack. When this met with no challenge, she dared to steal out into the room. Without even a glance at Miss Sennett, she hurried from the room and made her way back to her own bedchamber, where she closed the door and stood against it until her heart stopped pounding enough that she could take a normal breath. She went to stand at the fire that blazed on the hearth, for she was shivering uncontrollably. She was huddled in the chair at the fireside when the maid came in to help her dress for dinner.

"I wonder," Julia said, "if you would ask Mrs. Ferguson if I might have my dinner on a tray?"

"Certainly, madam. Are you ill?"

"I am exhausted and, in truth, I do feel unwell. I am sure Sir William will excuse me."

"Yes, madam."

The housekeeper herself appeared some minutes later, looking harried and concerned. "Oh, Miss Townes, I am so very sorry if we have neglected you in the midst of all that has happened. Sir William has just told me of your recent ordeal. It is, indeed, no wonder that you feel unwell."

"Thank you, Mrs. Ferguson, but, I think I am just weary."

"I will have your dinner brought here, and Sir William instructed me expressly to say that you are to rest and to ask for anything that he or the staff might provide you."

"Thank you. It is a great relief."

"The funeral for Miss Sennett will be held tomorrow morning, but everyone will understand, I am sure, if you do not feel up to attending."

Julia said yet another thank you and Mrs. Ferguson went away.

Alone again, Julia returned to the fireside to stare into the flames. There was a strangeness in the room—a presence—and she slowly realized it was the same feeling that had comforted her when she had been ill, disappointed, or frightened in the night, and it had been her mother instead of Mimmie who came to her side.

She ate little of her dinner; her appetite for anything of Sir William's hospitality was gone. The memory of his face, his black eyes glittering as he exulted over the dead Miss Sennett were burned into her mind as she sat again by the fire in the dressing gown Miss Pierce had lent her.

The thought of the dressing gown brought another memory—that of Mary Belleville lying dead beneath a pile of oaken panels. There had, after all, been only MacKenzie to attest that his master had been ill throughout that night. And now MacKenzie was also dead.

Julia got up from her chair and rang for a maid.

"I am sorry to give you trouble," she told the servant, "but I do not feel I can be alone tonight. Will you ask Mrs. Ferguson if someone—one of the maids—might sleep in this room with me?"

"Of course, madam. I shouldn't want to be alone myself after what you have been through. I will gladly stay with you. I'll have one of the men bring a cot."

So thus attended, Julia slipped into bed to stare into the dying fire, listening to the maid snore, confronting the urgent purpose that had not replaced, but forced aside, that cold black ache and emptiness. She must, somehow, see that Sir William—Bellwether—paid for his evil.

Julia stood at the graveside beside Sir William as Miss Sennett was laid to rest. The local vicar, who had known Miss Sennett from a girl, called up his own testimonial to her fine character and modest ways, strong in the certainty that she would find a better life than the one she had just departed. Julia acknowledged this truth in grim silence.

It was a very great effort for Julia to behave properly as they rode back to Winderfields in the new carriage, to share a funeral meal with the others of the household and the friends of Miss Sennett who had come to join them, to behave naturally toward a man she had once regarded highly and now found repulsive in every way.

But she did it all the same, even to sitting alone with Sir William for a few minutes before the first guests had arrived, sharing a glass of sherry and listening quietly as he extolled the merits of his late cousin. And when Sir William was called to the dining room to approve the arrangements Mrs. Ferguson had made, Julia hurried to the desk. With a racing heart she tried the bottom drawer. To her great astonishment, it opened at her first tug, and she was instantly determined that, whatever the risk to herself, she would take the bottle, conceal it somehow, find a way to get it away from here, to be certain that it contained the poison she suspected.

The bottle was gone. Destroyed, no doubt, or cleaned and replaced with the others during the night. Bitterly disappointed, Julia lingered at the desk only long enough to open the top drawer and verify beyond doubt that the handkerchief was truly Miss Flagg's.

When the last of the funeral guests had gone and the little party reassembled in the drawing room, there came a sound of horses and clattering wheels in the drive below. Robert, who was nearest the window, turned to announce, "A carriage has arrived, Sir William."

Who could it be? No other guests were expected. It was days too early to hope that a carriage from Fainway had come for Julia.

Footsteps were heard in the hallway, the drawing room door opened, and the party were astonished to see Major Forbisher. Julia did not notice the look of sudden anxiety that paled Sir William's face, for her eyes were fixed upon the woman who had entered the room behind the justice of the peace.

"Mimmie!"

Heedless of her teacup clattering to the floor, Julia was out of her chair in an instant and flying into Mimmie's arms.

Chapter Sixteen

"It is very kind of you, Sir William," said Mimmie, "but we must be off without delay. There are still a few hours of daylight left, and if it clears, we shall have moonlight to illuminate our trip to Fainway."

"What?" Sir William's face was a picture of astonishment. "You cannot mean this, my dear Miss Chappel, er, Miss Payne. You surely can stay the night and set out tomorrow."

"I cannot in good conscience keep Julia from her father even an hour longer than necessary. But it is good of you to offer your hospitality at such a sorrowful time as this. Poor Miss Sennett was very dear to you, I know."

Sir William took his cue and bowed his head sorrowfully. "Very true, ma'am, but so are my friends, and I would be glad to have them by me now."

"That is kind of you to say," Mimmie repeated,

but she turned to Julia and spoke firmly, "Julia, you must see that your things are packed at once."

"I've little to pack. It would be nothing but for the kindness of Mrs. and Mr. Woodland. It will take only a moment to be ready."

Julia was already at the door when Sir William said, "You needn't trouble, Miss Townes. If you really must go, Mrs. Ferguson will see to your packing. I'll just ring for her."

When the housekeeper had departed on her errand, an awkward silence fell among the group assembled in the drawing room. But Mrs. Woodland was never one to suffer any sort of silence, and never one to hesitate in coming to the point. "But you must tell us what have been your circumstances these many months since you left York, Miss Chappel. I understood from Robert and Sir William that you had disappeared from sight under the most mysterious circumstances. Is it that you have come out of hiding now that these terrible ruffians have been run to ground?"

To this discourse, Mimmie simply answered, "Yes."

Another silence. After a few moments, Robert cleared his throat. "And . . . and are you well, ma'am? Have you suffered in this period of forced retirement?"

"It has been sometimes difficult, sir, but I have not suffered—unlike others."

Major Forbisher gave a little cough and said, "Miss Chappel is not at liberty to disclose much of what has transpired, but I believe I may tell you without harm that it was *she* who figured prominently in the apprehension of the miscreants in Leeds."

There was a chorus of surprise and wonder. Mimmie saw Mrs. Woodland forming eager questions.

"You must not think this was all an exciting and romantic experience," Mimmie said preemptively. "It was sometimes rather frightening and at more times exceedingly dreary. But as the major has said, I am not yet at liberty to speak."

Sir William, who had been wondering whether to mention the name of Bellwether, decided against it. "Then we must not press you for information which you are honor bound not to dispense, ma'am. I will only say that I hope I may extend the hospitality of Winderfields to you and to Miss Townes at some time in the future when all of us are more at leisure and in better spirits." He turned to Julia, who forced herself to look grateful.

"Thank you, Sir William. I will just go and see how Mrs. Ferguson is getting on with my things."

When Julia came downstairs a few minutes later, Mimmie was already in the hallway. Outside, the carriage stood waiting, horses freshly changed; the coachman was receiving a basket of food from one of the maids. Julia shook hands with the housekeeper, with Mrs. Woodland and with Sir William, murmuring words of gratitude and sympathy which she could only hope sounded sincere. At last she came to Robert.

"I pray that all will be well with you, Julia."

"Thank you, Robert. Will you come to see me at Fainway? And bring—bring your family? I cannot bear to think that we will not always be friends."

"Nor can I. Certainly we will come, and I hope we see you at York again one day."

A moment later she was in the carriage and driving away from Winderfields.

They rode in silence—Mimmie, Julia, Major Forbisher—through the park and onto the secondary road that would take them to the main highway. Julia burned with questions for Mimmie and to speak of what she herself had discovered, but, reading Mimmie's glance of caution and the tiny shake of her head, she said nothing.

A mile or two along the main highway, the carriage drew to a stop at an inn.

"Come, Julia, this is where we leave Major Forbisher," said Mimmie.

Julia followed Mimmie out of the carriage; the major escorted them to another carriage which stood waiting in the stableyard.

"Thank you for your escort, sir." Mimmie shook the major's hand.

"It was my very great pleasure, ma'am. I wish you a pleasant journey the rest of your way. And my best regards to Mr. Sommerville."

It was a physical stab of pain for Julia to hear that name spoken in sarcasm. Feeling instantly hollow and weakened, she took a seat in the new carriage and the journey resumed.

Mimmie collapsed against the cushions with a long sigh and breathed in a whisper, "Thank God!"

"Mimmie," Julia said urgently, "I have a lifetime of questions for you, but there is something I must tell you first. I believe—no, I am certain—that Sir William killed Miss Sennett. Poisoned her. It was he who killed my mother. Mimmie, Sir William is Bellwether!"

"Poor Miss Sennett." Mimmie spoke almost to

herself. "Philip feared another death, but thought it might be the servant."

Julia felt her mind threaten to scamper in two directions; she grasped at the most tangible fragment of conversation.

"MacKenzie is dead, too."

"Ah. Then he was right, after all."

"When—when you say 'Philip,'" it was a question barely breathed, "Mimmie, you don't . . . you can't mean Philip Sommerville?"

"Yes, of course, Philip Sommerville. Who else?"

"But—but is he not arrested? Is he not one of . . . perhaps the leader of the traitors who were seized in Leeds?"

Mimmie looked puzzled. "Julia, my dear, how could you ever come to imagine such a thing?"

"Mimmie, you must tell me now! Where is Philip Sommerville at this moment? And if he is not arrested, what is his part in this affair at Leeds? I will not believe that he is not somehow concerned!"

"He was, indeed, very much concerned. As an agent of the queen."

"Oh . . . oh, my." Julia fell back and stared gaping at the woman in the seat across from her. "Mimmie," she said firmly, "you must tell me everything. Everything you can. Please."

"I don't know everything." Mimmie opened the food basket and looked inside, handed Julia an apple and took one herself. "We came to Leeds some three months ago—"

"No! No, Mimmie, you must begin at the beginning. Begin on the day you left me at Fainway."

"Ah, that day." A meditative smile played on Mimmie's face. "I was sorely tempted, I must tell you, to drive straight to Winterhall and seek the protection my relationship to the family might gain for me. Frances and I had learned when we returned from France what had happened to my own family, and I knew that the estate was in the kinder hands of Mr. Parke."

"But you did not go there?"

"No." Mimmie sighed. "Prudence told me that I must lose myself, at least for a time, so I went to London. My thoughts were unsettled, uncertain as to what I ought to do, though I had determined at once that I must find employment."

"But you had some money—the emergency fund Mama had put aside."

"Yes. And I"—Mimmie looked a little ashamed of herself—"had kept a little fund of my own, without telling Frances—just in case."

Julia studied her apple intently and said, "So you went to London."

"I went first to a good hotel, but after only one night there, I found lodging in a private house. I had seen the lady's advertisement on the house as the carriage had passed it." Mimmie closed her eyes. "It was not at all an agreeable place—full of nosy women, all with a kind of desperate gentility, and the most dreadful food!"

Julia looked up to smile at the offended expression on her companion's face.

"I did feel reasonably safe there—just one of so many ladies of similar age and circumstance. I had changed my name, of course, and . . . and I'm afraid I wrote myself a rather glowing reference on the hotel's stationery concerning my value as a ladies' companion. I signed it with the name of a

Lady Claypool. All the old skills at deception and self-preservation came back to me rather easily, I'm afraid. I was actually on the point of taking employment with a perfectly pleasant lady in Sussex when Phillip found me."

"He found you?"

"And I had been congratulating myself on my skill at concealing myself. Clearly I was not so clever as I thought. I was only lucky that it was Philip who undertook to look for me and not—"

"But why was he looking for you?" Julia shook her head, puzzled. "Philip, I mean. You must tell me about . . . about Philip."

Mimmie, who had opened the hamper again, now closed it without taking anything. "It was you who first attracted his attention at the Beatrice, the evening of Sir William's party. He said he was instantly reminded of Mr. Townes when first he saw you. He told me that later he came into the room where we all were and saw the three of us together —you, me, and, of course, Frances. He was certain at once of what he had discovered."

"But why was he in York at all? Did he suspect Sir William was Bellwether even then?"

"Not at all. Philip was on his way to Leeds on this other matter and stopped in York only because it has a good hotel. Philip does not like to be uncomfortable unless it is necessary."

"And, having recognized us all, what did the gentleman do then?"

"He followed us home. And the next day, he arranged to take the house across the street. It could be useful as a retreat just a few hours from Leeds, and his intent was to bring Mr. Townes to

York and have him decide what ought to be done. About you."

"Oh."

"And then, never dreaming there was any danger to Frances after all these years, Philip went on with the business that had brought him north. It was several days later that he returned to York and learned what had happened to Frances." Mimmie turned to look out of the carriage window at the afternoon shadows. "This could only have been the work of Bellwether, and Philip was nearly persuaded for a time that Bellwether was connected to this group at Leeds, after all. Though that seemed most unlikely."

"Unlikely? Why? There must be a connection!"

Mimmie shook her head. "Bellwether always sought power for himself. He used the general disfavor with the monarchy only as a rallying cry to attract followers. The men at Leeds were different —quite selfless in their determination to abolish the crown and entirely willing to sacrifice themselves in the cause. That Bellwether should be one of them, much less their leader, made no sense at all. When Philip learned of Frances's death and that you and I had disappeared, he left Thomas in Leeds to keep an eye on the one man in the group they had identified. Philip returned to London to confer with his superiors. I believe, though he has not said, that he was actually taken to see the queen."

"The queen!" breathed Julia, much impressed.

"He also went to speak to your father, but unfortunately, when Philip arrived, Mr. Townes was not at Fainway."

329

"My father left at once—on the morning after my arrival."

"But Philip did see you quite by accident. When he learned I was not with you, he set out to search for me. When he found me at my lodging house, I was offered sanctuary. And employment."

"Did he tell my father that he had found you?"

"He did not."

"But why? Oh, Mimmie, I was so worried about you!"

"I know, my dear, but caution above all was what we had to observe. Your father would never knowingly reveal a dangerous secret, but . . . Well, Philip thought it best."

Julia had turned to look thoughtfully out of the carriage window and was noting that evening was fast approaching when she heard Mimmie laugh.

"The employment he gave me was to learn to be an accomplished housemaid. I was turned over to his housekeeper for instruction. And when she and Philip thought me sufficiently skilled, the three of us set out for Leeds. We took up residence there in a dirty, noisy portion of the town, and I presented myself a few days later at a house where the maid had, with Philip's assistance, been lured to leave her post."

"I can well imagine how *that* was done."

"I think it best not to inquire too closely." Mimmie smiled. "In any case, I was employed. This was how Philip had hoped it would progress, because I, of course, could not be installed as housekeeper in the house at York. That job fell to Mary."

"Mary?" said Julia with a sinking heart.

"She was most embarrassed to bring word to Leeds that you had run away."

"Escaped!"

Mimmie knitted puzzled brows. "I was surprised to learn that Philip had placed you there. I just supposed he had left you with Lord Wrayburn."

That name brought a rush of memory and conflicting emotions. Julia forced them aside to ask, "And you really took a place as a housemaid?"

"I did. And I did it well, too."

"But why? Was the master of the house suspected? Was that the gentleman Thomas was left to oversee?"

"No. One of the tenants. This was a lodging house, you see. I am not entirely certain how he—Mr. Davis—came under suspicion, though I do know that your cousin, Lawrence Christian, played a very important role in discovering the evil plot in which he was engaged."

"Lawrence? But he said not a word of it to me!"

"He could not, my dear, for he knew nothing of what was being undertaken. Even your father, who first brought Lawrence's information to Philip, was kept in the dark. Philip's theory is that what one does not know, one cannot reveal under any circumstances, and, indeed, I must agree that in this line of work, it is a very sound policy."

"I have heard Mr. Sommerville say similar words," Julia muttered.

"My assignment was quite simple—to observe the man's activities and his visitors, and identify them if possible. To make note of who came and went, to listen to and remember any conversations they might have within my hearing. What I learned,

I was to report to Mary on the Sundays that she came to Leeds to meet me at church. Or to Philip's servant, Thomas, who came by from time to time, posing as my son. Poor Thomas. He spent a great deal of time traveling between Leeds and the south."

"And was there a great deal to report?"

"For the first few weeks there was nothing. Our gentleman had visitors—three men, including one particular man—a Mr. Harkins. We had a sketch of him, provided by your cousin. But they were cautious. I was unable to learn anything of use."

"And what was Mr. Sommerville doing in the meantime?"

"I cannot say with certainty. On one occasion when I saw Philip, he did tell me that he had encountered you in London in company with Sir William and Mr. Woodland."

"It is true."

"He assured me that you were well. And that you were very beautiful." Mimmie's eyes twinkled in the dim light of the carriage interior. "I believe that was about the time he came to suspect that Sir William might be Bellwether. I am glad he did not tell me until . . . until he was able to assure me that you had been taken from Fainway and hidden."

"You will forgive me if I did not find Mr. Sommerville's arrangements entirely delightful!"

"Yes, dear. Traveling with the gypsies must have been uncomfortable for you from time to time. Mary and I found it so as we came north. But Philip thought it necessary that you disappear completely."

"Why?"

"Why, I suppose because of Sir William."

"I don't believe it!" Julia snorted. "Sir William, had he wished it, could have done away with me twenty times over."

"Philip told me that there had been a death."

"Oh!" Julia was startled out of her indignation by this reminder of poor Mary Belleville. "That is true enough."

"To be sure of your safety, an elaborate abduction was staged. It would, of course, be said that Bellwether was to blame. Poor Sir William must have been very mystified by it all."

"All the same, Mr. Sommerville has a great fondness for the obscure and the enigmatic."

"Perhaps he does, but he is a man who must, by necessity, exercise great caution. If he did not make his plans clear to you, I am sure he had his reasons."

With crossed arms and frowning eyes, Julia watched the moonlight bathe the winter night in a silvery glow. When there had been several moments of silence, Mimmie closed weary eyes, thinking that a nap would be lovely.

"Well, what happened?" Julia finally asked, her curiosity stronger than her bad temper. "At Leeds, I mean."

Feeling less enthusiasm than she pretended, Mimmie sat up, yawned and stretched. "Finally, we managed to have the tenant next door to Mr. Davis hear of better lodgings at a much cheaper rate. When he moved, Thomas and I began to prepare the room as a listening post."

"What did you discover?"

"Enough to convince us that we had found a very

dangerous group of people, indeed. But they
seemed leaderless. Nothing was decided. They
mostly ranted about the evils of the crown. And a
fifth man, of whom we had only a description—
younger and walking with a limp—never appeared. It looked very much as though this man,
and not Harkins, must be their leader, and Philip
sent for Mr. Christian to see if he could help us. Mr.
Christian, it seemed, had heard him speak.

"While waiting for your cousin, Philip and
Thomas had gone to see that all was well with the
gypsies, and then, I believe on the very night you
had been taken away to Lord Wrayburn's, Thomas
was to return to York and to Leeds to see if Mary or
I had any news for Philip. He went first to York, and
there, to his great astonishment, he saw on the
street our own Mr. Harkins in conversation with a
much younger man who carried a cane. Realizing
he had discovered the fifth man, Thomas waited
until Harkins departed for Leeds, then followed the
other man, hoping to discover where in York he
lived. But Thomas was not careful enough. The
man waited for him at a quiet corner, struck him
down and made his escape. When Thomas recovered his senses, he rode through the night to bring
word to Philip."

"Yes," Julia said softly. "I was with him when he
received it."

"And, unfortunately that fifth man was not with
the others when we caught them. And although
Philip and the two gentlemen with him were able to
learn something of what they intended, they did
not hear the details." Mimmie shook her head in
sad frustration. "Now we may never learn it in

time, because Philip was discovered and . . . It was very terrible."

There now came to Julia a sudden rush of memory, sudden fear. "I heard that there had been violence."

"Philip was shot." In the dim moonlight, Mimmie did not see the blood drain from Julia's face. "It is just a minor wound to his thigh, but poor Thomas is dead, and so is Mr. Harkins."

"Dead." Julia sat for a long time without speaking, sorting distractedly through the emotions the last few moments had engendered. "Oh, Mimmie, you might have been killed, too."

"But I was not. Nor wounded, nor damaged in any way. Except for being terribly frightened, of course. And the next morning, Mary arrived in quite a state, to tell us that you had escaped. Philip sent me to find you and take you once more to your father. And he has charged me never to let you out of sight until he returns. When I learned that you had gone actually to Winderfields. . . ."

Julia shook her head, mystified, as the carriage rolled to a stop at the inn where they would stay the night.

"I wonder, Mimmie, if this will be the last incredible tale you tell me in a carriage!"

Chapter Seventeen

The next evening, with a nearly full moon on a clear winter night, Mimmie gave orders that the coachman continue the journey, and at half past ten, they arrived at the drive into the grounds of Fainway. Lights gleamed from the windows of the small family dining room.

"They are very late at dinner," Julia said as they stood in the light of the lantern that burned at the front door."

"Perhaps there are guests," Mimmie suggested.

"It must be Lawrence, then," Julia said, feeling a sinking of her heart. "Otherwise they would be in the larger portion of the dining room."

They were admitted by the butler, who beamed a wide smile. "Welcome home, Miss Townes! Your father will be most delighted. He thought there was little chance of seeing you tonight. Indeed, madam, so are we all delighted and relieved to have you home again."

"Thank you, Cobb. That is a very welcome . . . welcome. Mimmie, this is Cobb, our butler. Miss Payne will be staying the night, Cobb."

"Yes, madam, she is expected. Some dinner has been kept warm for you in the hope that you might arrive."

Julia went first into the dining room. Aunt Julia, from her position at one end of the table, was first to see her.

"Julia!" The old woman was on her feet in an instant, rushing to embrace her niece. "My dear girl, how very glad are these old eyes to see you again." And those eyes filled with tears as Julia kissed her warmly on the cheek.

"Thank you, Aunt Julia. It is more wonderful than I can say to be at home again."

Charles was on his feet as well. He stood awkwardly by for a long moment as Julia turned to him. But his eyes lit with joy as she embraced him.

"Father," she whispered. "How I have missed you."

"Julia. Thank God!"

They stood together, arms around each other, until Julia suddenly remembered Mimmie. "Father, here is someone that you know from long ago. I call her Mimmie, but you know her as Miss Clara Payne."

Julia was uncertain how her father would receive the woman who had fled with her friend, Frances Townes, on that long ago day.

But he smiled and took the hand she extended. "Thank you, ma'am, for bring my daughter back

337

to me. I was on the point of setting out for Winderfields when Philip's message arrived. I believe you will remember my aunt."

While Mimmie and Aunt Julia shook hands, Julia turned at last to Lawrence.

"Julia!" He took the hand she offered, but then pulled her into his arms for a brief, but not entirely cousinly, embrace. That same churning guilt returned to Julia's stomach as she let him lift her hand to his lips. "It is the greatest joy to see that you are safely home," Lawrence murmured.

"Good evening, Lawrence. Mimmie, this is my cousin, Lawrence Christian."

"Sit down, sit down," Charles urged. "Foster, set two more places and have some dinner brought for these hungry, weary ladies."

Julia took a place beside her father, sorry to realize that she must look into the eyes of Lawrence, who sat directly opposite. The feeling that she had betrayed him lay heavily on her heart.

"Lawrence," she said as her plate was placed before her, "Mimmie has told me that you had a most important role in the discovery of the plot at Leeds. Can you tell us about it now? I confess I am consumed with curiosity."

Lawrence laughed a little ruefully. "As much as I would like to have you think me a great hero in this matter, I must admit my role was very small. Last year, I guess it was in the last days of May, I was at Leeds, visiting with an old school friend. He had put me on to an interesting business proposition when I had seen him last in London, and I had gone to see about it."

Julia made a mental note to ask sometime just

what sort of business it was that Lawrence dabbled in, but she did not want to interrupt him now.

"On a Sunday afternoon, when everyone else at the house was napping, I happened to stroll alone near the church we had attended that very morning.There had been one of those early heat waves. The day and my friend's house were fiercely hot, and there behind the church I came upon a pretty park, shady and green, with a little fountain making a welcoming kind of splashing noise. To my surprise, the place was entirely deserted. I would have thought the whole neighborhood might wish to sit there in such weather.

"As I was walking toward a stone bench where I thought I might sit awhile, I passed beneath a window of the church just as someone opened it. I heard voices raised in very spirited argument, and I heard the words, 'But old William will be dead at any moment. When the wench comes to the throne will be the time, for when she is dead they must look very far for a monarch.' Or something very like that. I cannot be certain now of the exact words I heard. Another voice, a most distinctive, compelling voice, said something that curdled my blood. Something about remembering that none of them would escape alive, and they had to be certain they did not die without lopping off the head of the monsterous monarchy. I swear it made me shiver, even on that blazing day. This man, who seemed to be the leader, said they must have a plan that would not fail. Then another voice said, 'Yes, of course, they must have a plan and by the way, he had best close that window.'

"I flattened myself against the church wall and

was fortunate that the man did not look down to see me. I, however, had a brief look at his face. I forgot all about sitting in the cool of the park and waited in hiding until they left the church. I did not see the faces of any of the others—there were five of them—but I noticed that one of the group seemed younger than the rest, about my age, in fact, and he walked with a bit of a limp. When they were well out of sight, I went at once back to my friend's house."

"And did you tell him about it?"

"I didn't want to somehow. I thought I should wait and think about it. I didn't suspect my friend of any involvement, not really, but . . . There it is. Still, it kept preying on my mind. Eventually, it was your father whom I told."

"And, of course, that was the right thing to do," Julia said warmly.

"I suppose so, as it seems to have ended happily. At your father's urging, I was able to make a sketch of the one face I had seen. I heard no more about it until some days ago, when I was asked to come again to Leeds, to see if I could identify the voice of the man I had drawn. When I had verified that his was not the voice of the leader, I returned here. And that, Cousin Julia, is all I know."

"Well, not quite, Lawrence," Charles said. "The man Lawrence assisted in this matter is Philip Sommerville."

Lawrence took a sip of his wine. "The truth is that I have never especially cared for Sommerville, nor he for me, but as he did find Julia after all, despite his fears to the contrary, I certainly will think more highly of him now."

As Julia looked at her cousin thoughtfully, a

sudden truth washed over her: Her father had known all along of Philip's role in her abduction. But Lawrence had not been told, had even been a victim in that elaborate scheme. Why? That celebrated caution? Or ill will on Philip's part? With an effort, Julia put aside these questions as her father spoke to her.

"Philip's message came late last night, telling us he would arrive in due time, and in the meantime, you would be brought home by his cousin, Miss Payne. He said also that, as the danger is not entirely past, you were to be closely guarded, even now, until he himself arrived. We now will have two footmen on duty in the hall outside your room and I have given orders that Miss Payne is to have the room next to you."

"Oh, thank you, Father. I do not think I could bear to have Mimmie even so far from me as the guest wing."

Dinner was finished and the ladies moved into the large salon. There Aunt Julia described events that had happened in the neighborhood in Julia's absence. *My aunt rattles on as though I had just gone to Bath for a few weeks,* Julia thought, *like poor Miss Sennett.*

Mimmie listened, remarking now and then when she recognized a name or a place from her childhood days in the neighborhood, but at length Mimmie, who was near exhaustion, asked if she might be shown to her bedroom.

"I will go to bed, as well, Miss Payne," Aunt Julia declared. "You should come, too, Julia, for you look quite exhausted, as well you should be."

"I will go very soon, Aunt Julia. I do wish to speak to my father for a moment first."

"All right, dear."

Her aunt accepted Julia's kiss, then watched as Mimmie was also kissed good night. As the two women went calmly out together, Julia wondered if they were going to get along over time.

Julia sat down again in her chair by the fire, wondering how best to question her father about what had happened to her, debating whether she should be angry, even outraged.

But the fire was warm, the room was peaceful, silent, home. A half-hour later, Charles and Lawrence found her asleep in her chair.

Lawrence announced the next morning that he must return to London. "Since you are home again and out of harm's way, I can go without concern," he told Julia. "Except for the few days I spent going to and from Leeds, I have been here continually since you were taken." He shook his head smiling. "I think I am getting on your father's nerves."

"You mustn't say that, Lawrence. He has had a great deal to concern him."

"And so have you. In any case, with all that has happened, I have neglected my affairs, and if I do so any longer it will be at my peril. And there is poor Mary's business to be settled, too. I must go."

In truth, Julia was glad that she would not have so much of Lawrence's company just yet. She was in terror that a marriage proposal would come at any moment, and she could not bear the thought of having to answer him now.

When Lawrence was safely gone, Julia came downstairs to look for her father, determined to have the discussion that had been delayed from the night before. Hearing from the footman that Charles was in his library, Julia went there, and when she opened the door, her eyes fell first on Philip Sommerville.

"Julia," her father called to her, "Philip was just asking if he might see you."

"Good morning, Miss Townes. I'm much relieved to see that you are safe and well. I was just saying to your father that I hope you have forgiven us for our uncomfortable, but very necessary, deception.

Julia's eyes flashed at him for an angry moment before she replied, "How do you do, Mr. Sommerville?" She did not offer her hand, but went to sit in the chair her father was placing for her. "It is as well that you are together, for I have something I wish to tell you both."

She told them of her discovery at Winderfields, of her certainty that Sir William was Bellwether. Philip stood silently at the fireside as she spoke, frowning in concentration.

"I have no doubt myself that Sir William is Bellwether," he said when she had fallen silent. "And have even told your father so. In the intervals available to me while working on this business at Leeds, I was able to spend a day in York now and then. I am satisfied that it was Sir William who ransacked your house. The baker saw him on your street one morning just at dawn, walking out his grief, of course. Also, I attempted to learn precisely how Sir William had spent the morning of your mother's death. I found the inn where he and Miss Sennett were delayed, ostensibly by a faulty carriage wheel, and discovered that Sir William had not remained at the inn. He had taken a horse, presumably in the company of his coachman, and ridden out to view some property that had attracted him. I have not yet confronted the coachman about it."

"And you will not, Mr. Sommerville," Julia said softly. "MacKenzie is dead."

"When? When did he die?"

"About three weeks ago, according to the man who has the job now. It is said that he died in his sleep."

"That would be far too convenient for my tastes."

"And for mine," Julia remarked. "It was, after all, only MacKenzie who declared that Sir William was ill the night that Mary died."

Julia heard her father draw a sharp breath and saw that he looked pale and angry. She thought he would speak, but after a glance at Philip, he only turned to stare into the fire.

"And now Miss Sennett is dead, too," Philip said. "He must have felt her a threat to his safety."

"But she seemed so devoted to him!" Charles protested. "I cannot think she would betray him."

"Unless she herself were betrayed," Julia said softly. "Or thwarted." Oddly, she found herself looking into Philip's eyes for an instant before she dropped her gaze.

Charles said, "Philip, is there anything that can be done now?"

Philip shook his head. "I'm not certain. Nothing presents itself in the form of a solution just now. I fear that without some proof, or some witness, other than what Miss Townes has told us, we can do nothing just yet."

They sat silently for several minutes, then Philip said that he would think the problem over and asked if he might see Miss Payne. And Julia, sensing that the moment to speak (complain) of her abduction had passed, said that she would go and find Mimmie.

The next day was Sunday, and after services, Julia took Mimmie to the place where Frances was buried.

"Do you think, Mimmie, that my father has done right in bringing her here?" Julia asked. "Knowing what happened between them, do you think she would wish to be here, rather than at York?"

"You are here, Julia. And she would want you to be close to her."

"So my father said to me."

"Frances, you know, would always be at home wherever she were placed in life. I cannot think it would be different for her in death."

"Is your brother, Richard, buried here in the churchyard?"

"No. My parents did not wish it. Before I went to Leeds, I visited his grave at Portsmouth. Now I mean to have a proper headstone made. Philip has said that he will see to it."

There were guests invited to Sunday dinner at Fainway—Mr. Parke and Mr. Sommerville—and after dinner, Philip said, "Miss Townes, would you care to ride? It is a fine afternoon, and an outing would give us a chance to continue our discussions."

Torn between the intense desire to be with him and the absolute certainty that she should have nothing whatever to do with him, Julia hesitated a long time. But she finally drained her wine glass for courage and said, "Very well, Mr. Sommerville. I will be ready in a moment."

＇ They were barely out of the drive when he said to her, "Julia. . . ."

She turned on him with blazing eyes.

"Well," he said, with a mocking smile, "I can hardly continue saying 'Miss Townes' after . . ." He stopped when he saw the red in her cheeks, uncertain whether it was embarrassment or anger. "Julia, I would have sent word to you had it been possible."

"Yes, of course. It is such a great distance, Leeds to York. Why it may be all of thirty miles. Odd that your housekeeper, the venerable Mary, could have made such an arduous journey so often!"

Julia heard him chuckle.

"Poor Mary. You will be relieved to know that she is undamaged, in any permanent way, by her acquaintance with you."

Julia's withering glance told him that she cared very little for Mary's well-being.

There was a long silence. They rode side by side, past the estate outbuildings and into the woods. Silently they moved through the trees to the spot on the ridge where she had been abducted and Lawrence detained.

Now he spoke again, very softly. "Would you prefer that I go away and wait until you send word that you are ready to speak with me?"

"Why?" she exploded as she turned to him in fury. "Why did you take me from my family, consign me to a tribe of dirty vagabonds, then abandon me, imprison me without a word of explanation?"

"I did it for your protection, truly."

"Because you suspected Sir William? Because he was staying in the household? I don't believe it! Sir William had any number of opportunities to do away with me if he wished it. And . . . and anyway, he was to leave Fainway the next day if you remember."

"I remember. And I remember also that Miss Belleville had died. And that, I assure you, was no accident."

Some of Julia's anger flowed away as she thought about this puzzle. "But . . . but even if he did mistake Mary for me, why should he have expected to find me or anyone else prowling about the house in the night? Why didn't you just warn me?"

She heard him sigh wearily, but he did not answer.

"You did not trust me." Her voice was still angry.

"I did not know you. Indeed, I wonder if I know you now."

She looked at him, frowning, but his face was turned away, his gaze fixed on the trees, some already showing fattening nodules where they would bud. She studied the hand that rested on his saddle, a strong, large, curiously sensitive hand. The memory of his hands made her catch her breath, and, as he turned to look at her, she stared intently at her own hands.

"I should like to hear now about the business at Leeds. Since that is a deed accomplished, you may surely tell me of it. What kept you there, unable to release me or even to send word that you . . ." She stopped. She had been going to say, "that you were safe."

"Julia, I could not be spared, even for an hour. There were only the three of us—Mimmie . . ." He laughed. "I call her that myself. Mimmie, myself and Thomas."

"Oh, Thomas. I am very sorry about your servant, Philip," she said quietly. "And about Mary, too. But I didn't know!"

Silence fell between them again as they sat looking down on the Druid's Circle. After a time, Philip asked, "Would you like to go down and look at the stones?"

"Yes. I have never seen them at close range."

He led the way along the ridge to a spot where the path led onto the grounds of Winterhall.

"How large they are!" she exclaimed when he had helped her from her horse. "They look so much smaller from above."

"Everything depends on one's point of view," he said. "At least, I have always found it so. And from your point of view, I suppose I must have seemed a scoundrel."

"You lived up to your reputation in every way, Mr. Sommerville."

"Ah. I suppose it is Miss Merryweather who has been telling tales."

"Yes." She looked at him solemnly. "But I do not at all believe that she is the only lady you have . . . disappointed."

"What a delicate way you have with words, Miss Townes."

Suddenly he drew her close and kissed her. His

hands—those hands—moved surely along the line of her back and came to rest on her hips, pressing her closer to him. Julia felt the fires begin and grow; very soon the point had passed that she might have resisted him, and she called herself seven times a fool as her arms went around him helplessly. When he released her, she was breathless and tingling with desire and anticipation.

He turned, holding her hand and drawing her along, away from the stones and into the stand of trees. Julia supposed at first that he only wanted to be out of sight of anyone who might be riding on the ridge above, but they did not stop when they reached the seclusion of the timber. He drew her on many yards along a trail through the trees until they came to a spot where the trail ended and a gypsy wagon stood.

He helped her inside and, stooping, led her to the bed, pushing her gently down, laying her back against the cushions.

"Why, Philip?" she asked him. "Why is it I that came here? I know that this is wrong."

"No, my beautiful Julia, it is not wrong. It is lovely. It is perfection. And so are you."

He began to undress her expertly; of course he would do it expertly, with no hesitation or fumbling with hooks or bows or buttons, and placed searing kisses as each part of her became naked. And his hands, so sure and knowing, stroked and caressed her, each touch unexpected but exactly true, until she was pleading for release from her torment of longing.

With what seemed a single movement, he plunged his hands beneath her hips, lifting her to join their two bodies with an eager thrust, causing her to cry out at the force of it.

His eyes glittered and gazed into hers as all time was suspended, all thought abandoned. It might have been moments or even all eternity during which they moved together in this ancient, exquisite dance until the inevitable mounting of passion would no longer be held at bay.

"Julia!" he cried hoarsely, and molded her body as close to his as was possible. In her ear were whispered words of delight and, yes, of love, as they were swept into the sweet black fire of ultimate sensation.

When they could at last lie quietly together, he took her face in his hands and kissed her eyelids and temples and her hairline.

"How lovely you are, Julia. And how surprising. Those icy eyes would make a man think you cold and passionless."

"Is that what makes me interesting to a man like you? Do you seek the challenge of igniting a fire where only dead ashes seem to be?"

He laughed, but Julia thought she heard a note of discomfort.

"Miss Townes, you ask the most disturbing questions." He left her and began to dress.

After a few silent moments of watching him, Julia began to retrieve her own clothes.

"Philip," she asked as he was fastening her dress for her, "do you truly love me?"

He turned her around to face him. "Can you not trust me, even now?"

"I might ask you the same question."

The words hit home. He hesitated, uncertain, but

at last he shook his head, Julia thought with regret.

"I promise I will tell you everything as soon as it is prudent."

She stared at him silently, unsatisfied.

"What do you say to this?" he asked. "When all of this business is finished, I will come and court you properly."

"Court me?"

"Yes. Bring you flowers, read you poems, dance with you at the neighborhood parties." His green eyes twinkled, making her smile as he kissed her on the forehead. "I find it a charming idea."

"So it is," she replied softly, but thinking that it sounded most unlikely.

On the ride back to Fainway he told her that he would leave the next morning for London.

"How long must you be gone?"

"I don't know. It make take a good many days, even weeks. And I must take your Mimmie with me."

"It is important, isn't it, that you find this last traitor?"

"It is beyond important, Julia. He is the one who is to carry out their plot. Only Harkins knew the details of the plan to assassinate the queen, and he was shot deliberately by Davis so that he could not tell what he knew. We know only that the attempt to murder the queen is to be made at the coronation."

"Why did you—"

"Please, Julia. No more questions. I . . ." He turned sharply. "Someone is coming."

A moment later Julia heard the sound of the carriage rumbling along the drive behind them.

They turned their horses off the drive to permit the carriage to pass.

"It is Miss Merryweather," said Julia. "And her mother."

The two ladies had seen them and were waving out of the window as the carriage passed. Miss Merryweather did not look at all pleased to see who was riding with Miss Townes, and when the two young ladies sat together in the drawing room, Miss Merryweather took the opportunity to whisper a repetition of her warning about the gentleman from Winterhall.

Julia knew she must not try to persuade Mimmie to stay a few days longer, but the idea of parting was a heavy burden.

"It is so very hard to let you go when I have just found you again."

"I have promised Philip that I will return with him to London. He has a good many things for me to do."

"You know, Mimmie, you needn't continue with this . . . this employment you have found. Come here and live with us. My father will—"

"Oh, my dear, I know that your father would gladly have me remain to give you comfort. But I . . ." She laughed, almost embarrassed. "I find that this sort of life appeals to me. It is more excitement than I have known, except in those long ago days when I was fleeing with Frances. And this time the cause is entirely a just one." She smiled at Julia. "We will see each other often, my dear. I know I will be staying with Philip at Winterhall from time to time. And there is no reason that you should not visit with me in London now and then.

Indeed, I believe your father means to go there very soon."

Charles did find it necessary within the month to visit London, and he took Julia and her aunt with him. They stayed at the same hotel as on their previous visit to London, even in the same suite of rooms.

How different life is when one has means, Julia thought as she watched her maid unpacking. *My mother must have missed this sort of life, must often have regretted that she gave up this comfort and indulgence for a passion that came to nothing in the end.* It made Julia wonder what *she* might find she had given up for passion. Her honor? Her principles? Certainly. Her peace of mind? Very likely. What would she be left with in the end? Philip had *said* he loved her, but she could not put aside that last remaining anxiety. It would be with her until she heard him ask her to be his wife, more probably until she stood beside him at the altar.

But would it really be wise, prudent, sensible to marry Philip? Julia knew very well that she was much better suited to a life of tranquility, of harmony, with Lawrence.

Philip and she were so different, knew so little of each other. It may well be that they had only passion in common. And no doubt, she thought bitterly, he had that in common with other women, too. Was it possible for her to find contentment in such a union? Frankly, she doubted it.

"I have been to see Miss Flagg this afternoon, Julia, while you were at the lawyer's with your father. I told her that you mean to call upon her as soon as the business with your father will permit it."

"Thank you, Aunt Julia. I do mean to go soon." It was something Julia must do. She had to try to learn whether Sir William's affections for Miss Flagg were returned in kind. And if so—what? Warn her? No. Tell Philip. "How is Miss Flagg?"

"Glowing! Truly quite glowing. Her mother confided to me that she is certain that Narcissa has determined upon a husband at last."

Julia's startled fingers barely saved her crystal scent bottle from disaster. "Oh, Aunt Julia! Is it. . . . Do you think it is someone we know? Did she say anything of the gentleman?"

"She was unable to do so, for Miss Flagg has said nothing of the matter to her mother, but Mrs. Flagg, who knows her daughter best, is persuaded that she means to marry. And I had other information from Miss Hathaway, who had tea with me while I was waiting for Miss Flagg to finish with one of the parents."

"Yes?"

"Miss Hathaway, who has always had a tendency to talk too much, told me that Miss Flagg might be thinking of retiring from the school. The silly woman has hopes of being Miss Flagg's successor!"

"Most unlikely," was all that Julia could stammer.

"Miss Hathaway hinted that there *is* a gentleman in the question and that no one has seen him because Miss Flagg is fearful of a new young teacher who is exceptionally pretty!"

"Well," Julia said distractedly, "having given a scholar's mind to the business of choosing a husband, it is only reasonable that Miss Flagg would do the same in the matter of securing him. I certainly will call upon Miss Flagg as soon as possible."

"Oh, yes. Do that, my dear."

It was still a few days later, however, before Julia could make time for Miss Flagg. For three days in succession, she accompanied her father to the lawyer's office. Charles was amending his will and settling money on his daughter.

"Of course"—he smiled—"I intend and expect to live a long time yet, but it is well to have these things settled."

"Yes, indeed," said Mr. Craig, the attorney. "It is only prudent. I could tell you stories, Miss Townes, of the most astonishing instances of sudden death . . ." Catching the sharp glance from Mr. Townes, he stopped short and coughed to cover his embarrassment. "Well, I mean, it is only prudent."

"I have reason to know it, Mr. Craig," said Julia quietly.

"Craig and I have been discussing the question of where you might live if I were to die before you marry," Charles said. "As you know, Fainway must pass to Lawrence at my death. Your Aunt Julia, I know, would not care to stay on there under those circumstances, and it seems to me that the two of you might like to remain together."

"Oh, yes, certainly. I would never think of leaving Aunt Julia, not in all of her lifetime."

"That is good of you, Julia."

"Not at all, Father. Having had so little family for most of my life, I can hardly think of abandoning the people who are so dear to me now. If I should . . . marry, I would take her with me, if she would consent."

"The question is where you might wish to settle in the meantime."

"I see," said Julia, who had never thought about it.

"Your aunt, I am certain, will wish to remain in the country, for she has had every opportunity to choose city life and has declined it."

"That would be my wish, too, Father. I find country life very much to my taste."

"That settles the question, then, Craig. We need think no more about London properties. In fact"— Charles stood up—"I think we need do nothing more on this until Julia and I have had a chance to look at a little place I had in mind to buy in any case. It is not large, Julia, really not much more than a cottage, but it is pretty and very sturdily built, and it is not far from Winterhall."

"It sounds lovely, Father, though I am certain that I shall live on at Fainway with you and Aunt Julia until . . ." And here she stopped for she could not bear to finish the thought.

Julia was fearful that Aunt Julia would want to come along on the visit to Miss Flagg, but a timely return of goutiness kept her aunt in the hotel that day. Julia was driven in the carriage past the newly finished railroad station, disappointed once again that there was no sign of a train, to the doors of the academy. She was shown into the parlor but informed that Miss Flagg had not yet returned.

"But she is expected any moment, Miss Townes. I hope you will not mind waiting."

"I don't mind at all, Miss Hathaway. Miss Flagg's time is not her own, I know."

Miss Hathaway sniffed pointedly but said nothing.

"Miss Flagg keeps well, I hope?"

"Very well, indeed, Miss Townes. Never better, I should say."

"How glad I am to know it. The school continues to prosper, then?"

"Oh, the school. Yes, I daresay it is doing as well as ever. One only hopes it may continue to do the same."

"Oh, Miss Hathaway," Julia said, surrendering to the obvious ploy, "I do hope there is nothing wrong!"

"Wrong? Well, I am sure I cannot say so, Miss Townes."

"Oh. I mistook you. I rather thought you were suggesting that the school might be in some danger."

"Well, the truth is, Miss Townes"—Miss Hathaway hitched her chair a little closer—"some of us on the staff are thinking that Miss Flagg might choose to leave the school behind. It must not be spoken of, for it is not, I believe, a settled thing, but," her voice dropped to a whisper, "I believe it is likely that Miss Flagg may be married soon."

"Indeed?" How happy I am for her. Who is the lucky gentleman?"

"That I cannot say, Miss Townes, for he has never been introduced to any of us!"

"I see. Perhaps she may still be making up her mind."

Miss Hathaway sniffed again and looked doubtful. "Miss Flagg rode out with him about an hour ago." Julia felt a sick dread that might have been tinged with fear. Sir William was actually here! "They should return at any moment and," Miss Hathaway had the decency to blush as she went on, "I rather think we might be able to catch a glimpse of him from this window."

"Oh," Julia breathed, "do you think that would be—"

"Well, after all, there is no harm in looking out the window! It is fortunate that we are in this room, for it is the only one that overlooks the drive."

Julia, determined to know the worst, followed her guide to the window and took her position. They did not wait long; within a couple of minutes, a small rig drove into the courtyard and drew to a stop before the steps. Julia recognized the peach-colored dress Miss Flagg was wearing, but the large matching hat obscured her companion's face. Then, as the two ladies gazed down, they saw something very shocking. Miss Flagg gave her hand to the gentleman, the dark head bent to kiss it, then he seized the other hand and rained kisses on them both. Miss Flagg did not shrink from this intimacy, but threw back her head, laughing.

It seemed a very long time until the gentleman drew away and was stepping down from the carriage. He came around to help Miss Flagg to alight, and Julia's heart leapt to her throat and froze there.

It was Philip!

Chapter Eighteen

On the drive back to the hotel Julia felt only numbness. She stared straight before her into nothingness, seeing none of the March sunshine that struggled through scuttling clouds to brighten the London cityscape. The coachman had to tell her twice that they had arrived at the hotel.

"Thank you, Rogers," she said vacantly as he helped her to the street and saw her into the care of the hotel doorman. She spoke automatically and without the warm smile Rogers had come to expect from Miss Townes.

Julia was relieved in arriving at their rooms to find that her father was not in.

"The master has gone to meet with Mr. Sommerville, madam," the sound of that name seemed to ring shrill and deafening as the maid spoke it. "Indeed, madam, you cannot have missed him by more than five minutes."

Julia took off her hat and sat down in the elegant, but uncomfortable, chair that was nearest at hand. Still staring unblinking and dry-eyed, she forced herself to concentrate, to take a cold, clearheaded look at her situation.

The worst of her dreadings had proved to be true, and she realized with a sick little pang that she was not surprised.

Philip did not love her. Or at least he did not love only her. She had been the greatest of fools to suppose that he *could* love only one woman. And what was worse, she believed now that she must have known this in her heart of hearts, even as she gave herself to him. Yet she ignored every warning and her own better judgment.

She rose and went to stand at the window, staring down into the busy street below, now dampened by a light rain. So, how could she blame him, blame anyone but her foolish self? Just as her mother had done, Julia would have to live with the consequences of her own actions. In that moment she resolved that she would not be angry, not be vindictive; she simply would forget him. She laughed bitterly at herself. Well, she would learn to live without him.

That evening Julia pleaded indisposition and declined dining downstairs with the others when she learned that Mimmie and Philip were invited to join them. And the next day, too, she refused to emerge from her bedroom when told that Philip had called.

"I am sorry that you are feeling so unwell, Julia." Mimmie said as she stood beside the bed where Julia had just retreated. "Philip is leaving early in the morning to return to the north, and he did wish to speak to you, however briefly, before he goes."

"Please wish him success for me, Mimmie. And, of course, he can leave any message or instructions he may have for me with you. Unless . . . Oh, Mimmie, must you return with him?"

"No. He has given me a task here in London. One that he does not wish to leave to, well, to anyone else.

"Is it dangerous?"

"I don't think so. At least not for me."

Julia was puzzled by this but knew better by now than to press for more information. And whatever Mimmie's new employment was, it could not have been overly demanding, for Julia saw her every day. She was there when Lawrence came one morning to invite Julia out to drive.

"I should like to have you come with me to Mary's little house," Lawrence said. "I must begin to put it in order to offer for sale."

"I suppose that must be done," said Julia. "I will help in any way I can, certainly."

"Her will has just been settled, and it seems there was a bit more money than I thought. Her investments have prospered of late."

"I think my father had helped her with some investment advice."

"Actually, I think I might like to have you look at my house as well as hers. I have need of only one house, and I am not certain which would be the better to keep. A woman's ideas are always more to the point on such matters."

"Very well, then. Both houses."

Mimmie had already risen to don her hat to go

with them when Julia, fearful of jealousy on the part of her aunt, invited her to go along.

"You see, Lawrence," Aunt Julia told him as she took up her parasol, "what a bargain you have made. You shall have the ideas of three women rather than one." And Lawrence, to his credit, did try to look pleased about it.

It was not a difficult choice which house should be kept. Lawrence's house, while comfortable enough, was not so well designed or built as Mary's pretty home, which Julia remembered visiting on her last trip to London. Nor was it so well located, for Mary had settled in an up-and-coming portion of the city, while Lawrence's neighborhood, though not far away, seemed poised for a slide in the other direction. Julia pointed this out as tactfully as she could to Lawrence, and she heard the other ladies echo her thoughts.

When the tour of Mary's house was over, Lawrence invited Aunt Julia to show Mimmie the porcelain figurines Mary had collected, and suggested they each might choose one for themselves. While they were so engrossed in the drawing room, Lawrence drew Julia next door into the music room. As she followed him, she suggested that Lawrence might wish to consult her father on the question of the houses, too.

"I believe Mary once told me that my father had, some years ago, advised her on the purchase of her home."

"Julia."

She turned from the window where she had gone to look out on a pretty garden. "Yes, Lawrence?"

"Julia, I love you. You must know it. Julia,

dearest, will you become my wife and make me the happiest man on God's earth? I promise that I will do all in my power to make you happy, too."

"Oh, Lawrence, how good you are. But I . . ." No point in hesitating. She must not falter. She must tell him. "But I cannot marry you."

"What?" His face was ashen with disappointment, even a hint of panic. He led her to a sofa and sat down with her. "Julia, my darling, I will understand if you do not feel you can return my love in full measure as yet. That will come in time, as we grow to know each other better."

"Lawrence, I cannot marry anyone," she said firmly. "I will tell you why, but you must swear that you will not tell my father. Or anyone."

He sat looking at her dumbly.

"You must swear it, Lawrence."

"Yes. Yes, all right then. I swear it," he managed to say.

"Lawrence, I did not emerge from my captivity completely unblemished. I . . ." She took a long breath, "I am not a virgin, Lawrence."

His face at first was immobile, perhaps with the shock of it, then it contorted with rage. "Which one of them?" he rasped as he stood up stiffly. "You must tell me which of them is responsible for this, Julia. The authorities must be informed so that this may be added to his offenses. So the world can see what sort of villains these men really are."

"Sit down, Lawrence. I will do nothing of the kind—for my own sake, not that of . . . of the man responsible. I want no one to know of this. No one. Nothing can be done to remedy what has happened, and I do not propose to speak of it to

363

anyone. I must just let it be. But I cannot let you propose to me in ignorance of this fact."

"Julia"—he did sit down and take her hand—"I understand. You are concerned for those who are close to you, who would be hurt by this knowledge becoming public. I tell you now that what has happened to you makes no difference in my feelings for you. I am angry only on your behalf, that you had to endure this atrocity. I ask again that you marry me."

"No, Lawrence. At least not now. You say it does not matter, and I believe that you truly think so at this moment. You are sorry for me and concerned for me, and, of course, you are fond of me. But later, when the outrage has faded, when the indignity of it all becomes more familiar, you may well think differently."

"Julia . . ." he started to protest, but she held up a hand to stop him.

"Lawrence, in your heart you know that I am right. When some time has passed, when you have had time to think on what I have told you, if your sentiments are unchanged, you may ask me again."

She stood up and gave him her hand. He kissed it gently. She put the hand to his face for a moment before she smiled at him and said that they had best be getting back to the others. They departed with Lawrence more than ever undecided as to what to do about the houses.

That evening was spent at the theater. Lawrence sat beside Julia, but he was quiet and withdrawn and did not laugh with her at the foolishness taking place on the stage—still outraged, Julia supposed, by what he had learned. But in the intermission between acts, it was Julia who was outraged at the tittering comments she overheard from the theater-goers regarding an unfortunate situation in the queen's personal retinue.

"Do you mean to say that the queen intends to dismiss her?" a bejeweled matron asked of her companion as they swept by Julia.

"It is true, my dear," replied the stout lady in gray lace. "Her Majesty declared that the woman was obviously with child and without a husband, and such behavior cannot be countenanced in a lady-in-waiting."

"Well, of course not, if there were any truth to it, but my husband's cousin's wife knows Lady Flora rather well, and she declares that such a thing is impossible. I have heard it said that our queen is a prude and dreary in the extreme. I only wonder if they will come upon a prince desperate or dull enough to marry *her*."

"But Lady Flora is said to have grown very large in recent weeks, giving every evidence of an expectant mother. What other explanation could there be?"

The ladies drifted out of Julia's earshot, and she did not hear the reply.

It was mid-April when the family returned to Fainway. There had been no word of Philip. Mimmie did not mention him on her infrequent visits, and Julia pointedly did not ask. She heard no mention of his name except her father's casual remark that Philip must still be engaged in searching for the remaining traitor. Julia tried not to think of him at all except to plan very carefully what she would say when they did meet again.

A week or so after their return from London, Charles took Julia and her aunt to view the Stonebridge Cottage. It was a very short drive through the village and along the river, then across the pretty stone bridge for which the house was named.

"This is certainly more than a cottage, Father," Julia said as she was helped from the carriage. "And it looks as though it grew here, as though it has been here since time began."

"I have always admired this place," said Aunt Julia, "though it has been most unfortunate in its occupants. I recall when old Colonel Merton lived here with his black servants and all those dogs. Your Uncle George, Julia, used to ride over to visit him every time we came down to Fainway. And, of course, that meant he had to be invited to dine. And what a bore he was! You remember, Charles?"

"I do. And Mr. Witherspoon lived here briefly while the new vicarage was built."

"Who lives here now?" Julia asked as she surveyed the three stories of gray stone that rose out of a cobbled courtyard.

"Until her death last November, Mrs. Todd lived here. It has been unoccupied since that time."

At the mention of Mrs. Todd, Julia cast a quizzical glance at her aunt, but she was already leading the way to the heavy front door.

The cottage did not have a great many rooms, but they were large rooms, furnished at present with pieces of unserviceable daintiness and elaborate design. French, Julia thought. To her eye the place cried out for solid, serviceable English furniture.

"Do you think it would make a satisfactory home, Julia?" her father asked when they were descending from the servants' rooms at the top of the house.

"Indeed I do. And Aunt Julia likes it, too. But if we buy it, what will be done with it at present? I have no need or wish for any home but Fainway."

"You must offer it on a lease, of course. It will be a fine retreat for a young man in the city, or even for a small family who wish to be away from London for a holiday now and then, or for weeks at a time in the hottest of the weather."

"That sounds most sensible. A very good idea."

"It will be a source of income for you, too. I should think, though, that you must choose carefully whom you accept as a tenant."

"Me? Whom *I* accept as a tenant?"

"Yes. It is to be your house one day. You might as well have the management of it now."

Julia's eyes widened at the idea of it. "But you will not mind my asking advice from time to time, I hope?"

"Never."

"Let us have a look at the gardens, Julia." Her aunt came out of a bedroom, rubbing her gloves together to remove the dust she had triumphantly found. "The old colonel, as I remember, had grapes in the area just behind the summerhouse."

The grapes were there and showing fine spring promise. So were the kitchen gardens and the many roses that grew in well-arranged beds. Aunt Julia walked about exclaiming at the prettiness of it all, and, Mrs. Todd's insults to the place notwithstanding, the question of buying the house was quickly settled. That evening Julia talked with her father about placing an advertisement offering the house for lease.

A few days later, word came in the form of a note that Mimmie had come to Winterhall to stay as Mr. Parke's guest. The whole Fainway family drove over to pay a formal call of welcome.

Mr. Parke seemed a little confused about the status of his guest. "It was Philip who told me she was coming," he whispered to Aunt Julia, but loudly enough for Julia to hear quite plainly. "Wrote to me on Thursday last. I thought Philip himself would be here by now, but he has gone straight to London." He jerked his head in Mimmie's direction. "*She* has seen him."

"So he *has* returned from the north?" Aunt Julia wanted to know.

Mr. Parke growled and shuffled toward a chair. "I do not understand why he wants to concern himself in all this dreadful political business when he could and should be here at home tending to Winterhall's affairs."

Julia went to embrace Mimmie, wondering how she was bearing up under her less than enthusiastic welcome, but Mimmie's face was serene.

"It is a pleasant thing indeed to be back in my old home," Mimmie replied to Charles's inquiries. "Mr. Parke has been so kind as to allot me my old bedroom."

Mr. Parke turned quickly, and his face said that he had done this courtesy by accident. But he managed to say something unobjectionable and muttered that Miss Payne might as well pour the tea.

"I do wonder, though," said Charles as he accepted a teacup, "what has taken Philip to London. Perhaps he has had some success to report. Can you tell us nothing, Miss Payne?"

"Nothing, I am afraid, Mr. Townes. As always where Philip is concerned, I suppose we must just be patient. I have, however, received some news from York. I have had a letter, Julia, from Mrs. Ponder. I wrote to her, you know, as soon as I could."

"Dear Mrs. Ponder," Julia said. "She keeps well, I hope?"

"Quite well. She writes that Mr. Woodland is to be married to Miss Pierce."

"Oh!" This news, though expected, left Julia rather desolate. "I wish them joy, I'm sure."

"Yes, dear, and so do I. Though I expect the happiest person at this news is Mrs. Woodland."

"Most probably. When are they to be married?"

"Not until July. Mr. Simmons is expected to be recovered and returned from Bath by then. Miss Pierce, it seems, does not care for the curate."

"Odd. I never heard her say so. Perhaps it is . . ." She stopped.

"Oh, Julia," Mimmie said with an unmistakable twinkle, "go ahead and say it. Of course, it will be the ultimate triumph for Miss Pierce to be married *to* the man she wanted *by* the man who wanted her. She is just the sort of silly girl to fancy such a scene."

"Do you suppose the thought of it is what has made Mr. Simmons ill?" Julia grinned.

"I wouldn't wonder, though Mrs. Ponder does say that the poor man has been ailing some time."

Julia remembered then that it had been the curate whom she had seen at Mrs. Woodland's house the day of her escape, but somehow she could not bear to mention that day, those circumstances. She only said quietly, "Then we must not suspect him of malingering in the grip of unrequited love."

"Oh," Mimmie continued with a knowing look at Julia, "I might add that Mrs. Ponder has now met the gentleman in the house across the street. It seems he has lately spent much time in York. She finds him quite charming and believes that Miss Pierce thinks so, too. Perhaps *that* is the reason for the delay in the wedding."

Julia tried to return Mimmie's smile, but found herself perilously close to tears. She stared hard into her teacup and said they mustn't continue to talk of people the others did not know.

"I hear that you're negotiating for Mrs. Todd's cottage," Mr. Parke said to Charles.

Charles admitted that it was so.

"Can't think what you want with the old place," Mr. Parke continued. "I remember as a boy hearing stories of serious flooding in the basements. Bad location there just on the river."

"There was some problem with flooding many years ago, Mr. Parke," put in Mimmie. "But Colonel Merton, when he had the place, did some work on the drainage all around the house. A new system of ditching, I believe. Do you remember, Mr. Townes, how . . ." She paused suddenly, and a flush came into her face. Julia knew that Mimmie had touched by accident on a memory that would give him pain.

"I do recall, Miss Payne." Charles's voice was

low and grave, but it did not waver. "I recall riding over with you and Frances"—only the slightest hesitation over the syllables of the name—"to see what the colonel had been bragging about. I must say that his devisings were just the improvement the landscaping needed. There has been no difficulty with flooding since that time. Miss Payne is quite right there."

Another low grumble was emitted from Mr. Parke, and he turned to glower at Mimmie, who smiled at him with gracious charm and offered to refill his teacup.

"But, Mimmie," Julia interjected hurriedly, "as you have been in London these past weeks, what can you tell us of this business with the queen? The papers are full of hints and innuendo. Those of us not in London hardly know what to think. Is it truly a scandal?"

"Well, if Mr. Parke will excuse my repeating what he has already heard, I will tell you that it does, indeed, seem to be a scandal."

"What a pity," exclaimed Aunt Julia, "with the coronation so near at hand."

"I agree with you, ma'am," Mimmie said, "but it does appear that the queen has been in serious error about poor Lady Flora. Not only is she not in a state to be a disgrace to the queen, but the woman is actually gravely ill. It is feared that she might die."

"Oh, no!" cried Julia.

"Yes. I fear the queen will be placed in the uncomfortable position of having to apologize for her mistaken suspicions."

"Heavens!" said Julia, to whom the idea was

most foreign. "Still, if it must be done, it is best to do it at once. Then she—and we—can all forget it and think of the coronation."

The next morning, Mimmie visited at Fainway, and as it was a fine day, Mimmie and Julia walked again to the churchyard to visit Frances's grave. Julia placed a bouquet of tulips below the headstone.

"I never told you, Mimmie, but when I was at Winderfields, I felt my mother's presence very strongly. Just at the moment that I felt myself in danger from Sir William. I rather believe that she was trying to warn me. Do you think this can be possible?"

"I confess I have had similar sensations from time to time throughout this work I have done lately. I see no reason that Frances would not try to look after those she cares for, from wherever she might be."

Julia put her arm around Mimmie and asked, "Do you think we will ever see Sir William brought to answer for her death?"

Mimmie sighed. "I don't know, my dear. Perhaps Philip will be able to give full attention to the question when this other affair is finally settled. But he has said to me, and perhaps to you, too, that with Miss Sennett dead and the coachman, too, it will be a difficult thing to obtain proof."

Julia moved now to Mary's grave and placed a smaller bundle of flowers beside the few camillias she knew had come within the last few days from her father.

"And here is his other victim, Mimmie. You did not know her, I suppose, but she was a kind and deserving woman. She was very good to me when I first came to Fainway. Had she lived, I believe she would have become my stepmother. Sir William has deprived my father of two wives."

Spring advanced, and the country around Fainway burst and blossomed into a place of exquisite green and beauty. Julia knew she should be reveling in the sights and sounds and smells of approaching summer in the country, but her senses perceived little of the glory of the season; they were dulled by the loss of another kind of beauty, a more intense kind of glory which had once enveloped those senses in a way no amount of apple blossoms or thriving crops could hope to imitate.

"As I grow to know my daughter better," Charles said to Mimmie one morning, "I find her to be quite a solemn girl. Has she always been so, Miss Payne?"

"Julia was always rather serious," Mimmie said, "though she seems more withdrawn to me than in former days. I rather think she may be just thinking of the many changes that have come to her life since her last birthday."

"I daresay she still grieves for her mother."

Mimmie took a long time to answer. "Julia loved her mother very much. One must always love Frances, you know. I sometimes felt that Julia was a little overwhelmed by her, overshadowed by her. Often it did not seem fair."

"Yes," Charles said thoughtfully. "I see very well what you mean. Then what do you think?"

"She misses her mother, of course. But I tell you most sincerely that she loves you, Mr. Townes. And her aunt, too. She is content with you both, and, in time, she will be cheerful once more."

Charles decided that a party for Julia's birthday on the twenty-fourth of May might hasten the cheering process. It was the queen's birthday, too, of course, and a toast was drunk to Her Majesty.

Mimmie had a present for Julia, a pretty cameo she had purchased in London, and some most astounding news. "I have received an invitation to the coronation," she told the group assembled for Julia's birthday dinner. "It came only yesterday. I was certain that Philip would be invited, after all that he did in this matter, but I never supposed that I would be singled out in such a way."

"But it is only right that you should, Mimmie!" Julia declared. "You took a very great risk on behalf of crown and country. It should be recognized."

"I agree," said Lawrence, who had come down from London for the occasion. "Women who serve in such a way deserve the same recognition as a man would receive."

"I wonder if the queen sees it in that light, or if she hopes to show her subjects that a woman can be so devoted to the monarchy as to risk death on its behalf. Perhaps she hopes to discourage further plotting." Mimmie said this with a half-serious smile.

"Well, whatever the reason, I am delighted for you," said Julia.

"I must say, Miss Payne," Charles remarked, "you have outdone my surprise for Julia. I have only invitations to one of the coronation balls. You will be present at the coronation itself. You will actually see the queen, while we will merely toast

374

her along with all the other thousands of people in the city for the event."

But to Julia, the thought of attending a coronation ball was an astonishing prospect. To be a part of the excitement, to dance with Lawrence, perhaps —it was a delight she could never have imagined a year ago from her distant vantage point of York. As her father had hoped, this distraction did much to improve her cheerfulness, as had Lawrence's renewed proposal of marriage, uttered as they sat a little apart from the others after dinner.

Perhaps he truly will continue in his love for me as time passes, Julia told herself. *He looked quite desperately unhappy when I had to refuse him again.*

The next morning Julia was busy with the assortment of fabrics that had been purchased on the trip to London. She must have a new gown and there was not a moment to be lost.

Mimmie came each day to Fainway to help with the design and sewing of the gown. Julia had chosen a fabric very much like that of the dress that had been Mimmie's previous gift. It was a satin of palest, shimmering blue, and she had some lovely sapphires which she would wear on that important evening. When the dress had reached a certain point of completion, Mimmie took it home with her to Winterhall to sew the special ruffles for the sleeves herself.

Julia rode over almost daily to Winterhall to see Mimmie and to check on the progress of the gown. And since her father was not at home to object she rode alone. Now that Sir William was known (if not proven) to be Bellwether, there was no unknown threat to be feared. Julia felt herself safe anywhere on the grounds of Fainway or Winterhall.

The first day of June gave her a particularly fine morning for her excursion. As she rode beyond the last of the outbuildings of Fainway, she waved a greeting to several of the workers in the wheat field. She took the turn in the path that went past the woods and onto the grounds of Winterhall. There were workers in the fields there, too, and it looked as though the wheat was doing well.

The ladies had the house to themselves; Mr. Parke was out on a call to a gentleman on the other side of the valley, and Philip, to Mr. Parke's continued great annoyance, remained in London.

Mimmie produced the ruffles; which were delightedly approved of by Julia. She had brought along her sewing basket and helped tack them into place. The effect was stunning; Julia could not resist trying on the gown then and there before turning it over to the seamstress who would do the final stitching.

At four o'clock, Julia mounted her horse for the return ride to Fainway. She had just turned onto the path when she saw a rider approaching. In an instant, she had recognized him.

"Lawrence!" she said as he drew alongside her. "Whatever are you doing here? I thought I would not see you again until we came to London."

"The city has become a madhouse, Julia. I am sorry to say it, but I will be truly glad when this coronation is a done thing."

"I suppose the excitement is growing quite feverish."

"It is dreadful. No one can speak of anything

else. The women care for nothing but their gowns for the event. The men only wonder how they are to pay for the extravagance of their wives and daughters. And all of us are wondering what it is costing the treasury."

Julia laughed. "I guess we must hope that Her Majesty will live and reign a very long time, so that we needn't do this sort of thing any time soon."

"I could not agree more. Shall we ride through the woods rather than on the path and road? I came that way and found it most soothing."

Julia had stiffened before she realized it. She had avoided the Druid's Circle, had not even ridden to the ridge to look down on it since that day with Philip. But that day must be forgotten.

"Yes, of course. I have been wondering if there is any activity there. It is nearly midsummer, and I suppose the Druids will be coming for their famous celebration."

"I did not notice any signs of them as I rode through. But there is something most unusual in the woods nearby. I will show it to you."

Julia's heart sank. It could only be the gypsy wagon, and she was not at all sure she could return to those woods, to that wagon, and not lose her composure. But she told herself that she must. It would be a test, an important test.

As they rode along, Julia realized that Lawrence was chatting, telling her something, some story of an incident that had to do with poor Mary. She forced her mind to focus on his words.

"And so you intend to offer Mary's house for sale instead of your own?" she asked when he had paused.

"I do."

"Lawrence, I hope it has nothing to do with my not accepting your proposal. I did think you had decided on the other course of action."

"Well, of course, if we were going to be married in the near future, I would not have parted with it, but the truth is that a friend of mine is most anxious to have the house. He declares that it is perfect in every way for himself and his new bride. She is just as eager, and I do not see how I can refuse them in my current circumstances. He has offered quite a lot more than I judged the place to be worth."

"I see." Julia was unable to say why she felt so disappointed.

"Julia, if you fancy the place and think that you may soon change your mind, you have only to say the word. It is not a deed completed."

"Forgive me, Lawrence, it is just that I was surprised. I am sure you are doing the right thing in the matter of the house."

They had reached the woods and ridden into the trees. As Julia had feared, Lawrence led her along the trail to the spot where the gypsy wagon stood.

"There, now! What do you think of that?" Lawrence asked as he helped Julia from her horse.

"Why, it is one of the gypsy wagons, isn't it? It certainly looks the same."

"I thought so, too. Do you know what this means, Julia? They must mean to return here. I only hope they do not come at the same time as the Druids again."

"I wonder." For a moment, Julia closed her eyes and saw again the gypsy band. Milus, Jacob,

Jonetta, Fellie. Where were they now? Somewhere in their wanderings, thinking of the time they would return to the haven Philip had provided them? With a start she realized that Lawrence was speaking to her urgently.

"Julia, you must give me some hope. Tell me how long you intend to keep me waiting, my darling." He took her basket from her, held her in his arms and now he drew her gently near him. "I love you so much, Julia."

He kissed her then, tenderly at first, then with a growing urgency. With a conscious effort, Julia tried, really tried to respond. She knew in her mind that she should love him, but in her heart was the certain knowledge that she could not. Her heart belonged to Philip Sommerville, and though he did not want it, it could not be given to another.

She drew away from him. "I'm sorry, Lawrence. I think I had best go home now."

"No!" He caught her arm and pulled her back to him. "I do not ask that you marry me at once, Julia. I'll not insist on that. But I must know when. I must know for certain that one day you will be mine!"

She stood looking into his anguished face, but she could only shake her head sadly. "I cannot marry you, Lawrence. Not now. Not ever." She picked up her basket and turned toward her horse.

"You fool!" With a fierce movement, he snatched her basket from her and swung it against the trunk of a nearby tree.

Julia cried out as she saw it burst and splinter; thread and needles and pins flew out in all directions. "Lawrence! What are you doing? Have you gone mad?"

"Never more sane, my dear cousin." He moved back toward her deliberately. "Why, Julia? Why would you not just marry me? Now"—he took her roughly by the arms—"now, I will have to kill you after all."

Julia shook her head at him in confusion and disbelief. "Lawrence! Now I know that you are mad."

"You are such a perfect little fool, Julia." He took his riding crop from his horse. "I would have made you a good husband, too. I am quite fond of you, actually. And it all would have been so suitable. But now . . ." He shrugged.

Julia's absolute disbelief at what she was seeing and hearing was washed away in a wave of fear as he pushed her against the tree and brought the riding crop up to her throat.

"Lawrence, why? Why are you behaving in this way? It makes no sense!"

"Why? Money. Why else?"

"Money? But I have no money. And . . . and you are to have Fainway in any case. It is entailed. You must know that."

"And a lot of good it will do me, with no money to keep it up. Your precious father has seen to that. Everything that would have been mine—all the other properties, all the many thousands of pounds are to go to you now. But, of course, if you are not alive to inherit—well, you see, my dear Julia, I simply have no choice."

"You are crazy! Lawrence, you know you cannot do such an evil thing!"

"Why not? I have done it before to protect my interest in Fainway. Do you think I could let that scheming fool of a Mary marry your father? Suppose they had a son? What then? Fainway would go to him as well as all the money. No, no."

Julia's furiously racing brain told her she could not spare time or thought for this impossible revelation. Every effort must be turned to saving herself. "But, Lawrence, you will be found out. They will know that you came to Winterhall to fetch me. You must stop this crazy talk!"

"I will not be found out. Do you think I am such a fool as to let anyone know that I am anywhere near this place? I followed you when you left Fainway, keeping well out of sight of anyone on the premises. No one saw me either at Fainway or at Winterhall. Besides, my household knows that I am on my way to Brighton. In fact, I am already there and enjoying the hospitality of a special friend of mine. As for you, Cousin Julia, I am afraid that by the time you are taken from the river, most likely at that sandy bar some twenty miles or so downstream, there will not be much left to explain how you died."

A stifled scream escaped from Julia's lips as the riding crop was pressed against her throat, stopping her breath and making her eyes swim in pain and flame.

With an effort beyond any strength she thought she possessed, she struggled and twisted the crop away. Thrashing blindly, she brought her nails hard into his face, and when the force of him against her was lessened with the shock of her attack, she kicked out to strike him. Finding herself suddenly released, she turned herself around the tree trunk, putting its bulk between them.

They circled the tree trunk, he lunging for her, she twisting and wriggling to escape his grasp. When the time seemed right, Julia made a dash for her horse. Keeping the animal between them, she took the reins from the branch where the horse was tied, then, with a foot in the stirrup, she was pulling herself into the saddle when, with a single stride from those long legs, Lawrence was beside her and pulling her down onto the ground again. He held her now with her back to him, and the riding crop was again at her throat. She managed a single scream that was cut short in a choke and a gurgle. And then she was falling and he was falling with her. They were in a kneeling heap in the damp summer moss and he was breathing, cursing in her ear as he increased the pressure against her throat. All the time that she was scratching at his hands and struggling against the weight of him, Julia was seeing the beauty of the summer woodland and thinking, bizarrely, how incongruous it all seemed. And then the sight of the woods faded into a gray blur, creeping steadily to the center of all consciousness.

Dimly, very dimly, she heard a sharp crack and wondered if it was the breaking of one of her bones. The grayness faded for an instant and she seemed to be no longer imprisoned by that fatal grasp. The pressure of his weight was gone, and she found herself, suddenly unsupported, pitching headlong onto the ground. Another of those out-of-place thoughts found her wondering if this was the same terror her mother had known at her own violent death. Then, still faintly, came the sound of a struggle. With the greatest of efforts, she opened her eyes to see Lawrence on the ground nearby, locked in fierce combat with—yes, it was Philip!

Slowly, by concentrating on each and every movement, she was able to get to her knees, and then to sit up. She watched, mesmerized, though not fully comprehending, as the two men exchanged blow after blow. Though Philip surely had the advantage of size and skill, Lawrence was a cornered beast, and he fought with desperate intensity. It was not until a singular and very brutal blow sent Lawrence pitching head first against the trunk of a tree that he was unable to rise again to the fight.

Philip stood sweating and panting for a moment, making certain that the fight was ended, then he rushed to the spot where Julia sat.

"Julia," he cried as he gathered her into his arms, "if that devil has hurt you I will kill him here and now, I swear!"

"Philip? What are you doing here?" She could barely speak through her bruised and aching throat, and her gaze was blinking and unfocused.

"Sh. Don't try to speak. Just stay quiet until help comes. They should find us soon."

Bewildered and exhausted, but somehow oddly comforted, Julia closed her eyes and drifted into blessed unconsciousness.

Julia knew that she was in her own bed when she came drifting and floating back to wakefulness. Without opening her eyes, she lay still and tried to remember. When one could get beyond that memory of Lawrence, so cruelly vivid, there were only snatches, vague and almost dreamlike. Her peace and contentment in Philip's arms disturbed by shouts of men, answered, rough and booming, by a call to them from Philip. A crush of people, hands helping to lift her, to carry her gently to the gypsy wagon which she supposed might have carried her home. A glimpse of Lawrence, stirring and moaning on the ground, then hauled roughly to his feet. Her lunge to recover her precious basket, someone placing its mangled remains in her hands. The feel of strong arms—Philip's?—carrying her up some stairs. More hands, gentle and familiar this time, undressing her, bathing her bruises, putting her to bed. And then, she knew, there had been dreams, for once she had been awakened by the sound of her own cries and had been soothed and comforted and coaxed back to sleep by a voice that had belonged to Aunt Julia.

She opened her eyes and judged by the amount of summer daylight that it must be very early morning. As she turned her eyes from the window, she saw that Aunt Julia was dozing in a chair not far from the bed.

One of the maids was there, too, and noticing now that the patient was stirring, she got up and came to the bedside. "How are you feeling, madam?" came the whispered question.

"Hello, Molly. Rather thirsty, actually."

The maid poured a glass of water and brought it to Julia. The sound made her aunt stir and open her eyes.

The maid said, "I will go and bring some tea, madam."

"Yes, do that," said Aunt Julia.

"What time is it?" Julia wanted to know.

Her aunt consulted her watch. "Half past five.

You have slept very nearly ten hours, my dear."

Julia sighed and lay back on her pillows. "Have I?"

"Oh, my dearest Julia, I can hardly bear to think—"

"Nor can I, Aunt Julia. Nor can I quite believe it! You must tell me what has happened, for I have so little memory just now."

"I know little of the business myself, dear, except that Philip Sommerville found you in the woods by the Druid's Circle, and you were being attacked, actually attacked by Lawrence!"

"He was going to kill me, Aunt Julia. And he killed poor Mary, too."

"So they said. I found it all quite overwhelming. You were brought here, nearly out of your senses, and we put you to bed, and you have been sleeping ever since. The doctor has seen you and will come again later this morning."

"But how did Mr. Sommerville find me? How did he come to be there?"

"That I don't know, dear. And we are not likely to hear anything from him on the matter before tomorrow or the next day, for he rode to London directly from our door last evening, with Lawrence as his prisoner."

"Oh."

"But Miss Payne is to come to see you this morning. Very likely she can tell you—can tell all of us—something more about it."

"Oh," Julia repeated, and closed her eyes in weariness. When the maid returned with tea, Julia was fast asleep again.

Chapter Nineteen

"Mimmie!" Julia rasped, and put aside her breakfast tray to embrace the anxious woman who bent over her bedside.

"Julia. Oh, my dear, you are quite ... quite battered. What has that devil done to you?"

"Battered? Am I? Bring me a mirror, will you please?"

Mimmie brought a hand mirror from the dressing table and Julia took stock of herself. There was a large bruise running from just below her ear well down into the neckline of her nightgown. And at the center portion of her throat was an ugly red welt, swollen and angry.

"Oh, dear." Julia sighed. "I knew it *felt* this bad, but I am sorry to see that it looks it as well."

"Does it hurt to speak? It sounds as though it gives you trouble."

"Not so badly as earlier this morning. But I do

not want to speak. I want you to tell me what you know of this business. How did Mr. Sommerville come to be so readily on the spot?"

Mimmie drew a chair to the bedside and sat down frowning. "Not so readily, my dear. Philip is cursing himself for not finding you sooner. If he had, you would not have those dreadful bruises now."

"Not finding me? Mimmie, do you mean that he knew about Lawrence all along?"

"He was concerned, even before Miss Belleville died. Philip knew that Mr. Christian was in financial difficulties. He had borrowed heavily on his expectations from your father, and the concern was that Mr. Townes might come to harm, though, of course an attack on *him* would not be an easy matter. But when it appeared that Miss Belleville might become Mrs. Townes, well, she was a fairly young woman, after all, there might well have been another heir of Fainway. Lawrence *had* to prevent that marriage from taking place, and the only way to do it was to kill her. On that particular night, the circumstances were exactly right. He would make it appear to be an accident, and if the theory of an accident was not accepted, he very cleverly dressed poor Mary in the robe she had lent you so it might also appear that *you* could have been the intended victim, and the mysterious Bellwether the murderer."

"How very odd"—Julia laughed bitterly—"that Bellwether himself was staying in the house at the time! But, Mimmie, how did Lawrence—"

"Philip believes that he stole into Mary's bedroom and suffocated her with a pillow. Perhaps he struck her first. Then he carried her to the reception room and dislodged the panels so that they would fall in just the proper manner. When Philip heard of Miss Belleville's death, he knew at once who was to blame. He persuaded your father that you must be seen to be abducted. Mr. Townes did not require much persuading"—Mimmie lifted a quizzical eyebrow—"for it seemed that you had just proposed a most disturbing scheme to induce Bellwether to come and find you."

"Good lord! I had forgotten."

"As to Lawrence having murdered Mary, and perhaps thinking of murdering you, Philip was certain somehow that you would never have believed it."

"He would have been right, of course," Julia had to admit after thinking it over. "I hardly can believe it now, except . . ." She felt a knife in her heart as she wondered if there had been one time when Philip could have told her all—told her anything—and she would have believed him. She sighed. "Well, it does not matter now."

"So you were taken in a manner that would leave no doubt in Lawrence's mind, or Bellwether's for that matter, that you were out of reach. Meanwhile, each could hope that you might not survive. After our investigations at Leeds ended and you were back home, Philip again had to return north. We no longer feared an attack from Sir William, but I was left in London to keep track of Lawrence. And there, I must say, all appeared to be under control, for Lawrence apparently harbored hopes of a marriage that would bring him everything he wanted. Fainway, all your father's money, and you. But if Lawrence came to Fainway, I was to come to

Winterhall and be at hand to help your father keep an eye on you."

And with that statement Mimmie looked so unhappy that Julia felt it best to divert her. "But where does the question of Sir William stand now, Mimmie? Will he never be brought to account?"

"Philip *has* come upon something to be followed that might lead to Sir William's arrest, something he intended to pursue both in London and at Winderfields. But he has been unable to do much, because of this last, very dangerous traitor still remaining at large. Until he is caught, we cannot be easy about the queen's safety. Philip is back in London now, to stay until after the coronation, so I could be spared to come to Winterhall, with firm orders that if Lawrence appeared, I was never to let you out of my sight. For all the good it did!"

"You must not say that, Mimmie. No one knew Lawrence was here. It is certainly not your fault."

"It was a mistake, all the same. With Philip so busy, he was not immediately informed that Lawrence had disappeared from his lodgings. When neither Philip nor any of his people could locate him, Philip and a couple of others came at once to the country. They almost did not arrive in time."

And again Mimmie looked so unhappy that Julia searched for something to lighten her burden. "Mimmie, I think that in that bundle is my sewing basket. Will you bring it to me? I want to see how badly it is damaged."

Mimmie brought it from the dressing table, feeling gingerly the points of broken straw sticking through the burlap. Julia took it on her lap and unwrapped it carefully.

"Oh dear! He has smashed it pretty badly, I'm afraid," Mimmie said.

"Oh, well. It does not matter. My mother always said that the basket would have to be replaced one day. The tapestry is still intact, and that is the important thing." Julia took her scissors from the basket and began to snip the silken cording that held the lining to the remnants of the basket. "This basket might as well be discarded at once. It is of no use and might tear the fabric."

She gathered the basket's lining and removed it, placing the tattered straw into the burlap for disposal. She cupped her hand to support the bottom of the basket's liner, and a strange sensation overcame her. She sat with the tapestry in her hands as though puzzled and surprised. And then she lifted it up to look at what her hands had touched. Yes, there was a fold in what had been the bottom of the lining, that portion that had lain next to the basket. And from that fold, a piece of paper was emerging.

"Mimmie, look at this. What can it be?" Julia took out the paper and began to unfold it.

"What is it, Julia? What have you found?"

"It is . . . Oh, Mimmie, it is a letter from my mother!"

The letter read:

"My dearest Julia,
If you find and read this message, I pray that you are safe with your father. You will have learned some things about me that will have disturbed you. I will not attempt to explain my actions; indeed, from the perspective of so many years, I do not feel that I understand them myself.

390

"*I believe that Sir William Grant is the Bellwether whom Mimmie will have told you about in her relating of our histories. I have suspected it for some time—since I learned the name of the estate he was to inherit. My dear Richard told me that this mentor of his was a very ordinary-looking man and that his name might be Sennett or something like Winderfield, for Richard had heard these words mumbled as Bellwether slept. He told me also that Bellwether had a scar on his thigh (I do not know or do not recall whether right or left), the scar of a burn from a horseshoe just taken from the fire. It was inflicted by Richard himself in his last struggle with Bellwether before leaving his service for good. At Sir William's party last night, I learned from Miss Sennett, in the course of a carefully couched conversation about accidental disfigurements, that Sir William has such a scar, though, of course, Miss Sennett has never seen it. Her information must have come from MacKenzie, or perhaps from Sir William himself. In any case, Sir William has even confirmed it, having wandered into our conversation before I could prevent it.*

"*Sir William has agreed to delay his departure for Winderfields another day in order to speak to me tomorrow. We are to meet at the Beatrice. If he is indeed Bellwether, I will feel myself in greater safety in such a public place. But I am not entirely easy; Bellwether was a particularly evil and resourceful man, and there is, I know, some danger to my life. If he succeeds, and I do not survive, I want someone*

—you—to know of my fears and suspicions, though for your own safety, it is best that you not know at once, not know until you are safe with your father and any suspicion that Sir William might harbor has been quelled by the passage of time. I calculate that the basket I gave you—it was not a well-made one—will need replacement in two or three years' time. By then Sir William will have made himself very comfortable at Winderfields, and this revelation and subsequent loss of his wealth and his liberty will be a greater blow than now, before he has come to enjoy fully all his consequence and comfort.

"Of course, all this may come to nothing, in which case I shall buy you a much nicer basket tomorrow. Forgive me, Julia, if this message is incoherent or not explained with the sensitivity I should employ at this time. I am writing very late at night and feeling both foolish and frightened. The one thing I must say properly is how very much I love you. I hope with all my heart that I might embrace you at this time tomorrow and that one day I might tell you this story myself and we will have a good laugh together at my foundless fears. Failing that, I can only wish that you will find happiness and peace in a life with your father, who is a good man in every way.

Your loving mother,
Frances Townes"

Julia lovingly stroked the signature, the words swimming in the blur of her tears. After a moment, she passed the letter to Mimmie.

"Mimmie, please go and call my father. Mr. Sommerville must see this letter without delay."

"I beg your pardon, Sir William Grant, is it not?"

Sir William turned to see who had addressed him. "Mr. Townes!" He extended his hand. "What a pleasure to see you, my dear sir."

"I hope you are well, sir. I believe you will remember my neighbor, Mr. Parke, and his nephew, Mr. Sommerville."

The gentlemen bowed and exchanged "how-do-you dos."

"You have come rather early for the coronation, Sir William," Philip drawled.

"Good heavens," Sir William replied. "I hope and fully expect to be safely home again at Winderfields by that day. London will be an insufferable crush. I prefer to take it on faith that Her Majesty is properly installed."

"Sensible man," Mr. Parke growled. "It is only the young and showy folk like my nephew, here, who care about such things. Gentlemen, can't we have an ale? I declare I am weak with thirst on this hot afternoon."

"Why certainly, certainly," Charles said. "Sir William, will you join us? I believe there is an uncommonly fine ale to be had just across the street. Do come. It will do us all good to sit in the cool of the terrace and breathe the fragrance of the taps rather than the heat of the afternoon. And it will give me an opportunity to thank you more fully for your kindness to my daughter. And in your own time of bereavement, too."

"Not at all, sir. Your letter was most generous in

thanks for something that was, indeed, my very great honor and pleasure."

And, though doubtful about being seen with the frivolous and indolent nephew, Sir William recalled that the uncle, like his neighbor, Mr. Townes, was a wealthy and influential man. He allowed himself to be persuaded.

"Like you, Sir William," said Mr. Parke when they had sipped the first foam from their tankards, "I intend to be well at home before the madness of the coronation grows much worse than it is already. I would not be here now except for some tiresome business with my banker."

Charles laughed. "My daughter would think such an attitude quite traitorous. And I do admit to some excitement myself. After all, the queen is so very young, I think it unlikely that any of us will see another coronation in our lifetime."

"I will certainly drink to that!" Sir William raised his tankard and the others did likewise. "And so, Mr. Townes, it is you who have come early for the coronation."

Charles gave a long and painful sigh; Mr. Parke looked distressed; and Philip rather bored.

"I fear it is personal business of a most painful and embarrassing nature that brings me here," Charles said with a melancholy shake of his head. "I am surprised you had not heard or read that my young cousin, Lawrence Christian, was arrested some ten days ago for the murder of Miss Mary Belleville, his stepsister."

"Murder? But I thought—"

"So did we all think it an accident, Sir William. But it turns out to have been a most clever and diabolical murder."

Sir William sat thoughtfully, then asked, "How is Miss Townes bearing up under this development? I rather thought she might be fond of her cousin."

"She is most distressed, as are we all, Sir William. But it is yet another painful event that Julia must and will face up to, just as with the loss of her mother and all the things that have happened to her within this last year. She is a strong and sensible girl. She will be all right."

Sir William expressed his great relief at this reassuring information and inquired after Mrs. Carlyle. When this and other polite inquiries had been made and answered, a brief silence ensued.

"Well, Sir William," said Philip, signaling idly to the tavern keeper, "I trust that, if it is not the coronation which brings you to London, it is merely business and not such a misfortune as has befallen Mr. Townes."

Sir William hesitated, accepted a refill of his tankard and, unable to conceal his pride and delight, decided to share it with his companions. "No misfortune at all, Mr. Sommerville. And not even business as such. It is, happily, an affair of the heart."

There were murmurs of appreciation and congratulation.

Sir William continued, "I have come to meet the lady's mother. In fact, the two of them were supposed to have visited me at Winderfields this past month."

"Ah," Mr. Parke interrupted, "the better to survey both the man and his property." He gave a wink at Sir William, who appeared only mildly insulted.

"Perhaps. But the mother was taken ill, and the

visit had to be postponed. Now she suddenly wants to have a look at me without delay." He took another long drink from his tankard. "I'll not say names at this time, for it is not yet a settled thing, but I hope to return to Winderfields a married man."

"It sounds as though you'll have to take the mother as well," Mr. Parke growled.

"Ah, well. These things resolve themselves in time." Sir William smiled complacently.

"So they do," Charles agreed. Then he sighed again. "I only hope this business with Lawrence can prove to be some sort of wretched mistake."

And he looked so wretched himself that his companions had to turn from Sir William's happiness and exert themselves to reassure Charles.

Promptly at four o'clock, Sir William, dressed in his baronet best, lifted the brass door knocker at Miss Flagg's academy. He was admitted by a trim and tidy maid and shown into Miss Flagg's private sitting room.

Miss Flagg greeted him with a warm smile and extended hand. "Sir William, how glad I am that you have come on such very short notice."

He kissed the hand she held to him. "My pleasure, dear lady. I am only grateful that your honored mother is now recovered enough to receive me."

She led him to a chair placed near the window that overlooked the courtyard. "Mother, dear, may I present Sir William Grant? My mother, Mrs. Flagg."

The woman in the large heavy chair looked him over very carefully before extending a grudging hand. "How do you do, Sir William?"

"Very well, indeed, madam, and I trust that you are feeling better now?"

"Tolerable. Tolerable."

"Do sit down, Sir William," Miss Flagg said, "and we will have tea directly."

Feeling more than a little uncomfortable, Sir William took a chair and smiled hopefully at the older woman who still regarded him suspiciously. "I was most sorry, madam, that your indisposition prevented my welcoming you to Winderfields. I hope that you are better now."

"Tolerable, as I said," snapped Mrs. Flagg.

Miss Flagg smiled fetchingly at Sir William. "Since we have been unable to visit there as yet, perhaps you will be good enough to describe the place for my mother, Sir William."

"Why certainly, ma'am. It is located, as I have told Miss Flagg, just a day's journey to the south of York, where I lived before I came into the title and the estate. It would be only a two-day journey from London, and the roads are very good."

"York?" barked Mrs. Flagg. "What were you doing in a place like York?"

"I was a clergyman, ma'am. It was there that I was posted in the service of the church."

"The church, eh?" Mrs. Flagg settled back in her chair with a less hostile attitude. "Couldn't you have found a living in the country? Or at least in a village?"

"Perhaps. But York is a very pretty city, ma'am. And those who live in cities and towns must have a preacher, too."

"Well, so they must. And I daresay they are entitled to a good preacher as much as the next. Were you a good preacher, Sir William?"

She was looking at him narrowly; Sir William smiled at her. "I was, ma'am."

"Well," she muttered, "I am pleased that you are not a man of false modesty, Sir William. I cannot abide a man who pretends modesty." She suddenly smiled at him. "Now, tell me something about the estate of Winderfields. Is it a large place?"

"Not so large as some . . ." he began, then seeing her sharp look, corrected his course and began to describe the acreage and crops. At a question from Miss Flagg, he provided a description of the house and gardens. By the time tea was served, the atmosphere had become one of pleasant camaraderie, with the old lady fairly beaming at him.

When tea was cleared, Mrs. Flagg stood up and shook hands with Sir William, then invited him to call again at any time, even should dear Narcissa be engaged. "I always enjoy a chat with a sensible man." When she followed her maid out of the sitting room, Sir William was in a glow of happy anticipation. But his triumph must wait a little longer.

"I must ask you to excuse me for a moment or two, Sir William. I always go up with my mother to be sure that she is well settled. Do you mind waiting for a little while?"

"Not at all," Sir William declared with enthusiasm.

When Miss Flagg was gone, Sir William amused himself with a stroll around the little parlor, gazing at the furniture and bric-a-brac and thinking to himself that Miss Flagg was probably already receiving her mother's blessing on this most brilliant marriage.

He was still smiling to himself when the door opened and his three companions of the afternoon came in.

"Good afternoon, Sir William," Philip said.

"Why, why, Mr. Sommerville. Mr. Townes. And Mr., um, Mr. Parke. Gentlemen. I—I confess that I am quite astounded to see you."

"You will be even more astounded to learn why we are here, Sir William." Philip was moving ahead of the others as they crossed the room toward the baronet, in what seemed almost a menacing way.

"Why, I cannot say, I'm sure."

"We have come, Sir William, to look at your thighs."

"What?" Sir William looked in confusion from one to the other of the three men, then laughed uncomfortably. "I see. This is a jest. You have managed to determine the lady of my intentions and you have come here to tease me."

"No, sir," said Philip, and his voice was not the indolent drawl Sir William had heard in the past from this dilettante young man. It sounded like a voice of authority. "We are looking, you see, for a certain mark—that of a horseshoe burning through clothing. And"—Philip drew a pistol from his pocket and pointed it at Sir William—"we are prepared to see that you cooperate with us."

While Philip held the pistol a short distance from Sir William's head, Mr. Townes made a search of Sir William's pockets. "No weapons, Philip."

"I am glad to hear it. A weapon would be most unseemly for one so recently a man of the cloth. Now just stand very still, if you please, while these

399

gentlemen have a look at what might be found beneath those trousers."

A little sheepishly, Charles and Mr. Parke slipped Sir William's trousers down to his knees. There on the left thigh was the mark they had been seeking. Philip smiled at Sir William, whose outrage was slowly being replaced with alarm.

"Now, sir, There is a carriage outside with several very sturdy constables in it, and there are some gentlemen in the government who plan to stay up late to speak with you."

When Miss Flagg returned to her parlor, there were only Charles and Mr. Parke to receive her.

"It was true, then?" she asked.

"Yes. I fear that it was true," Charles answered wearily. "Sir William is this fiend Bellwether. A murderer and worse. It is a thing almost beyond belief."

"What a day it has been!" Miss Flagg sank onto her pretty sofa. "Gentlemen, I believe we need a little refreshment. And I don't mean tea. In that cupboard, Mr. Townes, is a bottle of very good whiskey. But you must promise that word of this never reaches the students or staff."

Julia met Philip in the rose garden, within the sight, but not the hearing of her aunt, who sat reading in the shade of a huge maple tree.

"Have you brought my letter?" Julia asked as they shook hands under Aunt Julia's watchful eye.

"Yes. And it has done its job very well. Last night Sir William was found dead in his cell. He must have had a quantity of poison somewhere on his person."

Julia could not speak for a time, then she said, "I am glad there will be no trial, to have all the old heartaches raised again."

Julia took the letter he now handed to her.

"Julia, I—"

"Wait, please, Mr. Sommerville. There is something I must say to you without delay." She took a deep breath and willed herself to do this calmly. "I do not intend that we shall meet again after today, except in the ordinary course of society which neighbors such as ourselves cannot avoid."

He stopped abruptly and would have caught and turned her to him, but she moved steadily ahead, and after a moment he followed.

"Julia, what can you mean by this? I—"

"I do not blame you, Mr. Sommerville," she interrupted. "I knew from the first that you are not a man of settled habits. You are attractive to women and they to you. It is how you are, how you have ever been, and, I am certain, will ever be. What I did with you, I did with my eyes open, knowing better, but unable somehow to persuade myself to prudence and . . . and caution."

"Julia, stop this."

"No. No, let me finish, please. It has taken a long time to bring myself to this point, and I must not weaken now." She turned to smile at him sadly. "I am afraid that you bewitched me, Philip, but I cannot deceive myself any longer. It will only bring trouble to both of us. You never made any promises to me, indeed, even in the height of the bewitchment, I don't think I expected any. I believe you are an honorable man in your own way. I am certain that every woman who has become involved with you would be forced to admit that you never used trickery or seduction. You wouldn't need to do so. Still"—she stopped, for they had come to the end of the path—"I find that I cannot continue . . ." She turned and moved a little ahead of him. "It simply is against my, well, my character. And certainly it is not for my own good to wait and hope that you might find me, in the end, the most . . . Oh, I cannot even venture to think what you truly want from a woman! I only know that I cannot be whatever that is. So, when we part today, it will be a final parting. I implore you, Mr. Sommerville, not to tempt me anymore." Her voice quavered. "I cannot bear it."

"Julia," he whispered urgently, for they were coming perilously close to her aunt, "will you not even listen to me? Permit me to—"

"No." She waited until they were safely past Aunt Julia before continuing. "I am sure that you will try to reassure me, to persuade me that I should be content to be one of the women in your life. I have still judgment enough to know that could never be so."

"But . . ."

"And, please, don't spoil my opinion of your honor by telling me that I am the only one. I have seen you, since our last meeting, with another woman. And your behavior, indeed, the behavior of the both of you demonstrated very clearly that yours is not a casual acquaintance." She stopped again. "Thank you for returning my letter. And for saving my life. And now I am going to sit with my aunt."

As she was turning away, he did catch her arm.

"Julia!" As she turned back to him, his face was urgent. "Julia, are you sorry?"

Her blue gaze, steady and direct, met his; she even managed a little smile. "Oh, Mr. Sommerville, I doubt that any of your women can ever be entirely sorry."

She turned from him and walked quickly to sit beside Aunt Julia in the shade.

Chapter Twenty

Midsummer eve. At dusk Julia was helped from her horse by her father and went to stand with him at the edge of the rise, looking down on the circle of stones where the Druids had gathered for their most special ceremony. The shelter that had offered protection from the elements on that evening six months ago had been removed, though the bench had been permitted to remain. But Julia had no wish to sit; indeed, she was not at all certain that she wished to be here. It was impossible to say what had drawn her to this place tonight. Perhaps it was another test.

At least there was not a large gathering as there had been on the previous occasion; in light of the unfortunate business of Lawrence, the Fainway family could certainly be excused from making this a social event.

Julia turned to look at Mimmie's eager face. "Is it really true, Mimmie, that this will be the first time you have seen the ceremony?"

"My father would never permit it to be conducted here," Mimmie replied. "He said it was because of its pagan nature and the offense it would give to his decent, Christian neighbors, but I always suspected that he had tried to charge the Druids a fee they thought exorbitant."

As they spoke, the first bonfires were lit in the meadow below them. The figures dressed in robes or skins began to move about, gathering in groups of two or three, separating to regather, sitting on the ground, leaning on the stones.

"One might almost think it was a drawing-room party," Julia said softly, "except for the clothing, and, of course, one knows what is to come."

"What is that?" It was Mimmie's voice, sharp and a little anxious.

"It is the flute. They will begin very soon now."

They stood still and silent—Charles, Mr. Parke, Julia, and Mimmie—as the eerie music came faintly to their ears through the scented air of the summer night. Then the chanting began, growing, cresting, falling away as the leader made his progress into the very center of the stones. Julia felt Mimmie stiffen beside her and put out a hand to reassure her, just as she had been reassured that other night. The memory brought an ache of emptiness that clutched her heart and tightened her throat and made her very soul sore and sensitive.

Julia's eyes beheld the ceremony, so mesmerizing, so disturbing, but her senses did not react as they had when she'd first seen the ritual. Those senses had been dulled and driven low by the loss of a love so consuming that only ashes of her charred feelings now remained. Though what was transpiring in the meadow below her was magical and mystical, there was now no threat to one's sanity. That came from another place—from green eyes and taut, finely muscled limbs and hands that . . . Julia realized that she had made a sound.

Mimmie had turned to her. "It is disturbing, isn't it? I don't know but that my father may have been right."

In the light of torches, they rode back to Fainway more subdued than when they came, and soon after arriving home, Julia and Mimmie both went to bed—Julia to stare into the darkness until the accumulation of hours would finally release her to sleep, and Mimmie to rest for her departure in the morning to return to London and Philip Sommerville's home.

It was only a day or two later that Julia, her father and her aunt went to London themselves. The coronation was to take place on the twenty-eighth of June; it would be a fine thing to experience a few days of the excitement in preparation for the event, but only a few days. They drew up to the door of their hotel on the afternoon of the twenty-fourth.

There was a party that evening, given in the home of old friends of Aunt Julia's. There were a number of young men to dance and flirt with Julia, and she tried her best to pretend pleasure.

"Julia, dear," her aunt said as they had conferred on Julia's packing the day before leaving, "I know that you have been terribly hurt and disappointed by Lawrence, and you will meet a good many young men on this excursion. You must not be too eager to find a new beau. Do not permit your head to be turned by their flattery and flirting."

"Yes, Aunt Julia."

"And don't be in a hurry to leave us to take up a new home with a husband. Now, you mustn't misunderstand. Of course your father wishes you to marry. It will be a fine thing for him to have a grandson to inherit Fainway in time, but you have been with him so brief a time, I will think it a sad thing if you fly away from him so quickly."

"I have no wish to go, Aunt Julia."

"The grandson of my friend, Mrs. Oliver, is quite a nice young man, very settled in his ways. He reminds me rather of that nice Mr. Woodland."

So Julia had gone to bed that evening thinking of Robert, to be married in the next month presumably to Miss Pierce.

That was yet another example of how swiftly change came. Not so very long ago, there were three men whom, for very different reasons, she had been tempted to marry. Now she could marry none of them. Two had chosen other women, and one was about to be hanged for murder.

Since her parting from Philip, Julia had given herself a good talking to, and she had tried to appear as cheerful as possible. She was going to a coronation ball, after all. Furthermore, she was only nineteen, and though she would never find another love to duplicate that she had known with Philip, in time, perhaps, there would be another Robert.

One of the things Julia meant to do in London was call upon Miss Flagg, and she determined to do it at once, before she could find reason or rationalization not to do so.

And so, on the second morning of their stay, Julia and her aunt were driven out in the carriage.

"I am beginning to think the train a myth," Julia told the old woman. "Or if genuine, it never really passes this way."

Julia was left at the academy, while Aunt Julia went across the park to visit with a friend who had fallen ill.

Julia turned from the carriage and walked into the courtyard toward the front door of the school. Looking up she could see the window of Miss Flagg's sitting room, its lacy curtains drawn aside to admit a welcomed summer breeze. A man stood there, his back to the window, a hand raised in gesticulation as he made a point of conversation with his hostess. Julia would have recognized that back had it been among a thousand. It was Philip. It was obvious he and Miss Flagg were no longer hiding their affair. Soon would come word that they were engaged, for Miss Flagg would settle for nothing less.

And suddenly Julia could not face it. She turned and walked blindly out the gate of the academy and into the street.

It was not a commercial street; Miss Flagg had located her school in a quiet and respectable residential neighborhood. Julia had remembered passing shops up at that corner. She could go and look through them while waiting for her aunt to return. No. She changed her mind even as she had begun walking. It was only two or three blocks to the station. She would see a train.

No sooner had she turned into the station than she saw one. With a roar and a wheezing, a giant black beast was steaming and snorting to a halt.

Passengers began alighting, pushing their way through those eager souls waiting to get on. Well-dressed ladies chattering to each other, top-hatted gentlemen with more weighty words and faces. A young man dressed in black.

There was something familiar about this last young man. Oh, of course, it was the way he walked—with a slight limp and leaning on a cane. With a start, Julia recognized that, though the cane was unfamiliar to her, it was the Reverend Mr. Simmons.

The waters of Bath can have done him little good if he now is forced to use a cane, was Julia's first thought. *He must be on his way home, even now. So Miss Pierce needn't wait any longer for the nuptials. He has been away from York a long time.* She stood staring at him as he moved away from her, walking out of the station. Perhaps he had been to Westminster, perhaps to have a look at the coronation site, for it seemed unlikely a lowly vicar from York could hope to attend the ceremony itself, unless, of course, he had some churchly function to perform.

Julia knew she should hail him, greet him, remind him of their acquaintance, wish him well and send greetings to her friends at York. But she did none of these things.

With her hand on the knob of the station door, Julia froze as knowledge of terrible, piercing clarity came rushing over her. Here was the man with the limp! With the compelling voice! She had often admired it herself! Philip had not found him in York because he had not been there! He had been hiding, waiting—waiting for this time to come.

Like a woman in a trance, she burst through the door of the station and searched the crowd for a

glimpse of Mr. Simmons. There he was, just entering the doors of a small inn across the street. Julia
now retraced her steps toward Miss Flagg's academy, slowly, thoughtfully at first, then more and
more quickly until she was flying at a dead run
through the gates of the academy and pounding
frenziedly on the door.

When she was admitted by the maid, she dashed
past the woman without a word, tore up the stairs
and fell into the door of Miss Flagg's dainty parlor.
The faces of the astonished couple turned toward
her.

"Philip!" she cried. "You must come with me at
once!"

"Mimmie, this cannot be so!"

"Indeed, it is so, my dear Julia. The queen has
asked—commanded, if you will—that you come
to see her tomorrow. After the coronation and
before the ball."

"But why?"

Charles stepped forward. "You ask why, child?
You may have saved her life! All the fine preparations that Philip and his colleagues had made for
her protection would have been worthless if this
suicidal fanatic had succeeded in his plan. Philip
found the choir robes in his room at the inn, and a
pistol as well. Knowing the ceremonies and the
workings of the church so well, he could easily have
concealed himself among the choir. With a single
shot he might well have brought the monarchy to
an end."

"He was entirely willing to die, if it meant the
queen would die, too," Mimmie said. "If he had

not been discovered, by your very clever reasoning and by Mr. Christian's identification of his as the voice he heard, I don't know what might have happened. Indeed, no one knows. The queen wishes to thank you. It is only natural."

Julia shook her head, still disbelieving.

"Julia." Her aunt came to take her hand. "I cannot fathom why you hesitate over such an honor. You are the one who has been ever a great supporter of the queen. Now you will meet her face to face. Do you not wish for this honor?"

"Of course I do, Aunt Julia. It only seems so like a dream. And really, I did nothing heroic. Not like Mimmie. She is the one who should be going to see the queen."

Mimmie looked a little sheepish. "Well, if that is your only objection, very soon I shall probably see her every day."

There was a chorus of astonished murmurings.

"Mimmie, what do you mean?" Julia demanded.

"Her Majesty has a vacancy for a lady-in-waiting, as you may have heard. The queen, at the urging of some members of the government, has asked me to assume that post. I have accepted."

Julia had to sit down. Mimmie came to her side and took her hand. "Please do not think that I did this without much serious contemplation, Julia. You must know that I never would leave you if I could not see that you have a dear and loving family now. And, of course, it is likely that you will marry soon."

Julia lifted stricken eyes to Mimmie, but did not speak.

"And it is not as though we will not see each

other. I am sure that the queen will spare me so that I may visit with you from time to time. In fact, I shall insist upon it!"

Mimmie looked so emphatic that the others, even Julia, had to smile at her.

"My dearest Mimmie. If I must lose you, I will try to be happy that someone else will have the benefit of your wise counsel and loving heart. Her Majesty could have no better confidante, no example of character so fine. I say God bless you both."

So Julia found herself dressing for the coronation ball a few hours earlier than she otherwise would have. And a carriage of the queen's came to transport her and her family to the palace through streets still full of those who had watched the coronation procession pass earlier in the day.

Through the very gates of the palace they drove in regal splendor, with prancing horses, liveried coach and footmen. It was like a fairyland, or one of those dreams from which one fears one will awake. And then they were actually walking through the stately halls, then through a huge and awesome room which was completely unoccupied, and at last into a smaller, almost intimate room where the queen herself was waiting.

Queen Victoria sat in a large carved chair, with her ladies standing behind and beside her. Among them was Mimmie, who smiled encouragement to the awestruck Julia as the little party came into the room. When they had made their bows and curtsies to the queen, they were taken to stand at one side of the room. There Julia had intended to spend some time scrutinizing the queen, memorizing every detail of the room, the gowns, the pictures on the walls—everything. But she saw none of these things, for across the room from her was Philip Sommerville, standing with his uncle and . . . Good Heavens! It was Lord Wrayburn.

She did not have very long to wonder what they all might be doing here as a ceremony was beginning.

Philip was led from his spot to kneel before the queen. A resplendent official read from a scroll of parchment, describing the deeds and service he had done for the queen which now merited his knighthood. Then, just as in storybooks, he was touched on each shoulder with a sword, and the queen said something to him which Julia could not hear, but she supposed it must have been "Arise, Sir Philip," because he rose, bowed and returned to his place.

A moment later a gentleman in somber black came to take Julia to make her curtsy before the queen.

"Your Majesty," said the gentleman in a deep and resounding voice, "Miss Julia Townes."

When Julia rose from her curtsy, the queen said in a soft thin voice, "Bring a chair for Miss Townes, please."

A chair was quickly placed next to the queen, and Julia was seated. Now she could see the queen at very close range, and the first thing that struck her was how tiny a woman she was. She made Julia feel excessive, too tall, just as her mother always had. Julia noticed another thing. The face of the youthful queen had hardened since the portrait drawn of her had appeared in the paper Julia had seen so many months ago. A year of being queen, of the fears for her crown and her life, of hearing and deciding between so many points of view, of deciding who might be trusted and who could not, perhaps even the scandal of Lady Flora Hastings had taken a toll on the small and vulnerable woman who was, like herself, just nineteen.

"Miss Townes," the queen was saying, "it is our wish to thank you personally for your assistance in the apprehending of this most dangerous traitor."

"That is very kind, Your Majesty."

"Sir Philip Sommerville has told me that, were it not for your clever reasoning and sharp eyes, this Mr. Simmons could have carried out an attempt upon my life during the coronation this morning."

"Well, I recognized him, Your Majesty, and it seemed to make little sense that he should be in London at this time. It is only fortunate that I happened to see him."

"Sir Philip tells me also that your cousin, Mr. Christian, has identified Mr. Simmons as the culprit whose voice he heard in this plot a year ago."

"Yes, Your Majesty. I believe that is so."

"And that is what I wish to discuss with you." Queen Victoria sat clasping and unclasping her fingers for a moment before continuing. "Mr. Christian has done a great service to the kingdom, and to us, by uncovering this plot in the first place. He is now, of course, imprisoned for a most foul deed. We are inclined to show him mercy, and it has been suggested that, rather than hanging him—"

Julia realized that she had gasped involuntarily at the pronouncing of these uncompromising words. "Oh, I do beg Your Majesty's pardon."

"Rather than executing him, we might require him to forfeit claim to any properties here in England, and banish him to a prison in Australia where he will be required to work very hard all his days."

The queen looked up from her lap where the fingers were again knitting themselves. Julia met her gaze and nodded silently.

"We do not wish," Victoria continued, "to take this step without consulting you, Miss Townes."

"Consulting *me*, Your Majesty?"

"Yes, Miss Townes. We have been told that, in addition to the death of Miss Bellville, Mr. Christian was guilty of a most brutal attack upon your person. It would not, in our view, be right to spare his life without your knowledge and agreement."

"I see." Julia sat still and silent for several moments, her eyes now on her own hands which lay folded in her lap. At length, she looked up to meet the eyes of the queen. "I believe I have just realized, Your Majesty, what a difficult duty it is to be queen. Your Majesty must be faced with such questions of life and death many times over the course of a year, or even a month. I am very grateful that this will be the only time in my life I must ever give even a moment's consideration to such a question, or to have such a grave responsibility as this. I certainly would agree that Mr. Christian should be offered the option of which Your Majesty spoke." Julia shook her head. "I only wonder if Mr. Christian himself will accept it."

"Would you accept it, Miss Townes?"

Julia again thought very carefully before answering. "Yes, Your Majesty, I suppose I would. I fear that I am not the romantic sort of woman to whom death would be preferable to a life of hardship and dreariness."

For a moment the queen forgot or abandoned the

imperial "we." "I will say that I think you a very practical woman, Miss Townes. And a candid one as well. I will admit to you that I should choose as you have done. Dreariness, after all, can take many forms."

Julia thought she heard a note of dismissal in these words, and was about to rise, but the queen now spoke again. "Sir Philip tells us that he hopes the two of you will be married very soon."

Julia could only stare in wide-eyed astonishment, with only the slightest shake of her head.

The queen smiled widely at her. "Oh, we know it is supposed to be a great secret, these things always must be a secret. We only hope that you will take our best wishes for your very great happiness."

"Thank you, Your Majesty," was all that Julia could think of to say. She rose, made her curtsy and returned to her place by her father.

Lawrence was hanged a week later, and a day or two after that, Julia received a letter, mailed from the prison. She read it by the window, looking out on a summer shower that had thoroughly dampened the grounds of Fainway.

"My dearest Julia,
I wish that you had come to see me. Though I know I have no right to expect it of you, I think it sad that the last sight I shall have of you will be that of a bruised and terrified girl who has every right to despise me.

"Her Most Generous Majesty has seen fit to offer me my life, but under terms which I find less appealing than death. You, very likely, will not understand such thinking, but I have con-

cluded after many days of consideration that Dame Fortune simply does not plan to smile upon me in this life, and I may as well end the trouble for us both. Having expected from a very early age to be a wealthy man and master of Fainway, I never thought, nor was I encouraged, to prepare myself for any other sort of life. If I cannot have those things which I most value, I do not choose to live in their absence.

"Good-bye, my beautiful Julia. My last thoughts will surely be of you. If you cannot forgive me, at least please believe that I love you most dearly, even now."

There were tears in her eyes as Julia put the letter aside.

"Ah, Lawrence. I was right about one thing. You had great finesse."

Julia was still standing at the window when her aunt came into the room.

"Julia, I have had a letter this morning from Miss Flagg."

The sound of that name made Julia start as she turned from the window, but she forced herself to ask calmly, "How is Miss Flagg?"

"Very well. And her mother, too. She writes that she wishes to take the Stonebridge Cottage for the remainder of the summer, and, if it proves satisfactory, to continue in an indefinite lease."

"Miss Flagg?"

Aunt Julia handed the letter to Julia. "I suppose she has been thinking about it since I happened to mention the cottage to her on our last visit to London. You may read it for yourself. She states that she has long wished for a retreat for herself and

her mother away from London. Not that I believe
for a moment they will be the only ones to occupy
the cottage. Her mother remains very certain that
Miss Flagg means to marry, even thinks that the
taking of the cottage is driven by that decision."

"I see." Julia looked at the letter, but the elegant
and rather flowing though entirely legible script
made no impression on her anguished mind.

"I think it a very fine thing, of course," her aunt
continued. "I can hardly imagine more desirable
tenants than Mrs. and Miss Flagg. If you agree, I
shall write to her directly to arrange for them to
view the cottage."

With a very great effort, Julia got hold of herself.
"That is good of you, Aunt Julia. I suppose I should
speak to my father before anything is undertaken."

"You are right, of course! You are a most sensible
girl, my dear." Her aunt drew on her gloves. "I
thought I would just drive over to the cottage to be
sure that the last of Mrs. Todd's things have been
removed. Should you care to come along? It looks
as though the rain will soon be over."

"Oh, no! No, thank you, Aunt Julia. My father
should return very soon. I will wait and speak to
him about Miss Flagg's request."

"Yes, do that." Aunt Julia kissed her niece, then
looked into her troubled blue eyes. "Julia, dear,
please try not to let this sad business of Lawrence
distress you so. He was an evil man, and he only
received the punishment he deserved, indeed, that
he asked for."

"I know, Aunt Julia. He *was* evil, but he was
charming, too. I'm afraid that I miss him. He could
always make me laugh."

Aunt Julia sighed heavily and straightened her hat at the mirror. "That wretched boy! Your father is fretting at the loss of Lawrence, too, though not at all in the same way. Now there is *no* heir of Fainway! Ah, well"—she turned from the mirror—"at least it will make him more resigned to the idea that you likely will marry soon."

Julia turned back to the window. Her aunt's words made her think of other words said by the queen, for which there seemed no reasonable explanation.

"I don't think I am likely to marry soon at all, Aunt Julia. I have had no offers, you know, and I can think of no gentleman from whom an offer is likely to come, even should I wish such a thing."

Her aunt stopped with her hand on the door. "Frances, I must say, raised you to have very modest ways. I believe you really *don't* think yourself quite the most beautiful girl in all the neighboring counties!"

Julia watched from the window as the carriage drew away from the family entrance, carrying her aunt to Stonebridge Cottage. She remained a long time in the same place, staring with eyes unseeing at the still-dripping trees that lined the drive. Miss Flagg wanted the Stonebridge Cottage during the month of August, when Philip would be at Winterhall. They must not be engaged, after all, if she was not invited to stay at the estate. She was coming to the country to continue the pursuit.

Julia supposed they were evenly matched. If it were not a thing to break her heart, it would be a fascinating thing to watch the contest proceed.

At length Julia put aside her musings and went to

speak to her father about Miss Flagg and the Stonebridge Cottage. She was disappointed, though of course not surprised, to have him endorse the plan enthusiastically. Julia decided to ask another ten pounds for the rental of the cottage.

Aunt Julia returned to luncheon and heard the decision about Miss Flagg with great delight. When she had gone to her room to write to the lady, and Charles departed on business in the village, Julia found herself at loose ends. She wandered from the small sitting room to her bedroom and back again, unable to sit or to read or to work. After an hour of this aimlessness, she asked that her horse be saddled and brought to the family entrance.

She set out in the direction of the woods. She knew that she must come to terms with the ghosts that haunted certain places in her most intimate neighborhood. The rise where she had first seen the Druids' ceremony on that unforgettable winter night and where she and Lawrence had been seized on that dreadful day. The circle of stones which always aroused such strange and unexplainable feelings. And especially the woods near the circle where the gypsy wagon had been. She wondered if it was still there.

She could not hope to exorcise all the ghosts on one outing; the plan for today was simply to ride to the far edge of the woods and look down on the stones. On another day she would venture farther.

The day was humid and growing uncomfortably hot as the July sun drew the dampness of the morning shower into the air. Julia was glad to reach the cooling shade of the trees, and she rode slowly along the path, feeling the lushness of summer around her. At the rise she dismounted and tied her horse in the shade of a large maple.

Yes, here was the place where the shelter had been; the bench was still there. That was where Lawrence had been tied. Poor Lawrence! Buried in the grounds of the prison among people he would never have associated with in life.

Perhaps she should speak to her father about having him brought to be buried beside Mary. A little sigh escaped her. Their churchyard would have quite a collection of stories to be told of the various graves, at this rate.

She moved now to stand at the edge of the rise, gazing down on the massive gray stones. In the glare of the July afternoon they had lost their sinister appearance; they looked almost reassuring in their permanence, as though, like the Stonebridge Cottage, they had always been there and would remain forever.

Encouraged by this knowledge, Julia sat down on a fallen log and studied the stones carefully, counting them, memorizing their placement, wondering what had happened to make that single stone fall from its place in the circle. And as she sat, she knew that there was one more ghost she could confront and put to rest this day. She rose, got back on her horse and began to make her way down the steep and tangled path that led to the meadow below.

She found shade for the horse up against the ridge; she left him there and walked to the stones, holding her hat to one side of her face to block out the blazing sun. First she walked all around the circle, touching each stone, even leaning for a time on the one that had fallen. Then, after taking a deep breath and squaring her shoulders, she went to the very center of the circle.

Julia closed her eyes and tried to picture what it would have been like on that midsummer eve to have stood here as leader of the Druids. She willed her mind to recall the flute, the chanting, the otherworldliness of it. Her mind tried to obey, but it was a sorry effort and she opened her eyes with a frown. It all seemed very foolish here in the heat and glare of an unremitting summer sun. Well, then, she would try something else.

Julia closed her eyes again and willed herself to see this place as it was those centuries ago when the stones were first raised. There must have been a meadow then, although the woods may have encroached a little closer to the stones. Perhaps animals had grazed here then, just as the sheep of Winterhall sometimes did now. Men and maybe women would have gathered to observe their mystical and awesome rites. They would have been dressed in skins, she supposed, or in roughly woven clothing, perhaps made of bark or even grasses. Their chanting would have been in a language that no one in this time, not even the Druids of today, would recognize.

She could almost hear it. Strange, disembodied voices, some deep, some shrill, a chorus of pagan intensity. The heat on her face must be the heat of their bonfires and not of the sun that gave life to this earthly plane. She was swaying along with them, humming a melody she could not identify and knew she had never heard before. Swaying, listening, humming, praising, waiting for the leader to appear. He must come soon. The fires were growing hotter, the brightness against her closed eyes was becoming unbearable. She put the heels of her hands to her eyes to ward off the fires, then to her ears to shut out the sounds that were growing louder and louder in her head. She felt herself sway once more and then she fell helplessly to her knees.

"Julia!"

With the greatest effort she opened her eyes to see Philip running, reaching her side, bending to lift her to her feet.

"Julia, what has happened? Are you all right?"

"Oh, Philip." She stood blinking at him. "Mr. Sommerville. Yes. Yes, I am all right. I must have been overcome by the heat."

But that was not so. The sun was low now, casting long shadows from the stones. She stood in such a shadow herself. Where, she wondered a little wildly, had she been while the shadows had lengthened?

"Just sit here on this rock. Whatever possessed you to come here like this?"

She looked at him steadily; it would be less difficult perhaps to claim that she had only wanted a closer view of the stones, but . . .

"I was exorcising ghosts, Mr. Sommerville. And I see now that it was not the heat that overcame me, but the stones themselves." Her voice dropped. "It was rather beautiful in a terrifying way."

He sat down beside her. "When I was quite a small boy, I had a very disturbing experience here. It was on the day that I came here for the first time . . . with my cousin, Frances."

Julia met his eyes for an instant, then glanced

away again. "And what are you doing here on *this* day, Mr. Sommerville?"

"I was riding to Fainway to call upon you, when I saw you here, swaying and singing, and . . ." He reached into his pocket and drew out a small book. "Here, you see, is the poetry, and I planned to pick a bouquet of daisies there in the meadow. Just as I promised I have come to court you."

Julia drew herself up, then turned resentfully away from him. "I recall having told you, Mr. Sommerville, that I did not wish to see you in anything approaching courting circumstances. I will not be one of your women!"

"Julia, won't you be my wife?"

She shook her head, frowning. "I don't know what you mean by these words, Mr. Sommerville, but I can tell you that they are in very poor taste." She stood up. "I am going home now."

Philip caught her hand and pulled her back onto the rock. "Julia, listen to me. I love you. I have loved you from the first moment I saw you. I will never love any but you. Here I am, even on my knees, begging that you will marry me. Why won't you believe me? Or at least believe the queen!"

"Because there is still the matter of Miss Flagg."

"Miss Flagg?" He leaned back on his heels. "Yes, I rather feared the problem was Miss Flagg." He stood up, grasped her by the hands and pulled her up and into his embrace; in an instant he was kissing her with the well-remembered tenderness, persuading, urgent, irresistible.

But Julia did resist. After the first heady instant of surging desire, she pushed herself away from him. "Let me go, Mr. Sommerville."

"Julia." He still held her fast as his green eyes glinted down into hers. "You may have seen me kiss Miss Flagg's hands in the carriage. You never saw me kiss her like this. And you never will, nor any other woman. Miss Flagg deserved more than the kisses of gratitude I bestowed upon her that day. She had just agreed to do what I had asked of her, to lead Sir William on to think that she would be persuaded to marry him. To go with her mother to Winderfields to discover what they could about how he might have murdered Miss Sennett. In the end it was not necessary because of what was contained in the letter from your mother. But even there, Miss Flagg played a most important role, and played it beautifully. She is a most extraordinary woman."

"So she is." Julia released herself and sat down again on the rock. She looked at him thoughtfully as he stood above her. "All the same, Miss Flagg intends to marry you."

"I assure you that she does not."

"Her mother believes, and so does my aunt, that Miss Flagg has settled on a husband. She has rented my cottage for the month of August, and, I believe, Mr. Sommerville, it is common knowledge that you always spend the month of August at Winterhall."

Philip was smiling widely. "My darling, beautiful Julia. This time your clever and clearheaded reasoning has led you very much astray." He sat beside her again. "I agree with you that Miss Flagg has settled on a husband, but it certainly is not my humble self."

"It must be you. She would not leave the object

of her desires to come to the country for a month. And there is no other person in the neighborhood wealthy and appealing enough to attract her."

"Oh, come now. No one?"

When the truth finally came to her, Julia nearly fell off the stone. "Oh! Oh, my God!"

"Yes." Philip nodded solemnly, but his eyes held a twinkle. "I am certain that Miss Flagg has determined to become the next Mrs. Townes."

Julia realized she had been holding her breath and released it in a hiss that became a sigh at the end. "Poor Father. He hasn't a hope of resisting. And I think I am rather glad. Miss Flagg does everything so extremely well, she is certain to be the perfect wife to him. And she is young enough that children will be likely to arrive."

"All the same, Miss Townes, I think it is your duty to marry and insure that Fainway has an heir. And you have had a proposal most recently."

"So I have, Mr. Sommerville." She looked at him with a grave expression, then a smile spread slowly from her eyes to her lips. "And as we must not deceive the queen, I will accept it."

He was on his feet in an instant, gathering her to him and kissing her with joyous abandon. It was the sweetest, most exquisite kiss Julia had ever known, more surprising than the first, more lovely than any of those exchanged in the passion of their lovemaking.

They stood together, closely embracing, as the sun made its way behind the trees of the woods of Fainway. Then Philip held her away from him and smiled at her. "I should like nothing better than to take you to the gypsy wagon this minute. I long for you more with every day, every hour that passes."

"Oh. The gypsy wagon." She had grown slightly stiff in his arms.

"But I am going to take you home instead. I must speak to your father. He will be sorry that I mean to take you from him, but I do not mean to take you far."

"Philip, where *shall* we live? I . . . I do not think I care especially for London."

"Nor do I. What say you to Winterhall?"

"I say it would be lovely, but—"

"I am finished with all that other business, Julia, except when called upon from time to time to offer advice or consultation. It is a life I could never find satisfying. It makes one hardened and sour. There are others who can do it now. I have told my uncle this morning, to his great delight, that I am coming home to settle down to my duty as a farmer and a gentleman."

Julia closed her eyes for a moment to savor the contentment that this last great difficulty would no longer trouble her. Then she opened her eyes and looked into the green light of his eyes which smiled down at her.

"We must be married very soon, Philip. My father needs a grandson, and if we delay very long, I will be tempted to meet you daily at the gypsy wagon."

He laughed and kissed her, then they walked past the brooding stones to retrieve her horse for the ride back to Fainway.